NOT ALL HIMBOS WEAR CAPES

C. ROCHELLE

CONTENTS

Typos & Languages	vii
Warning, Content & Triggers	ix
A Note on Superhero & Villain Identities	xiii
Stalk C. Rochelle	xv

1. Xander	1
2. Butch	9
3. Xander	17
4. Butch	25
5. Xander	31
6. Butch	37
7. Xander	43
8. Butch	51
9. Xander	59
10. Butch	67
11. Xander	75
12. Butch	83
13. Butch	89
14. Xander	99
15. Xander	107
16. Butch	115
17. Xander	123
18. Xander	133
19. Butch	139
20. Xander	147
21. Butch	153
22. Butch	159
23. Xander	167
24. Butch	175
25. Xander	181
26. Butch	189
27. Butch	199
28. Xander	207
29. Butch	215
30. Xander	223
31. Butch	231

32. Butch	241
33. Xander	249
34. Xander	259
35. Butch	267
36. Butch	273
37. Xander	281
38. Xander	289
39. Butch	297
40. Xander	305
41. Butch	313
42. Xander	321
43. Xander	329
44. Butch	337
45. Butch	347
46. Xander	355
47. Xander	363
48. Butch	373
Epilogue	381
Reviews	389
Villainous Things Playlist	391
(Censored) Butch & Xander Prints Available	393
Books by C. Rochelle	395
About the Author	397
Author's Note & Acknowledgments	399

Copyright © 2022 C. Rochelle

First Printing: 2022

All rights reserved. No part of this publication may be reproduced, distributed, or transmitted in any form or by any means without the prior written permission of the author, except in the case of brief quotations embodied in critical reviews and certain other noncommercial uses permitted by copyright law.

Author's Note: The characters and events portrayed in this book are fictitious. Any similarity to real persons, living or dead, is coincidental and not intended by the author. All characters in this story are 18 years of age and older, and all sexual acts are consensual.

If you've read this, your villain arc begins.

ISBN: 9798359274258

Cover design by divineconception

TYPOS & LANGUAGES

While many people have gone over this book to find typos and other mistakes, we are only human. **If you spot an error, please do NOT report it to Amazon.**

I *want* to hear from you if there's an issue, so I can fix it.
Send me an email at **crochelle.author@gmail.com**
or **use the form** found pinned in my FB group or in my link in bio on TT & IG.

SLANG NOTE: There is always a bit of slang peppered into my writing. When in doubt, use Google, or contact me using the methods above if you truly believe it's a typo.

WARNING, CONTENT & TRIGGERS

Not All Himbos Wear Capes is an MM romance between a superhero and a villain. Our men find other men in tight supersuits incredibly attractive. **This is not your kid's superhero book.** This is *Sin City* and *The Boys* having a love child with extra spicy Spideypool and is **meant for 18+ adults** who can handle such things.

The **Villainous Things** series contains standalone books (each with HEAs) that feature interconnected characters and an overarching plot. You should read them in order.

Please do not hesitate to email the author directly with any questions or suggestions for adding to the TWs.

NOW THE GOOD STUFF

Content, Tropes & Kinks:

- MM romance (love is love)
- Dual POV
- Grumpy/sunshine
- Star-crossed lovers + fated mates

- Hurt/comfort + found family
- Lovers-to-enemies-to-lovers (yup)
- Mutual (slightly psychotic) obsession
- "I've never done this before"
- "Who hurt you?!"
- Absolutely filthy dirty talk
- Soft dom with a big beefy bottom having a very enthusiastic bi/sub-awakening
- "Good boy" + "Yes, Daddy" (light D/s - more bedroom dynamic than lifestyle)
- Praise + light degradation
- Edging, spanking, crawling, boot licking
- Docking + foreskin fixation
- Territorial cum play
- Purposefully gagging during blowies
- Snowballing (some might say excessive)
- Supersuit fetishes that result in supersuit sex
- All the stretching, blow jobs, rim jobs, frotting, and dicks in asses because this is an MM romance

Possible triggers (please also check above list):

- Sweary dialogue (plus cringey non-swears)
- Naughty, medium-dark humor
- Using religious phrases in an overtly sexual context (oh, my God/Jesus Christ), along with the use of the words slut/brat
- Morally gray characters (both heroes + villains)
- Psychotic ideation + vague (but fond) memories of maiming + killing
- Mention of gory human remains in villain lair
- Violent hero/villain battle scenes with minor gore
- Controlling + neglectful parents with some physical (superpowered) abuse
- Lack of autonomy + indentured servitude

- Restraints + kidnapping (non-sexy kind)
- Detailed descriptions of humans' negative effects on coastal wildlife, specifically with pollution
- Seagull autopsy (the only detailed part is the contents of its stomach)
- A mouthy opinionated man who prefers cock and is very vocal about how much he personally prefers cock as his personal preference
- A cutthroat, dubious moral code for supes that isn't meant to be understood by normies - "It's how the game is played." *(Please also see the following page for a note on supe identities)*

A NOTE ON SUPERHERO & VILLAIN IDENTITIES

A SUPE'S IDENTITY IS SACRED!

In this world I've created, superheroes and villains are supposed to guard ALL secret identities from normies—including their own, that of their family/clan, and even their enemies.

And when one supe addresses another as their supe name, that is a not-so-subtle way of making it clear they are considered the enemy at that moment. (Siblings may also do this to show the battle has begun—especially during notoriously cutthroat, annual White Elephant gift exchanges.)

To further clarify:
Captain Masculine = Supe name
Butch Hawthorne = Civilian name (for use around normies)
Butch Holt = Secret identity

Doctor Antihero = Supe name
Xander Marin = Civilian name (for use around normies)
Xander Suarez = Secret identity

STALK C. ROCHELLE

Stalk me in all the places!
(by joining my Clubhouse of Smut on Patreon, my Little Sinners FB Group, and subscribing to my newsletter)

For anyone with a penchant for hot men in tight supersuits.

Embrace your villain arc, bestie.

CHAPTER 1
XANDER

How does he make that Lycra look so fucking good?

I angrily shoved another handful of Cheetos into my mouth as I squinted at the TV, wishing my glare alone could somehow penetrate Mr. Perfect's invincible supersuit.

Maybe if I adjusted the lasers in my ray gun to harness the power of the sun...

Shaking my head, I refocused on the televised ceremony, grinding my orange-dusted teeth when the Mayor presented the heroic himbo with his newest Medal of Honor.

"Once again, Captain Masculine has saved our fair city from the clutches of evil!" she simped, looping the medal over his Lycra-covered head. "Thanks to his unshakeable heroism, the latest plot of Doctor Antihero was foiled before innocent lives could be lost."

Oh, is that *the narrative they're going with?*

I rolled my eyes so far back I saw my enormous brain. The Captain didn't do shit to 'foil' me. My *morning* foiled me. First, my rescue Himalayan—Neil deGrasse Meowson—was struggling to cough up a massive hairball, so I had to rush to the vet to pick up some meds. Then I spent an hour wrestling the salmon-scented paste into his fanged mouth, which ended with me bleeding everywhere and smelling like a combination of jock strap and putrid swamp.

Since I had an image to maintain, I then got *back* into the shower to replace the fish scent with coconut and lavender. Only after re-coifing my luscious hair and throwing an embarrassing *trench coat* over my waterproof supersuit to save time, did I discover I'd locked my goddamn keys in the car.

With absolutely zero cabs available, I was forced to hop on the *city bus* to get to my secret warehouse in time. To continue the theme of disaster, the A/C on the overcrowded deathtrap was broken, and we were further delayed because some little old lady got mowed down by a douche in a Lamborghini.

I'm sure they'll find a way to blame that *on me, too.*

By the time I arrived at the warehouse, boarded my WaveRunner, and raced down the secret aqueduct, I was in danger of losing the tides. Even though all signs pointed to mission impossible, I couldn't abandon my task—not this close to a breakthrough.

That's when *he* showed up with his big dick energy. As usual.

I swore Captain Masculine had some kind of creepy intuition with me. There was no other explanation for how skilled he was at knowing exactly how to piss on my parade. If my morning hadn't been such a shit show, I would have activated the submarine function on my WaveRunner before he sent a giant fireball up my tailpipe, but I was off my game and didn't react in time.

The least he can do is stop looking so hot while destroying another one of my toys.

It's just rude.

Luckily, my Shark Suit™ kicked in as I dove into the icy depths to avoid being blown into chum. It was the only positive since I completely lost my chance to collect the algae samples I needed.

So I'm back at square one while Captain Cockblocker gets another medal.

It was times like these that I debated leaving Big City for good. I had more than enough money to start fresh elsewhere —to see what sort of trouble I could get into without a do-gooder breathing down my neck. But my experiments were centered on Awakener's Bay, the bodega on the corner made the best goddamn fried chicken I'd ever had, and Meowson really didn't do well with change.

Plus, I'd love to stick around long enough to knock the Captain down a peg.

Or... something.

As if lusting after that hourly rate, my cognitive therapist's voice rang in my head. *"You need to take charge of your mental habits, Xander. Instead of fixating on what went wrong, redirect your thoughts in a more productive direction. What can* you *do to improve your life?"*

Sighing, I dropped my head back against the buttery soft Italian leather sofa and considered Dr. Ownit's words. The thing that had *always* kept me going—no matter how much the haters hated—was my work, and this time would be no different. All I had to do was refocus on the next step toward reaching my goal.

Or, I could pick up some fried chicken and eat my feelings.

Fried goodness won out, and fifteen minutes later, I was standing in the Sun-Mart deli, breathing in the glorious grease while a pink-haired manic pixie dream girl chattered in my ear.

"Seriously, Xan, just give Bangers a *try*. You are so fucking tense that I can hear you grinding your teeth through the walls. Which also means I *don't* hear you getting laid."

I nearly choked on my orange Fanta. "You are *such* a fucking creeper, Kai. I should slap a restraining order on you for unsolicited voyeurism."

She scoffed. "Oh, please. If you got a restraining order against me, I'd have to move out of the building. Our apartments are so tiny, there's no way I wouldn't be arrested for simply existing within 600 feet of you at all times. And I hate to break it to you, but you are quite vocal when taking a dick up the ass, so if you ask me, you're inviting an audience."

Rolling my eyes, I accepted the to-go box of heaven from the fry cook, giving him a hard look in return at the way his gaze raked over my body.

"Keep dreaming, Felix," I snapped. "Despite what this stalker says, I am a *top*."

He shrugged. "That's cool, bro. I'm a switch. We could make it work."

Why is everyone up in my business?

I pinched the bridge of my nose. "Listen, Felix, I like you, but I like the fried chicken here more. If things ended badly, I would be forced to go elsewhere for my emotional support nosh, and I'm just too old to start over again like that."

Kai smirked. "Which is exactly why you need a profile on Bangers—so you can swipe right on the hottie bottoms who match your anal-retentive criteria."

Giving her a noncommittal snort, we headed back to my apartment, where I mindlessly scrolled through Netflix for impending food coma entertainment while Kai fucked around on her phone.

"That one looks good," she murmured, hazel eyes still fixed on her device.

I scowled at the superhero movie splashed across the screen, noticing how much the chiseled brick house of an actor resembled Captain Masculine. While Kai enjoyed piping hot tea, there would be no way to explain my irrational hatred of heroes without telling her too much about my background. This chick may be the closest thing I had to a friend, but she could never know who I *really* was.

The nefarious, algae-collecting villain of Big City, apparently.

Supes and normies were discouraged from forming relationships of any kind with each other. We were *definitely* not supposed to reproduce, thanks to some sort of weird, enhanced bloodline class system I didn't fully understand. However, it got tricky for someone like me. My parents were both supervillains—two of the most notorious—but I'd never manifested actual powers myself.

Besides an obsessive interest in marine biology.

Not to mention, I had less than zero interest in pussy, so any concerns about keeping my super bloodline 'pure' didn't really apply to me. Regardless, I practically double-bagged my dick before sticking it anywhere, just to be safe. For all I knew, I was carrying super-swimmers capable of inducing mpreg and did *not* need that kind of scandal in my life right now.

"I'm not really in the mood for a superhero," I gritted out, quickly scrolling to my favorite reality show about man-eating sea creatures, to see if a new episode was out yet.

"I doubt he's a superhero," Kai laughed, shoving her phone in my face. "It says here he works in accounting or something, but *my* Spidey sense says he really knows how to spread those sheets, nawmean?"

Realizing her attention had been on trolling Bangers, I snatched the phone away for a closer look. Kai sampled from both sides of the salad bar, and apparently, men were on the menu today, judging by the enormous dude-bro filling the screen.

Butch, 22
He/Him
Finance

Enjoys long flights, walks by the Bay, and doesn't really know what he's doing on here! Just looking for some fun, I guess!

He was gorgeous, despite the unfortunate fact he was wearing what appeared to be a polo shirt and *smiling* while doing it.

Definitely a serial killer.

His blond hair and blue eyes screamed all-American, serial-killer-next-door, and his profile literally said he enjoyed long walks on the beach. All crimes against humanity aside, even I had to admit the dude looked like he was packing a weapon of mass D-struction below the belt.

But I would definitely still tap that.

I tossed the phone back into Kai's lap and chose the latest episode of *Bored Trophy Wives of Awakener's Bay*, since my self-proclaimed bestie here loved it. "He's not your usual type, but you do you, boo."

She cackled like a true supervillain. "Oh, no, sir, this one's for *you*." Before I could send the phone sailing out my sixth-floor window, she tapped a series of buttons before deftly shoving the device into her cleavage where she knew it would be safe. "And you just asked him out on a date."

This is why I don't have friends.

"You made me a profile, didn't you?" I sighed as the opening credits of *Trophy Wives* echoed through the small space. Kai's answering grin had me briefly wondering if I could somehow bury her beneath the floorboards without the authorities finding out.

"Sure did!" she sang, grabbing a deep-fried wing and settling back to watch the drama. "And Butch here is your perfect match."

"I highly doubt that," I scoffed, thinking of how a few tweaks to the AI would vastly improve Bangers' clearly faulty algorithm. "But you're right—it *has* been a while since I gave you an orgasmic show through the paper-thin walls separating our lairs, so I guess I'll let you live."

CHAPTER 2
BUTCH

Well, that's not what I was expecting.

My latest spreadsheet on Dr. Antihero had just been completed when my phone dinged for what felt like the millionth time. It had been going off all day, making me question two things. One, why exactly I'd created a Bangers profile in a 4 am moment of weakness, and two, how the heck to turn off notifications for the app before I lost my dang mind.

I'd long given up on answering either question, yet *something* made me tap my screen to see who the latest incoming match request was from.

Xander, 31
He/Him/Yes, Daddy
World Domination
Enjoys fried chicken, reality TV, and long walks on the beach to bury bodies. Is also not in the mood for your bullshit.

The last line made me snort, even as I quickly peered around my cubicle to make sure management at Biggs Enterprises hadn't noticed the disturbance. Biggs himself wasn't in his office, which meant he was gone for the day or enjoying sex in the copy room with his secretary.

Note to self: Wipe down the copier before using it next.

Sarcasm aside, what really caught my attention about Xander's profile was his face, especially his eyes. They were brilliant amber—like shards of gold reflecting the sun—and something about the color paired with the particular cut of his jaw...

Do we know each other?

I shook my head with a quiet laugh. Bangers was a dating app for normies, and although the occasional supe discreetly joined for casual encounters, it was highly unlikely that I knew anyone on here—especially a human like this one.

And I'm sure I would have remembered him.

It wasn't until the chime rang for closing time did I realize two more things. One, I'd been staring at Xander's face for a good 20 minutes, and two, I had originally created a profile seeking women only.

I wasn't necessarily *opposed* to the idea of dating a man—I'd just never done it before. Actually, dating in general wasn't something I dabbled in very often, since defending Big City took up most of my time.

Well, that and filing my reports.

To most people, I probably appeared to have a fairly easy life. I grew up as the son of two of the most decorated superheroes in modern history, which meant I was destined for fame myself.

My impressive powers manifested at a young age, but I insisted on joining my peers at Superversity, despite being told

I didn't need to attend. Once I was there, I worked my tail off—often choosing to study over socializing—and graduated early. I never wanted it to be said that I hadn't earned my place.

Not that anyone would dare speak badly of me.

I was Big City's golden boy, the savior of mankind, the beloved superhero publicly known as Captain Masculine.

Yeah, my life looked pretty easy, but the truth was that I hated everything about it. For all the benefits I'd enjoyed simply for being born, there was only one word to describe this privileged existence of mine.

Sucky.

I sharply inhaled, realizing I'd just *thought* a word that was dangerously close to… *a swear.*

I'M PRACTICALLY A VILLAIN!

Hurriedly shutting down my computer, I gathered my things and prepared to leave, hoping Biggs didn't reappear to witness the guilt surely written all over my face. Not only had I checked my Bangers profile on company time, but then I had ungrateful thoughts that would shame my family for generations.

I should delete Bangers before things get any worse.

My trembling finger hovered over the delete app button, but I hesitated. Despite my deeply ingrained instinct to 'do the right thing,' I couldn't bring myself to let this go.

Just one date…

Knowing a flight would clear my head, I quickly headed for the roof. Securing the head-covering mask I was *required* to wear everywhere in public, I shot home faster than a speeding bullet, landing on my penthouse balcony, and accepted Xander's match request before I'd finished kicking off my boots.

> *"Hi Xander! Thanks for reaching out! Does this Friday night work for you? I see you like fried chicken. I could take you to a place! Let me know what works for you!*
> *Best, Butch."*

The instant I hit send, I felt *lighter,* which was odd, considering the circumstances. Joining a dating app like Bangers—one created primarily for random hookups—wasn't *prohibited* for supes, but it certainly wasn't encouraged. If Biggs discovered my profile, I'd probably get put on double overtime data entry duty until next quarter. If my *parents* found out, they'd simply frown in the language of severe disappointment and sternly remind me that my one goal in life is to 'be the hero others need you to be.'

But what about what I need?

Stripping off my Biggs Enterprises-issued Lycra supersuit, I caught my reflection in the mirrored closet doors, moving closer before finally removing my mask and tossing it aside. What remained wasn't Captain Masculine, but Butch Holt, the secretly disgruntled 22-year-old son of famous superheroes with the fate of an entire city resting on his shoulders. It didn't get any *suckier* than that.

I wonder if Doctor Antihero ever has moments like this.

There was no reason for me to be thinking about my nemesis, not when I was as naked as the day I was born. Antihero wasn't the first villain I'd been tasked with monitoring since being assigned to Big City, but he *intrigued* me—to where I downloaded a dating app just to get him out of my head.

He didn't behave like the usual villain. His behaviors seemed more systematic than psychopathic. Even when I thwarted his schemes, he didn't strike back—just doggedly tried again.

His determination is impressive.

I didn't know where exactly his hideout was located, but Awakener's Bay seemed to be his favorite playground, so I usually just hung out in the area until I found him. More often than not, I didn't interfere. I was content to simply observe the mysterious villain who'd turned into an unhealthy obsession.

While he wasn't stacked like me, Antihero was still tall and muscular, with more of a swimmer's build than a bodybuilder. He had no shortage of cool seaworthy vehicles, equipped with various confusing attachments he used to poke at the water before twisting the throttle and speeding away to his next destination.

And the way he handles that throttle...

As if compelled, my hand dropped to my dick, giving it a rough stroke that almost had my knees buckling. Masturbating was *not* the sort of activity a superhero had time for, and engaging in it while fantasizing about your enemy was about as wrong as you could get.

But I'm so tired of doing the right thing.

Leaning my other arm against the mirror for stability, I began pumping with a vengeance, squeezing hard enough that I gasped. Because of how completely our supersuits covered us, there was no way to know what Antihero really looked like—which only made my imagination run wild.

Antihero in that green spandex suit I loved the most... leaning over to collect a water sample with his round butt in the air. Antihero fitting his scuba equipment into his mouth in a way that had me wishing it was a specific part of *me* sliding between those lips…

I came so hard my head banged off the mirror, temporarily whiting out my vision. When the earth finally righted itself, I looked down to see my cum sprayed all over the mirrored surface—clear evidence of what I'd done.

"Oh, sugar," I cursed under my breath, darting to my bedside table for a tissue, somehow both satiated and humiliated at the same time.

Which is not the worst feeling, for some reason.

My phone dinged just as I'd finished wiping the cum from between my fingers—a notification from Bangers.

Xander had replied to my message.

Using my still slightly sticky hand, I tapped the notification to open the message, my breath catching as I read his reply.

> **Xander:** *"Are you a serial killer?"*

I gaped at the message, unsure if I was offended or somehow more interested. Based on his profile, Xander obviously had a sense of humor, so I assumed he was joking.

Flirting was not my forte, but the illicit orgasm had loosened me up. Biting my lip, I quickly tapped out a reply and hit send before I could overthink it.

> **"Why? Are you into serial killers or something?"**

His reply was instantaneous.

> **Xander:** *"Yes, I am."*
> **Xander:** *"But what I'm trying to determine is if you truly*

> *are one or just don't know how to communicate in a way that doesn't sound like a corporate email."*

I had to laugh at that, especially after I scrolled up to reread my original message.

> **"Haha! Guilty as charged!"**

> **Xander:** *"So which one is it? Serial killer or corporate lackey needing to get bent over a desk and flogged with a quarterly report?"*

My mouth dried up. This conversation had just gone from flirty to something else entirely. Gaze drifting to where my cum still decorated the mirror, I wondered whether I should continue down this dangerous path, or respond to one of the countless normie girls who'd been filling my inbox since I joined Bangers less than 24 hours ago.

Just one date…

> **"Whichever one you want me to be."**

I hit send and held my breath.

His answer made me dizzy.

> **Xander:** *"Good boy. Send the details for this wondrous fried chicken place we're going to on Friday and be waiting there for me at 8. If the food pleases me, I'll bend you over any surface you choose."*

I was fully hard again—painfully so. Never in my life would I have guessed I could get so turned on by nothing but two little words.

Good boy.

With a groan, I threw myself onto my hands and knees on the bed, bent over just like Xander wanted, and gripped my dick. My mind went blissfully blank as I imagined him behind me—a rolled-up report in one hand and dog leash of all things in the other—telling me how *good* I was.

Good.

Boy.

This time, I came so hard I really did pass out, waking up the following morning stuck to my sheets and more rested than I'd felt in a long time.

CHAPTER 3
XANDER

"Tell me, mother dearest, why aren't you asking Violentia to do your bidding today? She's better equipped for the task, being a raging lunatic and all."

Her icy laugh skittered down my spine. The unspoken power behind it reminded me that—shared blood or not—I was on the phone with the indomitable Glacial Girl.

The world sat up and took notice when this arctic terror settled down with none other than Argentina's Apocalypto Man. When they started popping out babies, the hero-sympathizers at the United Super Nations freaked the fuck out and wrote up a peace treaty. It offered my parents leniency if they promised not to combine all that hereditary power to reduce the planet to a pile of dust.

It's not like I could join in the fun, anyway.

Unlike my five suped-up siblings, my greatest contribution to the Suarez family was my ridiculously high IQ and countless unpatented inventions. Most of the time, this energy went into my personal research. However, I knew damn well that it was in my best interest to share my gifts, especially since they paid me a pretty penny.

And it keeps them from seeing me as deadweight.

"Oh, Xanny," my mother cooed. "You know Vi is too volatile to trust with a drop this delicate. If *you're* the one supervising the exchange, the odds are good that far fewer people will die than necessary."

I didn't bother asking how many deaths she considered 'necessary,' since that number fluctuated depending on the day and her mood. The real question was whether I was going today because I was more expendable than the infamous Ultra Violent.

But I already know the answer to that.

Glancing down at my understated Cartier watch, I saw I had a few hours to kill before my date with Butch. It also couldn't hurt to get some aggression out of my system first. The goons I'd be meeting on my mother's behalf were usually the type of scum who wouldn't be missed if something were to tragically go wrong.

Something that could take the edge off.

"Very well, my icy empress," I sighed, hearing the alert as a cool two million was instantly deposited in my account. "Just send me the coordinates, and I'll ensure your merchandise is handled with the utmost care."

"Much appreciated, *Antihero*," she chuckled. "You could still become my favorite, after all." Without waiting for a reply, she hung up, leaving me to seethe.

That ice-cold bitch.

I knew hell would sooner freeze over before I became a favorite child, but the added dig was just unnecessary. 'Doctor Antihero' was an embarrassing moniker given to me by Biggs Enterprises, Big City's ruling governmental body. While I was slightly flattered to be identified as a villain worthy of Captain Masculine's notice, they could have come up with a better name.

There wasn't much to be done about it. Hero and villain names were officially chosen and announced by the supe clans they hailed from. Since I didn't have worthy powers, I'd never been publicly acknowledged. As far as the world knew, Glacial Girl and Apocalypto Man only produced five supervillain babies who were now full-grown terrors.

Nothing like being your family's dirty little secret.

To my annoyance, I saw the port of arrival was the Royal Cove Yacht Club on Rose Island—the main setting of *Bored Trophy Wives of Awakener's Bay*. Unfortunately, the high-profile location meant I probably wouldn't be killing anyone after all.

The red tape alone would be a nightmare.

I wished I could tell Kai what I was up to, because she would have lived for the *Trophy Wives* drama it provided. It would be nice to talk to anyone about what I did all day, but that was a pipe dream, considering who I was.

Hopping in my limited edition Audi, I employed some of Dr. Ownit's breathing techniques as I drove to the docks. I had to use every trick at my disposal to turn the helpless rage coursing through my veins into more productive emotions.

Like a defiant five-year plan.

Three hours later, I was parking near the Tick Tock Diner on 57th, eager to erase this dumpster fire of an afternoon. Any assumptions that the scum I'd be dealing with today would somehow be *less* scummy simply because they were loaded were completely misguided. Their morals were looser than the *Trophy Wives* they married, and their twisted joy when they checked my mother's goods made me sick to my stomach.

She no doubt chose that *merchandise for me specifically.*

I paused outside the door of the blindingly silver 1950s-style diner, willing my mask of self-control to slide back into place. While I'd been annoyed at first that Kai created a Bangers profile for me, she'd uncannily tracked down the exact type of man I preferred to fuck the pain away.

Big, hot, and dumb as a box of rocks.

Of course, I didn't actually know if Butch was stupid, but he seemed to fit the big and hot requirements to a T. This was confirmed as the bells over the door jangled behind me and I met the gaze of the biggest, hottest, and hopefully, dumbest piece of ass I'd ever seen.

Thank you, Kai, for what this dick is about to receive.

Plastering on a charming smile that felt halfway real, I strode down the narrow aisle toward the booth where Butch was sitting. An even more genuine smile curled my lips as he *stood up* to greet me—like some sort of adorably oversized little gentleman.

"Thanks for coming, Xander," he murmured, as if he were truly *grateful* for my presence.

Maintaining eye contact as we both sat, I licked my lips. "You can thank me for coming later," I winked, almost losing my shit when he BLUSHED LIKE A GODDAMN SCHOOLGIRL at my suggestiveness.

Lord, take me now!

Needing to calm myself before I bent him over the questionably clean table, I threw an arm over the back of my bench seat and glanced around. "So this place has amazing fried chicken, huh?"

"Yeah, it does!" he exclaimed, bouncing in his seat like a big blond puppy until he suddenly looked shy again. "I mean, I really hope you agree…"

I cocked my head at his change in tone, scrutinizing how oddly nervous he seemed, considering this date had been arranged on a notoriously casual dating app.

No. Not nervous.

Eager to please.

Jesus H, this man was perfect. Not only was he built like a mountain begging to be climbed, but I highly suspected I was dealing with a dormant submissive on the verge of eruption.

Let's test this hypothesis by adding another variable…

"What are you going to eat?" I softly asked, purposefully keeping my voice low and calm so he'd become comfortable enough to let down his guard.

It hadn't escaped my notice that Butch's Bangers profile stated he was looking for women only, yet here he was with me. My guess was he'd probably never been with a man before, but was very, *very* curious about it. This thought alone was threatening to turn me absolutely feral, so I was forcing myself to at least *try* not to be overly aggressive.

As painful as it is.

He shrugged, a single dimple making an appearance as he nibbled his tasty bottom lip. "I usually get the chicken and waffles, but that's only if it's a cheat day."

I swept my gaze over his impressive form, bulging muscles straining beneath his freshly ironed designer dress shirt. Clearly, he was someone who took care of himself—both in and outside the gym—which I greatly appreciated. Unfortunately, this observation only conjured up a vision of my date, bent over a weight bench, naked and sweaty.

Begging for it.

Maybe it was because I had such a shitty afternoon doing shitty things for my shitty family, but I decided *'fuck it'* with trying to act civilized. I wanted to see Butch blush again. I wanted to know if his ass would color just as nicely as his face after I was done with it. As soon as I filled myself with fried chicken, I was gonna take this man home and bury myself so far inside him he'd remember me until next calendar year.

Assuming I don't scare him off first.

I knew I was an intense individual, with both nature *and* nurture to blame, but at least I owned it. We supes were required to wear masks when suited up in public. All that accomplished was to make me more determined to be as true to myself as possible at every other opportunity.

Let's see what you can handle, himbo.

"Is today a cheat day, Butch?" I lowered my voice, tasting his name on my tongue, pure predatory instinct roiling just below the surface of my skin.

He swallowed hard, his Adam's apple bobbing, capturing my attention. "It could be…" He gazed at me, searching my face for…

Permission.

Good LORD, I was going to *ruin* this man. I was going to repay Kai for her excellent matchmaking prowess with the voyeur's special full orchestra performance. My cock was probably going to Hulk its way through the wall separating our apartments with the sheer force of our fucking.

Taking a steadying breath, I leaned across the table, practically purring as he instinctively moved to meet me halfway. He smelled like fresh air on a windy day, and a visceral image surfaced of being out on the Bay, riding the waves—temporarily distracting me.

"What I think," I whispered, hooking a finger into the collar of his shirt, reeling him in until I could feel his breath on my lips. "Is that you should eat whatever the fuck you want tonight. Because I want you to enjoy yourself."

The change that came over him was practically orgasmic. Butch's pretty blue eyes fluttered closed, his enormous body almost melting through the greasy table and onto the floor as he exhaled, fully accepting the permission I gave him.

Holy fuck.

This was someone who *needed* to be dommed, who'd probably never realized until this moment that this was what he'd been craving like the air he breathed. Forget bi-awakening, I had a *sub*-awakening on my hands, and I had never been more here for anything in my entire goddamn life.

Come. To. Daddy.

CHAPTER 4
BUTCH

There was only one other man who'd captivated me the way Xander did. Since a date with Doctor Antihero was never going to happen, I was determined to appreciate every minute of this experience while it lasted.

The rash decision to create a Bangers profile came in the middle of another sleepless night, and it was pure dumb luck that I'd attracted someone like this. If it wouldn't have been super weird, I might have pinched myself to check I wasn't dreaming.

I can't believe this is happening!

He was just so... *handsome.* Tall and leanly muscular, with hands I couldn't stop staring at. I didn't think I'd ever noticed a man being attractive before, but Xander's light brown skin and pitch black hair perfectly complemented his amber eyes... eyes that kept settling on my face—really *looking* at me as if he *saw* me.

I wish he could.

We'd only been at the diner for an hour, but my date already had me wrapped around his little finger. I was fascinated with his graceful gestures—with how he ate his food—and fixated on every word that came out of his mouth. The way my body reacted to him speaking felt like a light switch was turned on, illuminating a room that had always been dark. Everything he said felt *important.*

"Well, *fuck me,* that fried chicken was excellent," he huffed a laugh, as if surprised, but delighted to be surprised. Those arresting eyes focused on me again, lighting me up. "You did good, Butch. Very good."

Oh, my GOD!

The uncontrollable moan that slipped out of my mouth made my cheeks heat. I normally wasn't so *awkward* in front of other people. In fact, I had been intensely coached on how to remain calm and composed even under the most insane circumstances—but that didn't seem to matter here. With Xander, I was apparently doomed to be a total loser who got hard when complimented on my food choices.

He chuckled softly, a warm sound that made me feel better instead of worse. "You like it when I praise you, huh?"

Is that a thing?

"Yeah," I rubbed the back of my neck, unsure what the correct answer was. "Maybe I do…"

"You do," he said, blessedly leaving no room for argument. "You're a complete *slut* for my praise, and I think you'd do just about anything I said if it meant you got to be my… *good boy.*"

"Sugar!" I gasped, my entire body reacting to him, starting with my dick. It was a struggle, but I regained my composure, suddenly suspicious of what sorcery was going on here. "Are you… using some sort of," I lowered my voice, so as not to disturb the elderly couple in the booth across the way. "*Sex magic* on me?"

He threw his head back and laughed, and dang if it wasn't a beautiful sound. "You got me, sweetheart. My secret superpower is that I'm a sex wizard."

I laughed at that, peeking up at him while I smiled like a fool. "Sweetheart, huh?"

Xander smirked, handing the waitress—Barb—his platinum credit card before I could stop him. "Yeah. Because you're sweet. Gonna look even sweeter on your knees." Barb choked on her gum as she scurried off, making his grin turn downright evil.

"Listen, Butch," he sobered, watching me closely. "It's no secret that Bangers is an app for people who want to fuck…" When I shifted in my seat, his smirk returned. "That's right, sweetheart. I said *fuck*. As in, what I'm going to do to you as soon as I take you home. But right now, I need you to focus and tell me if this is what you really want."

Is the drool not convincing enough?

"Yes," I croaked, barely above a whisper.

Seriously, look at me—I can barely form words.

He didn't look convinced. "I'm asking because your profile said you were only interested in women, and I hate to break it to you, but I have a cock. A *huge* one, in fact," he loudly added, causing the elderly couple to turn and gape. "And I'm a top, which means *you'll* be the one taking my huge cock. I'd be perfectly fine starting off slow tonight—fucking that pretty mouth I've been staring at since I arrived. But I want to make sure we're on the same page here and that I'm,"—he lewdly gestured toward his crotch—"what you want."

Sugar, honey, iced tea, I've never wanted anything more in my life!

Frustrated and horny as heck, I sat back to better look at him. "Why do you keep asking me? Isn't the top in control?"

His lips pressed into a thin line, a distracting wrinkle forming between his eyebrows. "That's not how it works. I need you to use your words to agree first—it's called *consent*." He cocked his head. "Has no one ever asked what *you* want before?"

"Never," I replied, which was the truth. I had *never* been given a choice for anything in my entire life. Since birth, my path had been chosen for me, and until this moment, I'd assumed that was how it was always going to be.

My eyes widened. I suddenly understood that even if I would give up control once Xander took me home with him, he was giving *me* control of the overall situation. Taking a deep breath, I geared up to follow his instructions, as foreign as they were.

I can do this!

"Yes, Xander, I want *this*—with *you*. I want to…" I faltered, a blush creeping up my neck again, but I powered on, "Get on my knees for you and… take your huge…"

God, I can't even say it.

"Fucking hell," Xander rasped, running a hand down his face as if he were also struggling with this conversation.

Barb reappeared with the receipt. "Right answer, honey," she whispered to me. "This one walked in like he has a huge cock, so there's a good chance he's telling the truth."

"Of course, I'm telling the truth," Xander snapped at her, his expression murderous. "It would be foolish to lie about the size of my cock when he's about to be face to face with it."

"Oh, god," I whimpered, my body shaking at his words and uncaring that Barb was still hovering over us, smacking her gum. "Yes, I want that. I *need* it… please."

Xander's amber eyes flashed gold as he abruptly stood, stuffing his credit card into his wallet before grabbing my hand and yanking me off the bench. "We're leaving. Now."

Despite me having a good fifty pounds on him, Xander easily dragged me out of the diner, the door barely chiming shut before he slammed me against the wall of the adjacent building.

"Say it again," he growled against my lips, setting my nerves on fire. "*Beg* me for it."

Anything.

"Please," I rasped, realizing I would not only beg but *crawl* through the streets of Big City for this man. "Please, I need your huge…"

"Say. It." His teeth were bared, his expression feral as his long, beautiful fingers wrapped around my throat, pressing lightly on my pulse points, owning me.

"I need your…" I was shaking. "Huge…" Absolutely helpless. "*Cock.*"

The scandalous word barely escaped me before he was crushing his lips to mine. I groaned as he invaded my mouth—his tongue forcefully demanding entry before tangling with mine, sweeping around, claiming every inch as *his.*

I'd kissed countless women at the after-parties for my heroic deeds—the forgettable memory of each blending together into one sloppy, booze-soaked puddle. But *this* was a nearly indescribable experience I knew I would never *ever* forget.

How will I survive this man?

As if recognizing how close I was to dropping to my knees on 57th Street, Xander slid his other hand down my body, languidly tracing my abs through my shirt before heading lower…

Oh, sugarrrrr.

"Mmm," he smiled against my mouth, giving my bottom lip a sharp bite that had my dick nudging his hand through my jeans. "It appears you might have a *huge* cock as well."

When I simply whimpered, he released me and took a step back, not a hair out of place, while I probably looked like I'd been hit by a bus. "All right, sweetheart, I'm going to take you home now. My car's right over here, and if you behave on the drive, I'll…"

As he trailed off, I tore my attention away from his captivating face to follow his gaze. I didn't know much about cars—had never needed one since I could fly—but a few parked along the curb looked like they might be the kind he would pick.

"Where's yours?" I breathlessly asked, lips still tingling from his delicious assault and dick practically bursting through my zipper to reach him.

I'm so ready for this.

"Not here," he sighed, sounding more exasperated than panicked as he pulled out his phone. "It's apparently been stolen."

CHAPTER 5
XANDER

"Cheese and crackers! Someone stole your car?!"

Even Butch's adorable non-cursing couldn't turn my murderous frown upside down. I was ready to take this man home and crucify him on my cock until he begged for salvation, but now I had to deal with this shit.

"Yes and no," I sighed, already seeing the not-so-humblebrag in the Suarez family group chat. "It was my sister."

Butch furrowed his brow, understandably confused. Most sane people would be. "I don't... why on earth would your *sister* steal your car?"

I felt my blood pressure skyrocket as Violentia sent a photo of my Audi precariously perched over Dead Man's Ravine. To add insult to injury, she was balancing on the hood and shooting a flamethrower into the air.

Which one of these fuckers took the photo?!

Shoving my phone deep into my pocket, I took a slow, calming breath, determined not to let this ruin my night. "I assume it's because I was asked to do something for my family earlier today that she believed *she* should've done. The irony is, she would have been the better choice for it and I would have loved nothing more than to not be involved at all. But I had little say in the matter, as usual."

I laughed bitterly before freezing, realizing I'd just shared more with Butch about my day than I ever had with anyone outside of the sociopaths who shared my blood.

And even they don't know much about me.

To my surprise, he laughed with a similar bite to his tone. "Yeah, that actually sounds really freakin' familiar. Honestly? Going on this date was probably the first real decision I've ever made in my entire life."

I turned to look at the man next to me. As in, turned my entire body to really *look* at him. He was still achingly attractive—still fitting the big and hot requirements my dick needed to survive—but I now suspected there was more beneath the himbo-esque exterior.

This shockingly *wasn't* a deal-breaker.

I'd always believed that the best way to determine compatibility was through your shared *dislikes*, and if family was also numero uno on Butch's hit list, then we were gonna get along like two resentful black sheep together.

Wait... together?

It was probably because of compounded stress, but the idea of having someone to *talk* to—aside from the filth I planned on whispering in his ear—was unexpectedly appealing. Now that the lust-filled haze from earlier had faded, I realized Butch was someone I might want to get to know.

Slow down, Xander.

Start with fucking his brains out through his throat first.

Pulling my phone out of my pocket again, I quickly muted the group chat before bringing up my membership apps. "Well, sweetheart, I'd still love to take you home, but it looks like it might be a while for an Uber Black. Should we…"

"I live nearby," Butch blurted out before blushing again in that way that made my cock practically leap out of my pants. "I mean, that's why Tick Tock is my spot for fried chicken. They all know me there." His blush deepened. "Oh cheez-its, I can't believe Barb saw me begging for your…"

A grin stretched across my face as he once again failed to get that terrible, horrible, no good, very bad word past his pillowy lips.

That's fine.

I still plan on getting it IN there tonight…

"Now, Butch," I purred, moving closer until I'd backed him against the wall. "How am I ever going to give you my *cock* unless you're able to ask for it?"

He whimpered, the sound lighting up my entire nervous system. I rested my hand on his cheek, noticing once again how instantaneously the change came over him. His shoulders dropped as he leaned into my touch, trust flavored with desperation, like a rescue mutt trying to convince a potential new owner to take them home.

"How far away do you live?" I growled, needing to get my dog to heel immediately.

"Right around the corner," he mumbled, deliciously dazed and already leading the way, unflinching when I wrapped a hand around the back of his neck as we walked.

It's not as if I'd never encountered someone with submissive tendencies before. But it didn't seem like Butch was even *aware* of how naturally he was falling into the role—how willingly he was letting me take over.

How has he gotten this far in life not knowing himself?

The strangest feeling began to wash over me as we reached The Gloucester—one of the priciest apartment buildings in the city. This unfamiliar sensation only amplified as we entered the expansive marble lobby and mirrored elevator beyond, so foreign that it took me a minute to internally articulate it.

I… care.

It was *not* on brand for me to give a shit. I wouldn't say I completely lacked empathy for other people, but it was an emotion fairly low on my personal agenda, despite Dr. Ownit's annoying attempts to convince me to develop it.

Who has the time?

As we entered the penthouse apartment on the 98th floor, my stomach sank at what I saw. I wasn't bothered by the overstated opulence, the couch that probably cost a few hundred thousand, but by how miserably out-of-place Butch looked surrounded by it.

Physically, he fit right in, no doubt raised with a silver spoon in hand, but I somehow sensed this wasn't *him*—that he hated everything about this place. How I could know that about someone I'd just met was troubling. It was so unsettling that I released Butch's neck from where I'd still been holding it and began backing toward the door.

I have to get the fuck out of here.

Butch turned to face me with confusion and concern on his handsome face. He probably thought I was intimidated by the wealth—never mind that I could buy this entire building—

and that was fine by me. It would be a good enough excuse to end things before they escalated further.

I didn't need a weird dating app to get laid. I could drive through midtown, whistle, and have no less than twenty suits clawing their way into my car. But what I *really* didn't need in my life was the unexplainable urge to protect this man at all costs.

Villains don't protect.

"Xander," his voice had gone low and rough with need.

And then he dropped to his knees.

Fuck.

There had never been a more gorgeous sight than this man kneeling before me. The moonlight was streaming through the floor-to-ceiling windows, glinting off the gold accents and illuminating the ridiculous white upholstery and even whiter surfaces, but all I saw was *him*.

Oh, fuck.

"Please," he whispered, placing his palms on his thighs like the perfect little accidental sub he was.

I'm fucked.

"You look so good like that, sweetheart," I praised without a second thought, hands unbuckling my belt of their own accord. "So ready for me."

Butch bit his lip with a soft smile, his baby blues locked on mine while I unzipped my pants and pulled myself free. His gaze dropped, eyes widening at the sight of what was, in fact, a *huge* cock, already rock-hard as I stroked it.

"Open your mouth," I moved closer, slowly, to give him time to change his mind. "And stick out that pretty pink tongue."

He obeyed without question, and I groaned at the sight of him. We hadn't even taken off our clothes or bothered to find the bedroom, but I was beyond ready to unload down this angel's throat in the middle of all this no doubt scandalously dirty *family* money.

I've never been harder in my entire life.

I used my thumb to spread precum over the head of my cock before placing it on his tongue, giving him his first taste. My usually unshakable self-control was tested as he remained perfectly still aside from a satisfied flutter of his eyelashes. The urge to grab hold of that soft blond hair and ram myself into his guts was blinding, but I oddly wanted to make this as enjoyable for him as it would be for me.

Maybe something was in the fried chicken…

I kept my voice soft. "I assume you've never done anything like this before, so I'm going to take over." His eyelashes fluttered, and I couldn't help but stroke his hair—petting him. "If you need me to stop, tap my leg three times, but otherwise, I want you to relax and enjoy yourself. And I promise *I'm* going to enjoy anything you do."

As soon as the words left my lips, I realized they were true. This man could probably do nothing but breathe on me and I'd spray him like a goddamn firehose. Again, that unfamiliar urge to *take care of him* flared up within me, but I quickly buried it, refocusing on my noble mission of introducing Butch to the wonderful world of sucking dick.

Hold on tight, sweetheart.

CHAPTER 6
BUTCH

I hated feeling like a newbie at anything, usually preparing to the point of practically being an expert before I took my first step. I'd admittedly done a little research before tonight's date—which flustered me to no end—but nothing could have prepared me for *this*.

Xander wasn't exaggerating about his size. We were fairly matched in that department, except he was uncut, which was something I hadn't seen up close before, since all superheroes were required to get circumcised at birth.

Somehow, it makes him even hotter.

He was thick and long, with tempting veins along his length that I couldn't wait to trace with my tongue, even though I'd never even *considered* doing anything like that before. Right now, I was trying to remain as still as possible, wanting to be *good*.

The weight of him on my tongue was thrilling, and the salty taste had my dick uncomfortably straining against my zipper. But more than anything, his approval—his praise—was the drug I needed more of.

I'm already addicted.

"Okay, sweetheart, now close those perfect lips around my cock as I slide in and... oh, *fuuuck!* Are you sure you've never done this before?"

I hadn't, but it felt like second nature to tightly seal my lips around his dick and suck him in as far as he could go.

Give me all of it.

Xander began slowly thrusting, sliding his hardness against the inside of my cheeks, my jaw aching as I strained to accommodate him. Back and forth he went, clearly taking it slow, letting me explore him as much as I could with my tongue as he inched his way down my throat, so freakin' far down...

Until I gagged.

Tensing, I looked up, unsure if the sound would gross him out... if it would make him immediately stop everything and leave my condo, and my life, forever.

I shouldn't have worried. The look on his face was *primal*—barely contained lust and hunger, and something darker flickering beneath the surface. His jaw was clenching and his chest heaving as he breathed heavily through his nose, his hand tightening ever so slightly in my hair.

Maintaining eye contact, I moved forward, taking him deeper, making myself gag again.

"Je-sus," he gritted out. "You *like* choking on my cock, don't you?" I nodded as best I could, gagging myself again. "Fuck. I am trying to be *nice* here, Butch. But I want to fucking *own* you right now."

I moaned, but he gripped my hair, stopping me as I tried to swallow him deeper. "Very well. Take off your shirt and get your cock out. I wanna watch you fuck your hand while I fuck your throat."

He pulled out completely, taking a step back and stroking himself with my saliva while I tore off my dress shirt and wrestled my dick out of my jeans.

"Mmm... look at that big thick cock," he licked his lips. "I can't wait to drink your cum as you ride my face."

"Sugar!" I gasped, desperately squeezing the base so I wouldn't embarrass myself.

"I bet you taste like sugar," he chuckled, stepping closer again. "Are you ready to find out what I taste like?"

Use your words, Butch.

"Yes," I rasped, beginning to pump with my fist, squeezing so hard it hurt. "I want you to f-fuck my throat like you... own me."

All humor left his face, his expression morphing into something almost *inhuman* as he roughly grabbed my hair, burying himself so deep, his balls slapped against my chin. Then he did it again, and again, making my eyes roll back in my head.

I almost came from how he was handling me, desperately thrusting upward into my hand to match his movements, gagging and moaning so loudly it echoed off the walls.

"My perfect little cumslut," he snarled, planting his other hand in my hair and holding me in place while he pummeled my face. "I want you to explode like the messy slut you are, so I can lick it off you after I fill your fucking throat."

Tears were streaming down my face and I was perilously close to losing it already, but I had never, *ever* been happier.

I want to be his perfect slut.

This was paradise. It barely registered that *multiple* very inappropriate words had crossed my mind and lips in the past hour alone. I never wanted this to end—this date, this night, any of it. It felt like something was finally snapping into place in my otherwise ill-fitting existence, something I couldn't quite put my finger on.

"So. Fucking. Perfect." Xander punctuated each word with a violent thrust that had my legs tensing. "Such a good, *good* boy."

That did it. Thick ropes of cum shot out of me, splashing up my abs and chest while I shuddered, loudly sobbing around Xander's dick, blissfully uncaring about how much of a mess I was making.

"FUCK!!!" he roared, holding my lips flush against his groin as he came in shuddering pulses. "Fucking fucking Jesus fucking Christ… that was… oh, fuck *and* you're swallowing? Christ on the cross…."

Of course, I was. He tasted like heaven, like the only sustenance I needed to survive from here on out. I'd barely finished drinking my fill when he was suddenly kneeling in front of me, his tongue claiming mine, collecting *his own cum* out of my mouth while I groaned.

"Look how sloppy you got," Xander hummed, the approval in his tone like fresh air. "Coming all over that ten-pack of yours like a good little slut. Let me clean you up, sweetheart…"

My back hit the mahogany floor as he lowered his mouth to my stomach, licking me clean with a gentleness that simultaneously turned me on and deeply comforted me.

"Let me take care of you," he murmured, so quietly that I wondered if he'd meant to say it out loud.

For some reason, this statement made a lump form in my throat, and before I could stop it, stupid tears began rolling down my stupid face.

What is happening?!

"Shit, shit, *shit*," Xander's face was suddenly above mine, his hands frantically wiping at my tears. "I was too rough with you, wasn't I? I was trying so fucking hard to not be too intense for your first time, and instead, I acted like a goddamn unhinged sex maniac. Jesus fuck, I'm sorry, Butch."

My heart stuttered as I wrapped my arms around his back, pulling him flush against my chest. "No! Stop it. I... I have no idea why I'm crying, but it's not because of anything you did. It was... perfect. *You* were perfect."

Perfect.

Xander froze, his expression dangerously close to how it looked earlier when he seemed about ready to bolt from my condo.

I tightened my hold. "Please spend the night."

He sharply inhaled, and I grimaced, wondering if I'd just ruined everything by crying like a big baby and then begging him to cuddle.

God, what is wrong with me?

After a tense moment of him staring down at me with those gorgeous eyes that saw everything, he slowly exhaled, brow furrowing. "You want me to... sleep in your bed? With you?"

I could feel a smile threatening to break free at how genuinely *confused* he sounded. "Yeah. I mean, unless you'd rather hang upside down like a bat, like you probably do at home."

Xander barked a laugh, his body relaxing enough that I dared to let him sit up without me clinging to him like a spider monkey. "You really have me pegged, huh? I'm a bat-man sex wizard with intimacy issues."

I hoisted myself onto my knees, stealing a kiss, which seemed to please him. "Well, I didn't know the intimacy part, but thanks for the freebie. If you stay, I promise I'll try not to be too needy."

Try…

He got quiet again—thoughtful. "It's okay to need things, Butch. I want you to be yourself with me. We should all be able to be ourselves…"

I had to mentally *force* myself not to start blubbering again, wishing more than anything that I *could* be myself with this man.

But that's never going to happen.

Smiling tightly, I rose to my feet, giving Xander a hand before leading him into my bedroom. I offered him some of my pajama pants, but he chose to sleep buck naked, which somehow didn't shock me one bit.

What did surprise me was how *natural* it felt to let another man spoon me. At first, his hold on me was awkward—as if it wasn't something he did very often—but it didn't take long for him to fully snuggle against me. Then his lips brushed along my neck and shoulder as one hand lazily traced my abs, his touch that odd combination of arousing and soothing.

In his arms, all the tension I'd been holding on to since accepting my position with Big City melted away, and I had a moment of absolute, startling clarity.

THIS is what's been missing from my life.

"So perfect," he sleepily mumbled in my ear, echoing my thoughts exactly. Soon after, his breathing evened out, lulling me to sleep as I dreamed about what the future might hold.

In the morning, Xander was gone.

CHAPTER 7
XANDER

"Is that my little brother, slumming in the fancy part of town?"

I rolled my eyes, shifting the paper bag I was holding under my arm as I approached my precious Audi. Violentia had rolled down the heavily tinted driver's side window just enough for me to register her smeared eye makeup and slightly unhinged expression—evidence that she'd probably been joyriding all night.

It's okay, baby. You're back with Daddy now.

I'd been buying egg sandwiches at the deli across the street from Butch's high-rise when my psycho sister texted me. The contents of his fridge were much too healthy for my taste, and since he was sleeping like a log, I figured I could slip out and back before he woke up.

To surprise him with breakfast.

Like some sort of weird boyfriend shit.

Who even am I right now?

Because she was a worse cockblocker than Captain Masculine, Violentia delayed my return by bartering my car for a favor. So I got stuck waiting for her on the curb like a vagrant, stubbornly refusing to eat until Butch could.

I glanced over my shoulder, my gaze drifting to the top floor where an extremely delicious man was waiting for me. "What's your problem with The Gloucester Apartments, Vi? Besides the interior designer catering to the Vegas octogenarian crowd."

She snorted. "Well, ignoring the fact it's full of normies who've made their money off the sweat of supes, I've heard some pretty important *heroes* live here."

My phone buzzed in my pocket. Once I wrestled it out, I saw it was Butch messaging me on Bangers, reminding me we still needed to exchange phone numbers.

> **Butch:** *"Why did you leave?"* [sad emoji face]

Oof.

Normally, I would have immediately blocked someone for that level of clinginess, but I *liked* Butch sending me sad little emojis for reasons I didn't want to examine at the moment.

I'm definitely blaming the fried chicken.

Ignoring my sister's stare, I quickly typed a reply.

> ***"I was grabbing us breakfast across the street. Hot and ready, just like I expect you to be when I get back up there."***

"Fascinating," I vaguely acknowledged Violentia's idiotic statement, in no mood to gossip when I had a bacon, egg, and cheese to inhale and some grade-A cum to wash it down with. "Now what was this big favor you—"

"Like Captain Masculine," she smoothly interjected, one perfectly on-fleek eyebrow arching as she awaited my reaction. "Big City's greatest hero supposedly lives right behind you in The Gloucester."

She's just trying to get a rise out of you, Xander.

"I'll be sure to keep an eye out for him." My tone was disinterested, despite now having *two* very compelling reasons to get back inside. I'd already decided my dick was sold on a second date with Butch—maybe more—but the idea of infiltrating my nemesis' *home* made me just as hard.

Smothering Masculine to death with a three thousand dollar designer pillow would be orgasmic.

"Dinner at the compound," Violentia's voice drew me out of my vengeful reverie. "In two weeks. Father wants to speak with you."

My heart stopped. It was one thing to be at the beck and call of Glacial Girl and my aggravating siblings, but Apocalypto Man was a final boss-level villain. I tried to avoid the Suarez family compound, but even when I was summoned, I rarely saw my father. This was fine by me. He was a literal world-ender who could just as easily snap my neck as Thanos-snap the universe into oblivion. Whatever he wanted with me couldn't be good.

Maybe I can hide at the bottom of Awakener's Bay...

"Breathe, doofus," my sister cackled as she opened the door, finally peeling her black leather-covered ass out of my car and handing me my keys. "You know he doesn't need to *see* you to *kill* you."

Not. Helpful.

She lazily stretched before retrieving a device I recognized from her jacket pocket. "Besides, I think you'll *like* what he has in mind for you since it apparently involves one of your evil genius toys."

With a flick of her wrist, the palm-sized cylinder Violentia was holding transformed into a douchey Segway I'd designed for her out of spite. Unfortunately, she ended up loving it *and* figuring out how to disarm the self-destruct mechanism I'd originally programmed it with.

A complete waste of my time and talent.

I didn't even want to *consider* what sort of 'toy' Apocalypto Man wanted from me. Any intel I was deemed worthy of knowing would come through in the family chat, so I banished it from my mind for now.

Especially because I have a more important toy to think about.

"As thrilling as this chat has been, Vi, I need to get back to my date," I airily dismissed her with a wave of my hand. "Which you interrupted."

I instantly realized I'd fucked up. Her cool gaze swept over me, instantly assessing my day-old clothes, the egg-sandwich aroma wafting from the bag in my hands, and that I was lurking outside this supposed lair of Supes Most Wanted.

Shit.

"What'll it take to keep this walk of shame out of the chat?" I sighed.

My sister smirked. "I want a new toy, too." She fired up the Segway. *"Without* a doomsday device built in this time."

"I make no promises!" I shouted after her as she sped off, playing chicken with an oncoming city bus until it drove up onto the sidewalk.

Fuck my life.

Taking a deep breath, I turned and walked back into the marble lobby, tossing my car keys to the on-site valet. As soon as the elevator doors closed, a fresh wave of Apocalypto-related panic washed over me. Yanking my phone out of my pocket again, I stared at my therapist's number, wondering if Ownit could squeeze me in sooner than my weekly Tuesday afternoon slot.

I will not allow my triggers to control me.

The elevator dinged at the 98th floor, doors sliding open as a strange sense of *calm* washed over me. I cautiously walked along the thickly carpeted private hallway, wondering if what I was experiencing was actually the lull before a psychotic break.

Reaching Butch's door, I swung it open and stepped inside, noticing how my relaxation only amplified, despite the questionable taste in decor. As my confused gaze drifted to where Butch stood—facing the street side windows, shirtless with all those drool-worthy muscles on full display, blasting me with that fresh scent of his—I suddenly felt as if everything was *right* in the world.

Oh, fuck.

It's… him.

I really am fucked.

Clearing my throat in an attempt to dislodge this terrifying truth, I walked to the granite kitchen island to unpack breakfast.

"I come bearing gifts!" I exclaimed, determined not to infect my date with my Violentia-induced bad mood. "All I found in your kitchen was nut milk and protein powder, so figured some grease would do that body good. Every day's a cheat day with me, sweetheart…"

My nervous babbling trailed off as Butch turned to face me, his broad chest heaving, sweat beading on his brow, looking as scared as an ultra-jacked bodybuilder could.

WHO HURT HIM?!

That someone had threatened what was *mine* while I was gone made a murderous rage swell in my chest. My vision tunneled until all I could see was the perpetrator's head brandished on a stake as I howled my victory through the streets of Big City.

"Who was that woman you were talking to down there?" he quietly asked, immediately bringing my attention back to reality.

What?

"W-what?" I stuttered, momentarily thrown off my internal rampage.

Butch advanced on me, grabbing my shoulders and spinning me to face him, his blue-eyed gaze raking over my body as if looking for evidence of... something.

Oh. Ohhh...

He thinks Vi is my secret girlfriend.

Gross.

"The woman on the douchey Segway?" I hedged, trying to determine if he'd seen Violentia exit my car or not. Then I remembered this normie lived 98 stories up, so unless he had superspy-level binoculars, there was little chance that he saw much of anything.

You're just used to dealing with supes, Xan.

He nodded, and I flashed him a charming smile in return. "Just some lost tourist looking for where they filmed *Twilight*. I sent her to the very tip of the peninsula."

I could have told him it was my crazy-ass sister returning my car, but there was an understanding among supe families not to openly associate with each other as unmasked civilians—just in case covers were blown. While there was no love lost between my siblings and me, in the end, it was the Suarez clan against the world.

Blood is thicker than murder.

He swallowed hard and nodded, gaze meeting mine with so much concern I wanted to drop to my knees and suck it out of his dick. "She didn't... *touch you*, did she?"

This is adorable.

"No, sweetheart," I cooed, hooking my fingers in his belt loops and yanking him closer. "She didn't. And I wouldn't have let her anyway—not only because I don't do pussy, but I knew I had something better and *bigger* waiting for me up here." I illustrated my point by roughly palming the enormous bulge in Butch's pants and squeezing until he moaned.

"Sugar..." he whispered in that helplessly breathless way of his that made me feral. "I'm sorry I'm being so weird, I just—"

"You just have a huge crush on me, I get it," I chuckled, licking my way into his mouth for a deep kiss before pulling him toward the kitchen area. "That's cool. I kinda like you too, big guy. Now let's eat our breakfast while it's still hot... because *I'm* still hot, especially thinking about what a *good job* you did last night."

His blush almost had me coming in my pants. "You *like* me, huh?" He stifled a smile, seeming to recover from his sexy AF bout of jealousy. Then, his pretty eyes lit up at the sight of his egg sandwich, which only made me want to figure out twenty more ways to spoil him.

And fuck, do I want to spoil him.

"Yeah," I shrugged nonchalantly, taking a juicy bite of cheesy goodness and feeling my pleasure multiply as he did the same. "Just a little bit."

CHAPTER 8
BUTCH

Xander *seemed* okay, and I didn't want to push, so I had no choice but to believe him when he said nothing had actually happened between him and…

Violentia Suarez.

I took a big gulp of my all-natural orange juice, willing myself to swallow down the panic threatening to rise to the surface again. When I'd used my supe-vision to look down 98 stories and discovered that deadly menace talking to *my*…

My…

Regardless of what I was *supposed* to call the man who'd given me a near-spiritual experience on my knees, the sight of him in danger—helpless and within Violentia's reach—had nearly wrecked me.

Even if I'd flown down at top speed, I wouldn't have made it in time.

"Are you okay?"

I was startled back to the present at the sound of Xander's smooth voice, again feeling that snap of a puzzle piece falling into place in his presence. This entire situation had been surreal from the start, and while it felt *right,* it was also a little overwhelming.

"Totally fine," I replied, plastering on the smile I'd been taught to give to the cameras since birth.

Xander gave me a stern look. "Bullshit. What's on your mind, Butch?"

If you insist.

The opportunity to actually *talk* to someone was too tempting to resist, so I set aside my half-eaten breakfast sandwich, even though it was the best thing I'd ever put in my mouth.

Besides Xander.

"To be honest, I've been under a lot of stress lately with work, so this,"—I gestured between the two of us—"is just a lot to take in on top of everything else. It's just so *new* for me, and like nothing I've ever done before, so…"

His expression was impressively unreadable. "Let me guess. Now that you've gotten your side trip to Cocktown out of the way, you think you'd rather return to Pussyville, where it's safe and warm, hmm?"

"Are you kidding?" I yelped. "I like… Cock… town. It's the best! I think I might stay—maybe buy a house and live there forever."

What the heck am I even saying?

The phone buzzing in my pocket saved me from embarrassing myself any further. Pointedly avoiding Xander's smirk, I pulled it out, groaning to find a message from Biggs calling me into the office.

"It looks like I have to go to work," I grumbled. "Even though it's supposed to be my day off."

Not that heroes truly get days off.

Xander glanced around my condo, that cute wrinkle forming between his amber eyes again. "I have to admit, I assumed this setup was thanks to family money, and that you were just a layabout, yet extremely athletic, playboy who works on spreadsheets for fun."

I barked a laugh. "It *is* family money—in a way—but I've worked hard to get where I am."

"How hard?" he teased, licking his lips and making me wonder if I should call out sick for the first time in my life. His expression suddenly changed to mild annoyance. "Wait, what are you doing?"

It took me a moment to realize Xander was referring to me wrapping up my unfinished breakfast to throw away.

Maybe he has an issue with wasted food?

"I have to go to work," I repeated, slower this time. "But *thank you* for the egg sandwich. It was a treat. Maybe next time I'll get to eat the whole thing!"

His hand was suddenly covering mine, firmly holding me—and the sandwich—in place. "No," his voice sent a delicious shiver down my spine. "You're going to sit your tight ass down and finish your breakfast. I don't give a *fuck* if your boss wants you to jump when he says jump. You're not going to work hungry."

Oh, okay.

Whatever you say.

My entire body immediately responded to his command—my 'tight ass' sliding onto the bar stool while my hands dutifully unwrapped my sinful treat again. I was *contractually* expected to jump when Biggs said jump, but when *Xander* gave me orders, I actually wanted to obey.

He watched me eat with a half-lidded expression that reminded me of how he'd looked standing over me last night. It was as if I were giving him pleasure all over again, which made *me* warm and satisfied in return.

Sugar, I like pleasing him.

"So, what do you do for work?" I mumbled around another deliciously unhealthy bite. "I mean, unless *you're* an athletic layabout too?"

Xander's lips twisted in amusement. "Well, I try to lay about as much as possible, but I *do* work. Mostly on my own research, but it's ah… a lot of it is privately funded." He paused, as if debating how to explain, before hesitantly adding. "It's also family money… in a way."

My heart nearly thumped out of my chest at the similarities, although I tried to play it cool. "Mmhmm, with loads of strings attached, right?" When he nodded grimly, I switched gears. "Tell me about your research! What's your field of study?"

Xander smiled. *Really* smiled. Which made his handsome face even more handsome and activated the heart eyes I was no doubt beaming at him with.

"Marine biology. I'm working on a large-scale project right now that could completely eliminate human impact on Awakener's Bay."

I couldn't help but smile back at his infectious enthusiasm. "That sounds nefarious," I teased. "Like some sort of evil villain plotting the demise of the human race."

He went completely still. "What makes you say that?"

Before I could tell him I was kidding—*obviously*—my phone buzzed on the countertop with another message from Biggs.

Ah, fiddlesticks.

"That fucker," Xander growled, snatching my phone and immediately texting back a reply.

Nononono...

"What are you doing?" I hissed, attempting to grab the phone yet somehow failing.

Goodness, he's fast for a normie!

"I am telling your boss that you will gladly be in *after* you've eaten a balanced breakfast. Including my cock." When he spotted my horrified expression, he snickered. "I didn't actually say that last bit, sweetheart."

My phone immediately buzzed, and Xander's eyes narrowed. "Who the fuck *is* this clown? You'd think he was somebody import—Oh, you work for Solomon Biggs? Interesting..."

Internally groaning, I tried to grab my phone again, but he took a step back and continued texting. Biggs Enterprises was notoriously polarizing among humans—and some supes—as many believed a corporation shouldn't be in charge of running a city.

I mean, they're not wrong.

Of course, I would *never* voice this dissent out loud. The Biggs family founded Big City and only hired the best heroes to defend it. Being chosen for this position was an incredible honor, even if it was *my* family name that helped me acquire it.

It's just how it is.

"I really do need to get going," I sighed, realizing I would have to fly at top speed to avoid invoking more of Biggs' wrath. "But um… I would like to see you again. You know, if you want…"

Xander scoffed, and I immediately assumed the worst, but his slow smile soothed my fears. "Oh, sweetheart, I've already saved my number in your phone and texted myself, so I have yours." His breathtaking gaze met mine across the breakfast bar as he handed the device back to me. "And I'd also like to see you again. In my bed. As soon as possible."

"Tonight?" I blurted out, apparently physically unable to play it cool with this man.

What happened to not acting needy?

Because he specialized in sex sorcery, Xander brought me to full attention with nothing but a wink. "It's a date. Just tell me when mean ol' Biggs finally lets you off the clock, and I'll pick you up at the office."

Gliding over to where I sat, he leaned in and placed his large hands on my thighs—dangerously close to my aching dick. "And sweetheart? Don't you dare touch your cock before then. I promise I'll take care of you later."

He ghosted his lips over mine, brushing a finger down the bulge in my pants with a featherlight touch. Then he was gone, shooting me another saucy wink before breezing out of my apartment.

Definitely a sex wizard.

I waited until I heard the elevator ding before hurrying into my bedroom, yanking on my Lycra, and covering it with a civilian suit to save time. Quickly packing everything I'd need for a *sleepover at Xander's,* I grabbed my keys and phone, then raced for the roof.

And because I was a lovesick fool, I peeked at the text Xander sent to his phone from mine, somehow hardening more when I saw he'd saved his contact info as 'Daddy Xan.'

Sweet cheez-its, this man!

Another groan left my throat as I opened the text, wondering how I would fly with a boner and keep it down all day.

> *I can't wait to collect my reward for being such a good boy.*

CHAPTER 9
XANDER

Why would he take the stairs instead of the elevator?

After leaving Butch's apartment, I'd quickly hidden a couple of remote-access cameras in his private penthouse hallway before the elevator arrived. It was partly because I didn't like the idea of *anyone* coming over here, but I also didn't trust Violentia not to snoop around The Gloucester, now that she knew I might unmask Captain Masculine.

Anything to steal the glory for herself.

Besides the higher-ups at the United Super Nations and local governments, very few supes knew each other's civilian identities. It was a fail-safe insurance policy created by the USN, in case a powerful supe went rogue and needed to be taken out. High resolution photos of Signe and Ender Suarez—aka Glacial Girl and Apocalypto Man—were probably plastered all over Biggs Enterprise's situation room, but I doubted Violentia or my other siblings had ever been identified outside of their required registration with the USN.

Which means no one else knows what they look like but me.

The thought of anyone in my family getting near Butch made panic dance along the edges of my vision. I didn't have the superpowers they did, but I was smarter, stronger, and faster than most normies, and I would use every ounce of my above-average attributes to protect my…

My…

Good lord, why am I getting my panties in a bunch over a normie Bangers match?

I needed to get a hold of myself. Butch was nothing but a casual fling… albeit one who was a perfect specimen of manhood, sucked cock like a pro, and called to an overprotective alpha aspect of my personality I never knew existed.

Someone who takes the stairs from the 98th floor when he's already late for work…

Shaking my head, I banished what I'd seen on the camera footage from my mind. Butch was obviously a granola-eating gym buff. He probably took the stairs on the way up, too—before finishing his night with a protein powder enema and a cock cage.

Jesus, fuck. Now I have a hard-on.

Forcing myself to refocus, I used my scalpel to carefully slice open the distended belly of the Western Gull lying on the examination table before me. While I didn't particularly mind using these same tools to extract information from shitty lowlifes who crossed my family, today's work was unpleasant.

As expected, about a quarter of the deceased bird's stomach contents were styrofoam, with another 20 percent being unidentifiable bits of metal and glass. I also found some rope, part of a plastic knife, a Doritos bag, and an electric green condom.

Who wears a green condom?

Gulls were known for their cast-iron constitution and could regurgitate most foreign objects, so the trash probably wasn't what killed him. That's why I preferred using the last meals of these notorious scavengers to monitor pollution in Awakener's Bay—it allowed me to detach from what I was seeing. There was nothing worse than stumbling upon the corpse of a more fragile shorebird with a shopping bag's worth of microplastics filling its gullet. That sort of death-by-human made me sick.

My parents would say this makes me weak.

But they'd never taken the time to learn what I did when I was off duty, nor did they care. That was fine by me. I would rather my family call my research uninteresting than decide to use my life's work to further their own agendas.

I needed to take a step back from the table as I recalled my mother's distasteful cargo at yesterday's drop on Rose Island. The uber-rich weren't known for their ethical sourcing with the finest things money could buy, but the pelts of endangered species were next-level abhorrent.

The pelts of humans, on the other hand…

The phone vibrating in my pocket interrupted me from my Buffalo Bill fantasies. Removing my latex gloves, I pulled it out, smiling like an idiot to find a text from Butch—right below the delicious one I'd sent on his behalf this morning.

> **Hottie Himbo:** *Biggs is making me work a full day, so I won't be done until 5:00. You still want to hang out later?*

I snorted. He really made this too easy.

> ***Of course I do. And you'll be the one 'hanging out' by the end of the night.***

The three dots appeared, disappeared, then reappeared as Butch no doubt struggled to reply in a way that didn't inflame his delicate sensibilities.

__Hottie Himbo:__ Is that my...

More dots.

__Hottie Himbo:__ Reward?

I blew out a breath, placed my phone down on the examination table, and walked away—more for self-preservation than to tease. If I replied immediately, I knew I would end up driving to that phallic eyesore of 19th-century architecture just so I could bend Butch over Solomon Biggs' desk and pound him into next week.

And I'd rather defile the hornet's nest in more strategic ways.

The corporation known as Biggs Enterprises was originally funded by railroad money in the late 1800s by Solomon's great-grandfather. This wealth was then reinvested in steel, oil, plastics, shipping, banks, real estate, big pharma, and Big City itself—including its poisoned politicians and unstoppable police force.

Led by a certain superhero, of course.

My phone buzzed again, and I narrowed my eyes, praying for Butch's sake that he wasn't being impatient. He didn't seem to have a brat bone in his body—and I had no interest in being a brat handler—but his inexperience meant missteps were bound to happen.

It buzzed again.

To my horror, my feet were already propelling me back across the cement floor of my secret warehouse lair, as if I couldn't stand the thought of keeping this man waiting a second longer.

For real, did I hit my head?

I frowned to discover I *had* received some bratty messages—from the Queen Brat herself. Kai.

> **Bestie:** *Excuse you, sir? I heard your slutty ass fumbling around your apartment this morning before you left again WITHOUT TELLING ME ANY DETAILS ABOUT YOUR HOT DATE WITH THE HIMBO.*
>
> **Bestie:** *I fed Meowson like you asked.*
>
> **Bestie:** *I expect payment. In the form of DETAILS.*

I rolled my eyes at her behavior, not least of all that she'd apparently changed her name in my phone.

Probably when she was installing Bangers.

With a sharp inhale, I realized I not only wanted to delete the dating app from *my* phone but Butch's as well. It wasn't just that the idea of anyone else touching him triggered a caveman-level possessiveness, but with how *innocent* he was...

It would be extremely easy for someone to take advantage of him.

I ran a hand through my hair—a nervous habit I thought I'd trained myself out of years ago. That Butch's naiveté was turning me into a mother hen instead of a fox in the henhouse was concerning. He'd already provided me with the perfect excuse to infiltrate *both* The Gloucester and Biggs Enterprises, along with providing the perfect dick, so I shouldn't care if some wannabe dom or domme sniffed him out on Bangers...

My vision went red as I clutched my phone so tightly that the screen almost cracked. A few deep breaths later—shout-out to Dr. Ownit—I realized I still needed to reply to my...

Mine.

> **That depends on you. Be outside at 5:01.**

It was a physical effort to *stop* myself from texting more than that—from telling Butch all the ways I was going to reward him. There was no doubt in my mind he'd been good for me, like I'd instructed. While I had every intention of showing him how much I appreciated his obedience, for now, there would be restraint.

Later, I'll blow his mind. And by blow, I mean...

A reply came through immediately, but of course, it was only Kai. Again.

> **Bestie:** *OMG, are you being super secretive and shady because you're CATCHING FEELINGS?!*

My eye twitched. Kai was out of her mind on a good day, but right now, she was grasping at straws to try to get a reaction out of me. I'd already planned on taking Butch out for dinner and drinks before bringing him home, and the last thing I needed was my next-door neighbor inviting herself to the after-party.

Just listen through the walls like you normally do, creeper.

I gritted my teeth as *another* text came through. My escalating tension bled out of me, however, when I saw it was from *him*.

> **Hottie Himbo:** *I've been good all day. I promise.*

My eyes closed, and a shudder ran down my spine at the thought of Butch's neglected cock aching for me for *hours*. He was just so perfect, almost to the point of being unreal. It was hard to believe there wasn't a catch.

> ***I know you have, sweetheart.***
> ***I can't wait to see you later.***

I hit send before I realized what I'd done. Sinking onto a nearby metal stool, I read over my disgustingly sweet text with growing panic.

Why the fuck would I say that?!

In the end, I reasoned Butch was so out of his depths that he would either take the tone of my text at face value or read so much into a deeper meaning he'd talk himself out of it again.

It's fine. Everything's fine.

Replacing my latex gloves, I scooted my stool closer to the gull's carcass. I was determined to focus on my research—something with tangible results and a clear end goal. Science, not *feelings*.

I can't wait to see him later…

CHAPTER 10
BUTCH

I need to get a grip.

Tearing my gaze away from the slowly ticking clock taunting me on the nearby wall, I refocused on the case file open on my desk.

An enormous man stared back at me from the grainy black-and-white photo clipped to the inside. His exaggerated square jaw made him look like a caricature mobster, and without even having his height and weight, I knew he could probably palm my entire head in one of his hands.

To then pop it like a balloon.

Shifting my focus to the other side of the folder, I reread the few stats we had on him.

Agent Penetrate
Villain - Strickland clan
Abilities: Super strength, impenetrable skin, abnormal bone density, punches with momentum equal to a bullet train
Number of hero kills: 7
Last sighting: Twenty miles west of Big City

I sighed. This was why Biggs had called me in on a Saturday, despite me begging for the day off earlier in the week. A villain known for clobbering heroes until they were nothing but a bloody stain on the sidewalk was headed our way, and I was the only one on staff who could take him on.

Without forcing my parents out of retirement, that is.

Penetrate wasn't anything I couldn't handle, but I would much rather not have to explain full-body bruising to Xander.

Something tells me he wouldn't take it well.

A loud clunk from the ticking clock told me another minute had passed, which made my dick jerk in anticipation. Blowing out a slow breath, I closed the file folder and discreetly readjusted my pants, making sure to not touch myself any more than absolutely necessary.

I can be good for three more minutes.

Being assigned this case was actually a blessing in disguise, since it had provided me with an excuse to poke around the highly restricted records room. I spent a few hours there this morning—longer than was necessary—but I *needed* to double-check if the woman I saw talking to Xander outside The Gloucester was truly Violentia Suarez.

It was.

We had full files on the entire terrifying Suarez family. Ender and Signe and their five children—Violentia, her younger siblings Baltasar and the twins Gabriel and Andre, and her older brother Wolfgang. Otherwise known as Apocalypto Man and Glacial Girl, Ultra Violent, Blunt Force, Shock and Awe, and The Hand of Death. It was unusual for Biggs Enterprises to care about supervillains' *spawn,* but every member of the Suarez clan was not only unusually powerful but actively engaged in villainy.

Not that we've been able to prove it.

I'd broken into a cold sweat as I stared at Violentia's deceptively attractive face. As Ultra Violent, she was known for falling into a berserker-like trance of fury while fighting her enemies, turning anything within reach into a deadly weapon. While I had little interest in taking her on—or capturing the attention of her family—I needed to be ready in case she threatened Xander.

Why was she even outside The Gloucester?

I could only assume she'd been staking out my apartment building for supes, saw Xander leave, and wanted to see what sort of information she could pry out of him. Dread weighed heavy in my gut as I once again realized I would have been powerless to stop her had she struck.

If anything happens to him, I don't know what I'll do...

The shrill sound of the closing buzzer snapped me out of my spiraling panic. Realizing I had exactly one minute to get downstairs, I shoved the folder in my desk drawer along with my discarded Lycra, grabbed my briefcase and overnight bag, and raced for the stairs. It was against regulation to exhibit any superpowers out of uniform, but the thought of disappointing Xander was more upsetting than being slapped with a misdemeanor from Biggs.

I'd better keep a lid on these rebellious thoughts.

Reaching the roof, I did a quick heat scan for any warm bodies in the neighboring buildings. Finding nothing near the windows, I deftly dropped 70 stories down into the back alley behind Biggs Enterprises before re-entering the building through the service entrance. The frigid air of the lobby instantly cooled my skin, but my heart was pounding so intensely I was sure everyone around me could hear it.

My excitement only intensified as I exited the revolving doors and saw Xander waiting for me at the curb. He was casually leaning against a sleek sports car, dressed like some sort of GQ model in a perfectly cut dark gray suit, wearing that expensive watch of his that probably cost more than my stupid condo.

Sugar, he looks good.

As soon as I got within arm's reach, he wrapped a hand around the back of my neck and pulled me closer. The touch was possessive and just shy of rough, and my entire body melted into a puddle of goo because of it.

"How was your day at the office, sweetheart?" he purred in my ear, rubbing two fingers along the lapel of my suit jacket as if testing the quality of the material. His lips brushed against mine for an agonizingly chaste kiss before he took a step back, running his disarming gaze over me as he opened the passenger side door.

"Torture," I admitted on an exhale, finally feeling like I could breathe again in his presence. "All I did was count down the hours until I saw you again."

For a moment, I worried I was being too open with my feelings—that maybe I should play harder to get. But then the skin around his eyes crinkled, a satisfied smirk turning up the corners of his lips, lighting me up. It was exactly like when I broke through heavy cloud cover to be suddenly blinded and warmed by the sun beyond.

I've got it bad.

"Mmm, I bet." His gaze pointedly dropped to my crotch before lifting to meet mine again. "I hope you can continue to behave through drinks and dinner because I need you fed. I have plans for you afterward."

"Yes, I can behave," I croaked, nodding eagerly as I brushed past him to sit in the passenger seat. My dick gave another kick as I noticed his tie had subtle green accents—the same shade as Doctor Antihero's Lycra...

Stop it.

That I was actually thinking about my *nemesis* while on a date with Xander made a sharp stab of shame course through me.

"You're sweating," he casually remarked as he slid into the driver's side and immediately adjusted the A/C. "Did you take the stairs or something?" That amber gaze swept over me again, missing nothing.

"No, the elevator was faster," I hurriedly replied, guilt assaulting me at the little white lie. "I'm just naturally sweaty."

Why the heck would I say that?

He smirked again as he turned his focus to the road and pulled into traffic. "That's fine. I'll just lick it off you later."

"Sugar!" I gasped, desperately pressing the heel of my palm against my groin. The memory of Xander *licking my cum* off my abs the night before had me clearing my throat, desperately scrambling for a safer topic of conversation. "So, I guess your sister returned your car, huh?"

"She did." He rolled his eyes. "Her point was made, so there was no need to continue holding my poor *baby* hostage." A long finger lovingly caressed the leather steering wheel, causing such irrational jealousy to flare up within me that my powers momentarily pulsed beneath my skin.

Cheez-its, I really need to get a grip.

"Are you... all right?" Xander was looking at me with a furrowed brow as we stopped at a red light. "If you're not feeling well, I could drive you back to The Gloucester."

His confusion gave way to concern, and I realized I truly needed to calm down so I didn't ruin this date. For a moment, I tensed, hoping I hadn't blown my cover, but I quickly dismissed my anxiety.

There was no way a normie could have picked up on my power flare, and the subtle display I just gave would only be detectable by an extremely powerful supe, anyway. I couldn't allow my ridiculous emotions—over Xander's safety or his affection for his car—to make me lose control like that.

I have a public image to maintain.

"No, I'm fine, I promise." I plastered on my best charming smile. "My boss just rode me hard today, so I may need a coffee, but I really want to hang out with you, promise."

"Good to hear." He tightly smiled, although his annoyance wasn't aimed at me. "Solomon Biggs should get the memo that the only one allowed to ride you hard is me."

Fudgesicles... How am I going to make it through drinks and dinner?

Another anxious thought suddenly occurred to me. "I hope I'm dressed appropriately for wherever we're going..."

Xander glanced at me as he shifted the car into a higher gear, the only expression on his face being bald hunger. "Butch, you look like a fucking *snack* right now. It's taking all my self-control to not drive you straight home and gorge myself on your cock. But I'll save that treat for dessert."

Sugar honey iced freakin' tea!

I couldn't help it. I rested my sticky forehead against the glove box and moaned in despair. The effect Xander had on me was unreal, and while I *enjoyed* how it made me feel, it was also complete torture.

Be good, be good, be good.

"We're here, sweetheart," Xander chuckled in amusement, placing a cool hand on the nape of my still sweaty neck, instantly settling me. "Time to tuck your *huge* erection away… first, I want to get you stuffed."

CHAPTER 11
XANDER

Fuck, he's such a big, tasty snack.

I couldn't stop staring at Butch's mouth as he sipped his espresso at the bar of Ars and Invenio. The tiny mug looked absolutely ridiculous in his huge mitts, but the way his plush lips skimmed over the ceramic as he took an adorably dainty sip had me swallowing a moan.

This dinner is going to torture me more than him.

Glancing down the polished mahogany bar, I casually took in the scene of one of my favorite haunts. Ars and Invenio had a Roaring 20s vibe that promised glorious excess under the guise of civilized debauchery, and I was *here for it*. The clientele skewed towards normies of the old money variety—but occasionally, I'd also spot a supe colleague or two of my parents.

Since villains throw money around almost as much as heiresses.

I may not have inherited superpowers, but I'd manifested more than enough villainous bourgeois tendencies to make up for it. There was nothing I loved more than buying the most expensive items on the menu before taking my sweet fucking time enjoying every last drop.

Just like I'll be taking my time with Butch later.

"Mr. Marin? Your table is ready."

At the sound of my fake civilian name, I swiveled to blast Chantal with a megawatt smile. The willowy hostess ran the front of the house with an iron fist, but when I'd called the private line earlier to request a last-minute reservation, she made it happen.

The tennis bracelet I sent via courier didn't hurt.

"Chantal, you look radiant as always," I cooed, grabbing my scotch and sliding off the stool. I spied her good-natured eye roll as she turned to lead us to a booth in a low-lit corner, but a response of a different flavor quickly caught my attention.

A pulse of power.

I shrewdly assessed the occupants of each table we passed, trying to figure out *who* had emanated the threatening energy. My ability to identify other supes out of uniform wasn't anywhere near as strong as the other members of my family, but it was enough to sense an impending attack.

Whoever just did that is pissed and powerful as fuck.

"Any important guests tonight?" I casually asked Chantal as she set down our menus. My gaze drifted to her new bracelet—the unspoken message being to spill the tea if she wanted the matching necklace.

"Not according to the books, Mr. Marin," she smoothly replied, gaze flickering to Butch. "Shall I bring your usual? And for Mr..?"

Another pulse

Who the fuck is it?

"Hawthorne," Butch replied, his baby blues fixed on Chantal with a colder expression than I thought he was capable of. I also noticed he offered his last name a beat too late—as if my sweet boy was distracted by… jealousy.

Be still my heart.

My dick, really.

"Yes, Chantal, my *date* will have what I'm having," I brusquely replied, noticing Butch immediately relax as I took over. "Plus a bottle of Moët, since we're celebrating tonight. That will be all, thank you."

I knew my brush-off served two purposes—telling our hostess to take a hike and bringing Butch back to baseline. As cute as it was that my hottie himbo had a possessive streak, the idea of him *actually* being upset made me weirdly unhappy.

"What are we celebrating?" Butch asked, shifting his delicious little glare away from Chantal's retreating back to bless me with more recognizable, wide-eyed innocence.

He really makes it too easy.

"A big first," I smirked, already salivating for his reaction. "Baby's first time sucking dick."

"Xander!" he hiss-whispered, turning so pink I nearly dragged him beneath the table for an encore performance. "We can't just… *talk* about—"

"Why not?" I interrupted, half-teasing but genuinely curious. "If you're worried about anyone overhearing us, I promise they're too busy talking about themselves. Or is the problem that you've forgotten how *expertly* you let my *huge* cock slide between those perfect lips and down your throat, like the good little cumslut you are?"

"Fu... Xan," he groaned, his almost-expletive paired with his hand disappearing beneath the table making my cock pull up a chair. "It's just... I just don't know what the heck I'm doing here."

His admission put an immediate stop to my teasing. Thanks to a less-than-stellar childhood, my knee-jerk reaction was to assume the worst—dismissal and rejection—but I forced myself to take a breath and get the facts, instead of retreating behind my protective walls.

Dr. Ownit better give me a gold star on Tuesday.

Tackling cock *was* a brand new experience for Butch, and while I probably wasn't the wisest person to go to for advice, I wanted to see where he was going with this.

I also want him sucking my dick again.

"That's fine, sweetheart." I sat back, projecting as much calm as possible while I casually sipped my scotch. "But listen, you don't have to beat around the bush with me. I'm a big boy—I can take it. And I can give it too."

He gaped at me a moment before an indulgent smile quirked his lips. "You can't help being suggestive, can you? It's part of your DNA."

If only you knew what my DNA was made of...

The thought of Butch discovering my infamous bloodline—and rightfully running in the other direction—made my breath catch. Normies were usually easy prey for me, with a cluelessness about my world that easily translated to no strings attached. But something was different this time.

Butch was nervously fiddling with his salad fork, probably debating how—or *if*—he should articulate his thoughts. I took the opportunity to study him, to notice that whatever was bothering him was important. My mouth suddenly went dry as I realized his hesitation was giving *me* the perfect opportunity to make an equally important choice.

The question is—how much of a villain am I?

Butch *needed* to be heard right now, but I could easily take over the conversation and nip this confession in the bud. He might even be thankful for the easy out, since my being in charge clearly spoke to his natural sub tendencies. But then I recalled a comment he'd made in the diner, mistakenly believing me being a top meant he had no say. When I'd corrected him, his entire countenance had changed—as if being given a *choice* was the most novel part about this entire situation.

Has he never had anyone listen?

Really *listen?*

Am I capable of being that person for him?

"Talk to me, Butch. Tell me everything that's on your mind."

The words escaped me before I could stop them, but instead of immediately panicking, I felt lighter—especially when his pretty blue eyes brightened. There was so much fearful hope in his expression that I wanted to wrap him up in a fluffy blanket and pet him until he purred.

Jesus, maybe I was adopted.

"Gosh, okay..." Butch stammered, clearly not expecting to be given the floor, which produced a hairline crack in my rusty heart.

Definitely adopted.

The waitstaff appeared to set us up with the champagne and some prosciutto-wrapped figs, supplying my date with a moment to collect his thoughts. When they dissolved into the scenery again, Butch swallowed hard, but met my gaze with an impressive level of resolve.

All at once, I realized I'd underestimated my himbo. I would bet that in all other areas of his life, this man *didn't* waver or second-guess himself. He was probably accustomed to things being easy—was born with so much natural talent he could simply coast by—but this situation had thrown him off his game. To admit that to me took an incredible amount of trust on his part.

And I'm not sure I deserve to be trusted like that.

"I'm a big boy too, you know," he began, before blushing profusely and clearing his throat. Seeing that I was refraining from taking the obvious opening to tease, he powered on. "What I mean is, we both know I've never been with a man before. That doesn't mean you have to take it easy on me. I mean, I *like* it when you… praise me. But I want to *earn* it."

My brow furrowed, but before I could jump in with a clarifying question, he continued. "I highly doubt the way I…" his voice dropped to barely above a whisper, "sucked your… cock… was even close to 'expertly,' but I *wanted* it to be. I want to be an expert here, and that starts with figuring out why I can't get you out of my head. You weren't anywhere near me today. You wouldn't have known if I'd disobeyed your directions and… touched myself, but I still didn't. That's how badly I wanted to be good for you. I want to be good at *this*—better than an expert—for *you*."

His almost breathless monologue ended on a forceful exhale as he scrubbed a hand over his face. "Cheez-its can you please say something? I'm just babbling like a teen girl with a crush at this point…"

If it had been anyone else, this stream of conscious confession would have been a cringe-worthy record scratch, triggering my well-honed fear of intimacy and successfully ending things instantaneously. Instead, pure caveman satisfaction was flowing through my veins. It wasn't only that I was the first man to have Butch like this—to brand him as *mine*, inside and out—although that was definitely part of it.

What he's saying is… validating.

The startling truth was that I *liked* Butch simping. It simultaneously boosted my ego while also making me want to reward him in every way possible, which somehow cycled back into pleasure for me. I relished him obsessing over me, because the truth was—I couldn't get him out of my head either.

It was already unusual for me to go on two back-to-back dates with the same guy. It was also out of character to have a sleepover, *cuddle,* send sweet texts, or daydream about someone when they weren't around. And it was so far out of left field—out of the fucking ballpark—for me to feel this level of *connection* with someone I'd only just met.

Not just a connection…

Recognition.

"I wanted to let you say your piece," I slowly replied, fighting to maintain a controlled facade while my heart tried to punch its way out of my chest.

My every instinct was screaming at me to end this before it got too serious. Before Butch started writing my name in his diary—hell, before I bought my *own* diary—but I knew it was already too late. It made absolutely no sense, but I felt like I was in danger of finding myself in *a relationship.*

With a *normie.*

Willingly.

I'd say I'm the one who doesn't know what he's doing here.

Realizing Butch was anxiously waiting for me to say more, I reached across the table and grabbed his hand.

"I already told you, sweetheart," I soothed, running a thumb over his knuckle. "I'm going to enjoy anything you do. That being said, I can be intense, so we need a safe word for you. Do you know what that is?"

He swallowed hard again, delicious color rising up his thick neck. "Um, yeah, I do," he replied, chewing his bottom lip before meeting my gaze. "I've been, uh, researching… things… since you found me on Bangers."

Good lord!

At the thought of Butch watching gay porn while poking around the BDSM dark web, my dick almost punched its way through the table and became the centerpiece.

"Very well," I replied, marveling over how fucking delicious this man was. "What would you like your safe word to be?"

I expected more squirming and blushing, but Butch surprised me yet again by steadily meeting my gaze. "Orca."

Be still my Ph.D.!

"Perfect." I licked my lips as our entrees arrived, although my hunger wasn't for my filet mignon with citrus caper herb sauce. "Now eat up. You're gonna need your strength if you want to become an *expert* with me."

CHAPTER 12
BUTCH

After Xander listened to my confession over appetizers, there was nothing I wanted more than to jump into his car like an overexcited puppy and get on with the night.

But I *hadn't* eaten much today—not since the breakfast sandwich he bought me—so I did my very best to clean my plate. The last thing I needed was to pass out from low blood sugar before things got good.

And I have a feeling they're about to get really good....

"Are you ready to go?" Xander's kissable lips twisted as he noticed me bouncing in my seat while he signed the bill.

"Yes!" I replied, a bit too loud, thanks to both the champagne and my nerves. "I mean, if you are… if that's okay…"

The hooded look he gave me relayed his approval. "I love how eager you are to please me, sweetheart," he cooed, gracefully standing and tossing his napkin on the table with a flourish. "And you've been so *good* for me all day, haven't you?"

I stood so fast I almost knocked over my chair, only to realize the semi I was sporting was proof enough of how neglected I was.

Talk about behaving like a teenager!

Of course, Xander missed nothing, his amber eyes dropping to the evidence of my desire. "I bet that beautiful cock is simply *aching* for me, isn't it?" he purred in my ear, steering me toward the exit—handling me rough enough that my dick ached some more.

Please don't let me come in my pants…

The valet had the car waiting for us at the curb, making me wonder how much of an Ars and Invenio regular he was. It was a little excessive here for my taste, but the ambiance fit him perfectly, and his menu choices were exceptional.

Xander ordering for me—the way he so easily took control—made my entire body relax in a way no expensive massage ever could.

What I *hadn't* enjoyed was how flirty the hostess had been—behavior I'd instinctively interpreted as a threat. It got me so worked up that my power embarrassingly flared up again, but luckily there were no supes around to notice.

All that aside, I begrudgingly appreciated her discretion when asked about any VIPs dining here tonight. There was no way for the staff to recognize me out of uniform, but I did occasionally come in with Solomon Biggs for lunch meetings with representatives from the United Super Nations.

That alone would be enough to classify me as being Captain Masculine-adjacent, although for all *Chantal* knew, I was nothing more than the Biggs Enterprises number-cruncher I pretended to be.

My boss does enjoy torturing me with spreadsheets.

However, my most recent visit to Ars and Invenio was for a date with a fellow supe, arranged by my parents. But that excruciatingly painful night was the last thing I wanted to think about right now. All I knew was that every previous experience at this restaurant had left a sour taste in my mouth —far from the giddy excitement I was feeling now.

"Take your cock out," Xander's smooth voice commanded my attention the instant the car doors were shut.

"W-what?" I stammered, my brain taking longer to register his instructions than the rest of me did. My dick was *straining* against the zipper of my dress pants, with all available blood rushing to my lower head—eager to obey my...

I want him to be mine.

When Xander gave me *a look,* I hurriedly unzipped, only to freeze and cautiously glance at the sea of pedestrians streaming by.

"The windows are heavily tinted, sweetheart." He smiled kindly before his expression hardened again. "Regardless. I. Want. To. See. Your beautiful cock. Now."

"Yes, Daddy," I rasped, wrestling myself free before realizing what I'd just said. Yes, *he'd* saved his contact info in my phone as 'Daddy Xan,' but that didn't mean he needed to know I'd been fantasizing about calling him that all day, while *not* touching myself.

Why am I like this?

It felt like an eternity before I dared to look at Xander, but just like when I'd gagged on him, all I found was feral hunger looking back at me.

"Is that what you need, Butch?" The way my name rolled off his tongue was criminal. "For *Daddy* to take care of you?"

I didn't move—barely breathed—my gaze locked with his while I gripped the base of my shaft. My entire body was *shaking* with the blinding need to be entirely owned by this man.

If he says no, I might die.

"Yes, please," I whispered, equally feral with desperation. "I'll do anything you say to make it happen."

"Fuck," he muttered under his breath, barely audible, before facing forward, putting the car in first, and easing us into traffic. It was a good five minutes before he spoke again—although whether the delay was to torture me or calm himself down, I couldn't be sure. "Very well. Let's see how good you can be… for *Daddy.*"

Oh, sugar.

His breathtakingly handsome face was the epitome of control, his cool gaze on the road ahead. "I want you to stroke yourself with no spit, and only enough pressure to feel your fingers barely glide over your skin. Don't you dare move your hips… and, sweetheart?" He quickly glanced at me. "If you spray my car, you'll be cleaning it up with that pretty pink tongue."

Fudging H-E-double-hockey-sticks!

I couldn't stop a whine from escaping me, but I dutifully stroked my full length, agonizingly gentle. My jaw was clenched, my glutes straining against the urge to thrust, but I was determined to pass this test.

"Mmm, I bet you'd actually *enjoy* licking your own cum off my leather seats," Xander absently mused, changing lanes before turning, seemingly in no hurry to do anything but destroy me.

I gritted my teeth as he continued. "I bet you'd *beg* me to play with your ass at the same time. How many fingers could you take, I wonder?" Another torturous pause. "Tell me, Butch— has anything fucked its way into that tight ass of yours yet?"

Oh, no.

He chuckled low as I whined again. "Or have you been saving that virgin hole for me?"

Nonononono…

"Xan!" I gasped, squeezing myself so tightly my dick almost popped off. "If you dirty talk me I'll never make it—"

"Oh, you'll make it," he interrupted, as casually as if we were discussing the weather. "Because you *want* to be good for me. And only a good boy gets to feel my mouth on his beautiful cock."

My entire body was shuddering, chest heaving as I panted through my nose, but with Herculean effort, I started stroking again.

I can do this.

Xander made a noise of approval as he pulled into an underground garage beneath what I prayed was his building. If I had to walk even a block in the state I was in, I might end up humping a fire hydrant.

Putting the car in park, he slowly reached across the console, running a featherlight touch along my neck, making me shiver. "I asked you a question, Butch. Has anyone or *anything* ever been inside your tight, hot hole?"

"No!" I yelped, strangling my dick to stop myself from exploding. "You'll be the first… I've never even done it to myself…"

I can be good.

He flung open his door, closing it with a decisive click before striding to my side. I feared I'd answered incorrectly, but then my door was ripped open and I was being yanked out of my seat and bent over the hood.

I gasped as my throbbing dick met the still warm surface of his car, groaning louder when Xander pressed against me from behind, trapping it painfully beneath our combined weight.

"You mean to tell me,"—his breath ghosted over the shell of my ear—"that you've never stuffed these *thick* fingers into your ass while you fucked your fist? Not even while thinking about what I could do to you?"

"No," I sobbed, quieter this time. I could feel him rubbing his enormous erection against my ass—like a wild animal marking its territory. "Not even when I thought about your fingers and tongue and c-cock in my ass. I've been so hard for you all day—for this entire week since we first messaged on Bangers—*only for you*. Please. *Please,* Xander. Let me show you how good I can be for you."

He sharply inhaled, immediately backing off, the cold air on my skin from his sudden absence making me whimper. A moment later, the elevator dinged. I tensed at the thought of a stranger finding me like this, but didn't move a muscle—not without *him* telling me I could.

Please let me show you…

"Fuck, you're perfect," he murmured, tone thick with praise and something else I couldn't place. He gently raised me off the hood before his hands dropped to efficiently tuck me back into my pants.

When I made a noise of discontent at the too-brief contact, he chuckled and sweetly brushed his lips over the back of my neck. "Welcome to my home. Let's go upstairs."

CHAPTER 13
BUTCH

I'd been so fixated on Xander during the drive, I didn't even know which neighborhood we'd ended up in. Even in the elevator, I couldn't take my eyes off of him—as if doing so might make him disappear.

When the doors opened again on the sixth floor, all I saw was a flash of blindingly white walls before I was herded to the end of the hallway by the man I was borderline obsessed with.

Wherever you want me, Daddy.

Because I was a total dork, Xander using his *fingerprint* to open his apartment door was the thing that managed to snap me out of my lust-drunk state.

"Hey, that's pretty cool," I chuckled. Of course, I'd encountered similar setups because of my job, but never in a civilian home. "It's kind of like you have a secret lair."

He smirked as he swung open the door. "It was a non-negotiable when purchasing this apartment, but my *secret lair* is actually off-premises."

"Maybe you could take me there sometime," I teased, assuming he was talking about wherever he worked on his marine biology research.

He simply cocked his head at me before wordlessly turning on the lights from an app on his phone. I didn't dwell on the non-reply, however, because I was now standing inside Xander's apartment.

I can't believe I'm here!

The decor was mid-century modern meets tech-geek man-cave. A black leather sofa faced a credenza supporting a ridiculously large flat screen hooked up to a dizzying number of blinking electronics.

Abstract art—red paint splashed across the canvas like blood spatter—decorated the gray walls, with the only illumination being track lighting on the art and a row of recessed bulbs in the stainless steel-dominated kitchen area. It felt so perfect—so *him*—except…

"It's a lot *smaller* than I was expecting," I blurted out. A faint glow was coming from beneath a single door off of the living area, leading to what I assumed was his bedroom.

Which is where I hope we're headed.

I blushed at my rudeness, but Xander laughed, tossing his car keys in a wooden dish near the door. "While I admittedly have a *huge* personality, I prefer a smaller footprint. Why live in some oversized monstrosity when everything I need can be at my fingertips here?" He cocked his head again, a sly smile playing on his lips. "Should we see where else my fingertips can fit in this *tight* space?"

"Yes," I croaked, immediately hard again—not that my erection had ever gone down. Just as I hoped, he placed a firm hand on my back and not-so-subtly pushed me ahead of him toward the bedroom.

A massive ball of fur—a *cat?*—shot out as we stumbled into the room, but the sensation of Xander's lips on mine combined with his hands stripping off my suit jacket quickly distracted me.

"I want you in my bed," he growled, loosening my tie only to then wrap it around his hand like a choke collar. "Naked except for this."

You would think a man strong enough to lift a tractor trailer and lob it at an oncoming villain in mid-air wouldn't enjoy being pushed around, but the way Xander handled me made my blood sing. It was all I could do to keep my powers locked down from the excitement. The last thing I wanted to do was accidentally injure him.

Although I'm dying for him to hurt me.

"What's your safe word, Butch?" He loosened his grip on my tie so I could speak, intently meeting my gaze while awaiting my reply.

"Orca," I repeated, fumbling to open my pants and attempting to shove them off without falling over. "But you can do whatever you want to me."

He groaned as if he were in pain, releasing me so he could start unbuttoning his shirt, methodically slow. "Oh, sweetheart, you have no idea how dangerous it is to say something like that to me."

His mesmerizing eyes tracked my movements as I finished tearing off my clothes—leaving the tie on, as instructed. By the time I was done, I was breathless, my dick straining toward him like it was magnetized.

"I want to experience everything, though," I insisted, hoping he could see how earnest I was in the dimly lit bedroom. "With *you*."

Only you.

Xander froze with his hands on his zipper, staring back at me with an unreadable expression. I knew I was being ridiculous—that there was a possibility he was just humoring my eagerness until he got bored—but I couldn't help it.

I want this too badly to pretend I don't.

Instead of addressing my latest confession, he slipped into his usual collected demeanor. "Very well. Lie back—feet on the mattress and legs spread."

Swallowing hard, I hesitated, suddenly unsure. I'd dropped to my knees for this man last night, but the position he was asking me to get into now was ten million times more vulnerable.

He'll be able to see my...

"I said I want you on my bed, presenting yourself to me," Xander hissed, suddenly inches away from my face, gripping the tie so tightly I choked. He shouldn't have been able to move that fast, but I blamed it on my nervousness and a trick of the low light.

Or that all the blood in my body has rushed to my dick again.

I frantically nodded, practically leaping onto the bed as soon as he released me—eager to please. Although I'd never dared look at myself from this angle before, I followed Xander's directions and spread myself wide for him, more exposed than I'd ever been before.

Thank goodness he doesn't have supe-vision.

"Look at you," he murmured appreciatively. "Look at that tight little hole I'm going to fucking *ruin*."

Yes, please.

Being one of the most powerful superheroes alive, I had a ridiculously high pain threshold. Xander had no way of knowing this, but it was why I'd told him to not take it easy on me. Being so concerned with consent, I hoped he'd take me at my word that I could handle whatever he could give me.

I want all of it.

Xander casually strolled to the bedside table, where a single cube of light on the wooden surface illuminated his gloriously naked body. He was built leaner than I was, but obviously had an exercise regime to keep up a physique like his. I wanted to reach out and touch him—run my tongue along his abs and feel him shudder beneath me.

Worship every inch of him.

I've got it so bad.

I expected him to quickly grab some lube, but when he slid open the top drawer, I saw it was only deep enough to hold a stainless steel surgical tray full of...

"How *big* of an expert do you want to be?" He smirked, holding up a metal butt plug so large my eyes almost popped out of my skull.

That's not a plug, it's a murder weapon!

Before I could agree, Xander warmly chuckled and set it back on the tray. "I'm just teasing you, baby. I'll give you *my* version of going easy tonight. Although..." His gaze drifted to my dick, already weeping precum. "You didn't lose your *enthusiasm* when faced with a monster, so perhaps I won't scare you away after all."

Never.

"I like everything you do," I whispered. "Especially when you call me baby."

This entire scenario was such a far cry from my public persona that it was almost laughable. As far as the citizens of Big City were concerned, I was the epitome of masculinity, dominating lesser supes left and right. If my adoring fans could see me now—spread open in submission and begging to be called a cutesy pet name—they'd probably revolt.

I'd lose everything.

And I wouldn't even be mad about it.

Xander looked at me so adoringly, my breath caught. "I'll call you baby if you want." His controlled mask slipped back into place as he slid the drawer closed and opened another to retrieve a bottle of lube. "Now, let's play."

He crawled onto the bed, prowling across the black comforter like a big cat on the hunt. Positioning himself between my legs, he poured a copious amount of lube onto his fingers, spreading it around while staring at my exposed hole.

Okay, maybe it is kind of hot.

Xander's gaze flickered up to mine as he traced my opening with the pad of his middle finger, making me jerk. "I'm only giving you my fingers tonight, no matter how much you want to jump right in."

As disappointing as that news was, it was fair. I was *desperate* to feel his dick inside me, but I also wanted to savor every moment. With the way his touch alone set my nerves on fire, I expected whatever Xander had planned for me would be like nothing I'd ever felt before.

Including these feelings I'm catching.

He slowly pushed his fingertip past my tight outer ring, closely watching my reaction. I tensed, and again, his searing gaze softened. "Relax for me, Butch. Let me handle things."

I breathed out and willed myself to calm down. What he was doing didn't hurt, but I was perilously close to coming already and really, *really* didn't want to embarrass myself.

But I absolutely want him handling things.

"Oh!" I exclaimed as he suddenly hit some sort of magical sex wizard spot I never knew existed.

His expression morphed into pure mischief. "There you are. How about another finger?"

I nodded eagerly, and he immediately slid it in, stretching me with a scissoring motion before crooking both to rub the magical spot. When all I could do was pathetically whimper, he leaned forward and used my tie to pull my lips to his—no doubt trying to distract me.

It didn't work. This entire night—every moment I'd spent with Xander since we'd met—was going to be seared into my memory for years to come. The feel of his muscular body pressed against mine, combined with the notes of smoky leather from his expensive cologne, was threatening to make me explode.

He's just pure sex.

Our tongues tangled, and I desperately attempted to lose myself in our kiss, despite the overwhelming sensations coming at me from all sides. His lubed fingers relentlessly pumped in and out, causing my slightly embarrassing moans to echo in the otherwise quiet space.

But I don't care what the heck I sound like at this point.

I'd clearly shown him how ready I was, as he released my tie and placed his hand on my pec as he sat back. Grazing my nipple with his thumb, he began traveling lower, tracing every ab, watching himself torture me as he slowly made his way to my aching dick.

Oh, please, please, please.

"You're so... *big* and *hot*," he rasped, almost angrily. "I just want to own you. Ruin you."

Pleeeeease.

I must have whimpered again because he chuckled, gripping the base of my dick to hold me steady. "I suppose I should stop teasing and give my *good boy* his reward."

As if my soul hadn't already left my body, he lowered his head and slid my entire length into his wet, hot mouth until his lips touched my groin—swallowing me whole.

Jesus, he's a pro!

Then he pulled his head back, hollowing his cheeks to squeeze out any bits of soul that were left, circling my head with his tongue before lifting off with an audible pop.

"Fuck, you taste so sweet," he sighed, twisting his fingers inside me, making me groan. "Do you think you could come down my throat, baby? Feed me some of that *sweetness?*"

There was a hint of sadness hidden beneath Xander's dirty talk, but I was too far gone to do anything other than beg.

"Yes, Daddy," I sobbed, unable to stop my hips from bucking, desperate for him to deepthroat me again. "Please... I'll give you everything, just please put your mouth on me again."

"Everything, huh?" he murmured, but dutifully sucked me down.

Apparently, the time for taking it slow was over. Xander devoured me as if he were as insatiably hungry for me as I was for him. He tirelessly bobbed his head, pounding into my ass with his fingers, hitting *that spot* over and over until my vision went hazy.

This. This. This.

"Xan! I'm gonna... I'm..." I panted, clawing at the sheets, scrabbling against the headboard, and burying my hand in his hair as the pressure building in my spine yanked my balls up tight.

He never slowed. Instead, he plunged *another* finger into my ass, stuffing me full, and booting me off the cliff. I howled as I shot what felt like a ridiculous amount of cum down his throat, violently shuddering while I babbled some combination of his name mixed with more pleas and promises.

Pro that he was, he simply slid off and out of me, calmly swallowing my load while watching me limply twitch on the bed beneath him.

"Lemme just..." I mumbled, weakly reaching for him. "Now it's your turn..."

Xander threw his head back and laughed. "Oh, you sweet, sweet thing. I appreciate the offer, but you don't look like you're in any state to reciprocate. Besides," his tone turned sultry again as he stroked my inner thigh. "It appears I'm all set."

Vaguely registering that my thigh felt damp, I peered down to discover Xander absently running his fingers through the mess he'd made—spreading his cum around, painting me with it. Realizing he'd gotten off from giving *me* pleasure made me drop my head back with a moan as my dick made a valiant effort to rally for another round.

"You did so good, baby," he praised, gently pushing his cum-covered fingers back inside me, claiming me as *his*. "Such a good boy."

I contentedly sighed, loving how cared for I felt, like nothing bad could touch me when he was around. The meticulous way he cleaned me up—that heady shot of comfort—only made my eyelids grow heavy.

The last thing I heard before drifting off to sleep was Xander's voice, his tone once again tinged with sadness. "I'll take everything you have to give."

Everything.

CHAPTER 14
XANDER

I am so royally screwed.

Not only had I invited Butch into my apartment, I *hadn't* fucked his brains out, and I'd *cuddled* with him again. All night long.

I was not a cuddler or someone who wanted to deal with seeing my one-night stands in the light of day. No strings attached was my preferred state of being, but suddenly, I wanted strings all over the goddamn place. I wanted to get completely tied up with this sweetly clueless, non-swearing slab of hot AF man muscle so I could cuddle him every night. I wanted to shibari myself so tightly to Butch Hawthorne as he fumbled his way through his bi-awakening that he'd never untangle the hold I had on him.

And while that realization scared the shit out of me, I'd apparently lost all sense of self-preservation, as I was no longer considering running in the opposite direction.

Meowson had woken me up twenty minutes ago, scratching at the bedroom door until I emerged to feed him his over-priced prescription diet food. Now I was standing next to the bed, petting the satisfied Himalayan while I watched Butch sleep.

Like some sort of creepy, lovesick fool.

So what happens now?

Before I could make any life-altering decisions, I heard my front door bang open, followed by a bratty, sing-song voice echoing off the walls.

"Oh, sluuuutbag! I've brought you breakfast in exchange for dirty detaaaaails!"

Shit, shit, shit.

"Who is that?" Butch was already off the bed and half-dressed, his blue eyes fixed on the bedroom door with the same oddly threatening intensity he'd aimed at Chantal last night at the restaurant.

My pre-coffee brain didn't know how to reconcile *my* Butch with *Blade Runner* Butch, or whatever the hell was going on here. Before he could stomp into the living room and give Kai the baseline test, I flung open the bedroom door and confronted the intruder myself.

"Cute manties, Xan," Kai cackled, holding a plastic bodega bag in one hand and a cardboard tray of coffees in the other. "Are those frogs?"

I glanced down at my boxer briefs, a gag gift from my brother Baltasar during our annual, notoriously cutthroat White Elephant exchange last Christmas.

Joke's on him because I love them.

"Pacific green sea turtles and *I had a date last night.*" I enunciated, hoping against all odds she would get the hint and take a hike.

She snorted. "Don't I know it? You two had an *excellent* time, from what I overheard. Now, put on *Trophy Wives,* bestie, because these breakfast burritos ain't gonna eat thems— *HOLY SHIT, he's still here!*"

Her rambling was cut short as Butch strode from the bedroom, shooting sexy daggers at Kai as he stared her down. He was fully dressed and just as tasty in the harsh morning light as he'd been while writhing on my bed, wearing nothing but his tie.

Please don't get a hard-on in your turtle briefs in front of…

"Well, dang," Kai murmured, her gaze roaming over him in an appreciative way I did not like one bit. "This might be the first time someone looked *better* in real life than in their Bangers profile pic."

An adorable wrinkle of confusion appeared between Butch's eyebrows as he turned to me, so I explained. "This is my extremely nosey next-door neighbor, Kai. She's actually the one who created the Bangers profile for me and reached out to you initially. I wanted nothing to do with the app before."

As soon as the words left my mouth, I regretted them, immediately worried that Butch would interpret this to mean I *wouldn't* have chosen him on my own.

I don't want him to doubt any of this.

Before I could have my *second* existential crisis of the morning, Butch turned to Kai and smiled so brightly, it was as if the sun rose again. "Well, shoot. I can't stay mad about being woken up when it's thanks to *you* I now have Xander in my life."

Oh, no.

It was like watching a slow-motion video of two speeding trains headed for each other down the track. I knew what was coming, but all I could do was shut my eyes and brace for impact.

As predicted, Kai released a deafeningly shrill sound, not unlike a train whistle. "Oh. My. God. *My babies!* This is amazing. This is fucking incredible, and we need to dig into these burritos while you tell me all about it. I brought extra of everything, so sit your ass down, big guy!"

She grabbed Butch's arm with her hot-pink tips and dragged him toward the couch. To his credit, he let her manhandle him, smiling sweetly as she sat him down and began spreading out breakfast on the coffee table.

"So… what do you want to know?" Butch asked, the epitome of innocence.

Oh, you sweet summer child.

Kai's supervillain smile would have made my mother proud. "Well—"

"Nope. Uh-uh," I cut in before Butch could fall into her trap. "Kai is a major voyeur and wants. Every. Dirty. Detail. I'm not kidding, baby."

Butch blushed furiously as Kai clutched her chest. "Baby?! You're calling him *baby?* Ugh. Just… okay, time-out on the cuteness because I have to piss like a racehorse. Hold the first date detes until I get back, lover boys."

She scampered through my bedroom to the en suite, leaving blessed silence in her wake. For a moment, Butch and I just stared at each other, until his gaze dropped to the giant ball of fur I was still holding.

"You have a cat," he remarked, his dimples popping out as he tried to suppress his smile.

"I do," I replied, giving said cat a scratch behind the ear. "His name is Neil deGrasse Meowson, but we peasants just call him Meowson."

To my astonishment, the furry overlord wiggled free and walked straight to Butch before jumping onto his lap. This was unheard of, as he was infamous for scratching the shit out of anyone who dared to disturb his life.

It's probably why we get along so well.

"You don't strike me as someone who'd adopt a cat," Butch added, running his huge hands through Meowson's floof while the little demon purred up a storm.

"Uh… he sort of adopted me." I rubbed the back of my neck, suddenly self-conscious about my cat and the fact I was still standing around in my turtle underwear. "He kept showing up on the fire escape, pawing at the window. I finally let him in one night because it was pouring out, and I'm not *that* much of a monster. He decided he liked me and wanted to stay. I decided I liked him and wanted him to. And that was it."

"That easy, huh?" Butch quietly asked, holding my gaze as the air seemed to ripple between us.

That easy.

I experienced both annoyance and relief when Kai loudly reappeared from my bedroom. "Whew, it smells like *nasty* sex up in there. Crack a window, Xan—air it out a little."

Butch was blushing all over again, but I just rolled my eyes. "Stuff a burrito in it, Kai. I'm going to put some clothes on before joining you. Please *try* not to scare away my date."

He's not just your date, Xan.

Kai gave a sassy salute as I walked into my bedroom, shutting the door behind me. As soon as I was alone, I sat on the edge of the bed and dropped my head into my hands. Whatever was happening to me went way beyond the emotional. My chest felt tight, and a strange buzzing sensation was running through my veins, making my fingers tingle—almost like they *itched* to do… *something.*

More than anything, I was excruciatingly aware of how much I wanted to tear my bedroom door off its hinges, simply because it separated me from Butch.

Jesus fuck, I'm fucked.

My phone chimed on the nightstand with a reminder for Tuesday's cognitive therapy appointment with Dr. Ownit. This made my anxiety ratchet up even higher because it meant I was going to have to talk about *this.*

About *Butch.*

Yes, I could just sit on Ownit's uncomfortable couch and rattle off a generic report of the past week, but that wasn't what I was paying a pretty penny for. Among the few things I believed in, one was that buying quality goods and services—and actually *using* them to their full extent—was my constitutional right as a man with exceptional taste and money to burn. Another was the importance of saving coastal wildlife from consumers like me.

I also previously believed I didn't need anyone else but myself.

Realizing Kai was probably strong-arming Butch into telling her exactly how my fingers felt buried in his ass, I quickly dressed in some activewear and returned to the living room. To my relief, the two of them were sitting on opposite ends of the couch, watching *Bored Trophy Wives of Awakener's Bay* while munching on breakfast burritos. At least *Kai* was.

"Why aren't you eating?" I pointed an accusing finger at Butch's untouched burrito, sounding way more demanding than I meant to.

My tone didn't seem to bother him, as those goddamn dimples appeared again. "I was waiting for you," he calmly replied, obediently reaching for his breakfast as I sat beside him.

I huffed, grabbing my own off the table, along with an extra large coffee. "You don't have to worry about your manners around me, Butch. I bet we were both raised with enough pomp and circumstance to last a lifetime."

"Agreed," he chuckled before eyeing me, almost shyly. "But the reason I waited was that I've noticed how much you..."—his gaze darted to Kai, but her attention was on the TV—"*enjoy* watching me eat."

I enjoy taking care of you.

"Come with me to work today," I blurted out through a mouthful of eggy goodness. While my plan for the day would probably bore Butch, the thought of us going our separate ways felt unacceptable.

He smiled before taking a bite of his burrito, the pleasure on his face making my insides hum with satisfaction. "Yes," he replied once he'd swallowed, like the good boy he was. "The answer will always be yes, Xan."

CHAPTER 15
XANDER

As expected, the northernmost cove of Awakener's Bay was a fucking mess.

Because of the North Pacific currents, a ridiculous amount of trash always ended up here, swirling in the shallows and lapping over the sand. Occasionally, some do-gooder normies would band together for a well-publicized 'Beach Cleanup Day,' but it didn't take long for the endless flow of flotsam to drift in again.

Forget beach cleanups—we need civilization cleanups.

I shook the tempting thought from my mind. Yes, with a few tweaks, the device I was working on could be used against humans—and supes—but that wasn't what I was trying to accomplish here. My focus was entirely on those most affected by the actions of us 'superior' creatures.

While empathy was *not* a trait modeled or encouraged in the Suarez household growing up, I'd somehow developed something close to it—for wildlife, at least.

I first noticed the unfamiliar emotion during a family outing when I was eight. A superhero-sympathizer pissed off my parents, so the entire clan had descended on his million-dollar oceanfront mansion to teach him a lesson.

By that point, we all knew I had no powers, so my job had been to stay outside and act as a lookout for fire boats and avenging supes. I obeyed—happy to be included—although what they thought a powerless kid could do against any would-be saviors was beyond me.

I was probably less of an accomplice and more of a sacrificial lamb.

As usual, my family had taken their sweet time torturing their victim, so I got bored and started exploring the beach. I'd always been drawn to the ocean—even once dreamed my powers would be water-based—but before that day, I'd never understood how *alive* it was. How fragile.

Until I saw the turtle.

In its early life, it must have gotten stuck halfway through a plastic 6-pack ring, which forced its shell to grow around the foreign object, giving it a gruesome hourglass shape. I watched in shock as the deformed animal slowly moved across the sand, periodically getting caught on rocks and other debris, thanks to the remaining rings dangling from its body.

I remembered how the hardened layer I'd constructed around my heart suddenly cracked as overwhelming *empathy* flooded my system. All I could think about was freeing the turtle from its man-made cage, but my family hadn't left me with anything I could use. Undeterred, I pounced on the poor animal, ripping and tearing at the unyielding plastic—even using my teeth to try saving it. That was how my family found me.

Sobbing over a fucking turtle.

Even though they were armed to the teeth to draw out their torture, nobody gave me a blade. Instead, they dragged me off the doomed animal, kicking and screaming, while they laughed and left it behind to die.

"I never want to see you crying over anyone or anything ever again. You'll make our family look weak."

"Are you all right?" Butch was eyeing me with concern, somehow looking even hotter in performance wear than he had in his tailored suit. I'd driven him back to The Gloucester so he could grab more appropriate clothing for today's outing, since there was no way in hell his massive body would squeeze into anything of mine.

I hadn't expected him to choose an all-black, form-fitting base layer that hugged every muscle, before topping it off with 'Please Fuck Me, Daddy' boots.

He looks like a goddamn supe in that outfit.

As much as I wanted to file away images of evil-villain Butch for my spank bank, I had to admit he looked more heroic than villainous.

Fuck, he's built just like Captain Masculine.

"Xan?" Butch's voice cut through my jumbled thoughts, saving me from addressing how that uncanny resemblance made my dick twitch.

Save it for Dr. Ownit's office, weirdo.

"I'm fine," I tightly smiled, bringing myself back to the day's work. "It's just that this never fails to disappoint me." I broadly gestured at the trash littering the beach.

I don't know what I expected. Maybe a good-natured eye roll or an empty platitude, but yet again, Butch proved there was true depth hidden beneath his himbo exterior.

"Yeah," he nodded, looking almost as angry as he did when he gave Chantal the stink-eye. "It kills me every time I come down here and see all this garbage. Don't people realize that when you throw something away, it doesn't just magically disappear?"

Marry me.

I'd never openly talked about my work with anyone before. Kai was nosey enough, and I only told Ownit that my family would disapprove of my job if they knew the specifics. By some miracle, Butch appreciated the natural beauty of this place as much as I did, but I couldn't help wondering what he spent his time doing down here.

"Do you surf?" I cocked my head, trying to imagine his massive body balanced on a board. This cove was harder to access than the touristy beaches, but the sudden drop-off with nothing but the vast Pacific beyond produced world-class waves, so some braved it.

Despite the pollution.

"Uh, no..." He deliciously blushed for some reason. "I just like to come out here to think sometimes, and... people watch."

There's rarely anyone out here but me.

And Captain Masculine.

I gazed out over the water—too choppy for anyone to bother surfing today, although it would have been fun on my new WaveRunner. Of course, with Butch with me, I couldn't access my warehouse, so we'd have to collect samples on foot today.

But it's worth it to keep this date going.

A rush of panic shot through me as I suddenly worried Captain Masculine would show up and attack us. Then I remembered I was out of uniform, so we'd just look like a couple of do-gooder normies conducting a two-person beach cleanup.

"Very well," I rolled my shoulders before digging into my bag for supplies. "The work we're doing today is a little gross, but it's for science. We need to collect samples of the microplastics that wash ashore, so I can test whether the device I'm inventing can successfully extract them from the water without hurting living organisms."

He gaped at me a moment before a wide grin stretched across his face. "*That's* what you're working on? Sugar, that's freakin' cool."

I laughed and handed him some rubber gloves and a gold panning tray. "We really need to work on your language, sweetheart. If I can't get you swearing like a trucker, I'll feel like a fucking failure."

Butch chuckled as he dutifully put his gloves on and followed me to the shoreline. "It's just how I was raised. I was always told my public image was the most valuable thing about me. If I tarnish that, I lose everything."

Jesus.

I couldn't stop my gaze from sweeping over his ass as he squatted down to work. "I'm guessing your parents are politicians or belong to a fundamentalist religious sect."

His laugh was strained this time. "A little of both, you could say." We worked side-by-side in comfortable silence for a few minutes before he spoke again. "My parents were pretty famous in their line of work, and I was always just expected to follow in their footsteps... which means *my* reputation reflects on them—on my family's legacy."

That sounds familiar.

While I appreciated Butch sharing more about himself with me, something wasn't adding up. "So, *did* you follow in their footsteps or not?" I kept my tone casual, but my gaze was locked on him, noticing how he tensed at my question. "I can't imagine your parents were world-famous *accountants."*

Let me in, baby.

His jaw clenched the tiniest bit, and for a moment, I assumed he was going to feed me some bullshit. But then he met my gaze with what looked like *tears* in his eyes.

"I did… because I didn't have a choice," he rasped, his voice thick with regret and bitterness. "It's why I work for Biggs, but I actually can't tell you anything more about what I do. I- I'm sorry, Xander."

Oh, sweetheart…

I wanted to pull this big idiot into my arms and hug the shit out of him. I also wanted to fuck him into the sand, but that was beside the point. If anyone could understand not being able to talk about their family—and the things they had to do in the name of said family—it was me.

And I can't tell him more about me either.

"It's all right, Butch." I smiled, making sure he could *see* that I meant it. "I'll just pretend I'm dating a super secret spy on a covert mission."

The tension bled from his body as he laughed, his pretty blue eyes sparkling. "Thank you for understanding, Xan." He grew serious again. "And I'm glad to hear you still want to date me."

I scoffed. "Oh, sweetheart, you won't be getting rid of me that easily. On that note…" I cleared my throat, knowing I was moving much too fast, but unable to stop this runaway crazy train. "I've been wanting to ask if you'd remove the Bangers app from your phone. If you'd consider... dating only me?"

Just laying all my cards on the table, no big deal.

Those tasty dimples appeared as he tried to stifle his smile. "You want me all to yourself, huh?"

There was no smile on my face as I stared him down. "Yes."

All mine.

Because he was perfect, he immediately stood and pulled his phone out of his pocket. "Done," he reported, turning his phone to face me so I could watch him do it. "To be honest, the notifications were driving me nuts, and I couldn't figure out how to turn them off. And to be even *more* honest, I want you all to myself, too."

"Done," I replied, rising to stand next to him. "But you should know, I've never attempted an actual relationship with anyone before, so this is going to be a novel experience for me."

He planted a kiss on my cheek, adorably bouncing on his toes in excitement. "I can't say I have either, on top of never being with a man before. So I guess we'll just figure this out together."

Together...

The idea of doing *anything* with another person by my side was so overwhelming, I was momentarily speechless. It was then that Butch's phone rang, interrupting the moment.

I caught 'Biggs Enterprises' on the screen before Butch brought the phone to his ear. "Hawthorne," he said, which was an odd way to answer when the caller knew it was you.

It must be part of his secret spy gig.

My senses went on high alert as his expression shifted to acute alarm. "He's *where?!*" he hissed, gaze shooting up to the sky as if it held the answer. "Yes, I'll be there as soon as I can."

Ending the call, his frantic gaze turned to me. "Xan, I'm sorry to do this, but there's an emergency with work. Are you okay with finishing up here on your own?"

What the hell is he talking about?

I quickly kneeled and efficiently gathered up our supplies and samples. "Take a breath, Butch. I will gladly *drive* you wherever you need to go, because right now, we're in the middle of nowhere. What were you gonna do, *fly* out of here?"

He looked at me like I had three heads, but slowly nodded. "Yes… what was I thinking? Okay, you could drive me to… the Navy Yard. I have a contact I can hook up with from there."

He's definitely a secret spy.

"Done," I repeated, leading the way as we hustled back up the cliffs. Biggs ran the city, so it didn't surprise me that the Navy was involved in whatever was happening. A sudden wave of concern for Butch's safety struck me as we reached my car. "Do you think you could call me later? Just so I know that the terrorists haven't won."

Understandably, he didn't laugh at my potentially inappropriate joke as he slid into the passenger side. When his gaze met mine over the console, I could've sworn I saw tears forming again. "I'll do my best, Xan. That's all I can promise you."

CHAPTER 16
BUTCH

I hit the brick building so violently that I blasted straight through and out the other side.

Fudge humper! His stats weren't exaggerated...

The blow would have killed a normie—and severely wounded a lesser supe—but besides a few cracked ribs, my biggest complaint was that my ears were ringing.

That's new.

Agent Penetrate stomped through the rubble to where I lay, his cape billowing in the wind kicked up by the Biggs helicopters circling above. The police force always provided backup for me, but we all knew their rocket launchers wouldn't do much to a supe other than temporarily slow them down. In the end, it was entirely on *me* to protect Big City.

If I fall, the city falls.

And it would be so embarrassing to lose to this *guy.*

Besides his cheesy cartoon mobster face, Penetrate wore a *cape*. That kids' superhero movie with the montage of why supes should skip capes wasn't far from the truth. Plus, they just looked lame and outdated.

My Lycra was so technologically advanced, it actually knitted itself back together after a hit, while applying first-aid to my already fast-healing injuries. It was also high-velocity-ready and fireproof, which was necessary for anything that came in contact with me when my powers came out to play.

It was probably because of the mild concussion, but my brain chose this moment to recall that Dr. Antihero's suit could also withstand my firepower. I only knew this because of all the times I'd playfully tossed fireballs his way while stalking him around the Bay.

I wonder who designs his suits?

Why the heck am I even thinking about Antihero right now?

With a grunt, I rose to my feet and brushed the brick dust off my shoulders, ready to finish off this villain. It was written into my contract that I had to keep the fight going until the press got their footage. Since the television crews had *finally* arrived, I didn't have to continue pretending it was a fair fight.

"Your famed Captain Masculine is proving to be a disappointing opponent!" Agent Penetrate sneered, projecting his unexpectedly nasal voice as he dramatically played to the cameras. "The citizens of Big City should prepare for my inevitable rule."

They never learn.

The cameras were locked on the action—keeping both of us in the wide-angle frame while every reporter and city employee in attendance eagerly awaited what they knew was coming.

Time to earn my paycheck.

Penetrate opened his mouth to monologue some more, but could only screech as I slammed into him—faster than a speeding bullet—and took off into the sky. The wind tore past us so forcefully his headgear was ripped off. This allowed me to glimpse the momentary terror on his ugly face, which pleased me way more than a superhero should ever admit.

That's villain territory.

Since I had his arms pinned tightly against his body, he reared back and slammed his forehead into my nose, causing the bone to snap and blood to spray all over us.

Mothertrucker that hurt!

All that move accomplished was me dropping him. I watched in irritation as he plummeted to the city streets a mile below, wildly cackling on the way down. Of course, someone with unbreakable bones wouldn't mind eating pavement, but I didn't plan on letting him touch the ground.

I spat blood out of my mouth and dove after the villain, focusing every ounce of my power into forming a massive fireball. For a moment, I felt compelled to reach beyond myself for more juice, but quickly banished the ridiculous thought.

A supe's powers are internal, not external.

Penetrate's eyes widened in delicious fear as I easily caught up with him, blasting flames outward to envelop both of us in a fiery inferno.

His bones may be unbreakable, but he can still melt.

And melt he did. By the time Big City's latest threat drifted down to the ground, he was little more than a charred husk of scorched flesh, with the cameras zooming in to capture the mess in disgusting detail.

Everything hurt, but I plastered a cocky grin on my face and gracefully landed beside my latest kill as the crowd went wild. A few minutes later, my head was *pounding*, but I struck a few poses for the press and signed autographs before heading toward the unmarked town car waiting for me.

Just my boss wanting to immediately torture me with a debriefing.

"Nicely done, Butch," Solomon Biggs clapped me on the back the instant the car door slammed shut. I winced—not because a normie like Biggs could actually injure me, but something felt… off.

Sugar, my head hurts.

"…and the Mayor will want to present you with another medal. In front of the Enterprises building, naturally…"

Something's wrong…

"…but first, I'm going to need you to enter Penetrate's information into a spreadsheet…"

I wish Xander was here to take care of—

"Xan!" I gasped myself awake, frantically groping the surrounding bed, desperate for him. It felt absolutely vital that I press my body against his—absorb his comforting warmth like a security blanket—but he was nowhere to be found.

Where the fudge am I?

I blinked the sleep out of my eyes and peered around the dim bedroom. The walls were painted a faint peach, with tasteful furnishings and zero personality. There wasn't a single identifying feature—no photos showing proof of life—which led me to believe whoever decorated this room was either a robot or…

Oh, no.

"Butch, darling! I'm glad to see you're awake."

My entire body tensed as my mother breezed into the room, eliciting a sharp twinge of pain from my newly realigned ribs. This frivolous discomfort was forgotten when I realized the sun was already setting over my family's estate—an hour's flight outside the city.

Xander's going to be so worried!

"Where's my phone?" I barked, patting the bed again as if all my belongings—and pride—weren't routinely stripped the moment I entered this house.

Definitely not *a home.*

My mother made a derisive sound before producing my phone from her pocket—holding it out of reach. "Yes, you've received no less than 30 text messages and a dozen phone calls from someone saved as 'Daddy Xan' in your contacts."

An uncontrollable pulse of power rippled under my skin. I'd promised Xander I would do my best to call him, and he was obviously worried about me, so if *this woman* thought she was going to keep us apart—

"Did you just *threaten* your own mother?" she hissed as searing, white-hot agony raced through my veins. My firepower came from this woman—aka Smoldering Siren—but where I could expel it, she could burn you alive from the inside.

"I'm sorry!" I choked out. "Please, I just need to call my… my…"

The flames instantly dissipated, replaced by my mother's icy tone. "I hope for your sake you're talking about *Nicole.*"

I couldn't stop the laugh that bubbled up through my parched throat. "Mother, I told you. That date you and father sent me on with Gemstonia was one of the most painfully awkward nights of my life. I don't want—"

"It doesn't matter what you want." My father was suddenly looming in the doorway, sucking the air from the room. There was no doubt he'd felt my disrespectful power surge and stopped whatever he was doing to come remind me who *he* was.

Vortexio.

My strength, speed, and flight came from my father, but I hadn't inherited his more awesome powers. This man could literally create a tornado on a windless day and fling an entire town into another dimension.

And he's looking pretty pissed off at the moment…

I swallowed hard, but forced my voice to remain steady as I attempted to advocate for myself. "I'm with someone now, and it's getting serious. His name is Xander—"

"Xander?" my mother interrupted, shooting a quick glance at my father before returning her gaze to me. "What is his last name?"

Why? So you can decide if his family is worthy of ours?

"Marin," I replied, dredging up the name the hostess had used to confirm our reservation at Ars and Invenio. "You won't know him. He's a normie I met on a dating app."

"Is that right?" My father snatched my phone and began scrolling, presumably through Xander's messages. Since I didn't have a death wish, I gritted my teeth and endured him invading my privacy. "And he believes you're a normie too?"

"Yes," I rasped, my entire body buzzing with the *craving* to hear Xander's voice. "We have something special and I want... Can I please just have this one thing? I'll defend Big City until my dying day, but I don't want to be randomly married off to another supe like some sort of... *breeding stud.*"

My father barked a laugh. "But that's what you are, son. It's thanks to the impeccable breeding of the Holt-Arella line *you* were created. It's the reason lesser supe families will make all manner of deals for the chance of their offspring reproducing with ours."

I don't want any of this!

"Gemstonia Lincoln is the closest we could find to a worthy match, darling," my mother cut in, awkwardly rubbing my arm in a sorry attempt at comfort. "So you'll just have to give it another try—"

"I can't," I choked out as my vision went spotty again. "Please. Everything hurts... I-I *need* to talk to him, please..." I shook off her hand as I doubled over in pain, uncaring if I appeared weak. Anything that wasn't Xander felt like knives on my skin—leaving gaping wounds behind where only he should be.

Is this what dying feels like?

My mother hissed in a breath and looked at my father in alarm. "Give him the phone, Harold. Then we need to talk."

With a scoff, my father tossed my phone on the bed before stalking out of the room, with my mother close behind him. Despite the rational side of my brain telling me to follow and insert myself into whatever conversation they were about to have, I pounced on the device like a starving man.

Xander answered on the first ring. "Butch?! Holy fuck, were you downtown when Masculine battled Penetrate? It was all over the news. You weren't hurt, were you?"

The acute pain ricocheting through my system instantly vanished at the sound of his voice. With a sigh of relief, I collapsed back against the pillows, wishing I had teleportation powers so I could instantly be with him. I would've done it in a heartbeat, even though my identity as a supe would then be compromised.

Xander would want me either way, right?

"Talk to me, baby. Tell me you're okay." His tone had evened out, but I sensed he was forcing his calm for my sake.

I'd *never* felt that wrecked after a fight before, but I didn't have the energy to think about what it could mean right now. If I couldn't be with Xander tonight—and I knew my parents would make me stay—then I was going to listen to his sexy as sin voice on the line until I fell asleep again.

He could read me the dictionary and I'd hang on every word.

"I'm okay," I replied, finally able to *breathe* again. "Everything's gonna be okay now that I have you."

CHAPTER 17
XANDER

Two nights without Butch in my bed and I'd turned into a fucking menace to society.

More than usual, that is.

His family was forcing him to stay inland with them for a few days, and it was all I could do to not demand he hand over the address so I could stage a jailbreak.

As soon as he's back, I'm putting a tracker on his phone.

I assumed his absence had something to do with Captain Masculine and Agent Penetrate leveling an entire city block on Sunday. Butch insisted he hadn't been anywhere near the action, but I suspected he wasn't telling me the whole truth. Then, I reminded myself he *couldn't* tell me, because of his job working for the puppet master of Big City's corruption.

With a frustrated snarl, I stomped into the shabby elevator and slammed my hand against the 53rd-floor button with more force than was necessary. It had taken everything in me not to cancel today's therapy appointment with Dr. Ownit, but I'd dragged myself here.

Like a goddamn *adult*.

Stepping out onto the ratty hallway carpet, I closed my eyes and took a few deep breaths to check in with my mental state. It wasn't as if I'd never come here in a bad mood before, but usually, it was because my mother or siblings had brought me their bullshit. Or the human race had annoyed me in general.

This feels different.

My adrenaline was stuck in fight-or-flight, but mostly fight. Every day inconveniences were sending me through the roof, to where I was legitimately considering injuring someone. This slightly concerned me. It wasn't as if I lacked the resources to cover up a murder, but I tried to limit my body count to those who truly deserved it.

But being around Butch is making me want to be less of a homicidal maniac...

Snapping my eyes open again, I decided *this* would be my reframe, in honor of today's session. Schooling my face into a mask of calm, I opened the door to my therapist's office and slipped inside.

"Ah, Xander! Wonderful to see you." Dr. Ownit beamed from across the cramped waiting room where he was watering the lone, dying Ficus. "Please, make yourself comfortable. I'll be in shortly."

As usual, I did my best to ignore the disarray of his office as I sat on the stiff vinyl couch. Besides the decor being a bit too 1970s wood-paneled basement for my taste, Ownit also employed the 'organized piles' filing system that made my eye twitch.

He hustled inside a minute later, clutching his signature *'I may not be totally perfect, but parts of me are excellent'* mug full of peppermint tea. Ownit rarely sipped on it during our sessions, which made me wonder if he was simply attempting a budget version of aromatherapy. I couldn't say if it worked one way or the other, but at the moment, the pungent odor was grating on my nerves.

Good luck with me today, doc.

What I liked most about my therapist—besides his Freud-like Austrian accent—was that he missed nothing. It was in such sharp contrast to the mess he surrounded himself with, but I appreciated how it essentially forced me to cut the shit when I was in his space.

Knowing him, enduring the mess may be a test.

"Thank you for waiting," he brusquely said, setting the mug on the wooden coffee table and picking up my file before taking the seat opposite me.

I couldn't help fixating on the fact he'd placed his mug one inch away from the coaster. The ceramic was wet—as if it had recently been washed—and the moisture was going to leave a mark on the wood. Just as I debated moving the mug for him, my gaze flickered up to Ownit's face to find him watching me shrewdly.

Fuck.

Definitely a test.

"I met someone!" I blurted out, desperate to focus on Butch and his sunshiny-ness instead of my doom and gloom. The last thing I needed was to fly off the handle and unalive my therapist—partly because I begrudgingly respected the man.

But mostly because I don't need the headache of finding a replacement.

Ownit's bushy eyebrows practically took flight. "Oh! Well, that's..."—he shuffled through my file—"*new* for you, isn't it?"

I laughed and slung an arm over the back of the couch, smugly delighted I'd thrown him off his game. "Most definitely. We only just met this week—on a dating app of all things—but I've already given up my lifelong commitment to being unattached by asking him to be exclusive with me."

"Fascinating," Ownit murmured, probably already composing the research paper he'd write on me in his head. "And what is it about this man, this ah…"

"Butch," I supplied, noticing the tension I'd been tamping down roil beneath the surface again at the mention of his name. "He's…"

I considered what it *was* about him I found so attractive, besides looking like a lifetime supply of snacks. We hadn't known each other long—despite me feeling like I'd known him forever—but I'd already realized there was so much more to Butch than what he displayed on the surface. He possessed core characteristics I'd never given much thought to before, but now felt like I couldn't live without.

Sharply inhaling, I immediately realized my mistake in bringing this up in the unforgiving setting of my therapist's office. "He's everything that I'm not."

Because he was merciless, Ownit just straight-up called out the elephant in the room. "What is he that you *think* you're not, Xander?"

I blew out a slow breath as my focus started to dangerously tunnel on the man sitting across from me. "He's kind, and open, and has a natural sweetness that I don't think anyone could corrupt."

Not even me.

"His smile just lights up the room," I gritted out, feeling my fingers start to weirdly tingle again. "And he wants to experience things—experience *life*—in this full-body, wholehearted way that I could never..." I choked on my words, suddenly finding it difficult to breathe.

Ownit was leaning so far forward he'd practically crossed the table and joined me on the couch. "What makes you think you're not capable of those things as well?"

Because I'm a villain.

"I'm just not," I croaked. "And I never will be." My heart was pounding, adrenaline coursing through my system as my vision started to go red.

How are things ever going to work between us?

Completely oblivious to the imminent danger he was in, my therapist calmly sat back to write a few notes in my file. "That's simply your core beliefs causing a cognitive distortion. Did he agree?"

"W-what?" His question caught me so off-guard, my rising fury instantly evaporated.

"Did, eh, *Butch* agree to be exclusive with you?" Ownit was back to watching me like a hawk.

"Yes," I rasped, as any remaining tension bled out of me. "He said yes almost immediately."

"The answer will always be yes, Xan."

Ownit made a noncommittal sound in his throat as he wrote more in my file. As usual, the man was letting a statement hang in the air to ensure I fully absorbed it. My attention had already moved on to Butch and the possibility that I might not see him tonight, either.

I don't think I'll survive it.

Before *that* core belief could send me down the path of negativity, a deafening explosion rocked the entire building.

Ownit toppled out of his chair in a flurry of papers, but I leaped over his fallen form to rush to the floor-to-ceiling window for a better view. A body suddenly crashed into the skyscraper the next block over, immediately followed by a blur of blue.

Captain Masculine.

The emergency lights started flashing in the hallway, signaling we needed to evacuate the building. Ownit took his cue to escape, shouting for me to follow him, but I was transfixed. During my run-ins with the superhero, I'd been too focused on survival to appreciate his godlike powers, but having this front-row seat—at eye-level, no less…

Look at him go.

It was like watching a ballet and a cage match at the same time. Captain Masculine moved as though the air—the entire universe—was created for the sole purpose of supporting his glory. A news helicopter hovered nearby, and I spotted a few snipers on a nearby roof, but the superhero was deadly focused on his target as they exchanged blows.

I vaguely registered that his opponent was Red Renegade—a member of the Strickland family, probably after revenge for Agent Penetrate's death. But all I cared about was seeing Masculine in action.

This is incredible!

Red attempted to make a break for it, but Big City's greatest hero snatched the villain out of the air like a bird of prey and violently slammed him against the building right next to my window.

Yessss…

I stepped as close to the glass as I could get, tilting my head so I could watch my nemesis pummel Red into the granite. Even when the villain had stopped moving—and looked more like roadkill than supe—Masculine kept swinging.

Fuck. Yes.

I'd seen plenty of footage of Captain Masculine defeating his enemies, and it always looked staged to me, but *this* display wasn't for the cameras. This was raw, unfiltered rage.

And there's nothing hotter than that.

All at once, I understood that the hero I saw on TV was just a persona crafted to inspire—by Biggs Enterprises, no doubt—but the unhinged man I saw before me was closer to the truth.

I see you.

I. See. You.

Masculine abruptly snapped out of his fury, backing off to let Red's mangled body drop to the pavement far below. To my surprise, he didn't immediately turn to the cameras to pose and preen and take his usual victory lap. Instead, he dropped his masked face into his hands, his impossibly broad chest heaving like he was trying to catch his breath.

I was so mesmerized by this sordid glimpse behind the scenes that I forgot I was still plastered to the window only a few feet away from the famous hero. As if sensing my presence, Captain Masculine's head suddenly snapped up, and I startled as his equally wide eyes locked on mine from beneath his identity-shielding headgear.

Then we just stared at each other.

I should have been terrified to be this close to the man who'd tried to kill me on multiple occasions, but I felt calm and weirdly safe instead. It was as if all the tension I'd been holding on to since dropping Butch off at the Navy Yard disappeared, simply from being in his presence.

This is some freaky shit.

Even though I was *craving* Butch, I couldn't stop my gaze from wandering over Masculine's *masculine* form. The sun was setting, casting shadows over his blue Lycra, bringing how stacked he was into sharp relief. Dude was built like a Greek god brick house, and I had the irrational urge to run my tongue over every inch of him.

When I looked up again, I saw he was doing the same to me—his gaze hungrily taking me in as if *I* somehow had the same effect on him as he did on me.

Fuck, I'm so hard right now.

Wait. What the hell is going on?

Before I could unravel this potentially unlocked kink, he *reached* for me.

Terrified, I jumped back so fast I stumbled over Ownit's overturned chair. This instinctive reaction broke whatever spell had come over us, as Masculine clenched his fists and zipped away faster than I could blink.

To be discussed at my next therapy appointment…

My phone buzzed against my rock-hard cock a minute later, and I fumbled it out of my pocket to find Butch texting me.

Well, this is awkward.

> **Hottie Himbo:** *I'm back in town. I need to see you.*

While I knew I'd have to address the weird-as-fuck encounter I'd just had with Captain Masculine, the only thing that mattered at the moment was that my painful separation from

Butch was ending. We'd talked both nights since he'd been gone, and texted throughout each day, but I couldn't wait to see him in person.

And who knows—maybe he'd be into a superhero fantasy?

> **Welcome back, sweetheart. I'll come pick you up wherever you are.**

Hottie Himbo: *I'll meet you at your apartment. Can I please spend the night?*

Grinning wildly, I turned and raced out of my therapist's office, leaving the door wide open behind me as I single-mindedly headed for the elevator. That Butch believed he had to ask to spend the night—to spend every waking and sleeping moment with me—was a misconception I would have to rectify as soon as possible.

But first, I need to get my hands on him.

As the elevator dinged, I fired off another text, no longer concerned about coming across as *too* interested. I wanted this man to know just how obsessed with him I was.

> **Baby, the answer will always be yes.**

CHAPTER 18
XANDER

Butch was not okay.

When I pulled into the parking garage below my building, I found him slumped on the ground next to the elevator, dressed in a worn tee shirt and basketball shorts with enormous bags under his eyes—looking as haggard as my hottie himbo possibly could.

Daddy's here now, baby.

"C'mon, sweetheart," I soothed, kneeling before subtly using my supe-strength to help the big guy rise to stand. "Let's go upstairs."

He nodded wordlessly and followed me into the elevator. Once we got to my floor, he simply trailed after me like a lost dog, which conjured up an image of him wearing nothing but a collar and leash while I fed him my cock.

Now is not the time, Xan.

Once inside, I immediately adjusted the lights and put on some Tchaikovsky, since the Russian composer never failed to relax me when everything went to shit.

I need to learn what he likes.

I need to learn everything about him.

"I'm getting you some water," I stated, striding to the kitchen area and filling a glass. He was standing in the same spot when I turned around again, so I did a quick body scan as I approached, trying to get a read on him.

Odd choice of clothing aside, his posture was slightly hunched, fists rhythmically clenching and unclenching at his sides, gaze fixed on the floor as he breathed heavily through his nose. As I slowly circled him, I saw the bags under his eyes were so bad, they almost looked like bruises.

Jesus, he looks terrible.

Still hot as fuck, but terrible.

"Let's go to the bedroom." I placed a hand on his lower back and began steering him toward my room.

His baby blues snapped to mine with a startling intensity. "Yes..." he murmured, lifting a hand to press it against my chest. "Take me to bed, Daddy."

Shit.

My cock was trying to punch its way out of my pants, but I somehow refrained from tackling him to the floor like an animal in heat. Despite Butch's daze, adrenaline was clearly coursing through his system—whether from lust or whatever had happened to him while we were apart, I couldn't be sure. The last thing I wanted to do was make things worse.

I want to make it better.

Blowing out a breath, I led him to the bed so he could sit. "Drink this." I handed him the water, determined to stay the course. "All of it."

He smiled indulgently—just like he always did whenever I bossed him around—before bringing the glass to his pouty lips. I started undressing, keeping my gaze on him to make sure he actually drank, and he watched me in return, his throat bobbing as he obediently swallowed every drop.

Good boy.

Butch lowered the glass, his gaze hungrily taking me in, eerily similar to how Captain Masculine had looked at me earlier. "I missed you so much, Xan. I'm sorry I—"

"Don't be sorry," I interrupted, moving to stand in front of him so I could grab the empty glass and set it aside. "Whatever you were going to apologize for—don't. And I missed you, too… more than I can explain. But we're together now and I'm going to take care of you."

I need to make it better.

He exhaled so forcefully that I was surprised he didn't fall off the bed. His broad shoulders slumped as he dropped his forehead against my hip, finally allowing himself to relax. The feel of his breath ghosting over me made me harden, but I focused on soothingly running my fingers through his soft blond hair.

"It physically *hurt* to be separated from you," he whispered, turning his head to nuzzle my aching cock, as if seeking comfort. "It felt like… like I was dying and the only cure was you. If I'd gone one more night without your skin on mine, I don't know what I might have done…"

I froze.

That's… interesting…

His description so perfectly matched *my* experience that I had a hard time believing it was a coincidence. A random memory brushed against the edge of my awareness—some ancient supe history I'd run across while researching my lack of powers in my family's archives several years ago.

"Xan..." he murmured, running his soft lips up my shaft, distracting me from my thoughts.

I groaned, wanting nothing more than to explode down his throat. "Fuck, Butch. I'm trying to take care of *you* here."

"But this is what I need to feel better." His pretty pink tongue peeked out, lightly teasing my retracted foreskin before depositing a sweet kiss on my crown. "Please, Daddy. Remind me that I'm good..."

Well, who can say no to that?

"You're *so* good, sweetheart," I praised, running my fingers through his hair again—petting him. "I was just telling my therapist today how sweet you are. How perfect."

He sharply glanced up at me. "That's where you were today? At your therapist's office?"

Smiling down at him, I nodded, realizing I hadn't mentioned my therapy yet—how there was still so much for us to learn about each other.

I want him to know me.

"Yeah. Things got a little... weird after my appointment, but I'll tell you about that later." I placed my hand under his chin, gripping hard enough to remind him who was in charge. "Right now, I want you to swallow my cock until you choke on it. Show Daddy what a good boy you are."

He moaned, his eyelids momentarily fluttering closed as if that command alone was enough to get him off. Then he grabbed my waist with both of his enormous hands, leaned down, and slid as much of me as he could into his perfect fucking mouth.

"Jes-us," I rasped as a jolt of electricity zipped down my spine. "I swear to god, baby, you're a natural at this."

In reply, he shoved the last few inches in, the sound of him gagging threatening to make me blow. This man sucked cock like he was starved for it—starved for *my* cock specifically—which only made it hotter.

That weird tingly feeling in my fingers was back as I tightened my hold on his hair, our connection somehow both easing and exacerbating the sensation.

Butch's throat was constricting around me—so sinfully tight and wet—and then he brushed his finger up the seam of my balls, confirming I wouldn't last long. Just before I reached the point of no return, he popped my cock out of his mouth with an obscene sound.

"Please come on my face, Xan," he gazed up at me, his lips puffy and tears streaming down his cheeks. "Show me I belong to you."

Holy fucking fuck.

How Butch always knew exactly what to say to set me off was a mystery, but the idea of painting his handsome face with my cum made me absolutely feral.

I roughly yanked him closer and began furiously pumping my cock, noticing how he kept his gaze locked on mine instead of watching what I was doing.

I see you, too, baby.

This deep connection between us made absolutely no sense considering we'd barely known each other for a week, but I didn't give a fuck. I never wanted this to stop. I wanted a piece of me buried in Butch at all times. If it couldn't be my fingers, tongue, cum, or cock, then I was going to permanently embed myself on his fucking soul.

Mine.

Butch slid to the floor and opened his mouth, as if this were some sacred act and he was about to receive the Holy Communion. Just the sight of him on his knees was enough to finish me. I came with a grunt, continuing to fuck my fist as thick ropes of cum decorated his face, gloriously marking him as mine.

All fucking mine.

"Thank you," he whispered, smiling up at me with a dreamy expression on his face.

I let my gaze take in the beautiful man kneeling before me, blissed-out as if I *had* made everything better simply by painting him with my cum.

What did I do to deserve this?

"Look at how *good* you are," I murmured, wiping my thumb through the mess before popping it into his mouth to suck clean. "And you're all mine."

It almost looked like his bottom lip trembled. "Can I always be yours, Xan? No matter what happens?"

I hesitated, only because something was nudging at my awareness again, demanding I pay attention—to *what*, I couldn't be sure.

Despite the secrets between us, I knew Butch was giving me every piece of himself that he could. Because he'd somehow decided I was worthy of his sweetness—his light—even though I still wasn't sure I could ever be as good as him.

"Yes, baby," I replied, helping him rise again, deeply inhaling the smell of *my* cum on top of his scent—memorizing it. "You'll always be mine. Now let's go take a shower and see if we can't wash our sins away."

The least I can do is try.

CHAPTER 19
BUTCH

Waking up in Xander's bed with him wrapped around me from behind was heavenly. After showering together the night before, I'd turned off my phone and tossed it into the bedside drawer. Even after a good night's sleep, and the near-spiritual experience Xander had given me on my knees, I had no interest in looking at it ever again.

Why bother when the one person I want to talk to is beside me?

Passing out in Solomon Biggs' car had been a blessing in disguise. My boss was so freaked out by my rare show of weakness that he'd shipped me off to my parents with strict instructions to not return to the city unless there was an emergency.

Of course, there was an emergency.

Red Renegade seeking revenge was its own stroke of luck, as it gave me an excuse to escape the Holt estate—and my parents' schemes. I hadn't planned on ending Red so brutally, but I was so untethered by Xander's absence, it felt like the only way to make the pain stop.

Seeing Xander at the scene of the crime immediately settled me. He'd seemed oddly comfortable watching me kill, and it was such a relief to feel *seen*, I'd almost pulled my mask off to show him who I was. For a moment, I also could have sworn the violence turned him on.

But he was actually afraid.

Big City citizens weren't supposed to *fear* me. I was their savior—their hero. Sure, a powerless normie might feel overwhelmed in my presence, but I'd done nothing to inspire the sheer terror I'd witnessed on Xander's face as he backed away from me.

I mean, unless you're a villain.

Thinking of supes inevitably brought me back to the excruciating events of Monday night. My parents invited Nicole—Gemstonia—and her family to join us for dinner, so the two of us could spend more time together under the watchful eye of four extremely invested chaperones.

I'd attempted to bribe Nicole into leaving me alone during our doomed date at Ars and Invenio, but she wasn't having any of it. It was clear she intended to see this through—all the way to the altar—because she wanted my family name and powerful children.

Opportunist.

At the time, I was most upset about being treated like a breeding stud who didn't get a say in his future. Now, the idea of spending my life with anyone other than Xander made my heart race and my hands itch for a villain to kill.

What if they force *me to marry her?*

"What's the matter, baby?" Xander's muffled voice against my neck, thick with sleep, simultaneously calmed me and turned me on.

Even though we couldn't possibly get any physically closer than we were now, I wanted more. I wanted to tell Xander everything—to crawl into his lap and cry over how nothing in my life was my own. Nothing except *him*.

If I lose him, I will burn this city to the ground.

Realizing my thoughts were drifting in a dangerous direction, I cleared my throat. "I was just thinking about how... *sucky* my last couple of days were. Without you."

"Mmm..." he hummed, sliding a hand down my abs to cup my dick through my boxer briefs. "Can I make it better before you have to go to work?"

I stiffened—in more ways than one. "I-I called in sick for the day," I mumbled this half-truth while desperately thrusting into his hand. "And I was hoping to, um... just stay here. If that's okay?"

No one knows where I am.

And I don't want them to.

Much to my dismay, Xander stopped what he was doing before abruptly sitting up and rolling me onto my back, still tangled in the sheets.

"Butch." He stared down at me with that almost scary level of intensity I loved. "What makes you think I *wouldn't* want you here?"

Blushing, I attempted to look everywhere except at him. "I just don't want to seem needy."

Even though I need you like the air I breathe.

Xander grabbed my chin and forced me to look at him. "Sweetheart. You're not needy. You need *me*—just like I need you. Since neither of us seems to have a problem with that, I say fuck what anyone else thinks about it."

My heart beat faster as a sensation of pure warmth filled me. Xander sighed, his gorgeous amber eyes fluttering closed for a moment—as if he also felt it.

Please feel it too.

I smiled up at him, feeling better already. "I wish I could be as confident as you in telling others to... eff off." His eyes snapped open again at my sorry attempt at swearing. "Maybe I need to try some therapy."

He huffed, but considered. "Therapy is an experience not for the faint of heart. It's a crash course in exposing all the dark pieces of your soul to the harsh light of day... but I do love dissecting things." Trailing off, he suddenly looked oddly unsure. "Butch, I need to talk to you about something that happened yesterday..."

That caught my interest. Whatever it was clearly bothered him, and if he wanted to share, I was more than happy to peel back another layer of the man I wanted to know everything about. "Sure, Xan. You can talk to me about anything."

I wish I could do the same with you.

"Very well, but consider yourself warned, it gets weird." He smirked down at me before sobering. "So, my therapy appointment was cut short because the fight between Captain Masculine and Red Renegade happened right outside the window. Did you see it on the news?"

I swallowed and slowly nodded, no longer sure I wanted to hear where this was going.

If he's weirded out by Captain Masculine, what does that mean for me?

For us.

He sat back, his gaze going distant as he mentally replayed what he'd seen. "Yeah, it was fucking wild. I mean, I've seen footage of the Captain defeating villains, but to get a front-row seat—to feel the building shake as he slammed Red into it? To see him *kill* his opponent with… with nothing but his bare hands and bottomless rage? *Fuuuuck…*"

Xander's chest was heaving, and when his gaze snapped to mine, I saw his pupils were blown out, making my dick throb in its cotton confines. "Is that weird?" he asked, his gaze searching mine. "That I liked it?"

I shook my head. "No," I breathed. "Keep going." To have confirmation that the violence he'd witnessed yesterday—the moment I lost all control—*turned him on* was everything I didn't know I needed.

He's just like me.

My hand dropped to my dick of its own accord, and his lip curled, tracking the movement. "Masculine reminds me of you—the way he's built and these bright blue eyes… It made me want to rip that sinfully tight supersuit off of him, bend him over, and fuck him until he begged for mercy."

"Xan!" I shouted, my eyes widening as a surprise orgasm thundered down my spine at this mental image. There was nothing I could do but groan as my vision went white and pulse after pulse of cum released inside my briefs.

Ah, fudge…

"You liked that, huh, baby?" he purred, his gaze darkening as he slid his hand under mine, feeling the evidence of my latest breach of control. "You wanna play superheroes in bed with me?"

Oh my godddd, yes, pleeeease.

"Maybe," I hedged, feeling my neck and face burn in embarrassment, even though I knew Xander was as into it as me. "But right now I just feel kind of gross, and I... I didn't bring any extra clothes."

Please don't make me go back to my condo to get anything.

He chuckled, batting away my attempts to remove his hand from the soaked cotton, making my dick stir to life all over again. "I like you gross, but yeah, I get it. Don't worry about the clothes. I have mine delivered so I don't have to, you know,"—he waved a dismissive hand—"deal with people. Just tell me your measurements and I'll call my guy. We won't even have to leave the house."

So much gratitude welled up inside me, I feared I might start crying again. "Thank you, Xan—" I abruptly sat up to hug the man, but a hiss of pain escaped as my newly healed ribs shifted the wrong way.

The change that came over Xander's face was startling. "Are you hurt? Take the blankets off—let me look at you."

Oh, sugar.

My mind raced for an explanation, even as I obediently pulled the sheet away from my midsection. Xander shifted on the bed so he was no longer blocking the light coming through the shades and stared at the fading bruises on my side with so much unbridled fury, I froze.

"Who. The *FUCK*. Did this to you?" he hissed, his amber eyes flashing gold. My powers pulsed in reply to... *something*, although I was too frantic to consider what it was.

"I-I got into a fight," I stuttered. "At a bar. I was out with some coworkers."

I hate lying to him.

"Who?" he repeated, his jaw clenched so tightly, I was afraid he might chip a tooth.

The realization that Xander wasn't angry with me—that he wanted to defend me against a threat—made that all-encompassing warmth flood my veins again.

"Why?" I teased, reaching out a hand to soothingly rub his biceps. "Are you gonna find the villain and kill him?"

"Yes." The way he looked at me suggested he wasn't joking.

This is so freakin' hot...

"Xan, I'm okay." I tried my best not to smile, but his possessive display was making me giddy. "I can handle myself in a fight. You should see the other guy!"

He's at the morgue.

Xander closed his eyes and breathed deeply a few times before resolutely nodding his head. "I'm sorry. I just—"

"Don't be sorry," I repeated his words from last night, shyly shrugging. "I kinda like you being all growly and protective."

Even though the roles would be reversed if it ever came down to it.

He laughed again, self-deprecatingly. "Well, good thing, because I can't seem to tone down the crazy when it comes to you. It's your own fault for being so goddamn *perfect*." His expression turned earnest, as if he wanted to say more, but he cleared his throat instead. "Let's get you in the shower again —*alone*, so you can get cleaned up—while I order some clothes. Then we'll spend the day on the couch before telling your boss you won't be in for the rest of the week."

My eyes nearly popped out of my head. "I can't take the entire week off! What if there's another emergency?"

Xander scoffed. "You got into a serious altercation that left you severely injured. There's no emergency more important than you healing. I'll have my doctor fax a note over to Biggs Enterprises, excusing you for a few days. If that idiot Solomon has a problem with it, I'll speak to him myself."

Tears blurred my vision, but I quickly blinked them away. "Thank you, Xan," I repeated, wrapping my arms around him so I could lay my head on his chest. "I've never had anyone take care of me before."

Not even my own parents.

"Same," he murmured, almost to himself, before clearing his throat again. "I will gladly make taking care of you *my* job, and while I can't promise to keep my hands to myself completely, I'll do my best to not involve you in anything too strenuous for the next few days."

When I whimpered in protest, he chuckled, untangling himself from my arms so he could stand. Helping me rise—sticky underwear and all—he planted a sweet kiss on my lips. "That's enough, baby. Go take a nice hot shower and see if you can squeeze all those hot muscles into one of my robes for now. Then prepare yourself for a Netflix and chill marathon."

CHAPTER 20
XANDER

If you'd asked me even a week ago whether I wanted someone inhabiting my sacred space 24/7, I would have laughed. After only a couple of days with Butch all up in my business, I was ready to move him in.

I wonder if that would be too soon?

"So, what did you do at your parents' house?" I asked around a mouthful of fried chicken. I'd introduced Butch to Felix and the wondrous Sun-Mart chicken, and got him to admit it was better than the Tick Tock Diner's. "Since I assume you went there *after* the bar fight?"

Butch's bruises were fading, thanks to Kai being in and out of my apartment for the last two-and-a-half days. She'd gone into full mother hen mode once she realized Butch was hurt, bringing over some weird herbal salve and organic cotton bandages. I couldn't scoff too openly, since they seemed to be speeding up the healing process to almost supe levels.

I still want to find whoever did this and take them apart.

Piece by piece.

Butch's silence brought me out of my daydreams of utilizing my beloved scalpel. "Yeah, it was after..." he finally replied, pausing to chew his tasty bottom lip, clearly struggling to share more.

I smiled encouragingly. "You don't have to tell me anything you don't want to, sweetheart. I totally get having a family who—"

"No!" he blurted out, before looking adorably embarrassed. "I *want* to tell you. It's just..."

I turned my entire body to face Butch on the couch, wanting him to see he had my undivided attention. While he was stumbling a little over whatever he was trying to tell me, I appreciated how he just laid his emotions on the table.

I'll get there someday.

He blew out a breath. "My parents are... kind of *formal*. While I was there, they hosted this big, extravagant dinner. I don't like that kind of thing anyway, but they invited over some family friends... including their daughter. For a while now, everyone has been assuming I'll end up with her."

It took every ounce of self-control to not immediately find this girl and eliminate the competition. Then my rage turned to anxiety as I suddenly worried Butch was gearing up to tell me *he* also saw this future for himself.

Because he could somehow sense me spiraling, Butch leaped across the couch and half-crawled into my lap—as much as a behemoth like him could. "Xan! Please don't worry. I have no intention of being with her. Even before we met, I wasn't interested, and now that I have you..." He cupped my face in his huge hands and stared deep into my eyes. "There's no one else I want to be with. I just wanted you to know what was going on, in case..."

My vision tunneled. "In case what?" I gritted out. While arranged marriages were common with supes, it didn't seem like something normies did much anymore—at least not in this country.

I swear on all that is holy, I will kidnap him if it comes to that.

He smiled, although it didn't reach his baby blues. "I don't know. There's so much I can't tell you about my… situation. But I don't want there to be any more secrets between us than necessary."

My heart sank as I remembered all the secrets *I* was harboring as well. It was strictly written into supe law that we weren't supposed to reveal our true identities to normies outside of sanctioned government officials and extreme circumstances, but I wondered if there was a loophole.

I need to visit my family's archives to poke around some more.

Since Butch was clearly stressing over this, I added some levity to the situation—for both our sakes. "Well, I have no intention of losing you to someone who doesn't even have a cock, especially now that we both know you're obsessed with mine. And we still have some superhero fantasies to explore, don't we?"

The cock *I* was obsessed with nudged me through the slutty gray sweatpants I'd ordered, along with an entire closet full of clothes. Butch had grown adorably flustered when the clothing arrived—so much so that I'd emulated Dr. Ownit and mercilessly dug for the root cause of the issue.

"What is bothering you about this?" I'd bluntly asked once my personal shopper had left the apartment. "I want to take care of you, I enjoy buying things for you, and I know for a fact you've experienced wealth before."

"Well, yeah," he'd stammered, his wide-eyed gaze darting over everything I'd purchased. "I guess I'm just not used to receiving anything without… earning it first."

I'd gripped his face so hard he grunted. "You don't have to earn this, Butch," I'd hissed, my anger entirely aimed at whoever trained him to think this way. "I don't mind you wanting to be a good little student in my bed, but my affection for you is unconditional. I intend to spoil you, and I expect you to accept it, like the good boy you are."

"Yes, Daddy," he'd smiled, and his protests were over.

"Yes, Daddy," Butch echoed my memory, subtly rubbing himself against me like he didn't even realize he was doing it. "I *really* want to do the superhero thing with you."

Fuck, he's so fucking cute.

Smirking, I brought him in for a sloppy kiss before grabbing the remote. "Hmm, I rarely watch superhero movies, but maybe we should put one on while I stretch you with my fingers some more…" Butch moaned so loudly, I expected him to need a change of clothes again, but then his gaze nervously flickered to the door.

I really need to revoke Kai's fingerprint access.

"Our Queen Brat has tap dance or some bullshit on Friday mornings, so I think we're safe from her barging in for a while. Although," I licked my lips, "maybe her seeing me buried knuckles-deep in your tight ass will teach her to knock first."

As expected, Butch attractively blushed as he squirmed in my lap. "Don't you think you've stretched me enough? When are you going to… you know…"

Teasing him will never get old.

"What, sweetheart?" I adopted an innocent expression as I pressed play, not intending to pay much attention to the random movie I'd selected. "What is it you want me to do?"

"I want…" he whined helplessly before something interesting passed over his face. Gone was the flustered insecurity, replaced by that unexpected calculation I'd glimpsed once or twice before.

Gracefully sliding off my lap, he laid back on the couch, spread his legs, and aimed his sweatpants-covered cock my way. "I want you to *fuck* me."

Look who's not playing fair.

"Don't you go turning into a brat on me," I growled, using every shred of self-control to not rip those sweats off and plow into him, sans lube. "I know you want to experience everything, but *I* want your first time to not hurt like a bitch."

He smiled with all his dimples—another sneaky move to get me to crack, no doubt. "What if I swear to you I can take it? Can we try? I promise I'll tell you the moment anything hurts."

This. Man.

Physically unable to say no to him, I sighed. "Let me think about it, okay? I assume you'll be spending the weekend, yes?"

Rhetorical question.

"Yes," he answered immediately, before chewing his bottom lip again. "But you need to say something if having me around all the time gets annoying."

I gave him *a look*, but before I could command him to move in with me already, my phone buzzed with a message from Kai.

> **Bestie:** *DUDE, I was just offered the role of Columbia for RHPS and my first show is TONIGHT!!! If you and lover boy aren't in the audience IN FULL FUCKING COSTUME, consider our friendship finished.*

As tempting as it was to test whether a break from Kai would be so easy, the vision of Butch experiencing a midnight performance of *The Rocky Horror Picture Show*—in scandalous dress—won out.

Plus, I should probably support my 'bestie.'

I texted back with the thumbs up, red lips, and two men in bunny ears emojis before scheduling another clothing delivery for a few hours from now.

Setting my phone aside, I reached for Butch's sweatpants and pulled them off his muscular legs. "All right, my brave little bottom. Let's get you limbered up while we get hard for heroes. This evil villain has another surprise for you tonight."

CHAPTER 21
BUTCH

"I'm not sure about this, Xan," I called from inside the bathroom. "I think Big City might have laws against being naked in public."

I could practically *see* the stern look he was giving me on the other side of the door—the one that meant he was about to boss me around and I was about to get a boner.

We both know I'll do anything he says.

"Sweetheart. You're not naked. You're wearing gold lamé briefs with an athletic cup underneath to protect others from losing an eye every time I take charge."

He gets me.

"Fine," I sighed, stifling a smile as I stepped out of the en suite for the big reveal. "Maybe once I see the movie, I'll understand why the heck I need to dress like—"

My words ended with a choked sound as I spotted Xander. He was sitting in the leather wing chair across the room with his legs crossed, casually sipping a bourbon so rare that when I'd secretly looked it up, the price tag almost made me pass out.

That wasn't what was threatening my consciousness at the moment. Xan was wearing what appeared to be a corset and fishnet stockings, topped off with a pearl necklace, dangerously high heels, and deep red lipstick.

How attractive can one man be?

"You look..." I couldn't even form words, since words were hard when all your blood had rushed to your dick.

He threw his head back and laughed before setting down his highball glass and rising to stand. Strutting toward me with way more grace than I could pull off in heels, he chuckled. "I look like a sweet transvestite from Transexual, Transylvania—but you can call me Dr. Frank N. Furter."

I was still gaping, taking in every inch of the man in front of me and wondering why we couldn't just stay home. "I don't understand a word you just said, but you look freakin' *hot.*"

Xander smiled and gave me an achingly sweet kiss. "And you look like my favorite obsession."

Stepping back, he retrieved a roll of oversized medical gauze from the bed. "The—albeit problematic—words will make more sense once you see the film. For now, let's get you all wrapped up and decent-looking. The audience may want to see what's on the slab, but I want them to shiver with antici—"

"—pation." Xander deposited a filthy kiss on my lips as we stumbled into his apartment hours later.

The Rocky Horror Picture Show had been like nothing I'd ever experienced before. At first, I didn't know what the heck was going on as everyone threw rice and put newspapers on their heads before spraying water guns into the air, but I soon got swept up in the ridiculousness. There were other Franks and Rockys in the audience, but Xan had waited until the correct scene to calmly lead me to the front and unwrap me in time with the actors on stage.

The crowd went wild—and when we went backstage afterward to congratulate Kai, she told me we'd stolen the show. She didn't seem too mad about it, especially since Xander apparently filled her dressing room with blood-red roses.

I don't know why he pretends she isn't *his bestie.*

"Did you enjoy yourself tonight, Butch?" Xander asked as he forced me to drink *another* glass of water.

I'd already incessantly babbled about the show the entire drive home, but I couldn't stop. "It was *so* fun, Xan! Can we *please* go to every one of Kai's performances? She was amazing as Columbia, with all the singing and tap dancing… hey!" A sudden realization had me bouncing on my toes. "It's our one-week anniversary tonight!"

He's never getting rid of me now.

I no longer worried about coming across as too eager or needy with this man. Xander made it clear he *wanted* to take care of me—that he needed me just as much as I needed him. Most importantly, he made sure I understood I didn't have to do anything special for him to treat me this way.

That I'm already worthy of it.

"So it is." He indulgently smirked, retrieving the empty glass from me and placing it on the kitchen island. "What do you think, sweetheart? In just seven days, have I made you a man?"

While I knew he was quoting the movie, I couldn't help using the opening to my advantage. "Not yet, you haven't," I whispered, giving him a meaningful look. "Please…"

A full-body shudder ran through him, as it always did when I begged. "Baby…" he murmured, his eyes growing hooded as he used his body to herd me into the bedroom. "I'm dying to fuck you, but I want your first time to be—"

"Special?" I interrupted with a scoff. Backing away from him, I peeled myself out of the gold briefs and wrestled off the cup. "Are you kidding? Xander, I'm so obsessed with you, I wish I could forget every random woman I've been with so that you could be my first time for everything. I honestly feel like I might *die* if I can't have your… cock inside me."

I'm getting so good at swearing!

"Is that so?" He advanced again, reaching behind his back to unclasp the corset and toss it aside. "We can't have my little cumslut wasting away simply because I haven't filled his tight ass until it's overflowing."

I dropped my head back with a groan, clutching my throbbing dick as I took a very slow breath. Unwilling to let this end in teasing, I met Xander's gaze again with the no-nonsense hero stare I'd been perfecting since my first set of Lycra.

Captain Masculine Blue Steel.

Xander cocked his head at me. "It's so odd when you do that, Butch. It's almost like you become a different person."

Oh, crap.

"I just really want this to happen…" I stammered, attempting to cover up my mistake. "So I guess I'll try anything to convince you to fuck me."

"What did you say?" His voice had gone dangerously low.

For a moment, I panicked, thinking I'd somehow given myself away, but then I realized what had caught his attention. I straightened and met his heated stare, forcing myself to ignore my deeply ingrained instinct to embody my family's version of 'good.'

I'm so tired of being good.

Unless I'm being good for him...

"I want you to fuck me," I repeated, keeping my voice steady and giving myself a rough stroke, which he narrowed his eyes at possessively. "And don't take it easy on me. I want you to fuck me how *you* want to. Please, Daddy. Please, ruin my... tight little hole."

My cheeks were *burning,* but the fleeting embarrassment was worth it for seeing Xander gape at me, momentarily speechless.

Especially if I get what I want.

"Jesus *fuck,* Butch, how do you keep surprising me?" He laughed good-naturedly before quickly slipping into stern Daddy mode again. "Very well, my eager little plaything. Get on the bed. On your back."

"On my back?" In my research, I'd mostly come across men taking it on their hands and knees—which looked just fine to me—but these unexpected instructions confused me.

Where's my dick gonna go?

Xander's gaze softened as he kicked off his heels and removed the fishnets—much to my disappointment. "Yes, sweetheart. On your back. I'm going to show you exactly how I want to fuck you."

CHAPTER 22
BUTCH

I excitedly leaped onto the bed, landing on my back so hard I bounced a little on the mattress.

Xander bit back a smile as he circled the bed, methodically opening the bedside drawer to retrieve lube and a brand new murder weapon butt plug he'd bought just for me.

The sight of it only made me wiggle *more,* which earned me that sexy stern look again. We'd been practicing with a few different plugs this week, which Xander's personal shopper delivered, much to my embarrassment. I got over it pretty quickly when I found out just how fun toys could be.

Why have I never bought one for myself before?

It didn't take an evil genius to answer that question. Growing up in the Holt household, the message regarding sex was a contradictory mix of 'let the adoring fans worship you,' but 'do not pass third base.'

Being a citywide symbol of masculinity, I often had vapid supermodels hanging off of me at afterparties, and if a blow job in the back cemented my reputation, so be it. As long as I didn't risk reproduction with a random normie, I was encouraged to play the playboy in public.

That's where it ended. *All* of my testosterone was otherwise expected to be funneled into eliminating villains. The more sexually frustrated I was, the more brutally I killed.

A breeding stud and *a show pony.*

The cool touch of Xander's lube-coated finger circling my hole demanded I stay present, and I was more than happy to lose myself in the moment. Come Monday, I would return to work—to protecting Big City with my life—but right now, I belonged to him.

I wish it could be like this all the time.

Xander crawled up my body to capture my lips with his, pushing the plug all the way in as he sucked on my tongue. I grunted into his mouth, involuntarily thrusting upward, smearing a trail of precum over his abs.

"Please!" I gasped when he finally came up for air. He simply smirked and lowered his mouth back to mine as he slid the plug in and out, psychotically slow.

"Patience," he teased, settling back on his knees so he could better watch himself torturing me.

My body felt like it was humming—like a swarm of bees was buzzing through my veins, ricocheting around my lungs as they tried to escape. It was all I could do to keep my powers under control, despite feeling like a magnetic force was trying to coax them out of me and into Xander.

I don't want to hurt him!

"Xan, please, *please*, I *neeeeed…*" I babbled, too horny and desperate to care what I was saying. "I need you inside me before I freakin' implode."

"So dramatic." He huffed a laugh, blessedly withdrawing the plug before guiding me to lift my thighs for him. "But I like you needy."

Xander must have lubed himself up when he did me because he was suddenly notched at my opening, making my heart race. We'd briefly talked about condoms a few days ago, and since both of us were recently tested, we mutually decided to skip them.

Just *thinking* about Xan's cum inside me almost made me miss the moment he squeezed past my outer ring—easing his way in with slow, shallow strokes.

I knew I needed to pretend it hurt more than it did, but there was no hiding my euphoria at us finally being connected in this way. Xander filling me so completely—to where I could no longer tell where he ended and I began—was everything.

"Fuuuuck," he swore, his jaw tight as he stared down at where we were joined. "Fuck. Why does this feel so fucking good?"

"Because it's you," I replied automatically, holding his gaze, wanting him to see everything I could show him.

Everything I wish I could.

For a moment, panic passed over his face—like that first night in my condo—but it disappeared as soon as I brushed my fingers down his arm.

He adjusted his angle and my eyes rolled back in my head as his dick glided over what I now knew was my p-spot. He circled his hips a few times before I felt his hand cupping my jaw—bringing me back to him.

"You okay, baby?" he whispered, pausing again while he awaited my reply.

I whimpered pathetically. "Yes, but… why aren't you fucking me *hard?* I told you I can take it."

His body shook as he silently laughed. "I will, I promise." Xander started thrusting—still torturously slow—but angling himself so perfectly that I arched backward with a moan. "I've never fucked anyone like this before, so I'm trying to savor it."

I snapped my attention back to him, unsure if I'd heard him correctly. "What do you mean?"

His expression was a fascinating mix of guarded and open. "Like this. Facing each other. I've always kept things… impersonal. But I didn't want to do that with you. I want to *see* you."

Tears pricked my eyelids. "I want you to see me, too."

Please see me.

"I see you, baby." He leaned down and licked an errant tear from my cheek before settling back on his heels. "Okay, enough of me being sentimental. Let's fuck how *you* want me to."

"You want it too," I choked out as he pressed my thighs flat against my chest, somehow going deeper than before.

Xander's smirk was sinful, even as his eyelids fluttered in pleasure. "Guilty."

Before I could demand he get going already, Xander pulled back before slamming into me with enough force to rattle the walls.

Cheese and rice, he's strong for a normie!

"Remember your safe word, Butch." He stared down at me intently, watching my face as he pulled out again. "If I don't hear it, I'll take that as full permission to ruin your tight little hole, as requested."

My powers fought to reach out to him again, but I held them back, shuddering as copious precum leaked out of my dick instead. "Please," I panted. "Please ruin me."

I'm already ruined for anyone else.

That feral expression was back on Xander's face, which caused a fresh pulse of precum to pool onto my stomach. When he looked at me like that, I liked to pretend he was a secret villain, tempting me over to the bad side.

Maybe a particular villain.

Without warning, he pulled out completely, slid off the bed, and then used his freakish strength to yank me to the edge. I tried to sit up, but he shoved me back down, lined himself up, and slammed home so forcefully, I actually yelped. From then on, he was merciless. Burying his hand in my hair, he curled his body over mine, trapping me under him and enveloping me in his scent while jackhammering me into the mattress.

"Look how good you're taking me," he growled in my ear. "It's as if you were made for my cock—like no one else belongs inside you but me."

"No one does," I gasped, pure bliss shooting straight into my veins while he ripped me open. "I belong to you."

He twisted his hips in reward for that statement, making me see stars. "Goddamn right, you belong to me. You're all mine, and I will *kill* anyone who thinks they're going to take you away from me."

Holy fudging shi…

Apparently, 'possessive psychopath' was my love language. I shouted in surprise as my back arched and what felt like a bucket load of cum shot out of me, coating both our chests.

Xander blessedly slowed his pace while I recovered, kissing my neck and rubbing himself through the mess I'd made. "Fuck, you're so pretty when you come for me."

I was *still* coming, but I somehow spoke. "Xan... that was..."

"Shhh, baby." He gave me a nip on my earlobe, chuckling against my neck. "We're not done yet."

Oh, sugar.

Straightening to stand, he grabbed my legs to anchor himself before starting up again, his skin slapping against mine when he resumed his punishing rhythm. I moaned and writhed, nearly losing my mind every time he thrust, desperately clutching the sheets to hold on. Every nerve in my body felt unstable—as if I were nothing but a live wire looking for a conduit.

As if this man was the only thing that could ground me.

"Xan!" I gasped as another orgasm started thundering down my spine. "I think I'm gonna..."

"Mmm, my sweet, perfect little cumslut," he effortlessly praised, his hooded gaze calmly locked on mine while I lost the plot beneath him. "So fucking tight and so good at milking my cock. Such a good, *good* boy."

I couldn't even make a sound—could barely breathe—as I came again, convulsing so violently, I thought I might buck Xander right off. He simply growled in approval, increasing his pace to near-inhuman speed as he found his own release with a groan a moment later.

The sensation of his cum filling my ass made my dick release one last valiant spurt. For a moment, I wondered how I'd survive if he wanted to go another round, but he seemed happy to gaze down at me, lazily pumping in and out while my ragged breathing returned to normal.

I wanted to ask if he meant what he said about me belonging to him—how he would kill anyone who tried to come between us.

I hope he meant it.

Not wanting to ruin the moment with questions, I was content to simply drink in the sight of him in return—gloriously naked and glistening with sweat as he finally pulled out of me.

I hope he knows I would do the same for him.

A grunt escaped me as his cum leaked out, but he simply smirked and pushed it back inside me, claiming me all over again.

"All mine." His serious gaze snapped to my face with an intensity that suggested he meant every word.

"Yours. Always," I replied, meaning every word in return.

CHAPTER 23
XANDER

When I dropped Butch off at the Enterprises building on Monday morning, I assumed I would pick him up at the end of the day. As far as I was concerned, there was no reason for him to return to his condo after work. He had everything he needed here, and I didn't want to be apart from him any more than was necessary.

It makes perfect sense to me.

So when he texted me in the afternoon to say he'd be working late and that it made more sense for him to sleep at home since it was closer, I was puzzled.

It didn't surprise me that Solomon Biggs would do the corporate boss dick move of enforcing longer hours to 'punish' an employee for taking time off. However, Butch *knew* he was welcome at my apartment no matter how late—and had claimed being away from me physically hurt. I didn't understand why he'd choose to torture himself.

Especially when that's my *job.*

He still called me as soon as he returned to his condo that night, which immediately eased the irritating ache I'd been battling all day. It sounded like he was in a goddamn wind tunnel—making it difficult to hear—but he said he was just out on his balcony for some air.

"I have to go out of town for a few days," he shouted over the wind. "But I should be back by the weekend." When I was too bereft to answer immediately, he added, "I miss you, Xan, and... I'm sorry."

Gritting my teeth against the dull throb already building in my skull, I somehow maturely replied, "I miss you too, baby, and I understand."

What I *wanted* to say was that he had no business being away from me for days at a time. That he needed to tell Biggs to eat a dick, put in his two-week notice, and get used to his new life as my trophy husband.

Jesus, I really am moving fast!

My superpower better not be codependency.

Dr. Ownit's building was closed for repairs following the Masculine-Renegade fight, and he didn't believe in teletherapy, so unloading on him wasn't an option. Kai would have been all ears to listen to me cry over my forced separation, but she was gone most evenings now because of *Rocky Horror*.

This left me with an unfamiliar—and slightly terrifying—sense of *loneliness*. After three decades of conditioning myself to not need anyone, I was suddenly faced with the harsh truth that my apartment felt *empty*, and my daily life even emptier.

You still have your work, Xan.

And fried chicken.

When I found myself lingering at Sun-Mart on Wednesday afternoon to chat with *Felix*, of all people, I knew I needed to find myself a new project. Tinkering with my microplastics-extracting ray gun was on hold while I waited for a part to be delivered, so I did the unthinkable.

I willingly visited the Suarez family compound.

The look of abject shock on my mother's face as I strolled through the front door was worth the discomfort of her company—if only for a fleeting moment.

"What on earth are *you* doing here?" She did a quick body scan, perhaps looking for missing limbs that would render me *less* useful to the clan. "Our family dinner isn't until Sunday."

I tensed. It wasn't that I'd forgotten father's 'invitation,' but I'd definitely buried it like a repressed memory since Violentia delivered the summons outside The Gloucester.

Plus, I've been distracted by a mountain of muscles.

"I'm here for the archives," I announced. My parents had amassed an impressive collection of supe artifacts and historical documents over the years, and all the Suarez kids had unrestricted access to their curated collection.

Knowledge is power, after all.

She pursed her lips together in thinly veiled exasperation. "Xanny, there's nothing else to find. You *don't* have powers. Accept it."

Oh, you want to play, mother?

Even though the real reason for my visit was to find a legal loophole that would let Butch into my world, I was eager for a fight. "Maybe my powers are simply dormant. I *have* been feeling a strange tingling sensation beneath my skin lately."

And a murderous rage when separated from a hot himbo normie, no big deal.

"Is that so?" The acute *interest* on my mother's face caught me by surprise. My parents—and my siblings, by extension—had long given up on me joining their ranks. Even though I was being honest, I hadn't expected her to take me seriously. "Who have you been spending your time with?"

That extremely specific question nearly made me drop my mask of indifference as *something* nudged at my awareness again.

"Oh, you know me—just fucking my way through the local bar scene." I gestured dismissively, keeping my tone sarcastic as I tacked on a pointed question. "Should I be concerned about *who* is ending up handcuffed to my bed?"

The indomitable Glacial Girl wrinkled her nose in disgust. Supes with lofty standards stayed away from normies unless they were horny and desperate. It was considered 'slumming,' but a powerless supe would never attract a more powerful one, so my family let my extracurricular activities slide.

Since nobody enjoys dealing with me when I'm not getting laid.

"Not if they're worthless *normies*," she predictably huffed, making me bristle.

The suggestion that Butch was anything other than the dazzling ray of sunshine he was inspired a fresh pulse of aforementioned tingling in my fingers. My mother's cold gray eyes shot to my hands with predatory intent and, for a moment, I worried she would not only detect the surge, but interpret it as a threat.

It would be a good excuse to eliminate me.

Instead, her calculating gaze returned to my face. "Perhaps you're a *late bloomer*. Have fun in the archives. I'll send Wolfgang to assist you with your research." Assigning my older brother—otherwise known as The Hand of Death—to chaperone me sent a clear message.

Don't step out of line again.

It was such a novel experience to be seen as worthy of such a warning that I let her stalk away with the last word. I'd never heard of a 'late bloomer' before. Most supes had powers manifesting before they could walk, so I'd often wondered why my notoriously detached parents had kept me around when I turned out to be powerless.

Maybe it's the high IQ.

Wolfgang was already waiting for me in the archives, reinforcing his reputation as not only the most powerful of my siblings, but the creepiest. He was the firstborn of Glacial Girl and Apocalypto Man, and the entire reason the United Super Nations started requiring supes to register their spawn with the organization.

Killing your nanny with touch alone tends to freak people out.

No supe could kill their own parents—an evolutionary precaution, no doubt—but all bets were off with siblings. Wolfgang was supposed to wear special gloves when he was around us, but he often ignored the decree for maximum intimidation. That my brother had worn his gloves and chosen to not terrify me today was promising.

"How can I assist?" His tone was uninterested, but I knew he missed nothing. "Mother says you believe you're finally developing powers."

Fifty bucks says the Suarez group chat is lit right now.

I was suddenly questioning why I'd divulged that random—mostly unproven—observation to my mother, especially if it meant my family would pay *more* attention to me. I'd solidified my standing with them through my inventions and comparatively cool head, but was otherwise—blessedly—left to my own devices.

Weighing my options, I chose the lesser of two evils. "I doubt it. To be honest, I'm really just here to refresh myself on the laws about supes and normies dating."

Unfortunately, this tidbit seemed to interest him more. *"You're serious about someone? Are they part sea creature?"*

I rolled my eyes. "Har har. Yes, hell hath frozen. Seriously, what else am I supposed to do? I refuse to end up as the Suarez spinster just because I'm not seen as prime breeding stock to other supes."

Plus, I don't do pussy.

Most villains were sociopaths to some extent—and most heroes too, in my opinion—so the *last* thing I expected to see on Wolfgang's face was *sadness*.

"At least you have options," he mumbled, glancing down at his gloved hands. "If mother and father ever accept any of the villain families currently bidding on me, any *breeding* will have to be accomplished via artificial insemination."

Well, shit.

I gaped at my brother, suddenly overcome with what could only be empathy. "Fuck, Wolfy, I never even considered that. You know I'm so far removed from this wheeling and dealing between families—"

"You won't be if it turns out you have powers," he absently mused before switching gears. "But don't cry for me, Xanny. Luckily, my *dick* is immune to The Hand of Death."

I cackled in appreciation of his dry humor. For all our petty spats—and outright death threats—my siblings and I did have rare moments of camaraderie.

And there's no way in hell I'm going to waste Wolfgang's good mood.

"Have you ever found anything in our archives about non-governmental normies being allowed to learn a supe's true identity?" I hesitantly asked. While it made my skin crawl to give anyone in my family ammunition against me, I was emboldened by my brother's rare show of vulnerability.

He scoffed, gesturing at the shelves and file cabinets around us. "Do you really think our parents would keep anything here that implied a *normie* could be treated as an equal?"

Touché.

Just as my hope for a future with Butch started to dissolve, Wolfgang tapped his bottom lip thoughtfully. "Although... When I was brought to the United Super Nations complex as a kid—for the hearing—I overheard some clerks discussing a petition they were working on. It was in favor of heroes and villains being allowed to wed, so perhaps they've been working on similar allowances for supes and normies."

My eyes almost popped out of my skull. "Why the fuck would I ever want to marry a *hero?*"

Regardless of any Captain Masculine roleplay I have planned for Butch.

Wolfgang threw up his deadly hands. "Don't ask me! It's probably why we haven't heard anything more about it in all this time. But I would bet the USN has *less biased* records if you could get to them."

Which I can't.

Unfortunately, heroes and villains were only allowed in that neutral zone by invitation, and heavily monitored while there. I opened my mouth to point this out, then promptly snapped it closed again once I actually considered his suggestion.

While all five of my siblings were registered at the USN—with headshots updated annually—I'd never been officially declared. It wouldn't be the easiest complex to infiltrate, even with me being an unknown villain, but everyone knew Biggs Enterprises had connections there.

And I have a connection at Biggs.

"You've thought of something." Wolfgang's tone turned dangerous as an evil grin stretched across his face. "Please tell me there will be bloodshed."

I couldn't help matching his wicked smile, always game to cause chaos. "I wasn't planning on it, but we'll see what happens. Either way, I suppose I'm done here, and you no longer have to babysit."

To my surprise, he didn't immediately leave. "Go on without me," he murmured, turning to the closest filing cabinet. "I have some research of my own to conduct."

CHAPTER 24
BUTCH

It happened again.

I'd been ordered to fly inland and eliminate the West Coast Strickland clan. This would normally be child's play for a supe as powerful as me—especially since I'd already killed two of their most dangerous family members—but I collapsed almost as soon as I was done.

Luckily, Biggs had sent a SWAT team in after me to collect evidence of the Stricklands' plot to destroy Big City. It was those officers who found me groaning on the blood-covered floor. Word couldn't get out that Captain Masculine was showing any sign of weakness, so—yet again—I was sent to my parents' estate to recover.

I really need to update my emergency contact with HR.

To my surprise, my phone was waiting for me on the bedside table when I woke up, so I immediately called the only person who could make me feel better.

"Hey, baby." Simply hearing Xander's voice magically fixed everything that was broken. "I was just thinking about how perfect you are."

"Oh, yeah?" I squirmed happily, even though he couldn't see how his praise affected me. In only a short time, this man had made me feel more worthy than anyone else had in my entire life—including those who worshipped me as Captain Masculine.

Because that's not really who I am.

"Yeah," he chuckled low—the only warning that trouble was imminent. "Like how *perfectly* you took my cock all weekend and how I can't wait to fuck you again."

"Xan!" I hissed, willing myself to not get an erection in my parents' guest bedroom. "I can't... not right now."

He laughed in that unapologetic way of his, making me *ache* to be with him. "What's the matter? Doesn't Biggs put you up at a nice hotel when he ships you out of town?"

"I ended up back at my parents' house..." I sighed. Xander already knew this aspect of my life, so there was no point in keeping it a secret.

Although it's not the entire story.

The truth was, after spending all of Monday in the Biggs Enterprises situation room, I'd called Xan en route, then snuck in some sleep before spending Tuesday night through Wednesday morning wiping an entire villain clan from existence.

"Way to kill my boner, sweetheart," he teased before clearing his throat. "You didn't have to sit through another one of those... *betrothal* dinners, did you?"

"No," I cautiously replied, since my parents could be planning a dinner as we spoke.

My powers roiled at the thought of being taken away from Xander—of being forced to be with someone else. As far as I knew, no papers had been signed between the Lincoln and the Holt families, but I knew how quickly these business deals went down.

I don't want to be a bargaining chip.

"Did I lose you, sweetheart?" The line crackled with static from my flare up.

You'll never lose me.

"I'm here." I forced some cheer, quickly regaining control of my powers so he could hear me. "But I think I need to grow a pair and go talk to my parents about this."

Xander's tone was soothingly bossy. "Just use your words, baby. No one should make you do anything you don't want to."

We said our goodbyes, and I took a few deep breaths, like I'd seen Xander do when he got upset. I needed to approach this conversation clearheaded—otherwise they wouldn't listen, and my mother might fry my veins again.

While my father would do worse.

After getting dressed in the preppy clothes left out for me, I stuffed my phone in my pocket and went searching for a—hopefully—fair fight. My tension lessened exponentially when I passed the dining room on my way and saw our housekeeper setting the table for three. With a smile, I realized Xander probably only ordered takeout because he'd also been raised in a house full of staff.

Maybe I'll learn how to cook for us...

Arriving at my father's home office, I froze with my hand on the doorknob. My parents were loudly arguing on the other side of the door, which was highly unusual. I wouldn't claim Smoldering Siren and Vortexio were in *love*, but their strategic union had always been a friendly match, and I'd never heard them outright *yell* at each other.

"...even you have to admit, this is an opportunity!" My mother was so worked up, I could feel her heat through the heavy door. "We may finally extract ourselves from—"

"Not like this, Tabitha!" my father boomed in reply. "I'm as eager as you to shed these chains, but this man cozying up to our son is nothing more than a disgusting..." His rant ended with a choked sound, as if he couldn't even bring himself to accept that I was with a normie.

How dare he talk about Xander that way!

Before I could fling the door open and confront them, my mother's quiet voice cut in. "So will this end like it did for Iron Axe?"

I furrowed my brow at her question, and the deafening silence that followed. Iron Axe was a legendary superhero from my parents' generation who'd met a mysterious and untimely end. No villain ever claimed responsibility for his demise, which was odd, since many would have relished the infamy of taking him down.

What the heck does he *have to do with my relationship?*

My father sounded more weary than anything, implying it wasn't the first time they'd discussed this. "Iron Axe was a means to an end—"

"It HURT, Harold!" Siren's power pulsed threateningly. "Far worse than simply being physically apart. And now you want Butch to experience the same level of suffering?!"

"The pain will be temporary." Vortexio's powers answered hers in challenge. "But it will be worth it for him to not be permanently handicapped."

I backed away from the door as if it were contaminated. While I didn't fully understand what my parents were talking about, plans were clearly being made—without my involvement or consent—that would end with me in anguish.

And my only weakness is Xander.

Racing back to the guest room, I pulled my supersuit back on and escaped through the window. Back at the Gloucester, I tore down the stairs from the roof—practically ripping the front door off its hinges to get inside. My father could fly, and I didn't plan on being anywhere he could find me once he realized I'd left without permission.

In my bedroom, I quickly stripped again and shoved my Lycra to the bottom of a drawer. As I straightened, my reflection in the mirrored closet door caught my attention. The last time I'd really *looked* at myself like this was the evening I'd first messaged Xander on Bangers, and the difference in my appearance was startling.

On the surface, I appeared the same, but my eyes were no longer dull and lifeless. There was a determination buried beneath my current anxiety that reminded me of how purposeful I'd felt after graduating Superversity.

When I believed a world of possibility lay ahead of me.

I remember how proud I was to officially succeed my parents as the defender of Big City—eager to prove to its citizens they could rely on me to keep them safe. It didn't take long for me to realize my beloved city was treated like a corporate conglomerate, where only the most powerful supes and normies called the shots.

The only information I was given on my opponents was the bare minimum I needed to defeat them. For all Biggs talked of foiling plots and plans, no one ever bothered to show me any proof.

I'm nothing but a weapon to them.

When the only thing that brought me joy was creeping around Awakener's Bay to crush on a *villain*, I knew something had to give. By the time I'd joined Bangers, I was desperate for anything to distract me from my reality. It was pure luck that I found someone like Xander.

He was the reason I no longer looked defeated when my mask came off. Xander may not be a supe—or my illicit obsession, Dr. Antihero—but he was the missing piece I needed for my life to feel whole. It was because of him I was learning to stand up for myself.

"No one should make you do anything you don't want to."

Since Biggs had already given me the rest of the week off—barring emergencies—all I had to do was quickly pull on some civilian clothes and send two texts before heading out. The first was to Xander, letting him know I was back and already on my way over—trusting the answer would always be yes, like he'd said.

"Use your words."

The second was to my parents, stating in no uncertain terms that I wasn't interested in Gemstonia—or a relationship with any supe—out of respect for my *normie boyfriend.* It wasn't the most heroic way to break the news, but hopefully it opened the door for a future conversation.

Unsurprisingly, neither of my parents replied, but Xander fired back a text almost immediately with exactly what I needed to hear.

> **Daddy Xan:** *Welcome back, baby. I'll be waiting for you at home.*

CHAPTER 25
XANDER

Butch was bad for my productivity, but I couldn't find it in me to care. Sure, I was excited to tinker with my ray gun some more, but I needed to wait until I found a supe-normie relationship loophole before I could do something as monumental as revealing my secret lair.

I guess we'll just have to suffer through more Netflix and chill.

"Hey, sweetheart," I murmured against his soft blond hair. Butch was laying with his back against my chest, half suffocating me underneath his delicious muscles as we watched yet another superhero movie, but I didn't give a fuck.

I would let this man crush my head with his thighs.

And I would thank him for it.

"Does working for Biggs give you access to the archives at the USN?" I kept my tone casual, even though Wolfgang's revelation had been bouncing around my brain the past two days. It didn't escape my notice that Butch tensed when I mentioned his boss, but he wouldn't be slaving for that asshat much longer if this all went to plan.

"Uh, yeah. Why do you ask?" He tilted his head back to give me a sweet smile.

Fuck, I missed that smile.

I hesitated a moment, finding it more difficult than usual to lie. "I need to double-check international water law, so that I don't end up pissing off the wrong country when I finally take my invention out for a test drive. The USN should have records of any treaties that were signed."

Instead of simply smiling and nodding, Butch twisted around, giving me his full attention. "That is so interesting! I've only dealt with international airspace before. I wonder if it matches up? Anyway, I'll look into it at work next week. It would be so *fun* to take you there on a tour!"

This man must be protected at all costs.

"You know, Butch," I teased, sliding my hand over the bulge in his sweatpants, just to hear him moan. "I might need a research assistant someday—think I could tempt you away from Biggs?"

He dropped his gaze with a sigh, presumably to watch me torture him. "I could match your salary *and* give you special employee benefits…"

"I'll just take the benefits, please," he whispered, rubbing himself against my hand until a tasty wet spot appeared through the sweatpants.

As much as I wanted to make him come in his pants again, his comment sparked a concern. "You do *spend* the money you make from Biggs, right?"

He stopped moving, his dazed expression meeting mine. "I mean, I buy things I need…"

"Oh, no, no," I released him and sat up, waving a scolding finger in his face. "I mean things you *don't* need—but deserve to enjoy, anyway." When he simply stared at me in confusion, I elaborated. "Like the most expensive steak on the menu, or a trip to Ibiza, or decor for your apartment that doesn't look like it came from Elvis' final years at Graceland."

Butch sat back on his heels. "I hate how my condo looks," he admitted—almost guiltily. "It was my parents' and I never knew if I was allowed to redecorate."

I forced back a smile. It was tempting to encourage him to gut the place, but he'd be moving in with me soon enough. "Okay, if you *could* decorate your own place, what would you choose?"

His deer-in-the-headlights expression pulled at my heartstrings, but then he rallied. "Well." He looked around my apartment. "It would probably look a lot like this. All the different shades of gray on the walls are soothing, and the leather and wood just feels… it feels *homey*. And I really like the art…"

I followed his gaze to the two large canvases on the far wall, which looked—for all intents and purposes—like monochromatic abstract art.

Even though it's more than that.

"What is it about the art that you like?" I shifted onto my knees and leaned forward, extremely invested in his answer.

He kept staring, mesmerized, his broad chest rapidly rising and falling. "The way the red paint sprays across the white canvas reminds me of…" His gaze flickered to mine. "Blood."

Oh, sweetheart, you have no idea.

It actually *was* blood—my very first kill in the Suarez name—and seeing Butch look at it like it turned him on was making me feral.

"What if it *was* blood?" I couldn't help asking, *needing* to know if this man was truly as perfect as I thought he was.

Butch licked his lips. "I'd like it even more."

That tingling sensation shot down my spine, and I had to clench my fists to calm my visceral reaction to his confession. I wanted to toss Butch onto his hands and knees and fuck him senseless while telling him every gory detail of that kill. I wanted him to come all over himself while admitting how hard that made him—how he wanted to *see* me kill.

How he wanted to kill someone with me.

Stop it stopstopstopstop.

My dangerous thoughts were interrupted when something smacked against the window, causing Meowson to leap off the sill with a yowling hiss. By the time I turned my head to look, Butch was on his feet and standing between me and the threat. His stance combined with the way he was backlit in the morning light made him look like a superhero—which only encouraged my psychotic hard-on.

Keep your crazy in your pants, Xander.

Before I could break the silence, he laughed and turned to face me, smiling sheepishly. "False alarm. Looks like someone lost their umbrella to the wind."

"My hero," I cooed, rising to stand. His smile faltered, but I kept going. "So big and strong—shielding me from nefarious bad weather gear."

Butch's expression was unreadable as he searched my face. "How secure *is* this apartment, Xan?"

Because he looked so adorably concerned, I humored him. "It's locked down, baby. Besides the fingerprint access, I have various security systems in place to keep me safe, I promise."

I didn't want to explain *why* the glass on the windows was blast proof, or that there was an escape hatch under my bed that led to freedom. He wouldn't understand why I had high-definition cameras aimed at every potential angle of impending attack.

Just like the one I installed in the hallway outside his condo door.

Most importantly, I didn't want to address how Butch in alpha-protector mode was doing all sorts of strange things to my insides. At this point, I'd accepted how much I enjoyed caring for *him*—despite being a villain—but him wanting to do the same for me was more than I could handle.

Especially without a session with Ownit on my calendar.

"Windy days are my favorite," I awkwardly segued.

It did the trick, as he rapidly blinked before blinding me with his megawatt smile. "Mine too." For a moment, he looked like he wanted to say more, but left it at that.

The gears were turning as I tried to figure out how to share as much of myself as possible without crossing any lines. "If I bring you to our beach, will you wait there so I can surprise you with something?"

Game for my schemes yet again, he nodded. "You know the answer's yes, Xan."

With that, I arranged for wetsuits and life jackets to be delivered before loading us into my Audi and heading for the Bay. Dropping Butch off at the beach, I parked at my lair and quickly swapped out my car for my largest WaveRunner, not wanting to keep him waiting. The look on his face when I zoomed up at full-speed made my heart feel like it was going to beat out of my chest.

"Cheez-its!" He gaped like a kid on Christmas morning. "You're taking me out on that?" The ocean was incredibly choppy—way too dangerous for a small craft like mine—but Butch's excited tone held no trace of fear.

Good boy.

I laughed and tossed him his life jacket. "Yes, now put this on and get your fine ass behind me."

He looked oddly confused by the life jacket, but managed to strap himself in. I was in no position to judge, since I normally didn't bother with one myself. My custom super-suits came equipped with emergency flotation, and I'd never heard of a supe *drowning* unless they were knocked unconscious.

But we're playing 'normies' today, so safety first!

Butch got situated, but before I could put us in gear, he surprised me by depositing a kiss below my ear. "Xan, would you ever let me behind you… you know… like *that?*"

My sharp inhale had him backpedaling immediately. "I'm sorry. I was just wondering, but it's totally fine if—"

"No, don't be!" I interrupted, turning to face him as best I could. "I've just… never done that before." Clearing my throat, I *forced* myself to maintain eye contact, despite how uncharacteristically vulnerable I felt.

Butch leaned forward to kiss me sweetly. "Me neither," he whispered against my lips before settling back again. A slight blush crept over his cheeks as he chewed his bottom lip. "In fact, I'd never had sex with anyone before you. I probably should have mentioned that…"

I blew out a breath, willing my dick not to knock us into full-throttle. "You absolutely should *not* have. If you'd mentioned you were a complete virgin on our first date, I wouldn't have shown so much restraint."

Might as well be honest.

He scoffed good-naturedly. "If *that's* what you call restraint, I wonder if I should be more afraid of you than I am."

The thought of Butch actually being afraid of me made sheer *panic* cloud my vision. "Never," I choked out. "I would never hurt you."

Unaliving me with his dimples, he quickly kissed me again. "I know, silly. I trust you."

This was not silly. It was life-altering to have this man implicitly trust me with his precious existence when I could end it so easily. Although it was highly unlikely that a normie could ever take me down—even one as jacked as him—it was suddenly imperative that Butch know the feeling was mutual.

"I trust you too," I whispered, meaning it with my entire being, even as every conditioned instinct screamed at me to trust no one.

We stared at each other for a minute—a lifetime—before I diffused the moment with a smile. "Now, hold on tight, sweetheart. Let's go play chicken with some waves."

CHAPTER 26
BUTCH

A few days later, we took the WaveRunner out for another spin. This time, we stopped for lunch at the Royal Cove Yacht Club on Rose Island, which had a 3-star Michelin rating and no apparent problem with wetsuits in its dress code.

Flash enough money, and anything's possible, I guess.

Xander made it his personal mission to select the most expensive items on the menu. I could barely pronounce most of them, but he smoothly ordered in flawless French, and I was more than happy to let him lead.

I wonder if I can get him to speak French to me in bed…

At one point, I noticed him glaring at a group of businessmen across the dining room. I assumed it was because they were being obnoxiously loud, but then one of them nodded Xander's way, almost in recognition.

Catching me watching him, he rolled his eyes. "Love the food here. Would love it even more if the clientele were forced to walk the plank."

I attempted to hide my laugh with a cough. "Not associates of yours, I hope?"

"Not by choice," he growled. "However, I've been unfortunate enough to deal with them on my mother's behalf. They don't deserve to inhabit a place as beautiful as this."

I vaguely remembered Xander mentioning the reason his sister stole his car was because he'd been pressured into doing something unpleasant for his family that *she* wanted to do. While I didn't want to exacerbate a sore subject, I knew enough about the billionaires who inhabited this island to show solidarity.

Since most of the Biggs Enterprises' board of directors are in this room.

Clearing my throat, I carefully spoke. "It's always those with pockets deep enough to make impactful change who rarely do—unless they have an audience."

Xander clutched my hand across the table, his amber eyes wild. "Exactly! The net worth of these fucking clowns could have fully funded several wildlife-focused capital campaigns, but they're more interested in exploiting the same natural resources that increase their property values. It's criminal."

Even though he was riled up, I couldn't help smiling at how *passionate* he was about his work. It also gave me an idea. "Are there any non-profits focused on preserving the Bay Area?"

He blinked at me. "Yeah. The largest is Cerulean Crest. I donate about a quarter of my annual income to them, but as they lack certain assets on their research team,"—he pointed at himself—"it's best if I funnel most of my funds into my own complementary projects."

This time, I couldn't contain my laughter. "What? No plans to intern at the organization?"

To my delight, Xander's stern Daddy look made a public appearance. "Could you honestly see me answering to anyone, even for a good cause?"

"No." I bit my lip and peeked up at him through my lashes. "You like to be on top."

His gaze darkened. "Eat your dinner, Butch. Then we're going home."

I practically inhaled my duck confit after that delicious threat, and my excitement only grew when Xander let *me* drive the WaveRunner on the way back to the mainland. With the way he possessively rubbed against my ass the entire time, I suspected he had ulterior motives for our seating arrangement, but we both knew I belonged to him.

He can do whatever he wants to me.

This domination continued after we finally stumbled through his apartment door and into the bedroom—drunk on lust and each other. In no time, we were both naked, and I was spread out on the bed while he hovered over me. With a hum of appreciation, he lowered his head and began kissing and nipping his way along my jaw and down my neck, making goosebumps break out over my skin.

"Fu…dge…" I grunted, tamping down my recurring primal *urge* to somehow connect my powers to a normie.

I should probably figure out what that's about…

The groan he let out was orgasmic. "Baby, if you keep almost-swearing like that, I'm going to come all over your cock." To punctuate his point, he reached down and wrapped his hand around both of our dicks, stroking us together.

My eyes started to roll back in my head from the sensation of his velvety skin gliding against mine, but I forced myself to *watch*. I couldn't help it. The way his foreskin moved over his shaft was fascinating—like a ripple on the water. Like a magic trick.

I'm still convinced he's a sex wizard.

"What does that feel like?" I asked, before realizing how stupid that sounded. "Being uncircumcised, I mean. Does it feel like you're rubbing inside… something? Like a sleeve?"

He released me and sat back on his heels to better look at me, continuing to lazily pump himself. As I'd now come to expect with Xander, instead of judging my ignorance, he always gave my questions careful consideration mixed with a large dose of mischief.

"Would you like to find out?" He licked his lips, his classic tell that trouble was coming.

"What do you mean?" I stopped stealing glances at his mesmerizing foreskin to focus on his face. "I don't have—"

"You do now," he snickered before lifting his chin. "Sit with your back against the headboard. You're going to want to brace yourself for this."

Whatever you say!

Scrambling up to sitting, I leaned back, ready for anything. Xander kneeled between my legs, pouring lube over both of us before grasping his dick with both hands and lining us up —tip to tip.

"Fuck," he murmured, rubbing our slits together before drawing back, creating a thread of precum between us. "I can't wait to have you inside me."

Inside him?!

Before I could get myself worked up over *that* mental image, Xander blew my mind with a different one. Lining us up again, he used his thumbs and pointer fingers to push his foreskin over my crown, encasing me inside the thin layer alongside him.

"Oh, my goddd!" I choked out, gaping as he secured the skin around me with one hand, sealing us in. Placing the other on the headboard above me for leverage, he started thrusting, and I lost what little grip on reality I had left.

It felt like heaven. It felt like my dick was encased in the warmest, slipperiest, tightest sleeve of goodness—made even better because it was in there with *him*.

I think I'm in love.

"Do you like that?" he purred down at me, in complete control as I fell apart.

As usual.

"Fuuu..." I groaned, clutching the blanket on either side of me as I bucked, already pouring sweat.

Xander stopped moving.

"What? What are you—" I stammered.

"Say it," he hissed, reminding me of our first date, when he cornered me outside the Tick Tock Diner and showed me in no uncertain terms that I was already *his*. "I want to hear you say the big bad F word as you fill me with cum."

Before I could reply, the hand he'd placed on the headboard shot down to grip my hair, tears pricking my eyelids at the delicious sting.

"C'mon, baby," he sweetly crooned as he began to move his hips again. "Swear for Daddy like a good boy."

Then he curled his body over mine and sunk his teeth into my neck.

"FUCK!" I roared, using every ounce of self-control to stop my powers from turning Xander's apartment into a blazing inferno of melted electronics. The pain, combined with his intoxicating leather scent and the suction on my dick, ripped the orgasm out of me. I exploded with a shout, coating the inside of his foreskin with my seemingly endless release.

Fucking fuuuuck.

Xander made a guttural sound against my neck, teeth still buried deep as he joined me, the overflow of our cum dripping onto me from between his shaking fingers.

"Fuck, fuck, fuck," I gasped, magically transformed into a foul-mouthed broken record by sex wizardry.

Unsurprisingly unconcerned with my swearing, Xander released me and began lapping at his bite marks—as if *that* wasn't going to get me hard all over again.

"What sort of sorcery *was* that?" I croaked, finally able to form more coherent words.

He laughed against my neck before drawing back and planting a chaste kiss on my lips. I melted, recognizing he was letting down his walls more often for cute little gestures of affection like this.

Although I'm a little too wrecked to fully appreciate it right now.

"While I wish I could take credit for that move, I didn't invent it. It's called *docking,* and it's a little easier if you're not as hard as we both were." Xander gazed down at me with an amused smirk. "Did you not stumble upon it during your scandalous gay sex research?"

My cheeks flamed as I shoved at his chest. I forgot to hold back my strength, but he still didn't budge, which was impressive. "No, I didn't. I was keeping it kind of basic to start. You know… vanilla gay."

He cackled. "Baby, I don't think you're vanilla." His thumb stroked my lower lip as he suddenly turned thoughtful. "And whoever made you believe that doesn't know you at all."

"I think you're right," I whispered, my heart pounding so hard I was sure he could hear it.

Xander held my gaze, and I couldn't have looked away if I tried. He was absolutely correct. The more time I spent with this man, the more I realized that since birth, I'd been molded into someone I wasn't. There was no one in my life who saw me for who I truly was—who *wanted* to see me.

Except him.

Our moment was broken when Xander slid off the bed and disappeared into the bathroom. When he returned, he silently cleaned me up with a wet cloth before sitting beside me, his expression a million miles away.

"Let me take you out for dinner tonight," I murmured, grabbing his wrist and tracing his veins with my thumb, wanting to feel his pulse like it was my own.

He grimaced. "I can't. I have a dinner... thing. At my parents' house."

"Oh, okay." I couldn't hide the disappointment from my tone, even though I had no right to be upset after disappearing inland on multiple occasions.

"Come with me," he blurted out, his expression almost manic. "Meet my family." Just as suddenly, the color drained from his face, as if he realized what this invitation meant. "No, wait, uhhh... I actually don't think—"

IT'S HAPPENING!

"Oh, no you don't!" I crowed triumphantly, grabbing him with both hands and pulling him down onto the mattress with me. "No take-backs! You want me to meet your family. You're *serious* about me."

There were a few security measures—and codes of conduct—for any supe allowing a normie into their *home*, but a house full of normies didn't have to do anything special. Because of my job, I was especially skilled at existing among civilians, so the Marins would simply think I was one of them.

Butch Hawthorne—total normie.

Xander's laugh was strained, but when he propped himself up on his elbow, I saw his smile was genuine. "I *am* serious about you, Butch. That's not the issue here. It just might not be the right time for you to meet them…"

My enthusiasm immediately fizzled out. Despite worrying about how my parents would react to him, I'd already been scheming about how to bring Xander to their estate. I knew our relationship was moving ridiculously fast, but I stubbornly wanted to experience every milestone that normal people did.

Especially with him.

Xander inviting me to meet his family meant he felt the same way about me as I did about him. Therefore, rescinding the offer almost immediately felt like a punch to the gut.

My disappointment must have been written all over my face as Xander pulled me up to sit beside him. "Oh, baby, don't be upset. It's not that I don't want to show you off—it's just…" He worriedly searched my face before sighing. "It would mean a lot to you, huh?"

I simply nodded, not trusting myself to speak.

"Okay. Okay, we can do this," he muttered, almost to himself, before snapping his attention back to me. "I do need to warn you that my family is a little..." He scrunched his face, searching for the right word. "They're... *intense.*"

"Yeah, that's a given. Exhibit A." I pointed at him as overwhelming joy flooded my system, causing me to laugh until tears came to my eyes. That Xander was worried about me meeting his weird family, after the unhinged, lethal supervillains I regularly faced...

This will be child's play.

"All right!" I clapped my hands as I jumped off the bed and headed for the closet filled with *my* clothes. While I assumed it wouldn't be a formal affair like my family preferred, I'd never seen Xander in anything that didn't look like it came from the pages of a fashion magazine, so I wanted to impress. "What should I wear?"

"Something where you can hide a variety of weapons," he grumbled, joining me and efficiently selecting an appropriate outfit. When I cupped his face and *forced* him to look at me, he sighed. "I just don't want them to scare you away."

You ridiculous man.

"Xan." I tried to emulate the sexy *Daddy* look he always gave me, realizing he needed *me* to be the confident one at the moment. "Please, don't worry. I can't think of a single thing they could possibly do to scare me away from you."

CHAPTER 27
BUTCH

We pulled up to Xander's parents' house just as it was getting dark.

The route we took was confusing. We doubled-backed a few times—and I swore we drove through a mountain—but I was too busy chattering to Xan to worry about it. I'd been half-expecting something that looked like Dracula's castle, so the futuristic compound we arrived at was a momentary surprise.

It explains why he's such a tech nerd.

Xander liked to fuss over me on a good day, but the amount of prep he put me through—before we even got in the car—almost had *me* calling this off. He told me how things would go tonight, with an insane amount of detail that still felt infuriatingly vague. There were a few conversation topics that were off limits, but the oddest thing was when he told me under no circumstances was I to shake anyone's hand.

Calm down, weirdo.

I was about to crack a joke about whether we were getting out of the car when someone knocked impatiently against

Xander's door. He cracked the window with a heavy sigh, but with the way we were all positioned, I couldn't immediately see who was welcoming us.

"Hey, doofus, way to ignore my texts."

Xander sighed again. "Vi, I simply had better things to do than answer your idiotic questions. You know, like clip my toenails, or rearrange my junk drawer, or literally anything else."

The mysterious woman snorted. "As if me contacting you wouldn't be the highlight of your existence. Although…" There was a slight scuffle as she attempted to open the door and Xander hit the lock. "Mother told us you were bringing a date…"

With a third sigh so heavy, I thought his soul might leave his body, Xander rolled down the window completely so we could meet.

And my entire world shattered.

The woman muscling her way through the window to get a better look at me made my heart stop beating. Long black hair fell in waves on either side of her familiar face. Familiar because the light brown skin and flecks of gold in her amber eyes reminded me of the man sitting next to me, but mostly because her mugshot was plastered all over the Biggs situation room.

It's a mistake. It has to be a mistake.

"Oh, look at that, Xanny," she cackled. "Your boy toy is so overcome by my beauty he's speechless." Her gaze roamed over me like I was a mouse caught between her paws. "What do you say, li'l bro? Is there enough of this big beefcake to share?"

It can't be... it's just a coincidence that she looks just like...

"*Gross*, Violentia," Xander grumbled, confirming without a doubt that this woman was exactly who I feared she was. Then he took his hand and palmed her entire face before roughly shoving her out of the car—as if she wasn't one of the most feared villains of our generation.

What the FUCK is going on?!

"Whatever dude," she scoffed, straightening her minidress with dagger-length nails. "Get in your butt-sex quickie and come inside. We're all fucking starving and if dinner isn't served soon, mother might start eating her young." Then she stalked away on towering heels, unknowingly leaving monumental wreckage in her wake.

Oh.

My.

God.

I sat frozen in my seat. The only reason I hadn't immediately incinerated Ultra Violent was because of the shock to my system—a hesitation that would have cost me dearly had she attacked. Now that she was gone, I was forced to accept that the man I'd let into my life—into my body—was not who I thought he was.

Xander was *not* a normie. His name was not Xander Marin. He was a Suarez—the offspring of Glacial Girl and Apocalypto Man, along with five formidable others. A supervillain who was undocumented and unknown by both Biggs Enterprises and the USN.

Who IS he?

Has this been a trap the entire time?

Oblivious—or uncaring—to my mental breakdown, Xander dropped his face into his hand with a groan. "So *that* was Violentia. I would say it gets better with the rest, but that would be a lie. The only silver lining is that you won't be meeting my father tonight since he doesn't eat with us… although I unfortunately need to slip away at some point because he wants to speak with me about something. But mother promised me everyone will be on their best behav— are you all right, sweetheart?"

My world tipped on its axis yet again. Xander wasn't looking at me like a villain who'd entrapped his prey. His gorgeous amber eyes were filled with concern, and he reached out a hand to gently caress my jaw with the same genuine care he'd always shown me.

He doesn't know who I am.

The realization that at least this intense connection between us was *real* calmed my racing heart somewhat. I was still sitting outside the home of the Suarez clan—and there was a high probability I would die or be captured tonight—but at least I would go out having experienced *this*.

It was worth it.

"I love you," I blurted out. "I just… I want you to know that before… before we go inside."

His eyes widened. "W-what? I… *Jesus*, Butch! Did Vi really freak you out that badly? You still have four more of these lunatics to meet, never mind my mother. Should I take you home? If you don't want to do this, I won't make you. Tell me what you need, baby."

The sweetness he was showing me caused tears to spring to my eyes. I wanted this more than anything. I wanted to hold on to what meeting Xander's family represented—a future together—even though now it was impossible. More than that, I wanted him to know how much he'd meant to me. How committed to this relationship I'd been.

How I'd risk it all for him.

"I want to meet them," I spoke evenly as the calm of inevitability washed over me. "I got a little nervous, that's all."

He scoffed, although his expression was kind. "Yeah, well, hot tip—if you show any weakness around these animals, they'll devour you whole." His lips curled as his mischief came out to play. "I'll tell you what, baby. If you make it through tonight in one piece, I'll reward my *good boy* in *any* way he wants."

Oh, this is just cruel.

Unknowingly twisting the knife in deeper, Xander leaned forward to deliver a scorching kiss, which I eagerly returned —knowing it was probably our last.

"I will admit, I'm a little angry." His gaze darkened. "You see… I had big dramatic plans in the works to tell you I loved *you*, but then you stole my thunder. What did I say about being a brat?"

"I'm sorry, Daddy," I whispered, holding his gaze and meaning every word with my entire soul.

Xander must have caught something on my face, as he cocked his head. "I'm not actually mad, baby, don't worry. And I love you, too." He deposited one last kiss on my lips. "Now let's go inside and get this over with."

I could only manage a clipped nod as we exited the car and I followed him to my doom.

As Xander opened the front door and ushered me into the foyer, I attempted to calm my nerves and think rationally.

Violentia clearly hadn't recognized me, so it was probably safe to assume none of the Suarez clan had access to the same high-level intel I did.

My hesitation to attack her had been a saving grace. If I controlled my powers, I could convince them all I was nothing more than Xander's normie boyfriend, and still leave here unscathed.

Although I don't want to think about what happens after that…

"Xanny." An older woman's frigid tone sent ice into my veins. Xander had already said I wouldn't be meeting his father—not that Apocalypto Man needed to be anywhere near me to inflict damage—but facing the infamous Glacial Girl was almost as terrifying.

And way above my pay grade.

Her gray eyes swept over me, and I could feel the subtle pulses of her power against my skin—testing me. I grimly held back from answering her in kind, determined to survive.

Maybe she doesn't recognize me either…

"What an unexpected surprise!" She grinned in a way that looked more like she was baring her teeth.

My guts twisted as I recalled Violentia mentioning their mother knew Xander was bringing a date. Signe Suarez had been expecting a clueless normie to arrive with her son, but who was delivered to her doorstep instead was a villain's wet dream.

Of *course*, someone as powerful as Glacial Girl would know exactly what every living supe looked like as a civilian—especially the only son of her greatest enemies.

I'm going to die.

"Go on, Xanny," she cooed, waving him ahead of us while she placed a hand on my back and roughly pushed me along after him. "Welcome to my home, *Captain Masculine*," she quietly hissed in my ear, sending a warning shot of frost skittering down my spine. "Let's hope you behave yourself better than you did with the Stricklands."

I'm definitely going to die.

CHAPTER 28
XANDER

As I should have anticipated, my family showed Butch no mercy.

Violentia continued to shamelessly flirt, Baltasar was his jerky jock self, the twins simply stared at him in their creepy *Shining* way—while telepathically plotting his demise, no doubt—and Wolfgang simply *watched* from his usual spot at the shadowy end of the table.

None of that was surprising, but the *attention* my mother gave him was. I'd expected her to be coolly dismissive and had already prepped Butch by fibbing that she was mildly homophobic. Her unwavering focus was unnerving.

This was a mistake.

Shaking my head, I banished the thought because to me, Butch wasn't some passing fling. This was someone I wanted to spend the rest of my life with, despite having avoided commitment like the plague before now. It was important for him to meet my family, even if just to show them I had a life outside of their schemes.

Who knows, maybe this will finally get them to cut me loose...

Being powerless meant I never fit in with the Suarez clan, so there had been little chance of an even *less* powerful normie impressing supes who thrived on dominance. Not for the first time, I wished Dr. Ownit took texts, because I desperately needed his professional opinion on why I would subject the man I'd fallen in love with to this shit show.

He said he loved you too, Xan.

Every time I thought about his confession in the car, my entire body felt like it was lit up from the inside—like little firecrackers were shooting off under my skin. And every time this happened, Butch would throw me a sharp glance as if he felt it too, holding my gaze a beat too long with a wariness in his expression I didn't like one bit.

You're safe, baby.

Returning my attention to the conversation, I found Butch had rallied to his usual charming self, albeit a slightly more subdued version. I knew he was nervous about this—hell, I was nervous about putting him within firing range of these psychos, even with all my coaching—but I had every intention of rewarding him for his courage later.

"So tell me more about your parents, Butch," my mother purred, using her fish knife to separate the meat from the skin on her plate with a surgeon's precision.

The decision to serve seafood tonight was an insult aimed solely at me—since everyone knew I wouldn't eat anything that came from the sea. Our family chef, a lesser villain named Betsy, had rebelled in her usual way by boldly preparing steaks for me and Butch. This was because she was a goddamn angel who'd not only seen this play out countless times before, but cooked too well for my mother to kill.

"I'm not sure there's anything else to tell, Mrs... Marin," Butch politely replied, calmly dabbing at the corner of his mouth with a napkin. "My parents are both retired and I'm doing my best to make them proud."

My mother's lips curved in a wicked smile. "I'm sure you are—especially with coming here tonight. What is it you do for Biggs Enterprises, again?"

Oh, don't start.

I didn't remember telling my mother that Butch worked for Biggs, but I'd been so stressed out when I called to ask if he could join me, I may have slipped up. It was no surprise she'd zero in on *that* bit of information, and unfortunately, her mention of Butch's workplace made everyone at the table zero in on our guest again.

"I'm an accountant," Butch smoothly replied, although I saw the tick in his jaw. "CFO, actually."

"CFO slash bodyguard?" Baltasar scoffed. "Dude, you look like you bench 650. There's no way scaredy-cat Biggs doesn't have you guarding his back, especially since so many villains want to kill him in the most painful way possible."

"Balty!" Mother admonished, although she did so with affection. "Assassination is *not* an appropriate dinner conversation. I'm sure Butch is being *completely honest* about what he does... aren't you, dear?" Her predatory gaze was back on him and my fingers twitched as that mysterious *tingling* flickered to life within me.

"Enough," I gritted out, bringing everyone's attention my way. My siblings mostly stared at me with blatant surprise, but Wolfgang's focus was on my *hands*, where the sensation was centralized. "We all know Biggs Enterprises is a government facility. Butch isn't able to tell us every gory detail about what he does."

My mother barked a laugh. "Perfect choice of words, Xanny. Tell me. How did you two meet again?"

I had no idea what the point of this dance was besides giving me a throbbing headache, but I humored the woman—if only so we could both leave here alive. "We met on a dating app we'd both only joined that day."

"Hmm," she hummed, tapping her lip. "Isn't that... coincidental?"

"It was." Butch's voice was as cold as my mother's powers—his expression as close to angry as I'd ever seen it—and we all braced for impact.

To my surprise, Glacial Girl's glare faltered, and she blinked rapidly at Butch, as if seeing him for the first time. A tense moment passed before she sat back in her seat, her thoughts suddenly a million miles away. "Interesting..." she mused, but said nothing further.

Jesus H.

My heart was pounding uncontrollably, and I discreetly grabbed Butch's hand under the table, giving it a squeeze, although whether it was to soothe him or me, I wasn't sure.

Most everyone had returned their attention to their meals—since the threat of death had sadly passed—but I noticed Wolfgang's gaze flickering between Butch and me as if he were trying to puzzle something out.

I used the distraction of Betsy replacing dinner with dessert to lean in and whisper in Butch's ear. "You're doing great, baby. I'm here."

He nodded once, somehow maintaining his calm demeanor despite the horrid way my mother was behaving, and I internally vowed to never subject him to this bullshit ever again.

I'll make it up to him somehow.

Unfortunately, that was the moment I was summoned.

We all sat up straighter as a pulse of unimaginable power thrummed through the room. Even Butch shifted uncomfortably, although he wouldn't understand what he was experiencing. Any normie who'd been unfortunate enough to encounter Apocalypto Man had been wiped from the earth, along with any memory they'd ever existed.

If I hadn't been so hasty in my invitation, I would have arranged for Butch to meet the family when I *wasn't* expected to speak with my father. Unfortunately, my impulsivity meant I would now have to leave the most precious thing in the world to me in the company of fiends. But it was that or take him with me into 'the workshop.'

And I would rather die than have him face my father.

Butch squeezed my hand as I rose to stand, so I bent down to sweetly kiss him, audience be damned. "I'll only be gone for a bit, baby," I soothed, willing myself to appear calm for his sake.

My father could choose to kill me at any moment, but I would try my hardest to please him, especially as I needed to make sure Butch got out of here alive. Straightening, I threw a glare around the table. "I expect him to be in one piece when I get back."

Violentia winked while Baltasar rolled his eyes. The twins had already tuned us out with their heads bent to each other, whispering in hushed tones.

My mother's mouth stretched in a Cheshire grin before she cooed, "We'll save you a *slice*." Before I could retort, she pointed at her German chocolate cake, as if *that* was what she'd been referring to.

My vision was dangerously close to turning red as I spun on my heel and began walking away. I knew I needed to get my shit under control before facing Apocalypto Man, but leaving Butch unprotected in such dangerous company was making my skin crawl, my insides buzz…it was making me want to kill…

Kill kill killkillkill….

"I'll keep an eye on him," Wolfgang spoke so softly as I passed by, I almost didn't catch it. When I abruptly stopped to face him, he added, "He'll be safe." Following his gaze, I saw he wasn't focused on Butch, but was intensely locked in on our mother instead.

"Thank you, Wolfy," I whispered in return, immediately returning to baseline. "I owe you one."

He chuckled low. "Careful, Xanny. You have no idea what I want."

That's not fucking ominous or anything.

Swallowing hard, I forced my feet to carry me from the room, leaving my heart behind as I went to face a nightmare.

"Enter."

I'd barely made it to my father's workshop when his command demanded I pick up the pace. I willed my body not to piss itself as I entered his lair, averting my eyes from whatever his current project was.

Apocalypto Man could cryogenically freeze a human—trapping them in their own bodies—before snapping them out of existence, but sometimes he kept them around to dismember. As if they were nothing but lab rats for his experiments.

At least I only dissect dead animals.

Mostly.

"Xander," his voice was as detached as ever, but his golden eyes flickered upward as if looking through multiple floors to the dining room far above. "It appears you've brought a guest."

I cleared my throat, not wanting to talk about Butch at all with this monster, but knowing better than to refuse. "Yes, his name is Butch Hawthorne, and he's a normie who works for Biggs Enterprises. We met on a dating app, and it's pretty serious, so… yeah, I thought he should meet all of you. Most of you."

Moving on…

My father did *not* care about me or my life. I was nothing more than a tool at his disposal who was forced to prove time and time again that I was worthy of the family name—and my existence. Clearing my throat again, I geared up to redirect the conversation when he surprised me by keeping it going.

"Why *him*, Xander?" His golden gaze was boring into my soul now, and I did not for one second believe he wanted the sentimental reasons I'd given Dr. Ownit.

"Um," I stuttered, desperately trying to determine what answer would keep me alive. "We… connect. I feel a *tangible* connection to him where I physically want him around me all the time. We fit well with each other."

"I'm sure you do," my father murmured before SMILING AT ME.

I actually stumbled backward, my lower back hitting the examination table as I narrowly missed putting my hand into the mess of leftover human spread over its surface.

"Your mother mentioned that you're manifesting powers," he calmly continued, as if he hadn't just SMILED AT ME. "How long has that been going on?"

"A couple weeks, tops," I stammered, surprised my mother had taken my claim seriously enough to pass along. "I would have told you immediately, but I didn't know if that's what was going—"

"The timing is intriguing," was all he said before sweeping a cool gaze over the examination table.

I was on the verge of a panic attack while he rummaged around inside the corpse, as casually as one might select produce at the grocery store. Just as I realized he'd brought up my developing powers as *fact*, he spoke again.

"This ray gun you're developing. Could you program it to detect something other than microplastics? Living organisms, perhaps?"

My blood ran cold. No one in my family bothered to ask what I did in my spare time. Ever. That my father knew exactly what I was working on—inside my impenetrable secret lair—made me realize how fucking godlike this man truly was.

"Living?" Was all I could manage.

"Yes," he stated, lifting his bloody hand so I could plainly see it. "Something *tangible*. Like DNA."

I swallowed hard, my brain already whirring with how to make this ridiculous request happen. "Well, anything's possible."

He chuckled, although at least that horrible smile didn't reappear. "That it is. I'll be closely watching what you do with this…"—he vaguely waved his gore-covered hand—"unique situation you've found yourself in. Perhaps I'll meet *Butch* myself someday."

CHAPTER 29
BUTCH

By the time Xander returned to the dining room, only three people were left sitting at the table—me, Glacial Girl, and The Hand of Death, who'd moved closer. The tension between us was so thick, I could have cut it with a knife.

Not that either of these two would need knives to kill me.

"We're leaving," Xander unceremoniously announced, striding to where I was and placing a firm hand on the back of my neck. The instant calm that washed over me at his touch and scent was immediately followed by a tidal wave of shame so deep, I felt like I was drowning.

"It's been a pleasure, Butch," Xander's horrible *mother* cooed, even as her gaze flickered to Wolfgang with blatant annoyance.

I was so eager to get the heck out of there, I thought nothing of it—not until Xander whispered his thanks to his older brother as he herded me from the room.

"Anytime," was The Hand of Death's reply, and I suddenly realized his nerve-wracking presence hadn't been to intimidate me at all.

Was he... protecting me?

That makes no sense...

None of this makes any sense.

"I'm so sorry about all this, baby," Xander rasped as we climbed into his car and sped away. "I should never have brought you here."

"I'm glad you did," I replied, suddenly exhausted. "It was... enlightening."

He had nothing to say to that, so we continued traveling in silence. Now that I was no longer in immediate danger, I could finally absorb all the information I'd been given—including the terrible knowledge of who Xander was. Not only was he a supe, he was the son of the two most notorious supervillains in recent history.

And not knowing his villain identity made my imagination run wild, envisioning all the distasteful things he'd done in his family's name.

You're one to talk.

A strange numbness washed over me. "I want to sleep at my place tonight." My voice was distant and emotionless—like it was coming from someone else.

"Whatever you want, sweetheart," he murmured, immediately rerouting.

"Alone," I added, bracing for his reaction.

Xander immediately slammed on the brakes and pulled over before twisting in his seat to face me. "Really? You... you don't want to... be with me?"

I want to be with you more than anything.

"I just need space to think," I choked out, shutting my eyes against the terrible sight of his astonishment and anguish—unwilling to see his beautiful face now that I knew where that beauty came from.

"Fuck. Okay, okay..." Xander muttered, pulling the car back into traffic. "Whatever you need, Butch."

Please don't make this harder.

By the time we parked in front of The Gloucester, my instincts were *screaming* at me to invite him up. I needed Xander on a soul-deep level, so there would be no sleep for me tonight if I wasn't in his arms. But if I let him inside, there'd be no turning back from this star-crossed match.

How did this happen?

"Butch." I snapped back to reality and realized Xander had been saying my name. "Look at me." When I reluctantly turned to face him, I almost gave in.

He's my home, that's how.

"This conversation isn't over," he stated, those intense amber eyes daring me to argue, calling to me, and turning me on all at once. "I'll give you space—tonight. But I expect to hear from you tomorrow as soon as you get home from work. Can you do that? Please?"

"Yes," I replied without question. The thought of facing the night without him was almost unbearable, but if I knew we were talking tomorrow...

No. Stop it.

"I love you, baby," he murmured as I exited the car, so low I wondered if he meant for me to hear it. "And I'm sorry."

"Me too," I replied—the sight of his face falling at my omission burning itself into my memory. Not wanting to see anything more, I closed the door and swiftly walked away before I could run back into his arms.

I love you, too.

Five minutes later, I was standing under scalding water, trying to scrub off the entire evening—to somehow magically return to how things were.

But we can't go back.

Can we?

As I dried off, I realized Xander still didn't know who I was or why I'd insisted on separating for the night. It broke my heart to imagine him home alone, believing I was on the verge of ending things for no other reason than a dinner with his family gone wrong.

I should call him to make sure he's okay...

The sound of my phone ringing had me tearing out of the bathroom at super speed. When I saw it was my mother, I almost didn't answer. But then I realized if I didn't pick up, I'd be left alone with my thoughts, and *that* was scarier than dealing with her.

"Hello, Siren," I used her supe name, so she'd know we could talk freely.

"Captain," she replied. "How are you?"

The uncharacteristic *concern* in her tone caught me so off-guard, I answered more truthfully than I normally would have. "Not great. Xander and I... had a fight."

Why am I telling her this?!

"Ahh," she hummed thoughtfully. "That's... actually who I was calling to talk to you about."

All at once, I remembered the unanswered text I'd sent to my parents a few days ago, declaring my devotion to Xander and swearing off supes for good. Sinking to the bed, I scrubbed my hand down my face and waited for the inevitable 'I told you so.'

It never came.

Then, I braced for my mother to briskly redirect the conversation to Gemstonia Lincoln, or another viable match waiting in the wings. Instead, she paused so long that I thought we'd been disconnected, before delivering the *last* words I expected to hear.

"You should see this through, Butch."

"W-what?" I stuttered, thinking I must have misheard.

She softly laughed. "Your father doesn't know I'm calling. We are in disagreement about your... *normie,* but it sounds to me like you have a special connection, correct?"

My heart felt like it was breaking all over again. "Yes, we did —do! We do. It's just... a truth came to light tonight that... changes things."

"Mmm," she hummed knowingly, as if she could possibly understand. "Would you like to tell me what you learned?" My mother's voice had sharpened—signature shrewdness lacing her tone—and I felt an immediate protectiveness over Xander and his secrets.

A supe's identity is sacred.

"I don't want to talk about it," I brusquely replied, assuming the conversation would be over now that she'd failed in her bid for intel.

"Very good," she replied, surprising me again with how *genuinely pleased* she sounded.

There was another long pause before she spoke again. "You know, Butch... I came in contact with a wide variety of people during my time as protector of Big City. Some lived their truth, and some chose—or were forced—to bury it, but neither stance changed who someone was at their core. The proof was in how they carried themselves and treated those around them. Money and power may rule our world now—with harsh lines drawn in the sand—but there was a time when the most deadly weapon... was *love*."

What the heck is she talking about?

Her voice became muffled as she began speaking to someone in the background—most likely my father—which gave me a moment to wonder if she'd been body snatched by aliens.

"Butch?" She came back on the line with my civilian name, sounding more like the detached woman I knew. "I must be going, but please let me know if you require anything further. We can't have Big City's greatest superhero being no match for *villains!*" With that, she hung up, leaving my thoughts more jumbled than ever.

Dropping my towel onto the floor, I climbed into my now unfamiliar bed, attempting to arrange the extra pillows around me to mimic another person.

It was no use. Xander wasn't here, and my body was already *aching* for him. Even though all I wanted to do was hear his voice, I knew it was in my best interest to sleep on everything that had happened tonight before contacting him.

If I can sleep...

In an attempt to settle my mind, I mentally organized what I needed to catch up on at work tomorrow, pretending I had control over my life. All that accomplished was reminding me I *didn't*. Just like my parents and theirs before them, I was an employee of Solomon Biggs and Biggs Enterprises, and every decision I made was actually decided by another, in the interest of the greater good.

Except Xander.

I sat up with a gasp. Regardless of everything I'd discovered tonight, *Xander* was my truth. From the moment I responded to his match request on Bangers, he represented an autonomy I'd never dared pursue—never believed I deserved. But he *cared* for me. He claimed I deserved to be happy, regardless of whether I'd 'earned' it.

And I believe him.

He did all of this as a *villain,* because his bloodline didn't change who he was at the core.

Mine.

Suddenly compelled, I grabbed my phone from the bedside table and shot off a quick text to Xander—so he wouldn't needlessly worry all night.

The answer will always be yes, Xan.

An overwhelming sense of peace washed over me at this realization, interrupted only briefly by the fact I'd have to come clean about who I was as soon as possible.

What if me being a hero is a deal-breaker for him?

Finding out Xander was a villain—an unknown Suarez—had hit me hard, and I assumed the same would be true for him in reverse.

My guts twisted at the thought of Xander rejecting me, but I banished the thought. I'd told him I loved him, and I meant it, even if my confession was badly timed. Most importantly, he felt the same. All I had to do was figure out how a hero and a villain could be together. Biggs Enterprises would never keep records on *that* subject, but the famously neutral United Super Nations might.

And I promised Xander I'd take him there anyway…

It went against all my training to aid and abet a villain—to give him access to the classified USN archives—even if all he was after was water law treaties. But I believed in Xander's research, and I believed in *us*.

And I refused to believe that something that felt this *right* couldn't survive anything.

I'm going to see this through.

CHAPTER 30
XANDER

"Ugh, it smells like swampy man-ass in here!"

I groaned and rolled over, reminding myself for the millionth time to revoke Kai's fingerprint access to my apartment and give it to Butch instead.

If he comes back to me...

"Where the fuck is Butch? Don't tell me you murdered him already."

With another groan, I hauled myself off the couch, squinting against the harsh morning sun as I stumbled over the sea of empty bottles littering the floor.

It had been a long time since I'd fallen into *this* deep of a self-loathing spiral. Between Butch running away after an inevitably disastrous family dinner and my father mildly threatening me with an impossible assignment, there hadn't been enough alcohol in the house to make it better.

I even drank the cheap shit.

"Boone's Farm wine?! Omg, you *did* kill him, didn't you?" Kai continued to squawk, even as she straightened up my shameful mess.

"Kai…" I weakly rasped, but she ignored me.

"Why not drink some White Zin and show me the body while you're at it? Jesus, Xander, this is practically a confession!"

"Kai!" This time my voice cracked with emotion, but I no longer had enough self-respect to care.

"Oh, no…" she gasped, bringing a hand to her mouth in horror as she finally got a good look at me. "Something happened. Here, sit your ass down and tell Mama Kai everything."

For once, I believed she actually wanted the details for reasons other than rubbernecking—or maybe I'd reached a new low. Either way, I sank back down to the couch and even allowed her to rest my head in her lap.

Maybe I'm coming down with something…

"I brought Butch home to meet my family last night," I haltingly spoke, ignoring her dramatic gasp as I concentrated on not giving her the wrong details. "My mother was so *awful* to him he asked to be dropped off at his place afterward. Alone. He didn't even want to sleep in the same bed…" I had to stop talking before something like *tears* got any ideas about making an appearance.

Don't show any weakness.

"Why would anyone be mean to Butch?" Kai absently mused, running her fingers through my hair. I usually wouldn't allow anyone to touch me like this—besides Butch—but the mother hen routine was working for me at the moment.

I will take that admission to my grave.

Swallowing hard, I rallied. "I never should have brought him there. It was so fucking selfish of me when I *knew* there was a possibility of the dinner going south. I still did it, because I just wanted us to be a normal couple, and now I've—"

"Oh, there's no hope for that," Kai cut in.

"What?" I snapped.

"You being a *normal* couple," she replied matter-of-factly, as if I wasn't perilously close to hiding *her* body and buying some White Zin from Sun-Mart. "I mean, look at you! Look at Butch!"

I sat up. "What do you mean, *look at Butch?*" I hissed, my focus narrowing on my ignorant prey, ready to defend my love. "He's the most straight-laced, 9-5er I've ever—"

"No, he's not," she scoffed, crossing her arms and bratting me way more than was wise, given the circumstances. "Never mind that he's chosen to shack up with *you,* have you seriously not noticed that something's... *off* about him? Not in a bad way—more like in the same way something's off about you."

When I simply gaped at Kai in reply, she added, "What I'm getting at is that neither of you is what I would call 'normal,' so why worry about doing things in the *normal* way? Pave your own path. Fuck 'em!"

"You're right," I murmured, unsure if I was more awestruck by the fact I'd insisted on such a traditional 'meet the family' in the first place, or that Kai had said something that made sense.

"Okaaaay..." she drawled. "So why aren't you immediately calling him?"

I sighed. "Because he said he needed space. I asked him to call me after work today—"

"Christ!" Kai shouted, so abruptly I jumped. "This is what happens when you don't date women. Idiot."

I felt miraculously recovered enough to herd her out the door. "Thank you for your Very Important Opinions, but Butch knows he can trust me to respect his wishes. I don't want to do anything to betray his trust."

Any more than I already have, that is.

"Okay, sounds good," she agreed—a little *too* readily.

I narrowed my eyes as she glided down the hallway toward the elevator. "What are you up to, Kai?"

She spun around with an exaggerated show of innocence. "Moi? I'm going to work and then rehearsal." The elevator dinged, and she danced inside, leaving me with nothing but the echo of her sing-song voice. "There's nothing to see heeere…"

And she wonders why I don't date women!

Slamming my door, I stalked to where I'd carelessly discarded my phone among the empties, intending to text Kai with a mild death threat. I cursed when I saw my battery was dead, but this annoyance turned to horror as I realized the phone itself was probably fried because of my proximity to Apocalypto Man last night.

FUCK!!!

Glancing at my watch, I breathed a sigh of relief to see I had hours to go before Butch got out of work and called me like I'd asked him to.

Unless he tries to contact me before then…

I raced into my bedroom to throw on some fresh clothes before acknowledging that I did, in fact, smell like 'swampy man ass.' Cranking up one of my few supe strengths, I took the world's fastest shower, quickly redressed, and headed down to the garage for my car.

An hour later, I was leaving the store with a new phone in hand and a splitting headache from being forced to deal with people. There were no new messages or missed calls from Butch, but the idiotic technician at the 'genius bar' said it may take another hour for everything to download from the omnipresent cloud.

They should try hiring some actual geniuses.

The last thing I wanted to do was return to an empty apartment, so I drove to my warehouse lair. Thanks to my father's request, the idea of working on my ray gun made my anxiety spike, so I gave up on being productive and took out a WaveRunner instead.

I didn't know what made me put on my supersuit. Maybe because it was one of the most comfortable things I owned, or that it had special features I could access if something went wrong. Most likely it was that, when I wore it, I got to feel like something more than a slightly enhanced human who didn't belong among either normies or supes.

Tearing around the Bay worked some of the angst out of my system, even if I was constantly looking over my shoulder for a Biggs police patrol or Captain Masculine.

I haven't seen much of the big guy lately…

Somehow, I ended up drifting offshore by the secluded beach I'd recently brought Butch to. *Our* beach. Just as I morosely wondered if we'd ever have another chance to pick through microplastics together, my phone buzzed inside my waterproof pocket. I almost dropped it into the depths when I saw it was a message from Butch.

Hottie Himbo: *The answer will always be yes, Xan.*

I dropped my face into my hands as overwhelming relief washed over me. There was no way to tell exactly when Butch had sent the text, but at some point, he'd decided this relationship was worth fighting for.

That I was worth fighting for.

The events of last night instantly dissolved, along with the stress I'd been carrying today. None of it mattered, because despite our seemingly incompatible existences, Butch and I were going to be together in the end.

As I finished resetting my psychological baseline, I considered my next steps. The first thing would be to see if the USN had information on how supes and normies could legally be together. Then I needed to figure out a way to fulfill my father's ominous request while laying the groundwork to cut ties with my family completely.

For Butch.

For us.

Before I could get too sentimental, a pulse of power brushed against my skin, making me tense. My head shot up, and I was startled to find *Butch* sitting on the cliff surrounding the beach.

No, wait...

The way the sun was positioned behind the figure made it difficult to see, but *something* was familiar about their particular build... the way they rose to stand.

Oh, fuck.

It was Captain Masculine.

He was close enough to attack, and I'd been too busy mooning over Butch's text to sense him watching me. Moving as subtly as possible, I slipped my phone back into my pocket and discreetly reached for the submarine function on my WaveRunner. Before I could hit the switch, the Captain raised his hand, and I braced for a fiery death.

Then he *waved*.

I gaped at the hero and cocked my head, as if a slightly different angle might explain the mystery of what had just happened.

Why the fuck is Captain Masculine waving *at me?*

Seeing that I wasn't returning the gesture, he slowly lowered his hand, and I wasted no time getting the hell out of there. Knocking my WaveRunner into sub-mode, I shot beneath the surface, escaping with my life and a plan for the future.

CHAPTER 31
BUTCH

Why can't we be friends?

I sighed heavily as Doctor Antihero disappeared beneath the waves. There was no good reason for Solomon Biggs to suddenly want me closely monitoring the mysterious villain once again, especially when the file we had on him was so vague.

It's not like he's hurting anyone.

Biggs sending me out to the Bay was a blessing and a curse. The last place I wanted to be was in the office—working on yet another spreadsheet—but coming to *this* beach only reminded me of Xander. Antihero had been MIA for the last couple of weeks, so it was a pleasant surprise to see him at all. It almost felt like we were drawn to the same place at the same time...

Shaking my head, I banished my misguided fascination with the villain. I didn't *know* him or even know who he was. Xander was the only villain I was interested in—the only person I wanted—and right now, my energy needed to go into not panicking over how he *still* hadn't replied to my text from last night.

He must be angry with me.

Xander had never *punished* me for anything before—and it didn't seem like his style—but the way I left things outside The Gloucester obviously hurt him deeply, so if ever there was a reason to ignore me...

I hope he gives me another chance.

Luckily, Kai had insisted on exchanging phone numbers the day we met, and she'd texted this morning to say Xander was a wreck without me. This made me feel better *and* worse, but when I swooped by his apartment on my way to the beach, his car was gone from the garage.

I didn't want to be annoying by texting him again, so now I was simply counting down the hours until I called him after work, like I'd promised.

Suddenly my phone vibrated in my pocket, causing me to almost drop it off the cliff in my haste to bring up the message.

Daddy Xan: *I just saw your text. Please call me.*

You don't have to ask me twice.

He picked up on the first ring. "Baby? Fuck, I'm sorry. My phone died, and I had to get all my shit transferred to a new one, so I didn't see your text until—"

"If anyone should be apologizing, it's me," I interrupted, desperate to make things right. "It wasn't fair of me to walk away like I did."

He was quiet for a long moment. "Actually, it was fair. My family was fucking *awful* to you, for absolutely no good reason."

It's because I'm your enemy.

"Your brother wasn't so bad," I offered. "Wolfgang…"

The freakin' Hand of Death.

Xander sighed. "Yeah, well, none of them do anything without an ulterior motive, so who the fuck knows what his agenda is… But regardless, I should never have brought you there. I don't give a shit what they think of you—of *us*—because we're going to be together no matter what."

I fought back tears, almost choking on the lump in my throat. Xander deserved to know the truth about who I was, but the idea of telling him now… after a declaration like that…

"Can you meet me at the USN?" I blurted out, too selfish to do anything but hold on to this bliss for as long as possible. "I, uh, got approval to bring you there for your research." It was another lie, but I decided it was safer in this case to ask my boss for forgiveness than permission.

What Biggs doesn't know won't hurt him.

"Yes," Xander answered immediately. "Just let me get changed. I'll meet you there in an hour."

"Okay, see you then," I murmured, feeling better already.

I had limited experience with the United Super Nations' archives, but the organization provided a fair and balanced venue for high-profile cases to be resolved—whether between supes and normies or heroes and villains. I trusted they'd have something on file that could help with our unusual situation.

Tucking my phone away, I shot into the air to fly back to my condo and change into civilian clothes. Less than a handful of normies in this city had the clearance to recognize me out of uniform, and as far as my boss knew, I was staking out Awakener's Bay all day. All I needed to do was maintain a low profile and everything would go smoothly.

If I can survive dinner at the Suarez compound, I can survive anything.

An hour later, I spied Xander casually leaning against a lamppost outside the USN visitor's entrance, with his attention on his phone. At least he was *trying* to look casual. I could feel the anxiety radiating off of him as if it were my own, and a fresh wave of shame washed over me.

Stop being an idiot, Butch.

I picked up my pace, but stopped short of reaching him, suddenly unsure of what was appropriate after last night. He glanced up and gave me such a *look* that I immediately closed the distance between us so he could pull me in.

"I'm sorry," I stupidly repeated as he hooked a finger under my chin, forcing me to look at him.

"It's okay." He examined me like he was trying to see into my soul. "We both know your parents won't like me, either."

For a moment, I wondered if he'd figured it out—if this was the moment we could come clean with each other—but then he smirked. "Since I'm physically unable to pop out mini-Butches wearing khakis and polo shirts."

I gaped at him, suddenly overwhelmed with a vision of mini-*Xanders* wearing custom suits and three thousand dollar watches while sipping scotch out of baby bottles.

Oh my god, I want that.

He grew serious again. "I missed you, baby. Please don't shut me out like that again. I'll listen to anything you have to say. Always."

I bit the inside of my cheek so hard I tasted blood, but managed to nod. "I won't, and I missed you too… But I need a little more time to get my thoughts in order before we talk about last night." When his eyes narrowed, I gave him my most charming smile and quickly added. *"With* you. I *am* able to think and hang out at the same time."

That beautiful smirk curled his lip again. "So efficient. Do you think you could demonstrate your multitasking abilities later, by swallowing my cock while you sit on the new toy I ordered?"

My cheeks went up in flames, and, of course, *that* was the moment I heard a familiar voice calling my name.

"Butch!" The balding man beaming at me as he strode down the brick path toward us was one of the few normies I trusted with my life—and one of the few USN employees *not* in Solomon Biggs' pocket. "What a lovely surprise."

"Sylvano Ricci," I smiled in return, using his full name so he knew I was in civilian mode.

He was the USN's Deputy Secretary-General, and his father had been one of the organization's original founders. It was this proud heritage that inspired Sylvano to staunchly insist on maintaining an unbiased approach to the Big City-enforced laws governing supe behavior.

Despite my boss' best efforts.

For a moment, I worried the USN had records on villains that Biggs Enterprises didn't know about, but when Sylvano's warm brown eyes took in Xander without a shred of recognition, I continued with introductions. "This is Xander Marin, my…"

Oh, sugar.

For how fast we'd been moving, Xander and I had yet to put any sort of label on our relationship. It hadn't mattered to me before—which proved how secure I felt with him—but right now, I was floundering with what to call him in the presence of others.

"I'm his handler," Xander smoothly answered. He then discreetly placed his hand on my shoulder, which simultaneously calmed me and reinforced who I belonged to. "But I'm also a privately funded marine biologist who was hoping to access your current records on international water law. Butch offered to escort me to your archives, so I wouldn't burn the place down."

I don't know if he's kidding or not.

Sylvano's smile broadened. "Of course! Any friend of Butch Hawthorne's is a friend of mine. Come this way. There's no need to bother with security when I can simply sneak you both in through the employee entrance."

My stomach sank. While I trusted Xander's intentions, Sylvano's trust in *me* was completely undeserved at the moment. My only consolation was knowing this deception was only temporary—that as soon as I straightened everything out, Xander and I could be completely open about everything, with everyone in our lives.

Hopefully…

I was quickly distracted from my guilt by Sylvano chattering away, filling me in on the latest USN legal cases while also asking Xander polite questions about his work. My 'handler' answered in a similarly professional tone, but a few glimpses of pure excitement slipped out when he talked about his one-man war against microplastics.

He's just the best.

Sylvano was sharing a recent case study on the quality of drinking water on Rose Island when we arrived at the thick steel doors leading to the USN's records room.

For a moment, I second-guessed the wisdom of giving a *Suarez* unfiltered access to such classified materials, but quickly tamped down my suspicions. There was obviously no love lost between Xander and his family, so it was doubtful he'd be infiltrating on their behalf. Besides the secrets all supes were required to keep from normies, he had no reason to lie to me.

And what he's researching checks out.

"Ah, here we are," our guide hummed, pointing Xander down an aisle of file cabinets that looked exactly the same as the dozens of others. "You'll find the most up-to-date treaties, including recent amendments created in the wake of jurisdictional immunities for refugees of…"

Already bored, I tuned out the overly technical conversation and allowed my gaze to wander around the otherwise unoccupied space.

The records room was depressing, with its only decoration being beige walls and an expansive cement ceiling broken up by flickering fluorescent lights and an emergency sprinkler system. A long oak table sliced the room in half, and I noticed a yellowed map taped to its surface, with each aisle clearly labeled with what it contained.

Gotcha.

Adopting an air of nonchalance, I absently traced a finger over the map, stealthily scanning it to find the exact subject I was looking for.

Interspecies marriage.

"I trust you can take it from here, Dr. Marin," Sylvano grinned at Xander before turning to me. "Don't be a stranger, Butch. It's good to see you outside of Biggs' overbearing shadow." Xander snorted in approval of the dig as Sylvano left us to our research.

"Doctor?" I eyed him appraisingly, even as I sidled toward my destination.

Xander hummed, already thumbing through a cabinet. "Well, I do have multiple PhDs." His gaze suddenly snapped to my face. "This won't take long, sweetheart, if you want to go catch up with Sylvano, or get coffee… or something."

"I'm good!" My voice was louder than I intended. "I'll just… poke around in here."

"Very well," he gave me an odd look before turning his attention back to the files.

That was close!

Casually turning down the aisle I was aiming for, I quickly located the cabinet containing supe-specific trials. Yanking out a thick file that looked promising, I noted the title 'Franco vs. Big City' as I flipped it open. Scanning the legal brief, I was surprised to discover an extensively documented case where a villain-turned-hero petitioned to marry another hero, only to mysteriously die before a final verdict could be reached.

How have I never heard about this?

The sound of approaching footsteps had me racing to the far end of the aisle and scurrying around the corner. Once I was safely out of sight, I spread the court documents on a nearby table and used my phone to snap photos of each page, intending to take a closer look later.

After demonstrating my efficient multitasking abilities for Xander…

Neatly collecting the papers back into the folder, I turned down the aisle again, only to freeze mid-step. Xander was hurriedly rifling through the next cabinet over from where I'd found my file, his gaze laser-focused on his research.

Research that apparently had nothing to do with international water law…

CHAPTER 32
BUTCH

My crushing disappointment quickly turned to confusion when I realized this aisle only contained domestic matters—like marriages, divorces, and paternity disagreements.

What the..?

"Fuck," Xander softly swore, and the obvious disappointment on his face almost had me stomping over to give him a hug. Before I could blow my cover, he slid the cabinet closed and turned his head in the opposite direction to call for me. "All right, I think I got what I needed, sweetheart. Where are you hiding?"

"Oh, hi, Xan!" I strolled toward him, as if I'd been aimlessly wandering this entire time—leaving the folder behind me and trusting a USN employee to get it back where it belonged.

He subtly stepped away from the incriminating cabinet—a move I wouldn't have noticed had I not been watching him like a hawk. The only reason I didn't call him out was that, instead of guilt hidden beneath nonchalance, Xander just looked... sad.

"Are you okay?" I couldn't help asking, hating to think of him being upset over anything, even if he was keeping secrets.

Talk about karma...

He pressed his lips together and slowly nodded, although he took a moment before he replied. "I will be. There's just some red tape I need to deal with before I can get what I want..." His voice caught, but he quickly cleared his throat. "How about a drink before heading home?"

Without waiting for my answer, he spun on his heel and walked away, clearly intent on burying whatever he was going through. I followed, but paused at the cabinet he'd looked at and quietly slid it open.

It only contained a few files, with a tab labeled 'Denied: Supers and Humans.' The brief in the first folder summarized that a supe and normie petitioning to marry was dismissed for reasons of 'scientifically proven biological incompatibility.'

Oh, Xan...

While I always thought it was odd that heroes and villains were considered different species, supes and normies definitely were. If I unleashed even a quarter of my full strength on a human, they would splatter like a bug on a windshield.

I could only imagine the potential complications of a normie woman giving birth to a half-supe, but such precautions didn't apply to two *men* wanting to be together. With a sinking feeling, I realized Xander might actually burn down the USN to get what he wanted. Namely, *me*.

I need to come clean asap.

Maybe after he calms down...

The sight of Xander waiting near the doors, looking as defeated as I'd ever seen him, made all hesitation disappear. I strode to my villain with purpose—invading his space and gathering him into my arms.

"The same goes for you, too, Xan," I mumbled into his hair, hoping I was providing some comfort. The man might have multiple doctorates, but right now, he needed to get out of his own head. "Anything you need to talk to me about, you can."

And I need to do the same for you.

He tensed for only a moment before melting against my chest. Xander was almost as tall as me, but I definitely outweighed him, and it felt good to be taking care of *him* for a change.

"My big, strong man," he crooned, lifting his head to scrape his teeth along my jaw, lighting me up. "Should we skip drinks altogether in favor of fucking the pain away?"

I sharply inhaled. While I was *craving* Xander inside me—and had been fantasizing about experiencing him in the same way—it didn't feel ethical to do anything like that without him knowing the truth about me.

The records room door banged open, saving me from my turmoil, but when I saw who was interrupting us, I internally groaned.

I'd rather confess everything than deal with this guy.

"Well, well, well… this is something I never expected to see."

Tobias Johnson was a high-ranking officer of the USN, although it was through no merit of his own. Like me, his family had worked for the Biggs empire for generations, but that was where the similarities ended.

Whereas I had been under contract to serve the city since birth, Tobias *chose* to exist in shadowy circles—more than happy to serve as Solomon Biggs' unscrupulous eyes and ears at the USN.

He was also always thrilled with an opportunity to taunt me.

"It's not every day I get to see Butch *Hawthorne* behaving so recklessly. Does Biggs know his pet *dog* escaped its short leash for a salacious tryst?"

"The *fuck* did you just say?" Xander had turned to face the intruder, his amber eyes flashing gold as the full force of his glare fell on the other man.

Tobias paled, stumbling back a step before regaining his usual haughty demeanor. "Excuse me, but who are you exactly? Does security know—"

"I'm Dr. Don't-Give-a-Fuck," Xander growled, advancing on Tobias until he towered over him. "And I will gut you—slowly—if you ever talk to or about Butch that way again."

A tidal wave of power thrummed through the space, rattling the file cabinets and causing the fluorescents to sway overhead.

Oh, shi…

Tobias was a normie—like all USN employees—and I was so accustomed to the disrespectful way he spoke to me that my powers hadn't even blipped.

That surge didn't come from me.

It came from Xander.

Not only did Tobias' eyes widen at the display, but *Xander's* did as well. He even turned to look at *me*, as if to check whether I'd felt it too.

Does he not know what he can do?

Before I could wrap my head around how the son of two extremely lethal supervillains could be so clueless about his own powers, Tobias huffed indignantly.

"You need to leave. Both of you. And you—*doctor whoever*—are officially banned from the premises."

Xander snorted. "Fine. This organization is no use to me anyway if it's corrupted from the inside. C'mon, sweetheart." He held out his hand for me. "Let's go do something salacious with a leash."

For once, I didn't blush. Instead, I held my head high as I walked to meet him, taking his hand before turning to stare Tobias down.

"The only leash you should worry about is the choke collar *you're* on the end of," I calmly spoke, even as I sent a warning ripple of flame down Tobias' spine.

"Oh, I will!" he shrieked as the archive room doors slammed shut behind us, his courage noticeably rallying with 10 inches of steel protecting him.

As if I couldn't melt those doors along with him.

I shook the thought out of my head. While the idea of burning Tobias Johnson to a crisp was tempting, murdering a normie for running his mouth was dangerously close to villain territory.

But really, being a villain sounds like so much more fun…

Xander was hurriedly pulling me through the marble lobby toward the nearest exit, his eyes flitting around suspiciously as we moved through the late afternoon crowd. I realized he was still trying to identify the 'threat' he'd felt in the records room.

We have to talk about this.

Now.

"Xan!" I forced him to stop and look at me. "I need to—"

"You need to quit your job with Biggs," he interrupted, chest heaving as if he'd run a mile. "I can't... I can't have anyone talking to you like that. If I think you're being mistreated at work—by Biggs or another employee—I... I don't know what I'll do..."

He released me so he could bend over with his hands on his knees, dropping his head and panting as his body worked through whatever intense sensations he was experiencing.

You know exactly what he's experiencing, Butch.

You've been feeling this way since you met.

Were the situation reversed, I would have torn Tobias limb from limb, burning each appendage to ash while he bled out and watched. Whatever this was between Xan and me wasn't a simple case of attraction. The physical *need* to be near each other, the intense emotional connection, and the almost blinding obsession to protect was unprecedented, and it was a thousand percent mutual.

Even stranger was how my powers had been trying to fuse with the ones hidden within him—somehow recognizing he *had* powers even before I did.

And obviously this is all new to him...

Reaching down, I gently cupped Xander's jaw, coaxing him to stand. "Let's go get that drink. I need to tell you what I do for Biggs."

He simply nodded and slipped his hand into mine, letting me pull *him* along this time, past security and out the door. I took a deep breath as the fresh air hit my face, and glanced around for the closest bar.

My gaze landed on a black town car idling at the end of the brick path, stopping me in my tracks. Solomon Biggs' personal chauffeur emerged from the driver's side and opened the back door before gesturing inside in a way that left little room to argue.

"Boss wants to see you. He got a call that you were here."

"That motherfucker," Xander muttered, tightening his grip on my hand and raising his voice. "If Biggs wants to call you into the principal's office, he gets to deal with me, too."

"Suit yourself." The driver shrugged before addressing me, "Butch—you should know that Biggs has a guest up there with him. Flew in on a tailwind just for you."

Oh, no.

"Xan," I gasped, attempting to pull away as I panicked. "Let me deal with this, okay? I-I'll meet you at home later."

Our home.

"No fucking way," Xander growled. "You are not taking the heat for this." Keeping my hand firmly in his, he stubbornly climbed into the car and dragged me along after him. The door was swiftly closed behind us, trapping us inside.

An anxiety attack was imminent. Yes, I was definitely in trouble for bringing an unapproved guest to the USN with me—an unregistered supe who threatened a government employee—but I wasn't worried about Biggs' punishment for me. In the end, he was still just a normie. I could endure his spreadsheets and arbitrary missions to annihilate entire villain families.

It would also be easy enough to fabricate a story for who Xander was, especially since there was no official record of his heritage. We could even offer to register him under a false identity, just to make everyone happy. I could manage that with ease.

The thing I absolutely could *not* handle at the moment was who else was waiting for us in Biggs' office. It was difficult enough for me to face Vortexio when he was angry, but giving him access to the son of his sworn enemies...

Hopefully, he won't know who Xander is.

I was terrified of the man I loved being in the same room as my father, but the idea of what might happen if I refused Xander's protection scared me more. If I forced him to sit this one out, his powers might flare up again—at the wrong time and against the wrong supe.

If my father tries to kill him, there'll be nothing I can do.

CHAPTER 33
XANDER

Butch was *shaking* by the time we pulled up in front of Biggs Enterprises, and I was dangerously close to imploding myself.

Hearing that sniveling *normie* speak to Butch so disrespectfully was a grave offense that deserved immediate punishment, preferably of the slow and painful variety. I'd been blindly wrathful when it happened—poised to strike--but the wave of power that blasted through the archive room distracted me enough to spare the tattletale from certain death.

But who did that power come from?

The more important question was, who *else* treated Butch in such an insulting manner?

Because I'm making a shit list and checking it twice.

"Who gave you those bruises?" I quietly asked, my teeth clenched so tightly my jaw popped.

"W-what?" Butch stared at me across the seat.

"When you showed up at my apartment after being inland. Was it your *boss* who did that to you?" My vision was flickering red as I imagined my hands closing around Solomon Biggs' neck, squeezing until I watched the life leave his eyes.

"What? No! No," Butch huffed a laugh, but it sounded nervous. "Biggs couldn't hurt me like that, and he wouldn't *want* to. I'm too... valuable to him."

Like property.

Like a dog.

It was amazing I could form words at all. "What sort of contract do you have with Biggs, Butch?"

He met my gaze with pure devastation in his pretty blue eyes. "Not one I can get out of."

My skin felt like it was on fire, like I would burst into flames as white-hot rage licked at my veins. I was going to burn Solomon Biggs until his corpse disintegrated, raze the entire Enterprises building to the ground, and dance in the smoldering remains of anyone who ever wronged—

"Xan. XAN!" Butch's frantic tone snapped me out of my murderous thoughts. "Please breathe. I can't tell you more *right now...*" He paused with a meaningful tilt of his head toward where the driver sat, reminding me he'd been about to explain his job before this goon picked us up. "And *please*, let me do the talking when we get up there. I just... I don't want you to get hurt."

The barely contained terror in his voice instantly doused my fury with ice water. Biggs Enterprises was clearly some kind of mafia, and since Butch still thought I was a fragile normie, I needed to humor him and behave as if I didn't have a death wish.

Even though I feel like I could take on anyone right now...

The town car rolled to a stop in front of the Enterprises building. When the chauffeur hopped out to open our door, it was all I could do to not throw Butch over my shoulder and make a break for freedom—contract be damned.

First chance I get, my lawyer is looking at that bullshit piece of paper.

Unsurprisingly, Biggs' driver stayed uncomfortably close, escorting us through the lobby and into the elevator, invading our personal space. Even once we were inside, he used his body to block the doors, as if I couldn't just as easily kill him from behind.

"Xan..." Butch squeezed my hand, searching my face as if checking my mental state. "Please remember that I love you."

If he was trying to soften me up, it worked, as I actually huffed a laugh. "Baby, if you continue to only say those words under duress, I may get the wrong idea."

He closed his eyes. "You're right," he whispered, his face scrunched in anguish. "I've messed this up. I'm *still* messing it up..."

"Hey, hey," I soothed, gathering him close and petting his soft blond hair. "You could never mess this up. I told you. You'll always be mine, no matter what."

A sigh escaped Butch as his enormous muscular body collapsed against mine, bathing me in that calming scent of his—although it barely calmed me now. "Say it again," he whispered, desperately.

"You're mine," I growled, feeling a ripple of power vibrate in the enclosed space, causing Biggs' driver to turn and eye us warily. "Always."

The elevator dinged at the top floor and we separated, even though no longer touching Butch made my fingers twitch.

This time, our third wheel gave us a wide berth as he led the way. The unnecessarily long hallway was lit by widely spaced wall sconces—for maximum dramatic effect—and led to enormous mahogany doors at the far end. The driver opened the doors and ushered us inside, before hurriedly backing out of the room and sealing us in.

Guess we creeped the creep out.

Good.

"Ah, Butch, thank you for coming!" Solomon Biggs rose from behind his massive steel desk, beaming as if we'd willingly arrived instead of being forcibly summoned. He looked exactly as he always did on TV—with cold gray eyes and perfectly styled white hair in a monochromatic contest to his patriotic blue suit and red tie.

His fake smile disappeared as he spotted me. "Is this the individual who threatened Tobias Johnson?"

Normies aged worse than supes, so although he was only a decade older than my parents, the deep frown lines on his face displayed the wear and tear that came along with being a complete and utter douchebag.

Before I could cut in, Butch straightened. "It wasn't unprovoked, boss. You know how Tobias speaks to me."

Biggs cocked his head, confused. "How else *should* he speak to you, Butch? You work for him."

This clown.

"I work for Biggs Enterprises. For the city," Butch calmly recited, his eyes cautiously flickering to a seating area to our left. I followed his gaze and was startled to see an older man seated on a leather Eames chair, impassively observing the scene.

How did I not notice him sitting there?

Icy-blue eyes took in every detail, his expression blank, but the slight tick to his jaw betrayed his displeasure. This may not have been his office, but his presence commanded the room—sucking the air out of my lungs until I found it hard to breathe.

"That's correct, Butch." The mystery man gracefully stood and glided over, as if carried by the wind itself. "Your every move should be in service to this city, and your every decision reflects on all of us. Do you believe your reckless actions today were an accurate representation of the city you supposedly love? That the... *company* you've been keeping lately," — his gaze raked over me and found me lacking—"is in line with the way you were raised?"

What the fuck kind of cult is this?

"He has a name," Butch's voice faltered, even as he defended me. "This is—"

"Xander *Marin*. Yes, I know." That judgmental stare found me again, although this time, it was more assessing. Calculating.

My eyes narrowed on him in return, no longer able to hold my tongue. "I don't believe we've met before."

He tightly smiled, although nothing about the expression was friendly. "Oh, we have, but you were just a baby." When I tensed, he chuckled. "My name is Harold Holt, and I know your parents well."

Holt...

Butch sharply hissed, distracting me from trying to place the vaguely familiar name. When I glanced at him, he looked horrified, his gaze frantically darting between me and Harold Holt. Biggs was eyeing our exchange with a detached curiosity, but my attention was already back on the actual threat in the room.

He'd used my civilian name because of the other normies present, but he still wanted me to know that my true identity was no secret to him. This implied he was high-level, perhaps even above Solomon Biggs. If it was true that he'd been aware of my existence since I was born, then this random normie knew more about me than most did—more than anyone should.

Who the fuck is Harold Holt?

That tingling sensation raced down my fingers, only this time, it felt like it was reaching outward, like antennae testing the air.

Harold blanched, a shocked expression passing over his face before he buried it beneath a genuine grin so wide, a dimple actually appeared on his disarmingly handsome face.

"Oh, now *this* is an interesting development," he chortled, as if my rising anger was delightful. His gaze drifted to the others. "Butch, I'm going to borrow your *friend* so you can discuss business with Solomon."

Butch paled, looking dangerously close to passing out. "No… please—"

Harold scoffed. "There are more important issues at hand than your misplaced attachments, but you can calm down." He sighed heavily, annoyance and resignation lacing his tone. "I'll do my best to return him to you in one piece."

How reassuring.

I wasn't particularly worried about my safety, but hated how frightened Butch looked on my behalf. "Everything's all right, baby," I soothed, taking great pleasure in how the term of endearment caused Biggs' eyes to widen while Harold's narrowed. "I won't let this big meanie make me cry."

"I'll talk to you later, okay?" Butch called after us as we left Biggs' office, but it sounded more like a plea to the glowering man leading the way than a promise to me.

We entered the elevator, but instead of taking us back down to the lobby, Harold Holt hit the button for the roof.

Intimidation it is, then.

While I didn't think he would actually try to throw me off the roof, as soon as we exited the elevator, I put as much distance between us as possible.

Harold simply smirked, as if my precautions amused him. "So tell me, Xander *Suarez,* when did *you* suddenly start manifesting powers? Are you the biggest secret in our community, or has this development only been since you and Butch started this… whatever this is between you?"

Okay, so he's a supe.

"I couldn't say." I shrugged, adopting an exaggerated show of innocence, even as I internally raged at his casual dismissal of what Butch and I shared. "Not when I'm flapping in the breeze with some random fucking stranger on a rooftop."

My mother had also asked *who* I'd been around when hearing my powers had manifested, but now wasn't the time to examine the coincidence.

He huffed a laugh. "Your choice of words is fitting, considering the circumstances." Quickly sobering, he gave me another appraising look as his powers pressed against my skin—testing me. "Even if I were to tell you who I am, you still wouldn't be properly motivated to cut ties with Butch, would you? We'll simply have to find another solution."

"Who the fuck are *you* to think you have a say in this?" I scoffed, no longer interested in niceties. "As if this is a problem that needs to be solved. As if Butch doesn't deserve someone in his life who *loves* him, especially with how he's treated around here."

Like property that can be beaten when he doesn't cooperate.

A sudden thought occurred to me, and my eyes narrowed. "Are *you* the one leaving bruises on him?"

He stared at me in astonishment before throwing his head back with a laugh. "Oh, this is marvelous. You truly don't know what's going on here, do you? Ender and Signe did you a grave disservice by keeping you in the dark. Regardless. No, *I* didn't put those bruises on Butch…" The calculating expression was back on his face as his lip curled. "But I know who did."

I knew I was taking the bait but couldn't stop myself—not when revenge was within reach. "Who?" I gritted out. "Who did that to him?"

"What do you think *you'll* be able to do about it, Xander?" He cocked his head, as if I were an odd specimen under his microscope. "You've existed as little more than a human for your entire life. You don't know what sort of powers are trying to emerge or how to properly wield them."

Harold Holt—whoever he was—took a single step toward me, still nowhere close enough to strike. "Unlike those of us who were *born* with the ability to *solve problems* with a flick of our wrists."

He lazily gestured, and a punishing wall of wind slammed into me, forcing me dangerously close to the edge of the roof. I panicked, but only for a moment. An unfamiliar sensation erupted in my chest, spreading outward through every nerve ending, pushing back at the powers attacking me with enough force to match.

My attacker stumbled backward, as if shoved by an invisible hand, and the wind pummeling me instantly disappeared. I slowly circled him as he straightened, grumpily brushing a wayward leaf off of his suit jacket before glaring at me with newfound hate.

And begrudging respect.

I had no fucking clue what I'd just done—or how I'd accomplished it—but this asshole didn't need to know that.

Jesus, I hope I can do it again.

Instead of throwing more wind at me, Harold calmly strode to the elevator. He pressed the button and entered the cab without indicating I should join him—not that you could have paid me enough to do so. He turned to face me, cocking his head with a secretive smile playing on his lips.

"Since I'm feeling generous, I'll not only let you live, but give you the name of who's responsible for those bruises on your beloved Butch *Hawthorne.*"

His smirk grew as the elevator doors closed. "The one you want is Captain Masculine."

CHAPTER 34
XANDER

I quickly realized the elevator at Biggs Enterprises had been programmed to take me straight to the lobby. When I stomped over to reception to demand access to Biggs' office again, I was told I could either leave the building on my own two feet or be dragged out.

Having no choice but to trust that Butch wasn't in mortal danger, I quickly hailed a cab back to the USN for my car before immediately turning around and driving back to the Enterprises building. I was hoping to intercept Butch as he left, but they must have snuck him out while I was gone.

When he later called to say he'd been sent inland again, I barely reacted. It was partly because I wasn't surprised that Butch had gotten punished for what happened today, but mostly that every atom of my being was laser focused on seeking revenge against the supe who'd hurt him.

Captain Masculine.

Captain fucking Masculine.

The very hero this idiotic city simped over was using his enhanced strength to intimidate and injure Biggs employees who stepped out of line. Masculine had put his hands on

Butch. He'd broken his bones and left visible marks. He'd hurt the man I loved until he could do nothing but drag himself to my apartment like a broken toy waiting to be fixed.

I'm going to fucking kill him.

"Xan?" Butch's voice on the other end of the line brought me back to the conversation. "Are you all right? Did something happen with… Harold… Holt?"

I blew out a forceful breath. "No, Butch, I'm *not* all right, but it's less about that asshole and more about how *you* are treated by your employer. Do you think you could get me a copy of your contract with Biggs? I want to look it over."

There was a long silence. "I-I don't know where it is," he stammered. "I've never seen it."

Excuse me?

"I'm sorry… what?" I squeezed the reusable aluminum water bottle I was holding so tightly it bent in half. "How could you have never seen a contract that you signed?"

Another pause. "I didn't sign it. My parents did. Before I was born."

I'M GOING TO FUCKING KILL THEM ALL!!!

At the moment, I was perilously close to either a nervous breakdown or a rampaging murder spree. "Baby… baby, listen to me. This is not okay. None of this is okay. When are you coming home? Because I-I *need* you here in my apartment —*our* apartment. I'll get you set up with fingerprint access and then we'll work on a plan together to get you the fuck out of this goddamn cult that you work for—"

"I don't think you should give me fingerprint access to your apartment," Butch interrupted, shocking me into silence. "Not until I tell you what I do for Biggs."

"Tell me now then," I demanded, beyond done with this entire situation. "Just tell me now and then we can—"

"I want to tell you in person," he cut in again, although his voice wavered slightly. "You deserve to hear it from me, face-to-face."

Enough of this!

"Are you actually a serial killer?" I huffed. "Or do you murder marine wildlife?"

He barked a laugh, and as it was the first one I'd heard out of him since our abduction to Biggs' office, I took it as a win. "No. I don't kill marine wildlife."

I smiled, even though he couldn't see me. "Well, since that's my *only* deal-breaker, it sounds like everything will be fine. Seriously, baby, there is *nothing* you could do to make me feel less sure about you—about us. About *this*. I promise."

"I'm not going to hold you to that," he whispered so sadly I almost demanded he come home immediately.

The arrival of a woman in the background—his mother, probably—stopped him from saying more. Their conversation grew muffled as Butch put the phone down to reply. When he came back on, he sounded even more defeated, if that were possible.

"I've gotta go, Xan. I think they'll let me come back to the city tomorrow, after a… thing I have to do tonight…"

Wiping a hand down my face, I sighed, annoyed that I'd forgotten to install a tracker on his phone when I had the chance. "Very well. But I'm not kidding—I want you to come *home* as soon as you're back, okay?"

"I will," he murmured.

"You will *what?*" I growled, suddenly needing to remind him who he belonged to. To remind myself.

Because he was perfect, he answered immediately. "I will, Daddy."

"Good boy," I praised. "I'll see you tomorrow."

Tossing my phone onto the couch next to me, I dropped my head into my hands. Something seriously fucked up was going on here and the answer was hovering infuriatingly just out of reach.

As soon as Butch gets here, I'm locking him in the bedroom.

My phone rang and I snatched it up, hoping it was Butch calling me back. I sighed heavily to see it was my mother. She'd been trying to get a hold of me since our disastrous dinner, but I hadn't trusted myself not to lay into her for how she'd behaved.

But I'm choosing violence tonight.

"Who is Harold Holt?" I barked into the phone, skipping hellos altogether.

"What did you say?" Her voice was dangerously low.

"Harold Holt. I had the pleasure of meeting him today at Biggs Enterprises," I laughed, sounding exactly as unhinged as I felt. "He took me up to the roof for a little chat, then tried to toss me off with a gust of wind. I somehow threw it back at him and oh! He says he knows you and father well. Old friend of yours?"

"You…" my mother choked out. "You matched the wind-power of *Vortexio?!*"

My blood ran so cold it froze and shattered. If I'd known the man I was giving major attitude was THE Vortexio, I would have shut the fuck up and taken several seats.

Okay, maybe not, but still.

More puzzle pieces fell into place while others disappeared entirely. Butch had clearly been nervous in Vortexio's presence, and even more frightened of leaving *me* in his care, which meant he knew what he was capable of. Harold had also given his real name in front of both Biggs and Butch, which meant Butch had much higher clearance than I'd originally suspected.

Maybe I should just tell him I'm a supe...

"What happened when you revealed your powers to Vortexio?" My mother's oddly concerned voice brought me careening back to our conversation. "He didn't... threaten you, did he?"

I scoffed. "Besides the attempted murder, no. He even gave me the name of the supe responsible for hurting Butch, so I could go after him. Captain Masculine."

"WHAT?!" she shrieked, nearly blowing out my eardrum. "That little shit. Just wait until I tell your father—"

"I know!" I shouted, glad we were seeing eye to eye for a change. "Big City's golden boy is nothing but a meathead bully, and now I have the evidence to prove it. Oh, I can't *wait* to get my hands on him. I will make him suffer and I will make it last."

It will be glorious.

"Wait. No, Xanny," my mother sounded distracted, no doubt already taking the elevator to my father's workshop to fill him in on the gossip. "You... *can't* go after Captain Masculine, because, ah...."

I glared at my phone, willing my rage to somehow travel through the ether. "And why not, mother? Because I'm not *strong* enough? Because my powers aren't developed? Whose fault is that?! You and father kept me in the dark for so long, I was practically existing as a *normie!*"

Before she could reply, I hung up and tossed my phone onto the coffee table, but immediately grabbed it again so I could fire off a text to Butch.

> ***There are things I need to tell you about myself as well.***

It was helpful that Butch already had insider knowledge of supes, but at this point, I didn't give two shits about our 'rules' for dealing with normies. I was going to drag that hottie himbo into my world so fast, he would practically become a supe himself.

It would solve so many problems if he were one.

Butch didn't immediately reply, and I remembered he said he had something to do. The idea of spending another night alone in my bed was depressing, so I packed up a few things and headed out, deciding I'd rather go to my lair and lose myself in work for a few hours.

After grabbing some emotional-support fried chicken to go...

A few hours turned into half the night, and I woke up stiff and cranky on my warehouse cot. Maybe because it was the lesser of two evils, but I'd chosen to focus on how to isolate DNA instead of microplastics with my ray gun, and actually came up with a solution. I still needed to test it out, but at least this meant Apocalypto Man would let me live another day.

I avoided using live animals in the lab, but pulled on my supersuit and boarded a WaveRunner, intent on trolling around the Bay until I found a fresh corpse of *something* to bring back with me.

If it's a human, even better.

Nothing turned up, and I found myself bobbing in the waves near 'our' beach again, thinking about the future. The possibility of leaving such a beautiful area to go into hiding sent an unexpected pang of loss through me, but I knew I'd do anything to keep Butch safe from those who'd hurt him.

There are plenty of other beaches in the world.

My gaze drifted to the cliffs and my jaw dropped to see a familiar figure watching me once again—making my rage flare and my vision go red.

Captain Masculine.

Oh, it's fucking on.

CHAPTER 35
BUTCH

Xander's going to be so angry with me.

The first reason was that I hadn't been completely honest about what I was up to last night.

Vortexio literally dragged me home in a tornado after what happened in Biggs' office and then invited Gemstonia Lincoln and her family over for another painfully formal dinner. I'd shocked everyone by refusing to go downstairs until my father swore to me he hadn't killed Xander. However, he refused to discuss our relationship any further before stalking away.

My mother then surprised me by discreetly slipping me my phone, saying she'd distract our guests while I called him. She was also unusually quiet during dinner, although I caught her glaring at my father over her chicken cordon bleu.

It looks like both of us are rebelling lately.

Luckily, no one mentioned marriage, not that I would have been included in any backroom deals between our parents. It was a small mercy that—as of now—I wouldn't also have to tell Xan I was engaged to someone else when I revealed my identity.

That might actually be worse.

The second reason he would be upset was that I *hadn't* gone straight to his apartment when I returned to Big City, although that wasn't entirely my fault. Father had escorted me back to Biggs Enterprises this morning, then met privately with my boss for an hour before I was invited into the office.

And ordered to kill Doctor Antihero.

As I gazed out over the Bay from my cliffside perch, my thoughts inevitably drifted to Xander. His fury over my contract with Biggs—over how uninformed I'd been in my own life—had made me question everything.

Since I was young, I'd believed heroes were inherently *good,* and that Biggs Enterprises only had Big City's best interests in mind. Now I realized I'd blindly followed orders I should have been questioning and trusted the wrong people—including my own parents.

Just because I was *told* a villain was evil didn't make it true. Yes, Xander's family was legitimately terrifying, but his brother, Wolfgang, had actually kept an eye on me, presumably in case their mother attacked. I couldn't even fault Signe Suarez for being suspicious when I arrived at her home, especially after I'd wiped the Stricklands from the face of the earth only a few days earlier.

I never even asked to see the evidence against them.

The realization that I'd been used as a mindless weapon to murder other supes—often unprovoked and possibly unjustified—destroyed something inside me.

What if Xander can't look past everything I've done?

Adding to my current distress were the abrupt orders to eliminate Doctor Antihero. It was because of monitoring *him* I'd started to suspect heroes and villains weren't that different. I never actually saw Antihero doing anything nefarious, and if Biggs hadn't insisted he was a villain, I wouldn't have assumed he was.

He seems just like me.

I tensed as Antihero himself drifted into view on one of his high-tech WaveRunners. He hadn't noticed me yet, so it would be easy enough to incinerate him with a fireball or swoop down like a bird of prey and throttle him with my bare hands.

But I don't want to.

Antihero finally spotted me, and I calmly waited for him to escape again. When he continued staring at me instead, I slowly raised a hand, assuming any movement on my part would send him running. Again, he didn't flee.

He drove straight for me.

My jaw dropped as he gunned the WaveRunner up onto the beach before jumping off and stalking to the base of my cliff.

Does this guy have a death wish?!

"Get the *FUCK* down here! Now!" His voice was distorted by his mask, but something in his tone had me scrambling to my feet.

I hesitated after that, gazing down at him while trying to get my jumbled thoughts in order. He did not like this one bit. Further proving he had serious balls, Antihero snapped his fingers and impatiently pointed to the sand in front of him.

Yes, Daddy.

What the heck is wrong with me?

Desperately hoping my growing erection wasn't too obvious through my supersuit, I stepped off the cliff. Softly landing, I immediately clasped my hands in front of my crotch to hide the evidence of my full-blown villain fetish.

"Fuck, you're big," he murmured, but it wasn't fear lacing his tone. If I didn't know any better, it sounded like... *lust.*

I cocked my head. I'd never been this close to Antihero before, but it was as if I needed to get closer still. My skin was *tingling* under my Lycra, and all I could think about was stripping off both our supersuits so we could roll around on the beach together.

There is something seriously wrong with me.

Antihero's gaze was roaming over me as well, his chest heaving as he took me in. Then he angrily shook his head and refocused on my face.

His eyes are so pretty...

"Listen up, Masculine," he growled, jabbing a finger into my chest. "I know all about you. I know how you *hurt* people—how you punish others for Solomon Biggs."

Oh, no.

He knows.

Of course, I would seem like a villain *to* villains. The only thing that differentiated us was that I had the official backing of Biggs Enterprises, sanctioning my disgusting actions with a government seal.

The *hatred* pouring off this supposed villain made me want to drop to my knees and beg for forgiveness. I also wanted to drop to my knees for other reasons, but all that awkward realization did was add to my overwhelming shame and confusion.

"Oh, you have nothing to say for yourself?" Antihero scoffed derisively. "I bet this is a novel experience—having someone actually stand up to you. You're a fucking *bully* who targets those who are weaker than you, simply because you can."

Everything he's saying about me is true.

I'm a monster.

Antihero continued, rage radiating off of him so intensely it felt like my own firepower. "But you've gone too far because you hurt someone I care about. Someone I *love*. This may come as a shock to you, but villains also have emotions. We're also *people*. You know what… we're gonna do it this way…"

Then he reached up and pulled the mask off his head.

And my entire world shattered a second time.

I stumbled backward, but that only made him advance, still snarling. "What? You don't want to *see* me? You don't want to acknowledge there's an actual man behind this mask?" He glared at me while pointing to his face with a circling motion —a face I knew better than my own.

Xander.

I could have killed Xander.

The emotions flooding my system were so intense that I thought I might actually die. Shock, terror, and self-loathing mixed with overwhelming relief and a desire so strong, I had to clench my fists at my side to stop myself from reaching out to touch him.

"There's an employee at Biggs Enterprises named Butch Hawthorne," he coldly spoke, pure venom glittering in his amber eyes. "If you ever lay a finger on him again, I will do everything in my power to destroy you."

Oh, my god…

A fresh wave of shame washed over me. Xander had just stood up to Captain Masculine—risked his precious life—to protect *me*.

I don't deserve him.

There was no way this could work between us. Despite being a villain, Xander was a far better man than I ever would be. Whether I pulled my mask off now, or later tonight, or ten years down the road, it wouldn't change who I was or what I'd done. Xander would never be able to look past the murderer I was, and he had every right not to.

He deserves better.

My heart preemptively splintered into a million shards of pain at what I had to do, but it was for the best. Bracing myself, I swallowed hard and met Xander's gaze, memorizing every inch of his face—accepting I would never be this close to him again.

"You're too late," I kept my voice steady, knowing my mask was distorting it enough to remain unrecognizable, like the faceless *villain* I was. "Butch Hawthorne is already dead."

Not waiting for a reply, I shot into the air, flying away as quickly as I could—but not fast enough to miss the howl of despair echoing off the cliffs behind me.

CHAPTER 36
BUTCH

"You may enter."

Steeling my spine, I walked into my father's home office. After leaving Xander on the beach, I'd flown back to my condo—half-blinded by tears—packed everything I needed into a bag, and slunk to my parents' house.

My plan was to stay here until I found a new place to live, far enough away from anywhere Xander would ever find me.

Not that he'll be looking for me, anyway.

I hadn't been lying when I said Butch Hawthorne was dead. As far as I was concerned, I no longer had a civilian name—or any name at all. I wasn't even Butch Holt. I was Captain Masculine and the only thing I was good for was being Big City's beloved murderer.

It's what I was born to do.

"Solomon called to ask if you'd completed your assignment, since you apparently didn't check in with him." My father was sitting behind his enormous oak desk, hands loosely clasped on the blotter, awaiting my reply with his usual mild disinterest.

I clenched my jaw and stared down at his desk, trying to ignore the fact he'd just asked if I'd killed Doctor Antihero in the same way one might discuss the weather.

"It's done," I gritted out, my heart shattering all over again at what those words actually meant.

A choked sound drew my attention to where my mother sat across the room. "Oh, darling… I'm—"

My father loudly clearing his throat put an end to whatever she was going to say, and I tiredly met his gaze again.

"Very good," he brusquely spoke with the efficiency of a man accustomed to wiping his hands of things. "Now that we've solved *that* little problem, your mother and I have something important to talk to you about. Please,"—he gestured to the leather chairs facing his desk—"have a seat."

"I'd rather stand," I replied with the same level of cold disinterest he was showing me. Doctor Antihero's true identity was never in his file, but that didn't mean my father had the right to refer to him as a 'little problem.'

Xander was so much more than that to me.

He was everything.

"Fine," he scoffed. "I can see you're in a *mood*, so I'll make this quick. The Lincolns finally brought an offer to the table that was worthy of this family, so the paperwork has been signed. You and Gemstonia will be married in a month, on live TV at the Royal Cove Yacht Club. You'll be expected to announce the engagement outside the Enterprises building on Monday morning so the press can—"

"No," I interrupted, outwardly calm despite every atom of my being having gone up in flames. "I won't be marrying Gemstonia Lincoln. Not in a month. Never."

"Butch…" my mother warned.

"Excuse me?" My father rose to stand, the papers on his desk rustling in the gathering wind. "I don't believe I heard you right—"

"DID I FUCKING STUTTER?!" I yelled, releasing just enough power of my own to let him know I was serious. "It's bad enough that you bound me in servitude to Biggs Enterprises before I was born, but now you're selling me off to the highest bidder so *more* little murder machines can be created? I don't want to marry a random opportunist like Gemstonia. I don't want any part of this bullshit. What I do want is a goddamn lawyer to look at every contract you've ever signed in my name so I can take your ass to court at the USN and get the hell out of this fucked up cult family!"

Xander would be so proud of me right now.

"Language, Butch!" my mother gasped, but my glare was fixed on the seething man before me.

"You want out of this family, hmm?" my father sneered. "You are nothing without the Holt name—without that mask you wear. Where could you possibly run to? Do you know how many villains want your head on a stake? It's only a matter of time before you finally meet your match, and since your little secret Suarez is no longer alive to protect you—"

My eyes widened as he abruptly stopped talking, but I'd heard enough.

"You… *knew* that Doctor Antihero was Xander Suarez?" I croaked, stumbling backward until my back hit the doorframe. "You knew, and you told Biggs to send me to *kill* him?"

He crossed his arms over his broad chest, unmoved by my anguish at this revelation. "Of course, I knew who he was. Xander was the third child of Ender and Signe Suarez—our greatest enemies, must I remind you? He was preceded by The Hand of Death and Ultra Violent. Do you not think *every* superhero worth his salt knew full well the day Xander was born? When he turned out to be a powerless dud—or so we thought—he was somehow swept under the rug before the USN or Biggs ever learned of his existence. The only reason your mother and I didn't expose him was because he wasn't a threat, and the knowledge gave us a bargaining chip against the Suarez clan, if we ever needed it."

Sitting heavily, he incredulously shook his head. "Never in my life would I have guessed *this* would happen." His gaze snapped to mine again. "But as I said, he was a problem that's now been solved. A problem that's been solved before."

My mother released another sob, and I used the distraction as an excuse to turn and race from Vortexio's office. I didn't stop until I'd reached the guest room and began throwing my few belongings back into my bag.

"Where could you possibly run to?"

I sank onto the bed, defeated. If I went to Xander, I would have to come clean about who I was, and if he didn't hate Captain Masculine before, he certainly did now.

There's nowhere for me to go.

As if the vision of a grieving Xander wasn't enough to torture me, I grabbed my phone and scrolled through the dozens of texts he'd sent since I abandoned him—all unanswered.

Because I'm a coward.

> **Daddy Xan:** *Call me right away.*
> **Daddy Xan:** *I need to know you're ok.*
> **Daddy Xan:** *Baby answer me.*
> **Daddy Xan:** *Please.*

I've really messed this up.

A light knock on the door had me quickly hiding my phone under the pillow. "Butch?" My mother's voice sounded strained. "May I come in?"

I sighed, but obediently stood and walked to the door. When I opened it, I found my mother looking as disheveled as I'd ever seen her—her eyes puffy and red-rimmed, as if she'd been crying.

What the...

"You didn't kill him, did you?" she whispered, clutching the front of my shirt and searching my face for the answer.

"I... I took care of the problem," I haltingly replied, unsure what the correct answer was at this moment.

Whose side are you on?

"You didn't," she stated as she entered the bedroom and shut the door behind her, sounding relieved. "You'd be in much worse shape if you did."

I crossed my arms over my chest. "How would you know what shape I'm in? You know nothing about me."

She flinched, but nodded. "It's true that I haven't been the most attentive mother..." Her gaze drifted to the window, traveling a million miles away before returning to meet mine again. "But I know how it feels to lose one's *inventus.*"

Something buzzed beneath my skin—a recognition. "What's an *inventus?*" I asked, although I had a feeling I already knew.

Xander.

My mother sighed as she sat on the bed, gesturing for me to join her. "An *inventus* is a superhero or villain equal to you in every way—able to receive any power you have to give, and return it in full. This closed circuit creates formidable teams, and sometimes the deep connection turns into more—making the pair truly undefeatable."

She swallowed hard, clearly struggling to continue. "These power couples are usually seen as a threat to the established hierarchy, so many seek to destroy them. Somewhere along the line, it was discovered that if you cut ties between two *inventus* early enough, they won't bond completely. The way to do that is to… kill one of them."

Fuck.

I dropped my head down, suddenly nauseous. "That's what father was trying to do—stop my connection with Xander from happening. What kind of man *does* that?!"

"The kind who's done it before," she murmured sadly. "Your father eliminated my *inventus* so he could marry me instead—to create the strongest heir." When she saw my horrified expression, she huffed a laugh. "It's simply how the game is played, darling."

This game is bullshit.

"So, what are you saying?" I growled. "If Xander was a *woman*, our relationship would be approved of—because then he could pop out supe babies to continue the proud Holt bloodline?"

She pressed her lips together and rose to leave, apparently finished with our heart to heart. "The only way it would be acceptable to your father is if you were both heroes."

Or villains…

My phone buzzed from under the pillow just as my mother left the room. I snatched it up, both hoping for and dreading another text from Xander.

Instead, it was from Kai.

> **Matchmaker:** *Did Xander murder you?*
>
> **Matchmaker:** *He showed up at my doorstep like a hot mess express and said I needed to take Meowson while he went to his parents' house for a few days. I asked where my favorite himbo was but he gave me that death look… you know the one.*
>
> **Matchmaker:** *C'mon, give me the tea from beyond the grave, bestie!*

I smiled, thankful Kai wasn't also worrying about me, and that Meowson was in good hands.

Scrolling through Xander's texts again, I almost replied, but then acknowledged I needed to grow a pair and go grovel in person.

Unfortunately, his location didn't just complicate things—it made them exponentially more dangerous. The Suarez compound was the last place I wanted to return to, especially now that I'd hurt one of their own. That I'd made it out of there alive previously was a miracle I didn't expect to see happen again.

With that in mind, I accessed my bank account and quickly emptied it before suiting up. Blowing out a slow breath, I realized this might truly be the end, but also knew it was the right thing to do.

It's time to show Xander the real me.

The man behind the mask.

CHAPTER 37
XANDER

I can't breathe. I can't breathe.

"Breathe, doofus," Violentia's snarky voice brayed from the doorway behind me. "Mother says if your boy toy was actually dead, you'd be in way worse shape."

"What the fuck does she know about it?" I rasped, lifting my head to sightlessly stare out the glass balcony doors, latching on to this kernel of hope. "She's an automaton lacking human emotion."

My sister snorted and came to join me on the bed. "Oh, come now, you fucking romantic. You don't think her and daddy dearest *lurve* each other?"

I almost threw up in my mouth. "One, I'm not even sure how they procreated, as I suspect father has an alien tentacle for a dick and two, never refer to him as 'daddy' again."

There's only one person I want to hear that word from.

What if I never hear him say it again?

"You're still not breathing," Vi sang out, delivering a punishing slap to my back to help me along.

Rising, she stalked to the balcony doors on towering heels before flinging them open and stepping outside. "Let's air this place out, little bro. It smells like dirty socks and depression in here."

She sounds like Kai.

I wish Kai was here to pet my hair again.

My thoughts were both dizzyingly full and frighteningly empty. Although I'd already exhausted every avenue to locate Butch, I was methodically scheming a dozen more—determined to track him down. At the same time, my survival instincts had kicked in, to the point that I was perilously close to disassociating and pretending this nightmare wasn't happening.

This can't be happening.

After Captain Masculine shattered my world with a single sentence, my immediate response was to find the hero and put his head on a stake. Then I took a breath, reminded myself the supe was a notorious asshole who was probably just fucking with me, and tried to call Butch.

When he didn't answer the phone or reply to my next five texts, I raced back to my lair to get my car and drove to The Gloucester. The doorman tried to stop me, but when I informed him I was investigating a potential murder in his schmancy building, he quickly made himself scarce.

The threat of bad publicity will have that effect.

Kicking down Butch's condo door revealed a suspicious scene. It looked as if someone had blown through and rifled through his drawers before disappearing again—and I had a suspicion who it was.

Collapsing onto his ridiculous white couch, I pulled out my phone and accessed the app connected to the remote camera

I'd installed in his hallway after our first date. I replayed the footage, desperately hoping for a clue while mentally berating myself for being so distracted by Butch's hot muscles to not stay on top of monitoring the feed.

All I saw was Butch or Captain Masculine.

Going back through the last couple of weeks revealed both men coming and going, always from the stairwell to the door, although days would pass when neither showed up at all. The last sighting of Captain Masculine was only a few minutes after I'd confronted him on the beach, meaning he'd come directly here.

Probably to remove any lingering evidence.

Now I understood why Butch never seemed to want to return to his condo—why he was *shaking in fear* when we were driven to Solomon Biggs' office. That he'd had been constantly bullied by the famous supe, including while we were together, made me see red.

I vowed to punish the Captain severely, even if it turned out he hadn't killed the love of my life. There were no signs of a struggle—or an incinerated body—so I deduced that whatever happened to Butch took place at a different location than his condo.

That left Biggs Enterprises as my next stop, but I barely made it through the front door before security appeared. I couldn't seem to access whatever badass windpower I'd conjured against Vortexio, but it still took six of the jacked up normies to drag me outside.

After that, I was at a loss. I couldn't call the police because they were in Biggs' pocket, and a Google search for the name Hawthorne in this state brought up nothing.

It's like he's a ghost.

So I called my mother—the last person I'd ever expect sympathy or comfort from, and she met those expectations. After listening to me tearfully relay what happened, she suggested I come to the compound. Before I could express my gratitude, she briskly added that I should bring my ray gun project with me, since my father wanted to see what I'd accomplished so far.

Thanks, mom.

"MOTHERFUCKER!" Violentia abruptly shrieked, and my startled gaze shot up in time to see her leaping over the balcony railing to the ground below.

From the shouts and chaos, it sounded like the entire compound had responded by the time I ran out onto the balcony to see what had sounded the alarm.

Captain fucking Masculine.

Ultra Violent and Captain Masculine were fighting hand-to-hand, although it looked more like the Captain was blocking her hits than anything. My mother was standing off to the side with her fingers on her temples, screaming at Vi to stop, and for my other siblings to stand down.

What the fuck is happening?!

Captain Masculine shoved Violentia off before saying something I couldn't make out, angrily gesturing at the house. Whatever he said made Vi stop attacking and cross her arms before vehemently shaking her head. When he tried to take a step toward the building, she blocked his path, and the resulting blue flames that danced over his suit were hot enough for me to feel from where I stood.

"I WANT TO SEE XAN!" he shouted, causing Vi to take a step back and my younger siblings to cock their heads in confu-

sion. The only ones who didn't look surprised by the familiarity were my mother and Wolfgang.

Wait...

Time seemed to slow as I followed Violentia's lead and hopped over the railing. The seconds ticked by at half-speed as I slogged through molasses to reach the clearly unhinged—but oddly familiar—superhero raging on my family's front lawn.

He was hunched over and panting, his enormous muscles bulging through his uniform, practically begging for my tingling fingers to trace their recognizable shape. And when he spotted me—when those pretty blue eyes met mine with way more desperate love than two strangers should have for each other...

Oh, no.

Oh, fuck.

"Xan," he whispered, before reaching up and pulling his mask off his head.

"Oh, fuck," I repeated out loud as every red flag I'd ignored wildly flapped in the breeze.

Violentia spun to face me, her expression a mix of shock and admiration as she jabbed a thumb over her shoulder. "You've been fucking Captain Masculine this whole time?"

Apparently, yes.

Butch shoved his way past Vi and dropped to his knees at my feet. "Xan, I am so sorry. I couldn't tell you who I was at first because I thought you were a normie, and I didn't realize who *you* were until we came here for dinner. But I didn't tell you who *I* was that night because I was confused and afraid you wouldn't want to be with me anymore. Then I decided to go all in and figure out how this *could* work between us before coming clean. And then all that shit happened yesterday, and it just seemed easier to make you think I was dead then have you leave me once you realized what a monster I was… and now that I'm saying it out loud, I realize how fucking stupid it sounds. I'm just so sorry for everything, but especially for being such a selfish, cowardly, himbo dumbass."

My brain had stopped functioning. *I* was now an automaton lacking human emotion. For a moment, I wondered if one of my siblings would have to attach jumper cables to my nipples to kick-start my heart.

I really hope Dr. Ownit starts seeing patients again soon.

"You just swore. A lot," I absently mumbled, choosing to focus on *that* random detail for some inexplicable reason.

"Yeah," he huffed, driving the knife in deeper by *blushing*. "I think it's the company I've been keeping."

As my heart started revving up again, I felt the strangest sensation—like pure energy traveling through my veins, powered both from within and from somewhere outside of me.

From Butch.

"I thought you were dead." My voice sounded as hollow as I felt, although life was coming back to me again. I was empty of everything that wasn't *him*—as if he truly were the sun I needed to survive on this insignificant planet.

I thought I was dead, too.

He gazed up at me with tears in his eyes, looking as perfect as ever on his knees. "I know, and I'm sorry."

My hand moved of its own accord, gently cupping his cheek. As always, he briefly closed his eyes and leaned into my touch, trusting me completely, despite the dangerous villains surrounding him on all sides.

As we then stared at each other for an endless moment, and I realized I didn't care *who* Butch was. He could be a normie or a supe, a hero or a villain, Captain Masculine, or just someone who played him on TV—it didn't matter. It didn't change who he was to me.

Mine.

"I never want to feel that way again," I said, holding his gaze, wordlessly sharing every ounce of bottomless love I had for him.

"Well, then you won't enjoy this," my mother sighed. "Wolfy?"

Before I could react, Wolfgang was standing behind the man I loved, and before I could stop him, he removed his glove and placed his hand on the top of Butch's unprotected head.

CHAPTER 38
XANDER

I woke up screaming, momentarily confused to find myself sprawled on the Suarez living room couch with Wolfgang lounging in the chair across from me.

Killkillkillkill...

"You fucking piece of shit!" I snarled, diving for my brother with both hands aimed for his throat.

He barely had time to leap over the back of the recliner before I collided with it. "Do you have a death wish or something?!" he shouted up at me from where he'd landed on the floor. "Don't touch me, you imbecile."

"You. Killed. Him," I gritted out, glaring down at him and wondering if I could successfully smother The Hand of Death with enough throw pillows between us.

"I did no such thing," he huffed, standing and indignantly brushing himself off. "I simply incapacitated him so *mother* wouldn't put him on ice. The intensity of my powers is affected by my opponent's strength, so I made sure not to touch him for too long."

This random intel pulled me out of my blind rage. "You… what?"

How did I not know this?

He sighed, incredibly put out by this entire situation, apparently. "Yes. As you know, when I touch another supe, I'm draining their life force. With someone as strong as Captain Masculine—*Butch*—I would probably have to maintain contact for a good five to seven minutes to truly kill him. With *you*,"—he sniffed, eyeing me judgmentally—"it would be more like two. Although, you're probably stronger now that you've met Butch."

Wolfgang tapped a gloved finger against his bottom lip to consider, as if I wasn't currently murdering him with my eyeballs.

"If Butch is safe, then where is he?" I hissed, near-feral with the need to be close to him.

I'm going to finally kidnap him and leave this goddamn circus behind.

"Mmm, I'm not sure how *safe* he is…" Wolfgang hedged, but took one look at my face and quickly elaborated. "He's in father's workshop."

Oh, my god…

"What the *fuck* is he doing down there?!" I shouted, panicking as I raced for the elevator.

To my surprise, instead of running in the opposite direction, Wolfgang followed me into the cab, still talking. "Well, father sensed we had a guest, and since he needed a test subject for that ray gun you brought over for him…"

OH, MY FUCKING GOD!

The elevator arrived at the basement level and I carefully squeezed past my brother to take off running again. I'd seen the various human remains from my father's lab rats, and the thought of Butch ending up as a similar pile of meat...

Please be okay, please be—

My breath rushed out in a whoosh as I stumbled through the workshop door. Butch was strapped down on one of the stainless steel operating tables in his supersuit, still passed out cold.

But still in one piece.

"You've arrived just in time," my father absently murmured as he fussed with *my* invention—the ray gun I'd created to extract microplastics from the Bay. The very piece of machinery I'd then reconfigured to extract DNA from a living thing.

The one currently aimed at Butch.

Stay calm, stay calm, stay calm...

Violentia, Baltasar, and the twins were standing off to the side with my mother, who was proudly watching her husband be a sociopath. Vi was picking at her nails while my younger brother tossed a skull fragment into the air like it was a baseball. The twins were staring at Butch, although Gabriel snuck a wary glance my way—rightfully so, since their hypnotism powers were probably to blame for putting me to sleep.

Little creeps.

Wolfgang strolled in and positioned himself on the opposite side of the room, his unnerving gaze fixed on me. Waiting.

"Xan?" Butch groaned as he regained consciousness. Before I could speak, he realized he was in a Very Bad Situation and immediately panicked, struggling against his restraints while his wide eyes frantically darted around the room. "Oh, my god! I'm sorry, Xan. I'm sorry, I'm sorry, please don't do this…"

Shitshitshit!

"No, baby, nooo, you did nothing wrong," I ran to his side, trying to soothe him despite the fifty shades of fucked up we were in. "I didn't do this—I would *never*. But I'm going to get you out of here, okay?"

"You're not," my father casually remarked, stepping into Butch's line of sight. "I'm ready to commence this experiment and I simply don't have the patience to find another body."

Butch was staring at my father as if the Grim Reaper himself had appeared to take him away. This was appropriate, since most supes who saw Apocalypto Man didn't last long.

I'll save you, baby.

"Father," I used every last tattered shred of self-control to keep my voice steady. "I didn't have the chance to test the device on a living creature before and, uh… I'd rather we *not* do it on someone I care about. Someone I *love*."

He looked at me in surprise, and for one stupid moment, I thought he might care. "Oh, Xander, don't concern yourself with that." He waved a dismissive hand as he turned and walked away. "I'm sure I'll be able to put the DNA *back* into Captain Masculine after I extract it. Now, I suggest you move out of the way so you don't get vaporized if something goes wrong."

"No," I calmly spoke, reaching behind me to grab Butch's shaking hand. My father stopped mid-step and turned to face me, an incredulous smile twitching his lips.

"Xander…" my mother warned, annoyed by my existence more than anything. "Your silly attachment to this *hero* is making this family look weak. Step aside and let your father work."

Not a chance.

"Why are you not moving?" Apocalypto Man asked, his gaze flickering to my mother before returning to me—mild annoyance quickly being replaced by dangerous predatory intent.

I gave Butch's hand a squeeze to let him know I wasn't going anywhere. "Because he's *mine*," I growled. "And I won't let you hurt him."

"This is fascinating to witness!" My father grinned, looking me over with genuine interest before addressing his wife. "It reminds me of our old friends Iron Axe and Smoldering Siren, hmm?"

Isn't Siren Butch's mother?

Butch's hand had become uncomfortably hot, and I realized he was trying to subtly use his firepower to melt the special straps holding him down—another one of my inventions. It wasn't working, probably because Wolfgang had drained too much of his power to go full throttle.

I'll just give him some of mine.

Wait, what?

How can I give him power I don't have?

Glacial Girl scoffed and rolled her eyes, but her full attention was on her husband. "Well, Franco was an idiot to think switching sides would save him. Regardless, Siren survived his death at Vortexio's hand. Xanny will live through this, too."

Butch had my hand in a death grip, and I willed myself to somehow send the unfamiliar energy fizzing through my veins his way, praying I was doing it correctly. I gasped as a blast of power was returned to me, ten times stronger than before, buzzing beneath my skin like angry hornets, ready to swarm and sting.

My father's gaze snapped to where Butch and I were joined, as if he sensed what was happening. "Stop," he commanded —*his* immeasurable power now thrumming through the workshop, making my teeth chatter.

I almost laughed at how absurd it all was—how *I* was suddenly facing down one of the deadliest villains who'd ever lived, father or not. Apocalypto Man casually lifted his hand to destroy us, and I tensed before realizing I could finally take him on.

This is not how it ends.

"No," I repeated, raising my hand as well. His infamous cryonic power hit me like a freight train, dry ice and antifreeze blasting into my veins, but somehow, I tossed it right back at him.

Apocalypto Man's eyes widened in alarm, his mouth forming a comical o-shape as his body froze in place, although his mind would continue to scream from its eternal prison.

Fuck around and find out, dad.

"*How DARE you!*" my mother shrieked as she unleashed a jagged wall of solid ice in my direction.

I threw dozens of ice daggers in return, slicing through her wall and embedding in her skin, sending her screaming to the workshop floor.

My siblings scattered in the chaos. The twins fled from the room—rightfully assuming they were next—Baltasar backed away with his hands raised in surrender, and Violentia ran to Glacial Girl's side to tend to her injuries.

Spinning, I prepared to fight off Wolfgang next, but his predatory gaze was fixed on our mother. Specifically, on the blood dripping from her wounds.

Wounds I gave her.

"Xan," Butch croaked, and I looked down to find him pale and sweating, still afflicted by my brother's energy drain. "I'm not strong enough to get us out of here. You're going to have to do it."

"What am I supposed to do?" I hissed, even as I somehow melted the straps from his body with only my fingertips. He weakly sat up and clung to me, his fresh air scent and the achingly familiar feel of his muscles against mine making me shudder.

"Blast a hole through the wall and fly us out of here," he murmured against my neck. "Take everything you need from me."

"I-I don't know how," I stammered, noticing my mother rallying for another round with murder in her eyes.

"You do," he whispered, his enormous body going slack as his remaining strength faded. "You're my *inventus*."

Maybe it was my vast knowledge of Latin, but the word sent a bolt of recognition straight into my core. Trusting my instincts—and knowing Butch was counting on me to escape—I used all our points of contact to somehow siphon his famous firepower, feeling it fill my veins with red-hot lava.

Holy shit, this is incredible!

With a flick of my wrist, I sent a massive fireball through the wall, carving a path to freedom. Turning, I shot a smaller fireball at my ray gun. I cringed as my hard work went up in flames, but the last thing I wanted was for something I invented to be used to hurt Butch—or anyone who didn't deserve it.

I guess I have some morals, after all.

Taking one last look around my father's workshop of horrors, I met Wolfgang's gleeful gaze, unsure what to make of the salute he sent me as I somehow levitated—holding Butch in my arms—and flew us the fuck out of there.

CHAPTER 39
BUTCH

I woke up with a groan on an unfamiliar cot before frantically patting the bed around me for Xander.

Is he alive?!

"Everything's okay, baby. You're safe."

I almost wept in relief to hear Xander's smooth voice. Rolling over, I saw we were in a large warehouse space that was half science lab, half man cave—most likely his lair. The enormity of being brought to this sacred place wasn't lost on me, but I already knew what we were to each other.

Xander was perched on a metal stool several feet away in his Doctor Antihero supersuit, his amber eyes assessing every inch of me.

Sugar, he looks good in that suit.

"I see you over there, undressing me with your eyes," he said with a smirk before sobering. "How are you feeling, sweetheart?"

Xander had previously made it clear he didn't want me to feed him bullshit, so I closed my eyes and took stock. "I feel mostly back to normal. A little tired." I met his gaze again as I sat up. "A little starved for cock."

Just as I'd hoped, he gave me *that look*, although he quickly huffed a laugh and shook his head. "This is wild. I can't believe I've been fucking Captain Masculine... or that I ever thought you were a normie. What is wrong with me?"

Nothing. You're perfect.

"I have years of experience hiding my powers from civilians, and I thought you were a normie, too—up until your family's dinner." I softly smiled, almost to myself. "Who knew I was actually with the man of my dreams this whole time?"

Oh, shoot... I didn't mean to say that out loud.

Xander cocked his head. "What do you mean?"

My cheeks were going up in flames, even as my dick hardened beneath my supersuit. "Well, I've kind of had this ridiculous crush on... Doctor Antihero," I stammered. "It's why I was always hanging out around the Bay. I liked watching you work—liked messing with you."

I am such a dork.

He snorted. "I thought you were trying to *kill* me. You blew up my favorite WaveRunner."

I grimaced. "I was just playing..."

He spread his legs, revealing the conversation was having the same effect on him. "You're so fucking cute, trying to flirt." Licking his lips, he palmed his dick through his suit. "It's too bad we didn't meet as supes. I've been so careful with you—thinking you were going to break. All this time, we could have been having angry hero-villain sex."

Oh my god, I want that!

I whimpered, and he chuckled darkly. "You like that idea, huh? You wanna play superheroes with me?"

When all I could do was breathlessly nod, all humor left his face. "Very well. I want you on your knees. Then I want you to crawl to me." He smirked as I immediately dropped to the floor. "And baby? Don't you *dare* come in your suit before you get here."

"Yes, Daddy," I replied, even though there was a strong possibility I wouldn't make it.

Especially if he calls me his good boy…

Blessedly, Xander didn't utter those words, but he did something just as dangerous. He pointed at the floor in front of his stool.

And snapped his fingers.

"Crawl."

I obeyed with a moan, keeping my gaze locked on his as I slowly approached. The truth was, I already would have crawled for this man. So him commanding me to do it—with the reward being his dick down my throat—was just icing on the cake.

"So perfect," he praised as I reached him. "Now show this evil villain just how *starved* you are."

For a second, I wasn't sure what he wanted, but then he slid his shiny black boot along the rung of the stool, positioning it in front of my face.

"Lick it."

Oh. My. God.

Without hesitation, I dragged my tongue from the toe of his boot all the way up to where it ended below his knee. I tried to keep my gaze on his face, but the smell of the leather, the feel of it sliding under my tongue, and the knowledge that he was as hard as I was for him had my eyes rolling back in my head.

"Fuuuck," he groaned, fumbling with the hidden zipper on his suit and wrestling his dick free. "I'm going to fucking blow if I watch you do that again. Up on your knees, sweetheart. Get that mouth on my cock, quick!"

You don't have to tell me twice.

Scrambling to my knees, I grabbed the base of his shaft and swallowed him whole. I wasn't just starved, I was ravenous—desperate to work him down my throat until my lips pressed against the green supersuit I'd fantasized about more times than I could count.

"Look at you," Xander growled, roughly gripping my hair with both hands. "Look at what a slut you are." He gave a violent thrust, making me gag. "My superhero cumslut, addicted to villain cock."

He's not wrong.

"Get your cock out. Then put your hands flat on my thighs." He waited until I was in position before starting up a rhythm, still holding my face tightly against him. "First, I'm going to fuck this pretty mouth, and then I have plans for the rest of you."

Yes, please.

If I'd thought Xander was rough with me before, it was nothing compared to how he handled me now. He pummeled into me from below, unrelenting, his hands painfully buried in my hair, dick so far down my throat he was cutting off my airway. Praising me the entire time.

Making me whole again.

"Fuck, yes, baby, you're doing so good. Listen to those slutty little moans. Choking on my cock like you'll die without it. I think you like being treated like a toy, don't you? It's like your only purpose in life is to be my little fucktoy."

It's all I want.

With tears streaming down my face and my drool beading on Doctor Antihero's waterproof suit, I was in heaven.

Xander suddenly lifted me off until only the head of his cock was still in my mouth. "Suck it out of me," he commanded. "And don't swallow."

I hummed with pleasure, suctioning my lips around him as he jerked off onto my tongue, exploding with a guttural groan. He immediately withdrew, and I snapped my mouth shut, feeling cum dribble down my chin as I struggled to hold it all in.

"So fucking messy," he murmured appreciatively, pulling me up to stand between his legs. "C'mere, baby. Give Daddy a kiss."

Placing a firm hand on the back of my head, he brought my lips to his, opening up to me with a contented sigh. Then he gripped both our dicks with his other hand, stroking us together—that hot as hell foreskin sliding against my shaft—while *drinking his own cum from my mouth.*

Holy fuck fuck fuuuuck!

I came so hard I stopped breathing, trusting Xander to keep me upright as I coated the front of his supersuit with all I had.

"Oh, my god. Oh, fuck," I panted, gazing down at Doctor Antihero's beautiful green suit covered in our combined release.

I can die happy now.

"Mmm, I love it when you get so worked up that you swear," he smirked, running a thumb over the mess on my bottom lip before popping it into my mouth. "And I love you all dazed and sloppy like this... when I know I'm about to fuck you in the ass."

What..?

Before I could fully absorb what he'd said, Xander spun me around and roughly tossed me to the floor. I fell to my hands and knees as he landed behind me, ripping my suit wide open in the back, exposing everything to him.

"What's your safe word, baby?" he demanded before spreading me wide and delivering a long lick from my balls to my hole—causing me to simultaneously clench shut and open for him, begging for more.

"Orca," I whispered, trying to fuck myself on his tongue as my dick rallied for another round. Feeling Xander back off, I looked over my shoulder and moaned to see him swiping a hand through the mess on his chest before using it to lube us both up.

I love how filthy he is.

"I assume you won't say it," he chuckled as he lined himself up. "Because you *want* me to fuck you as hard as I can, like the villain slut you are."

Helplessly whimpering, I lowered myself down to my elbows, dropping my forehead to the warehouse floor. "Yes, Daddy. Fuck me like I deserve to be fucked."

Xander ran his hand down my spine—a loving caress. "I'll give you everything you deserve, baby. Always." Then he brought his hand down on my ass with a resounding slap and I almost came on the spot.

Is he spanking me?!

"I thought I'd fucking lost you," Xander snarled, wrapping a hand around my waist to hold me in place as he delivered a thrust so deep I yelped. The sound turned into a groan as he spanked me again on the same spot as before, the sharp sting of contact lighting me up. "I was about to burn down this entire fucking city to find you and kill everyone who'd played a role in taking you from me."

Tears were blurring my vision again, only this time it was sorrow for the grief I'd unnecessarily caused him. The emotion was quickly replaced with gratitude for how he took care of me like no one ever had before.

How he never would have let me go.

"You are mine," he continued, picking up the pace until I could barely hear him over the sound of our skin slapping through our suits—of his hand spanking me raw. "You are mine because you deserve to be mine. You deserve everything I have to give you. And if you ever feel like you *don't*, you need to *tell* me, so I can remind you why you do."

"Yes, Daddy," I sobbed, nearly overwhelmed by the sensations coursing through me—his thick cock stretching me, the burn on my ass from his palm, his hand holding my waist so tightly, reminding me I was *his*.

Everything I was experiencing converged into one tangled mess of emotions, only to have his love instantly smooth it all away. "I deserve you," I gasped. "I deserve everything you give me."

From the moment Xander walked through the diner door, I'd sensed how inextricably connected we were—felt it in the depths of my soul. Discovering we were fated to be together simply made the last puzzle piece snap into place of what I already knew to be true.

He's my home.

Xander curled himself over me, grinding slow and deep as he emptied himself with a moan. The feel of his dick pulsing inside me had me coming again, leaving a puddle beneath me I immediately collapsed into.

I really do like playing superheroes....

Gently lifting my head, my *inventus* captured my lips with a lazy kiss that I devoured in return. "I love you, baby. You'll always be mine, no matter what."

Always.

CHAPTER 40
XANDER

I set down my phone on the examination table, staunchly ignoring the twenty texts Kai replied with when all I asked for was an update on Meowson.

After fucking Butch until he passed out on my cot again, I'd spent the morning ordering everything we needed to hole up here for a while.

Including a bigger bed.

I was fairly certain my lair hadn't been compromised. At least, I hoped that was true. My mother was especially impatient when it came to revenge. It stood to reason she would have shown up by now to turn us into ice sculptures if she knew where we were.

And if my father had pinpointed our location—through the same creepy mind-meld powers he used to learn about my ray gun—I had to assume he was still too incapacitated to spill the intel.

Fuck, I hope he's still frozen...

The idea of Apocalypto Man on our trail caused icy dread to pool in my gut, never mind Glacial Girl and the rest of my siblings. On top of the threat of my immediate family was the vast network of villains—and unsavory normies—the Suarez clan had aligned with over the years.

The more I thought about how *alone* Butch and I were in this fucked up situation, the more anxious I became.

I need to keep it together for his sake.

As if on cue, a still sleepy and still so fuckable-looking hero appeared beside me, his stealth-to-size ratio reminding me yet again how ridiculous it was that I ever believed he was a normie.

"Good morning... or, afternoon..." he mumbled, sweetly kissing me on the cheek before squinting at the heavily tinted, earthquake proof windows facing the Bay.

He tossed his phone on the table next to mine. "Dead," he stated. "Not that I want to see who's been trying to get a hold of me, but I should probably charge it."

I gestured toward my charging station and may have watched him walk away with way more supervision than was necessary

That. Ass.

When he turned and caught me staring, I smirked, unable to resist. "It looks like your suit survived being turned into a glory hole, hmm?"

This comment made him enticingly blush, and for a moment, my anxiety switched gears to worrying about whether he'd ever get so desensitized to my bullshit that he stopped looking so pink and pretty.

I'll just have to find new ways to shock him.

"My suit is self-healing and administers first-aid," he explained with a shrug before eyeing me warily. "I get torn up a lot."

Instead of reminding Butch who tore him up the most, I was hit with the reality of who he was and what he faced regularly. If you didn't count my recent altercations with Vortexio and my parents, I'd never taken on another supe—never could—but the man standing before me was numero uno on every villain's shit list within a hundred-mile radius.

This realization made my stress levels skyrocket through the fucking roof.

I think I'm going to be sick.

Because he was a perfect little psychic cinnamon roll, Butch was immediately at my side, cocooning me in glorious muscles and fresh, ocean air. "You're worrying about me," he murmured into my neck. "Please don't."

I huffed. "It was a lot easier when I only had to deal with the slim chance of my sweet, innocent normie getting caught in supe crossfire I was never involved in, anyway."

He lifted his head so he could meet my gaze, his expression as serious as I'd ever seen it. "Yes, but now I have *you* to protect me."

My jaw nearly dropped to the floor. Instead of pointing out the obvious—that Captain fucking Masculine could take care of himself—Butch was implying *I* could somehow save him from our enemies, who were multiplying by the minute.

"W-what the fuck am I gonna do?" I choked out. "I have nothing to—"

"Stop it," he snapped, grabbing both of my hands in his. "Does *this* feel like nothing?"

I gasped as scalding flames and punishing winds shot through my veins—unfamiliar sensations Butch had experienced since birth now dancing at my fingertips, begging me to play.

How does he not implode from the overstimulation?

"That's not me!" I vehemently shook my head, even as the euphoria of whatever was happening tried to tell me otherwise. "This power is all yours."

He sighed, his eyelids fluttering like he was getting off on it. "No, it's not. It's amplified—cycling back to me tenfold. My powers have *never* felt this strong before, and when you were blasting your mother with ice and your father with… whatever the heck that was, those powers became accessible to me, too. This is incredible. *You're* incredible."

I snatched my hands away as panic bubbled up in my chest. "But I don't know what the fuck I'm doing to make it happen. I tried to recreate the windpower I threw at Vortexio when security dragged me out of the Enterprises building, but I wasn't able—"

Butch stumbled backward, all color draining from his face. "What did you say? When did you fight my father?!"

Oh, shit.

"Yeah…" I grimaced, rubbing the back of my neck and realizing just how insane the past couple of days had been. "When your dear old dad pulled me out of Biggs' office, he took me up to the roof and tried to toss me off with some wind. When that didn't work, he told me *Captain Masculine* was the one leaving bruises on you. Clearly he was fucking with me…"

I trailed off as Butch released an inhuman sound, like an injured animal backed into a corner, ready to bite the first person dumb enough to approach.

"That fucking bastard set us up," he snarled. "The entire reason I was at our beach when you confronted me in uniform was because my boss suddenly ordered me to kill Doctor Antihero—right after my father privately met with him."

The realization that Vortexio knew who I was, both in and out of uniform, sucked all the pleasure out of hearing Butch swear and refer to the cove as 'our' beach.

I should kill the man for that alone.

"Why does your father care so much about us?" I ran a hand through my hair, desperate for this to make sense. "Besides the fact that his only son is banging a villain with a huge cock instead of some respectable hero chick."

Butch swallowed hard, although he looked slightly less rabid. "We're not just *banging*, Xan."

"Oh, baby, I know…" I immediately closed the distance between us to get my hands on those muscles again. "I'm sorry, I didn't mean it like that."

"I know you didn't." He smiled, although he still looked nervous. "What *I* mean is… the reason my father wants to keep us apart is because of the connection we share. It's also probably because—"

Before Butch could say more, someone knocked on the warehouse door.

Not the door near the loading dock—where any deliveries I'd arranged would arrive—but the door camouflaged so completely from the outside that not even supe-vision would help you find it.

NOT ALL HIMBOS WEAR CAPES

Who the fuck is out there?

And why are they bothering to knock?

Butch tensed as I brought up the app for both the camera and weapons aimed at the single square-foot of space outside the door—along with whoever tracked us down.

Wolfgang.

Somehow, my older brother was outside my lair, *waving* his Hand of Death directly at my hidden camera in that naturally creepy way of his.

When I simply gaped at the live feed on my phone, he dropped his hand and knocked again, tapping out the secret rhythm he, Violentia, and I used as kids to collectively exclude our younger siblings from whatever we were up to.

Oh, now he's just not playing fair.

I *knew* it was stupid to open my door to anyone right now—especially a member of either of our families—but when I glanced at Butch, he firmly nodded, and that gave me the confidence I needed.

It's two against one, after all.

With a few taps on my phone, the door swung open, and Wolfgang strolled inside as if this were nothing more than a friendly social call. Butch took my hand as the door slammed shut, allowing that almost orgasmic energy flowing between us to amplify.

Of course, my brother's gaze immediately snapped to the source of our connection, but instead of looking concerned, he smiled in triumph.

Which is way creepier than him waving.

With the air of someone who'd never been afraid a day in his life, Wolfgang began casually wandering around my lair, being nosey as fuck—no doubt trying to psych me out. Just as I was about to send a borrowed fireball up his ass, he dropped onto the couch and slung an arm over the back.

"Father's dead," he calmly spoke, meeting my gaze with the ghost of a smirk curling his lips. "I killed him myself."

CHAPTER 41
BUTCH

Even if Xander and I weren't so intrinsically connected, I would have felt his panic over Wolfgang's revelation. Apocalypto Man was a nearly unkillable supe, so if the man sitting before us had ended him, we both should be very, very afraid.

But I wasn't.

I may have only recently acknowledged how messed up my personal situation was, but I knew how our world worked. Any show of weakness was a death sentence. Supes were already the dominant species on earth, but within our cutthroat ranks, it was survival of the deadliest. Only those willing to do what was necessary survived.

Kill or be killed.

"What?" Xander finally choked out. "How? Supes *can't* kill their parents. It's biologically impossible."

Wolfgang spread his hands wide with a flourish. "And yet, here we are. All thanks to you."

My mind was whirring, already considering the possibilities of this bombshell. Only interested in the facts. "Tell us how you did it."

The smile that stretched across Wolfgang's face was villainous. "You're getting more intriguing by the day, Butch." When Xander growled possessively, he rolled his eyes. "Oh, calm down. He has too many muscles for my taste, but I appreciate his bloodlust."

His attention snapped back to my face. "That's why you're asking, right, Captain? You're thinking this might be your chance to overthrow your handlers?"

Internally, I bristled, but I impassively held his gaze. "It's how the game is played."

He smirked and licked his lips. If it wasn't for the psychotic glimmer in his eyes I didn't fully trust, I may have smiled back. "To answer your question, I took advantage of our father's sudden paralysis to sneak down to the workshop overnight and drain him dry."

Like a spider feasting on a fly caught in its web.

Xander gaped at him. "Fuck. That was a ballsy gamble. If it hadn't worked—"

"I knew it would," Wolfgang nonchalantly replied. "Because you drew blood on our mother by throwing her power back at her. If the stories told were correct—about a supe's parents being invincible—you shouldn't have been able to do that." He sniffed judgmentally. "If you'd possessed better aim, you could have sent an icicle through her heart."

"Jesus, Wolfy!" Xander laughed humorlessly. "Why not just say you were using me as an expendable grunt to take the hit if something went wrong?"

It was his brother's turn to scoff. "That accusation is unfounded and, quite frankly, rude. I've been simply biding my time for your powers to re-emerge, so you can finally bring something more to the Suarez name than a loophole for killing normies."

The silence in the warehouse was deafening. Despite being dragged into their villainy, Xander had hinted at his low-ranking status within his family. What I kept getting stuck on was how incredibly unusual it was for *any* supe family—hero or villain—to bother raising a powerless child.

Unless that's exactly what made them useful…

Besides outing another's true identity, it was the worst crime imaginable for a supe to purposefully kill a normie. Punishments ranged from banishment and status-stripping to execution, depending how well-connected you were.

A family as well-known as Xander's somehow kept their noses clean, despite Biggs Enterprises having an entire file cabinet of unsolved murders we'd been trying to pin on the Suarez clan for over a decade.

All this time, they had an unregistered, seemingly powerless supe doing their dirty work for them.

"Baby, I…" Xander turned to face me, looking as unsure as I'd ever seen him. "I have a lot of blood on my hands. I promise you, they were all the lowlife scum that my family dealt with… Not that it makes it any better, I'm sure…"

He thinks I won't still love him.

I huffed a laugh and reached up to gently stroke his face. "Xan. Do you know how many villains I've killed in only the past year since I took this job?"

"Seventy-seven," Wolfgang piped in, although his gaze was fixed on how I caressed his brother's face—fascinated. When he saw he'd captured my attention, he shrugged. "I enjoy following kill stats."

Even though Wolfgang was hovering nearby, I *needed* to reassure Xander—to make sure he knew his past didn't change a thing. "Every one of those kills was ordered by Biggs Enterprises, and I never once questioned whether they deserved to die. The only time I didn't follow through on an assignment was with Doctor Antihero…"

My breath caught as I recalled our confrontation on the beach —how wrong it could have gone—but I rallied for his sake.

"Before you get angry on my behalf, you should know that I wasn't only following orders because it was written into my contract. I also *enjoy* killing—way more than I used to think a hero should. So, there is nothing you could do, or have done in your life that I won't like. Especially if *you* also enjoyed it."

I wanted to add how hard I got just thinking of Xander with actual blood on his hands, but we had a very attentive audience at the moment.

One who probably likes to watch.

Xander released a shaky breath, even as he maintained a stoic expression. "Both Biggs and the USN could come for me over my body count now that I'm a confirmed supe. My mother might even throw me under the bus."

I scoffed. "Let them try it. In the end, it was your *parents* who kept your existence a secret, even if they didn't know you had powers…"

Wait a minute…

"Did you say *RE*-emerge?" I spun toward the couch as Wolfgang's earlier words finally registered.

The Hand of Death wore an expression that was probably the closest he came to a pity. "Yes. Xanny's had powers since he was born. However, I'm the only one who ever saw them in action."

"Ex-fucking-scuse you?!" Xander shouted, rounding on his brother. "How do you know more about my powers than I do?"

Wolfgang made a judgmental noise. "Because you tried to *kill* me when you were barely out of diapers. Granted, I was trying to kill *you*, but you fought back by draining me in return. You somehow turned my power back on *me*, so I had no choice but to let you live."

White-hot rage raced through me, uncontrollably exploding outward in a fiery blast that, thankfully, Xander was immune to. "If you so much as *think* of touching him again, I will incinerate you until no one remembers you existed!"

Wolfgang hadn't even flinched at my threatening display, although a single bead of sweat ran down his temple from the heat.

"Okay, that was mildly attractive." He leaned forward with his elbows resting on his knees. "Listen, Butch. I wouldn't expect an *only child* to understand sibling dynamics, but I assure you, it was a one-time murder attempt. After that, Xanny became my little secret—to hide and protect—although I *did* vaguely mention his powers to our parents, for reasons…"

Xander cocked his head, approaching his brother despite my growl of discontent. "Our parents *knew* I had powers all this time? What did you tell them, Wolfy?"

Some sort of sibling understanding passed between them, as Wolfgang sighed and resolutely nodded. "I told mother and father I'd witnessed you moving objects with your mind. A bullshit parlor trick, but it was enough to keep them interested in you…"

He watched Xander carefully as he added, "I had to ensure they wouldn't kill you before you were strong enough to kill them."

Xander swallowed hard. "You think they would have killed me?"

His brother pressed his lips together. "I *know* they would have. A few years after my discovery, I overheard them discussing how to finally dispose of you. They believed you were powerless and therefore of no use to the family. But you weren't useless to me."

"Why would you save me?" Xander rasped. "Especially after we tried to kill each other?"

Wolfgang shrugged again, although his nonchalance seemed forced. "I saw a long-game opportunity, but only if I played it right. That your powers only came out when threatened caused me to suspect your abilities weren't exactly the same as mine—but even deadlier. It was only a matter of time before mother or father got around to killing you, so I bet on you being able to defeat them when that happened." His expression turned hard. "No one gets away with threatening my family."

Says the villain who just killed his father.

I shifted closer to my *inventus*, drawing Wolfgang's attention back to me. "So you've been planning your parents' deaths since you were a kid?"

His amber gaze snapped to mine, unnervingly similar to Xander's. "When Apocalypto Man and Glacial Girl brought me to the USN for the original hearing on supes registering their offspring, it wasn't because they wanted to cooperate. I was paraded through that building as a warning—to show the world what they had at their disposal if need be. I've only ever been treated as a weapon. What our parents didn't know was that I was harboring a weapon of my own."

Xander moved closer to his brother, making every instinct of mine howl in protest. "What sort of weapon am I, Wolfy?" His whisper seemed to echo in the cavernous space, and I held my breath for the answer along with him.

Wolfgang genuinely smiled. "You have the ability to return whatever energy is thrown your way, and to pull power from any supe nearby—regardless of whether they're attacking you. This makes you nearly undefeatable on your own, but now your power is shared and amplified between you and Butch. In fact, I believe it was finding your *inventus* that coaxed your powers out of wherever they've been hiding all this time."

He knows about having an inventus?

As Xander looked understandably stunned, I cut in, "Why give us this valuable intel? Why help us at all when we're such a threat to other supes—including *you?*"

Wolfgang stood and languidly stretched. "Because I know my limits, but I still want to be on top. You two are clearly fully bonded, and I want the most powerful supes in my corner. Think of it as repayment."

Xander looked dazed. "You saved my life when we were young—"

"So I could ensure mine would be protected later on," Wolfgang softly replied before glancing at me again. "It's how the game is played."

Opportunist.

"And what about me?" I hissed. Although I was grateful that Wolfgang saved Xander, and watched my back during their family dinner, I didn't appreciate his strong-arm approach to securing our loyalty. "Besides my villain kill stats—all sanctioned by Big City—what could you possibly have on me?"

Wolfgang started walking for the door. For a moment, I thought he wouldn't bother answering, but then he paused with his Hand of Death on the doorknob.

He swung the door wide, tossing a smirk over his shoulder that reminded me so much of Xander, I startled. "It's not what I *have* on you, but rather, what I can *do* for you. I hear you have a little problem, Butch. A pesky contract that could put a damper on obtaining legal rights to protect your *inventus* bond. It's been all over the news."

Wolfgang paused for dramatic effect. "Apparently, the entire city is on the hunt for a golden boy runaway groom."

CHAPTER 42
XANDER

"Ah, sugar," Butch muttered as Wolfgang shut the door behind him—turning to me with an apologetic look on his face. "I didn't get the chance to tell you... my parents made a deal with the Lincoln clan..."

I shut my eyes and blew out a shaky breath, willing myself not to murder everyone at this exact moment. Butch belonged to *me*, and no shady backroom deal could change that. Besides that, the only daughter the Lincolns had was Gemstonia, a supe whose abilities involved extracting gems from the earth to create energy-infused vapors.

Totally lame.

"Xan..." Butch pulled me down to sit on the couch with him, wrapping his enormous arms around my midsection as if he thought I might run away. "I swear, I didn't sign anything."

"I know, sweetheart," I sighed, suddenly exhausted. "I'm mostly frustrated that I don't fully understand any of this bureaucratic supe bullshit, since I've always been so far removed from it."

"And I've been purposefully left in the dark," Butch muttered sourly before switching to a hopeful expression. "Do you think your brother actually intends to help us?"

I hummed thoughtfully. Wolfgang may be a creepy fucker, but I'd never known him to lie. If everything he said today was true—and it definitely tracked—he had more reason to side with us than against us.

And he wouldn't have come here without an ace already in his pocket.

"My family has its own archive on supe history—one of the largest private collections in the world," I explained. "I've poked around a bit, especially when I was researching my lack of powers, but Wolfgang has mapped it, inside and out. So, yeah, if anyone knows how to get out of a supe-signed contract, it's him."

"Your archives must be how he knew what an *inventus* was," Butch mused, absently tracing my triceps with his fingertips.

I shifted on the couch to better look at him. "You used that word yesterday, when we were escaping my father's workshop. It means 'found' in Latin." I gestured vaguely. "Something that's been found—"

Butch tackled me to the cushions, successfully shutting down my lecture with his pillowy lips. I groaned as our tongues stroked each other—the movement echoed in how he rubbed his hard cock against mine, creating delicious friction through our suits.

All at once, I realized I'd never been *beneath* him before—never felt all this stacked muscle and pure power handling me like I belonged to *him*.

I could get behind this idea.

I'd established my role as a dominant top long before Butch came along, but just for a moment, I considered what it would feel like to be the one owned for a change—by this man specifically.

Maybe even in front of it...

"You found me," he gasped as he came up for air. "That's exactly what it felt like when we met—like I'd been *found.*"

I gripped his perfect face in my hands, feeling my sad rusty heart rattle to life again. "That's right, baby. I found you, I made you mine, and I'm going to keep you forever."

And anyone who thinks otherwise will die.

Butch stared down at me with such a vulnerable expression, I felt that same heart crack wide open to match.

"That easy, huh?" he whispered.

"That easy," I replied, without hesitation.

Another ripple of intoxicating power passed between us, and I fought to stay focused. "So where did *you* hear about this whole *inventus* thing?"

Butch frowned. "My mother, actually—right before I flew to your family's house to apologize. She explained it's what you call two equally strong supes who can create a closed circuit of power together. They're perfectly matched and undefeatable once they fully bond, which I'm assuming we did already, since you used my powers to get us out of Apocalypto Man's lair."

His gaze darkened. "Other supes try to kill one or both of them before that power-sharing happens... like my father apparently did to my mother's *inventus,* so *he* could claim her instead."

What the actual fuck?!

My stomach flipped. This was much bigger than Butch being a runaway groom, or scandalously shacking up with a villain who had a cock. This wasn't even about aligning powerful families with backroom betrothals. Vortexio wasn't just playing the game...

He's playing to win.

A fractured memory arose from the chaos of yesterday. "Didn't my parents mention your mother during that shitshow in the workshop? Something about Smoldering Siren losing someone named *Franco?*"

"Franco..." Butch muttered before sitting up and pulling me along with him as his excitement grew. "I know that name! When I took you to the USN archives, I snuck off to research whether heroes and villains could marry each other..."

Butch abruptly snapped his mouth shut and turned the most delectable shade of red. The revelation that he'd *also* been looking for ways we could legally be together made me feel something I rarely had before.

Happiness.

Deciding to give my hottie himbo a break from my teasing, I smiled conspiratorially. "I was secretly doing the same research while we were there," I stage-whispered. "Only I still thought you were a normie, so I struck out on my end. Supposedly, our supercharged dicks are hazardous to a fragile human's health."

He shyly peeked at me through his eyelashes, tempting me to destroy his supersuit again. "I know. I saw you," he murmured before sighing heavily. "Shoot, Xan, I should have just *told* you who I was right after that dinner. There's so much I wish I'd done differently with this entire situation. Instead, I kept messing things up—"

It was my turn to silence him with a kiss. "None of that. Yes, you've made some... *reckless* decisions." I paused to give him the stern look I knew he loved. "But you're what... 22 years old? Fuck, I'm surprised I'm still alive with the shit I was doing in my twenties, and that was *without* having the weight of an entire city on my shoulders. You're fucking amazing, Butch, and I'm going to tell you that every damn day until you believe it."

Since none of these other assholes bothered to.

He tried to drop his head, so I gripped his chin, forcing him to look at me. "That being said, I'm incredibly thankful I was at my family's compound when you flew there in full supe mode. Even more so that I got you out of there alive. From now on, we *discuss* major decisions first, so we can make a plan—together. It's you and me, and everyone else can go fuck themselves. Sound good?"

Those goddamn dimples appeared as he tried not to smile. "Yes, Daddy."

"Good boy," I purred, running my fingers through his soft hair. "Now tell me about your clandestine research on this Franco character."

He laughed and rose to retrieve his phone across the room. "Well, I didn't look too closely because I was trying to be sneaky, but I took photos of everything that was in the file."

Plopping back down onto the couch, he held the phone where I could see it and began scrolling through his photos. The documents covered a confidential court case from around 25 years ago, where an ex-villain named Franco Marisi was suing Big City for the right to marry a superhero named Tabitha Arella.

"Is Tabitha your mother?" I carefully asked, not wanting to upset him.

Butch grimly nodded. "Yeah, and I believe Franco was a hero named Iron Axe."

"Iron Axe..." I sat back to ponder. "You know, I think I might remember this from when I was a kid. Not the trial, but when Iron Axe switched sides. My mother was all up in arms over his 'defection'—ranting to anyone who would listen about what a traitor he was to other villains. Of course, she'd make it about her..."

"I didn't even know a supe *could* switch sides," Butch mused, squinting at the phone as he zoomed in on a photo. "Huh. It looks like it was Sylvano's father defending Franco on behalf of the USN. He's passed away, but maybe I could ask Sylvano if he knows anything."

"About the court case?" I distractedly asked, suddenly recalling how Wolfgang mentioned the USN previously being in strong support of heroes and villains being allowed to marry.

It might be time to reopen this petition.

"About switching sides." Butch's unexpected answer wrenched me from my thoughts.

"W-what?" I sputtered. "You can't be serious. I am the farthest thing from hero material, and I'm not just talking about my background and bloodline. Heroes *protect* people. I don't care enough about anyone other than you to give a shit what happens to them."

Butch shot me a *look* that eerily mirrored the one I often gave him. "Xan, you care *and* you protect—and not just me. Look at Kai! It didn't escape my notice that you told her to bring Meowson to *her* place this time instead of going to yours to feed him. You didn't want her getting caught in the crossfire if anyone came looking for you."

He's on to me.

He apparently also wasn't done listing my better qualities. "You faced off against both Vortexio and *Captain Masculine* on my behalf, even when you believed you didn't have powers. That's a level of bravery most don't possess. And let's not forget all the work you're doing to save wildlife in the Bay—not for recognition, but simply because you *care*. You are one of the most protective, caring, *heroic* men I've ever met, so stop pretending you're not."

A strange feeling washed over me—more profound than the *happiness* I'd felt earlier. It was as if all the ancient cracks in my heart were being patched up and smoothed over with pure, unadulterated *love*.

Gross.

But I'll allow it.

To my horror, I also felt myself *blushing,* so I quickly deflected. "I appreciate the pep talk, sweetheart, but don't get your hopes up. Not only would heroes start a riot if a Suarez tried to join their ranks, I'm not sure I have any interest in switching sides. Being a villain is much less regulated and therefore, much more fun."

Butch bit his bottom lip as he tried and failed to hide another cheeky smile. "I know. That's exactly why I want to become one."

CHAPTER 43
XANDER

Be still my heart.

"You... want to be a... villain?" I haltingly asked, unsure if I'd heard him correctly.

Butch excitedly nodded with that infectious golden retriever energy of his. "Sure do! Like you said, it's less regulated and if there's one thing I'm tired of, it's how micromanaged my life has been. Not to mention,"—he blushed again, but held my gaze—"if the main issue with us being together is that I'm a hero and you're a villain, then I'll switch sides in a heartbeat."

He'd give up everything...

Even though all I wanted was to take this hunk of man meat to the floor for another round, I forced myself to focus on our next steps. "Very well. How about you contact your friend at the USN? Find out what he knows about Franco's court case, supe marriage laws, anything he might have access to that would be useful to us."

I purposefully left off the suggestion that he ask Sylvano for information on switching sides. While Butch insisted he wanted that—and the idea of an eager little student of villainy made me hard as a rock—he had a history of rushing into things without thinking them through.

And I would prefer his reputation remained intact.

Although he was nodding along, Butch's expression had turned grim as he scrolled through the countless missed calls and unread messages on his phone. I could only imagine the verbal abuse he was receiving from his father, boss, and anyone else who thought they owned a piece of him.

All because he did something for himself for a change.

"Butch," I raised my voice, demanding his attention. "None of those fucking douchebags matter. Call Sylvano. Focus on *us*."

I could *see* the tension leave his body at my command, his pretty blue eyes turning dreamy as his gaze met mine. "Yes, Daddy," he replied, like the perfect little accidental sub he was.

Not accidental—just dormant until we met.

Like my superpowers, apparently...

I rose and walked away—to give Butch space as he called Sylvano, but also to collect my thoughts before I contacted Wolfgang.

Everything my brother had said was suddenly hitting me all at once. That we'd almost killed each other when we were young before he foiled our parents' plot to dispose of me. How Wolfy had been scheming for decades to not only murder our mother and father and ascend the Suarez throne, but align himself with fully-bonded *inventus* mates to ensure he stayed there.

Mostly, I was struggling to wrap my head around having powers at all, never mind supposedly undefeatable ones. I'd grown up powerless. I had no fucking idea what to do with the overwhelming sensations now stampeding through my veins. Powers that were magnified exponentially by my *inventus*—one of the strongest supes alive.

How can I be expected to do this?

When I faced Vortexio and my parents, I didn't have time to think, only act. In those tense moments, I'd somehow instinctively *known* how to return my opponents' energies, canceling out their attacks to protect myself and the man I loved.

It can't be that easy…

Can it?

Needing to distract myself, I decided to see what scandalous spin was being put on this 'runaway groom' story situation by the others involved. Grabbing my phone off the table, I brought up my news app—and immediately wished I hadn't.

Gemstonia Lincoln filled my screen. She was posing outside the Royal Cove Yacht Club, perfectly styled in her supersuit with such glittering tears in her eyes, I wondered if she'd conjured up actual diamonds.

"I-I thought we were in love…" Her voice wavered just enough to catch in her elegant throat, while remaining perfectly articulate for the mics. "Captain Masculine and I have been planning this wedding together since we were children—it's all either of us wanted…"

Doubtful.

She paused to dramatically dab at her eye with a monogrammed handkerchief. "I'm not sure if it was our parents finally signing off on our union that gave him cold feet, or if there's another woman, but I am absolutely heartbroken by his disappearance. I simply don't know how my family's reputation will ever recover from the shame of me being left at the altar."

Good lord, someone give this girl an Oscar.

The shot suddenly cut to the studio, where a nervous-looking news anchor was sitting across from a glowering Vortexio.

"Here to comment on Gemstonia Lincoln's statement is Captain Masculine's father, Vortexio—the former protector of our city, alongside Smoldering Siren." The anchor turned from the cameras to face the supe with a practiced smile. "Will Siren also be joining us today?"

"No," Vortexio replied, his expression leaving no room for further discussion.

The anchor cleared her throat. "The Lincolns have taken the stance that your son willfully abandoned their daughter, despite a recent agreement that the two heroes would wed."

What I wouldn't give to see that contract...

"Captain Masculine would never disgrace the Holt name by running away from his responsibilities. He has too much respect for his family, his fiancé's family, and the citizens of Big City." Vortexio's tone remained steady, but I could see the papers on the anchor's desk fluttering as his windpower stirred them up.

I also noticed how Vortexio's stony gaze was fixed on the camera, instead of on the woman speaking to him. There was no doubt in my mind he was saying this so Butch would *know* how incredibly disappointed he was in his only son.

This guy is the fucking worst.

A quick glance at Butch across the warehouse space showed he was still on the phone with Sylvano, so I returned my attention to Harold Holt.

"Despite what Gemstonia is boldly implying, my son did *not* willfully abandon their engagement," Vortexio gritted out, the entire stack of papers now blowing away in a mini-whirlwind. "He was kidnapped by a member of the villainous Suarez family—an *undocumented* supe that Biggs Enterprises has been monitoring for quite some time. Doctor Antihero."

Oh, this is bad.

Unless it's not...

"Hey!" Butch appeared at my side so abruptly, I almost dropped my phone in my haste to close the app. "So, Sylvano says he can meet us in two hours at the Rolling Meadows cemetery."

"That's not morbid or anything. Are we going to end up in a mob grave?" I was only half-joking, suddenly deeply suspicious about putting my faith in a normie I barely knew.

"I trust Sylvano almost as much as I trust you," Butch replied to my unspoken concern, running his fingertips down my arms again, soothing me. "He's never been quiet about opposing Solomon Biggs' goal to give heroes more rights than villains—"

Excuse me?

"That fucker," I hissed, incredibly tired of continuously discovering more layers in this stinking pile of bureaucratic bullshit. "What gives *Biggs* the authority to decide that? He is *nothing* without the supes he surrounds himself with. The way he acts like he *owns* you—"

"He *does* own me," Butch quietly interrupted. "At least on paper."

"Thanks to your parents," I growled, itching to march down to the news station and slice out Vortexio's entrails on live TV.

"He owns them too," Butch grimly added.

That shocked me into silence, so he continued, "Ever since the Biggs family founded Big City, they've had superheroes on the payroll. I obviously don't know all the specifics, but it's not the type of job we can just leave."

"What the... what the *fuck?*" I stammered, too confused and ragey to access intelligent words.

None of this made sense. Solomon Biggs—and his forefathers—were all normies... normies who were inexplicably given ultimate power over much more powerful beings somewhere along the line.

Something isn't adding up.

Determined to destroy at least one contract by nightfall, I tapped my phone awake and texted Wolfgang.

> ***Find out what the terms are in Butch's marriage contract.***
>
> ***Then take care of the problem.***

> ***Big Brother is always watching:*** *Have you decided what's in it for me?*

Blowing out a slow breath, I looked at Butch, who was watching me type over my shoulder.

Again, he gave me a single nod of approval, only this time, he smiled sweetly. "I trust you to know what's best, Xan. For me and for *us.*"

I simply stared at him, willing myself not to cry. Never in a million years would I have thought I'd find someone like Butch—that I'd experience this level of connection and understanding with another person.

Why did I ever think villains were incapable of love?

After taking a moment to sufficiently tongue-fuck Butch—since he was too tasty of a snack to resist—I returned my attention to making a deal with Death.

My inventus and I will have your back.

Until the next time we need you to get your Hand dirty.

Big Brother is always watching: Consider it done.

I had zero idea what Wolfgang was going to do, and from my experience, it was better not to ask.

As Butch led me back to the couch, I realized I needed to tell him about the statement his father gave. This made me drag my feet to delay the inevitable, but Butch gave me that rare, *calculating* look I now knew came from what he did for a living.

If you can call indentured servitude a living…

"What did you learn, Xan?" he bluntly asked, pulling me down to sit with him. When I hesitated again, he narrowed his eyes, making my dick twitch from the stern Daddy vibes *he* was giving off.

Jesus, maybe I'm a switch.

"I saw your father on the news," I spoke slowly, *really* not wanting to upset him. "He was commenting on Gemstonia's almost-accurate claim that you abandoned her for another woman."

Butch dropped his head back against the couch and sighed. "Let me guess—there was a lofty speech about how Captain Masculine would never run from his duty because of all the people in his life he'd horribly disappoint?"

I smiled sadly at this wonderful man who'd put up with way more mistreatment than he deserved. "Oh, you've heard that script before, huh? Well, he *did* add some extra pizzazz at the end by announcing that an unregistered Suarez villain named Doctor Antihero had kidnapped you."

"THAT FUCKER!" Butch yelled, startling me more with the swearing than the volume. "Fuck! I can't let you take the blame for this, Xan. We need to go public and tell the world who we are to each other—"

"Baby, baby…" I ran a hand down his broad chest—mostly for his benefit, but also mine. "Take a breath. Then repeat what *you* said to *me* when I was freaking out over the possibility of my identity being outed by my mother."

Obedient as ever, Butch took a couple of slow breaths and nodded. "I said to let her try it, because the fact she kept you a secret will only come back to bite *her* in the end."

"Yup!" I grinned, almost giddy with how this was playing out. "Vortexio doesn't know we've split from my family, or that Apocalypto Man is dead. He thinks publicly revealing this ace he's been holding on to since I was born will flush us all out."

Understanding washed over Butch's face. "But all it's going to do is piss off your mother enough to come for him, as Glacial Girl."

"Maybe we'll get lucky," I cooed, lowering my head to suck on his neck, marking him as mine—all mine. "Maybe they'll kill each other off."

It's how the game is played, after all.

CHAPTER 44
BUTCH

Xander's warehouse lair was cool, but I now understood what he meant by enjoying a smaller footprint. I didn't mind the vast square footage and high ceilings—especially as someone who could fly—but I didn't like how *far away* Xander seemed.

I miss his tiny apartment.

"Do you need something, sweetheart?" he murmured, a smile twitching his lips even as his eyes stayed glued to the microscope.

I knew I was unnecessarily crowding him, but couldn't help myself. "What are you doing? Can I help?"

Xander silently laughed before lifting his head to look at me. "I'm watching algae reproduce. It's not as salacious as it sounds, but it's distracting me until we leave to meet your USN contact." He paused before awkwardly adding, "My work always helps me decompress."

He's opening up to me!

It was a ridiculous thing to get excited about, but I'd realized how unnatural it was for Xander to share even the most mundane things about himself, so I'd take any crumb I could get.

"I usually go for a long flight to take my mind off things," I offered, squeezing myself into the small space between his metal stool and the worktable. "Obviously, that's not an option right now, so... I guess I just have some nervous energy that needs to get out."

Xander was giving me his full attention now, as unbothered as always by how needy I was behaving. "What about taking a nice hot shower?"

I canted my head from side to side. "Mmm, not as good as flying, but yeah, showers work. I do some of my best thinking in there—especially if I'm trying to solve a big problem."

His smirk was now in full bloom. "Good to hear, because I have a *huge* problem I was hoping you'd help me solve."

Welp... I walked right into that one.

I couldn't even be mad about it, since Xander was already herding me into the bathroom while expertly locating all the hidden zippers on my supersuit.

"Fuck, I miss your slutty gray sweatpants," he growled against my lips, yanking my suit down my chest like it offended him. "Such easy access to that even sluttier cock."

I whimpered and backed away so I could quickly peel off the rest of my suit. Xander did the same, maintaining eye contact the entire time, making just the act of undressing together unbearably hot.

We may need a cold shower after this.

He stepped into the massive walk-in shower—enclosed in glass, with luxurious dual rain shower heads and a smooth ceramic floor sloping to an enormous drain.

Perfect for washing away copious amounts of blood.

At this point, I fully embraced that my thoughts went *there,* and that doing so made my already throbbing dick weep precum. Xander noted the steady stream trailing down my shaft for a moment before turning on the shower and shifting his gaze to mine.

"Get in here," he commanded, gesturing for me to enter with a dick-twitching snap of his fingers. "On your knees with your back to the wall."

Yes, Daddy!

I instantly obeyed, stepping inside and dropping to my knees against the wall of glass. Xander immediately positioned himself in front of me with his dick in-hand, sliding back his foreskin and rubbing the smooth crown over my lips, smearing them with precum.

"You're so good," he praised, petting my hair while nudging my mouth open, letting me lap up the overflow. "So good for *me.*"

"I love being good for you," I gasped, gazing up at him, knowing he could see how much I meant it. "Only you."

Xander's eyelids fluttered closed as he released a contented sigh. "All mine. My perfect little slut—perfect for fucking." His eyes snapped open, gaze darkening. "Because that's what I'm going to do. I'm going to fuck your perfect mouth and come down your perfect throat while you choke on my cock."

Perfect.

"I love choking on your cock," I whimpered, full-body shuddering, half-feral with need.

He smiled down at me so adorably, I almost started crying. "I know you do, baby. That's why you're perfect."

Slipping his hand between the back of my head and the wall, he slowly slid his way into my mouth and down my throat, filling me completely. My jaw ached to accommodate him, but the feel of his silky hardness gliding over my tongue made me moan in pleasure.

Then I gagged.

"*There* it is... fuck," Xander groaned. "There's no way I'm gonna last long—not with my perfect slut so eager to drink my cum."

He paused for a moment to compose himself. "All right. Tap my leg three times if you want me to stop, and keep your hands off your cock. If you manage to not come before I do, I'll give you a treat."

I was shivering with anticipation, trying so hard to be good, but he wasn't moving yet, waiting to see if I'd tap out.

Not a chance.

To make it crystal clear how on-board I was, I leaned forward and gagged myself again.

"Very well..." he smiled wickedly. "Hold on tight, sweetheart."

Knowing just how I liked it, Xander was merciless from the very first thrust, pounding into me so hard, I was surprised we didn't crack the glass. Of course, he kept his hand planted behind my head, handling me with loving care even as he fucked my throat raw.

So perfect.

Maybe it was all my pent-up energy—or that I couldn't stop fantasizing about it—but I boldly skimmed my fingers up his muscular thighs until I reached the curve of his ass. Glancing up, I found him watching me with one eyebrow cocked in amusement, as if daring me to try.

Taking that as permission, I continued on my path, placing one hand over Xander's taut cheek and spreading him open. When he sharply inhaled, I ran my middle finger down his crack, moaning around his cock as I grazed the puckered skin, feeling him clench.

"I know what you're thinking about, naughty boy," Xander panted as he increased his pace, tightening his grip on my hair to the point of pain. "You want to stuff that thick, beautiful cock into my tight virgin hole, don't you?"

Ah, fuck.

My plan had backfired. Now that exact scenario was all I could think about, and uncontrollable pressure built in my spine, my balls threatening to explode at any second...

Be good, be good, be good.

Desperate to make Xander come first, I pressed the pad of my finger against his hole, forcibly breaching his entrance until I was two knuckles deep.

"Fucking *FUCK!*" he bellowed, clearly caught by surprise, yanking his hips back so most of his load landed on my tongue.

My victory didn't last long as he quickly withdrew and slapped a firm hand over my mouth, leaning down to harshly whisper in my ear.

"You wanted my cum that badly, huh, brat? I sure hope you can keep this slutty mouth shut, because I don't want to see a drop until you've painted the wall. Now stand up, place your palms on the glass, and bend the fuck over. And *don't* swallow."

I hummed eagerly through my mouthful of cum, using my super speed to stand and get into position.

Xander chuckled and dropped to his knees behind me. "Such a slut for my tongue. So eager for me to eat your perfect ass…"

Absolutely.

Not giving me a moment to prepare, he wrenched my cheeks apart and punched his way into my hole with a forceful jab of his tongue.

I writhed and wiggled as he devoured me, fucking myself on his tongue like the needy slut he knew I was. Holding my ass open with a bruising grip, Xander softly ghosted his thumb along the seam of my balls—his signature combination of pain and comfort being the exact torture I craved. He could do this to me every day and it would never be enough.

Never.

The muffled noises I was making might have embarrassed me previously, but I didn't care what the hell I sounded like. Xander's tongue was in my ass, his lips were sucking on my hole, and his teeth were nipping at my skin. My entire body was an instrument created only for him—an instrument for him to play as he pleased.

His nails dug into my flesh, holding me in place while he dragged me toward release, so sloppy and wild, yet perfectly in control, showing me it was safe to just let go.

I sobbed as I tumbled over the edge. Pulse after pulse coated the glass only to instantly wash away, along with any stress I was still holding on to.

Knowing I passed my test, I attempted to swallow, but with my head still hanging down, I choked instead, coughing as Xander's cum poured down my chin.

Jesus, I'm a mess.

Xander spun me around, already back on his feet to prop me upright and get me breathing again. "What a good boy," he murmured, lapping at my lips and chin, rubbing my chest to massage my lungs. "Did you like coming on my tongue? Did it help with all that pent up energy?"

All I could do was nod, closing my eyes and resting my head against the glass, letting Xander take over until I'd caught my breath again.

I take it back... showers are better than flying...

———

"Are you fucking crazy? I can't... I can't *fly!*"

How can I help him accept this?

I adjusted my headgear and floated over to where Xander was stubbornly standing with both feet firmly planted on the ground. His black leather boots, to be exact. The ones that were extremely lickable.

Okay, Butch, now is not the time for a boner.

"Yes, you *can*. And you already *did*," I grinned, kissing that filthy mouth I lived for. "Remember, my *inventus*—we share powers now and are fully bonded. I bet you don't even have to touch me anymore to take off like a rocket and throw some flames around. Just try it."

He scowled, and I backed off, reminding myself Xander had lived his entire life as little more than a physically and mentally superior normie. I was levitating out of my crib and setting my stuffed animals on fire before I could walk, but this was all new to him—on top of the reality of our situation.

And he likes to be in control.

"All right then," I adopted a businesslike tone. "How would you like me to *carry* you to the cemetery? You can ride piggyback or I can throw you over my shoulder like a caveman... Or I can carry you bridal style—being a runaway groom and all."

Xander responded exactly how I'd hoped, kicking my semi into third gear with a sexy signature glare. "What did I say about being a brat?" he hissed. "The only way you'll be carrying me is if I'm riding that thick cock."

I dropped my head back with a groan, willing my aching dick to calm down. *"Fuuuuck,* Xan," I whined. "Stop teasing me about that if you don't plan on letting me do it."

All I could think about—all I'd *been* thinking about—was a gloriously naked Xander straddling me, sinking down until I filled him completely, making *him* unravel for once. Knowing he'd never done it before only made me want it more, knowing no one else could claim that piece of him but me.

No one else ever will.

"My apologies, sweetheart." His breath on my lips snapped me out of my lust-soaked daze. "I may have misspoken. The only way you'll be carrying me is *when* I'm riding that thick cock."

OH MY GOD!

His cruel tease was forgiven the instant I realized he was *also* floating in mid-air—apparently just needing a mild threat to his pride to get past his mental blocks.

"Now," he drifted around me to deliver a sharp swat to my backside, "get that sweet ass in front of me where it belongs and lead the way to Rolling Meadows."

"So bossy," I mumbled around a stifled smile, even though I loved his bossiness.

I love everything about him.

Xander was the missing piece to the formerly hopeless puzzle of my life. Everything he said and did made me feel cared for in ways I'd never experienced before. The best part was that I knew he needed to care for me as much as I needed him to do it.

While the thought of losing the right to defend the citizens of Big City saddened me, I would gladly give it all up to spend the rest of my days by his side.

"What's the matter, baby?" Xander called from far above me, where he was now lazily drifting around like he'd been born to do it. "Are you scared of heights?"

Who's the brat now?

With a huff, I shot straight up, kissing the smirk off his face before separating again. "Never!" I laughed, so happy to be sharing this with him—to share everything. "Just try to keep up."

Then I turned and took off in the cemetery's direction—maybe not at full speed, but fast enough to give Xander a challenge. I didn't need to look over my shoulder to know he was behind me. Not only could I *feel* him in my blood, but I knew without a doubt he'd always be there, backing me up.

CHAPTER 45
BUTCH

Xander and I circled above our destination a few times, heat-scanning the area in case any of the various parties looking for us had followed Sylvano to the cemetery.

After determining the coast was clear, we landed on the ridge overlooking where the Ricci family plot was located—giving me a moment to observe the man waiting for us there. Sylvano was seated on a stone bench facing the mausoleum housing generations of his ancestors' remains, including his well-respected father.

I'd never met Pasquale Ricci, but had heard enough about him to want to introduce myself to his son Sylvano after the graveside service. Of course, I was there with Solomon Biggs, but slipped away from my boss long enough to approach the newly appointed Deputy Secretary-General of the USN.

Our conversation was stilted at first. I always had to practice caution when speaking to normies, and I wasn't sure what he'd been briefed on yet. Sylvano somehow saw through my civilian act and casually mentioned he would continue his father's mission to give supes the equal rights they deserved.

Before asking me point-blank what I thought about his platform.

I gave him a politely neutral answer, mostly because I'd always been told my place in the food chain was established long before I was born. But I clearly remember my *internal* reply, even if I didn't fully understand where my rebellious thoughts were coming from.

Please, make it stop.

I hadn't thought about that day in a while, but it was at the forefront of my mind as I led Xander to where Sylvano sat. For a moment, no one spoke, but my old friend broke the silence with an incredulous laugh.

"Butch Holt," he chuckled, shaking his head. "You sly fox. Sneaking your *inventus* into the USN, right under my nose."

I grimaced, even as he stood and embraced me in a warm hug before turning to shake Xander's hand. "And if I'd known you were a *villain*—an unregistered member of the Suarez clan, no less—I would have offered you a tour myself."

Xander huffed, unsurprisingly unconcerned about any rules we may have broken. "I take it you saw Butch's father on the news?" When Sylvano nodded, he turned serious. "You don't, uh, have a sworn duty to immediately take me in to be registered, do you? I'm more than happy to cooperate with the USN in the future, but now's not really the best time."

Sylvano laughed again, a full-bodied sound that echoed off the mausoleum. "No, no, no, don't fret about that right now, Doctor Antihero. In fact, if you and Captain Masculine were so inclined to sneak out of the city altogether, I wouldn't be leading the charge to bring you back. However,"—he cleared his throat—"I have information that I hope will make you both stay, if for no other reason than to help get this city back on track."

Anything.

"Of course," I readily agreed. "It's the least I can do after lying to you… and sneaking a villain into the USN…"

"It's perfectly all right, Butch," Sylvano patted my shoulder in a comforting way my father never had. "If you'd informed me who your guest was, I might have suggested registering him, simply to get it over and done with. But then, none of this excitement would have happened, so it's all for the best!"

That's one way to look at it.

"Agreed!" Xander flashed one of his genuine smiles, telling me Sylvano had passed whatever mental gauntlet he ran people through before approving them. "A little chaos never hurt anyone. Now let's see what sort of top secret documents you've brought us."

Sylvano chuckled at that. "Yes, well, Butch mentioned he'd unearthed the 'Franco vs. Big City' case, so I thought I'd hand off copies of my father's notes from the trial. You may peruse these in your own time, but in short, my father never accepted the rumors of why Franco Marisi—Iron Axe—was killed. He didn't believe it had anything to do with Franco transferring allegiance, or that he was a former villain attempting to marry a hero."

I gaped at him. "What else could it have been? My mother told me Vortexio killed Iron Axe so he could claim her instead."

Oh, sh… it.

Sylvano looked understandably pained by my bombshell, but took a moment to consider before replying. "The Deputy Secretary-General in me would love to use that intel to reopen the Franco case in my father's memory. However, as your *friend,* I'm going to give you a choice. Would you prefer Vortexio be charged with murder—which will be tricky, since

Iron Axe *was* a former villain—or focus on his more serious crime?"

"What could *normies* think is more serious than *murder?*" Xander scoffed.

Read the room, Xan.

To his credit, Sylvano didn't seem fazed by Xander's psychotic musings. "Franco and my father knew each other well prior to the trial. Iron Axe first came to the USN months earlier for assistance with switching from villainy to heroism. This sort of request was unheard of at the time, and has understandably not been repeated since. Yes, he was doing it mostly because of his love for Siren, but Franco also strongly believed there was no biological difference between heroes and villains, and he wanted the USN to scientifically prove it."

Xander's gorgeous amber eyes were nearly popping out of his head, and I was certain mine looked the same. If heroes and villains were actually the same species, there was no fundamental reason my *inventus* and I couldn't be together.

This changes everything!

"Did that research ever happen?" I hesitantly asked, buzzing with anticipation.

"No." Sylvano sadly shook his head. "It was soon after we publicly announced Franco as the face of the USN's new supe DNA research project that he mysteriously disappeared. His body was never found, and the heroes and villains who'd anonymously signed on to donate blood all withdrew their offers to participate."

A horrifying thought occurred to me. "You don't... you don't think *your* father's death had anything to do with..."

If Vortexio killed Pasquale Ricci...

Sylvano placed his hand on my shoulder again, squeezing slightly. "No, Butch. It was a long illness that took my father. As distasteful as Vortexio's crimes are, they've also been *smart*. Everyone knows what happens to supes who indiscriminately kill humans."

Xander sharply inhaled, but attempted to cover it up with a cough. My old friend missed nothing, shrewdly glancing at him out of the corner of his eye.

"That being said," he casually added. *"Off the record,* I've always been a fan of vigilante justice."

Thank you.

This time, Xander cleared his throat for real—probably to cover up some pesky emotions bubbling to the surface. "So, your father believed Vortexio killed Iron Axe to stop this research from happening, *not* to sever the *inventus* bond with Smoldering Siren?"

Sylvano blew out a breath. "Yes, he believed it was his primary motive, and that marrying Siren soon after was more of an excusable cover-up. The lesser of two evils, you could say. It would be far better for Vortexio to admit to taking desperate measures to maintain an equal balance of power than to committing a crime against humanity." When he saw my confused expression, he clarified, "Since that's what obstructing a humanitarian effort like this research would be considered."

My mind was whirring over all the moving parts, trying to make them fit. This was clearly bigger than the severing of *inventus* bonds, but I didn't understand why my father would go to such lengths to stop the DNA research.

He must know something.

Sylvano turned to the bench to pop open his briefcase, but instead of the stack of papers I was expecting, he handed me a thumb drive. "Digital copies of my father's trial notes are on here. You'll also find documentation of the original terms binding so-called heroes in servitude to human governments, including *your* family's contracts with Biggs Enterprises."

Tears blurred my vision. Sylvano providing these files to us—when the USN may not even have the right to possess them—was a kindness beyond anything I could have expected.

His father would be proud.

"Thank you," I choked out, securing the drive in one of my hidden pockets. "If the USN ever wants to start up the supe DNA research project again, Xander and I would be happy to donate blood."

"Absolutely," Xander agreed, taking my hand in his before turning to Sylvano. "But back up. Why did you refer to those bound in servitude to humans as 'so-called' heroes?"

My old friend smiled in a way that suggested he was also a fan of chaos. "As you'll discover in the documents, the only true difference between heroes and villains is whether they agreed or refused to sign the original contracts."

There it is.

"It's never been about biology…" I murmured, realizing just how deeply messed up this situation was.

"It's fucking politics and power," Xander growled.

Sylvano laughed, but there was little humor in his tone. "It's usually politics and power, which is exactly why my father founded the USN in the first place—so both heroes and villains could come to us for unbiased representation."

His phone dinged, interrupting the conversation. When he glanced down at the screen, Sylvano's face paled and his gaze immediately snapped to the two of us, warily looking us over.

"Walk with me back to my car." His tone was casual, but I could sense anxiety beneath his words. "When all of this excitement is over, you might be too famous to visit your old friend Sylvano."

I rolled my eyes good-naturedly, but happily helped him collect his things before escorting him toward the main entrance with Xander trailing behind us. "If I get any more famous, I may need to go into witness protection."

"Not if I have anything to do with it," Sylvano muttered as we crested the hill. His expression immediately brightened when his car came into view. "Ah, here we are! Be sure to wave at Eddy, Butch. You know he's your biggest fan."

I turned to see his longtime driver excitedly waving from the curb. As usual, he pulled out his phone to take some photos, but given the circumstances, I tensed.

"You should have Eddy delete those," I whispered. "I don't want you to get in trouble for being photographed with us—"

"Absolutely not," Sylvano hissed from behind his broad smile. "Let him document that both of you were here with me *at this time*, paying your respects to my father's memory."

What is he talking about?!

Xander was watching Sylvano so intently, I worried he might attack, so I sent a low-grade burst of power his way to snap him out of it. When he sharply glanced at me, I subtly shook my head.

Trusting my friend, I turned to Eddy and waved, flashing my most charming Captain Masculine smile—the only part of my face you could see—while ignoring Xander's judgmental snort.

He loves it.

"Stay safe." Sylvano brought me in for another hug before heading for the car. "And be sure to check the news!" he called over his shoulder.

My brow furrowed at his odd choice of words, while Xander had already pulled up the news app on his phone. I watched the car drive off before turning to my *inventus,* freezing as I registered the shocked expression on his face.

"Well, Wolfy sure took care of the problem," he chuckled, shaking his head incredulously before meeting my gaze again. "Your fiancé, Gemstonia Lincoln, is dead."

CHAPTER 46
XANDER

When we returned to my warehouse lair, Wolfgang was sitting on my couch.

In the dark.

"Jesus, *FUCK*, Wolfy!" I shouted as I turned on the lights to discover him there—having to physically restrain Butch from attacking. "How the hell did you get in?"

Unfamiliar with boundaries, as always, he simply shrugged. "I signed for one of your deliveries at the loading dock. Nice bed, by the way." He canted his chin toward the sleeping area where he'd apparently set it up for us. "It's big, but I suppose it has to be to contain all those muscles."

Oh, my god.

Butch was staring at him with a half-shocked, half-disgusted expression, and an equally horrifying thought occurred to me. "Wolfy, I swear on all that is holy, you better not have set up cameras in here. Keep your lecherous voyeurism to OnlyFans, please and thanks."

Maybe Kai should be his *bestie instead.*

Wolfgang rolled his eyes, as if he wasn't exactly the type of person to creep on someone else's bedroom activities. "I was expecting more of a 'thank you, Wolfy, for taking care of the problem so professionally,' but perhaps you haven't heard—"

"Oh, we heard," Butch grumbled, pulling off his mask and blasting my brother with that sexy as fuck Captain Masculine glare. "Did it occur to you *we* might get blamed for Gemstonia's death? *Xander* especially?"

You're adorable.

Wolfgang scoffed, clearly offended Butch didn't know how our family operated. "Besides you two idiots somehow being smart enough to get photographed on the opposite side of town with Sylvano Ricci at the time of death, all evidence points to a certain ice-wielding villainess with a bone to pick."

Ice-cold, Wolfy.

"You framed your own mother?" Butch choked out.

My brother fixed him with an unimpressed look. "Says the *hero* who wants his father dead."

I closely watched Butch's reaction to this accusation. He supposedly wanted to be a villain—and now we knew it was semantics, anyway—but actually committing patricide was something else entirely.

Especially as supes value their own families above all others.

He considered for a full minute before replying, proving yet again he was a himbo in appearance only. "Vortexio is a rogue supe who has posed enough of a threat to require a response. Evidence has come to light that strongly suggests he obstructed humanitarian efforts that would have benefited countless supes—both heroes and villains—never mind the unwarranted murders and… attempted murders."

Butch's gaze briefly flickered to my face, the split second enough to reveal the burning *need* to avenge me simmering beneath the surface. The instinct to protect *him* had already become a habit I enjoyed way more than expected, but to have someone else feel that level of protectiveness over me?

I love this man.

"Can you two please stop eye-fucking each other for a minute," Wolfy groaned, earning him a glare from me this time. "I want Butch to tell me the *more interesting* reason he wants to kill Vortexio."

What the fuck is he talking about?

My attention snapped back to my *inventus,* and I almost throttled my brother to find *tears* threatening to form in Butch's gorgeous baby blues.

"I just want it to stop," he rasped, and I realized it was uncontrollable rage fueling his emotions. "This bullshit has been going on for generations, and my father did absolutely *nothing* to fight back, not even for *my* sake. I-I can't imagine not doing everything I could to free my son or daughter from these chains—to at least *educate* them on what they were up against. But he was more interested in selling his soul, my mother's, and mine to ensure he held as much power as possible, given the circumstances. I refuse to continue this cycle—contract or not—and I can't allow others to suffer in similar situations when I'm able to help them."

I really fucking love him.

While I didn't possess Butch's ingrained sense of duty to protect helpless normies, I appreciated how that aspect of his job mattered to him, regardless of his contractual obligation. This was a man who wanted to *help* people, who still had an unwavering belief in doing the right thing—despite the beating his moral compass has taken lately.

Not knowing if Butch would want me hugging him in front of Wolfgang, I mimicked what he'd done in the cemetery and sent a subtle burst of power through our bond.

I'm here, baby.

It worked as he visibly relaxed and I returned my attention to where Wolfgang sat, eyeing Butch thoughtfully, considering his answer.

"Blind vengeance would have been hotter than a Boy Scout code of honor, but that's why you're Xanny's *inventus*, not mine."

He sighed almost mournfully before quietly adding, "It's quite rare to have an *inventus*. I've extensively researched it in our family's archives, wondering if there's someone out there who could handle *this*." Wolfgang waved a gloved hand, making my jaw drop.

"Since when are *you* looking for love?" I blurted out, half-teasing but actually extremely invested. My brother showing an interest in a relationship of any kind was possibly the wildest thing that had happened this week.

Thoughts and prayers to whoever becomes the object of his obsession.

Wolfgang shrugged, unbothered by my disbelief. "Since I discovered that these marriage contracts are a fairly recent practice, and one started by supes themselves. It's all about amassing power, of course. But while some, like Vortexio, are simply hoarding it for themselves, it appears others are doing it for the greater good—to shift the power back to supes. I believe our parents were undecided on the issue, or uncaring, which is probably why none of us Suarez kids were married off yet."

Butch hissed in a breath, drawing our attention back to him. "I overheard my parents arguing when Xander and I first started dating. At the time, I thought it was because he was a normie. Now I realize it was about me being with someone from the Suarez clan. My mother was in favor—partly because of the *inventus* aspect, I'm sure—but she also must have recognized how beneficial it could be for *all* supes if our families aligned." His expression soured. "Unsurprisingly, my father was opposed. Despite how much power it would have brought him, he was unwilling to even humor the idea, simply because Xander was a 'villain.'"

A classist through and through.

His air quotes did not escape Wolfgang's notice, and my brother huffed derisively. "Yes, I always felt the titles of 'hero' and 'villain' seemed a bit… arbitrary. That being said,"—he clapped his hands together and abruptly stood—"there are some who are decidedly rotten to the core, no matter which side they're on. Mother has disappeared. Violentia too."

Excuse you?

I gaped at him. "You could have *led* with this intel, Wolfy, Jesus Christ! Where the fuck did they go? Should we be worried? What about the others?"

He slowly blinked at me before rattling off the requested info in a bored tone. "I would assume mother is going after Vortexio for publicly accusing her of Gemstonia's death. Oops. Baltasar and the twins know *I'm* the new head of the family and that *you* could send your beefcake boyfriend to incinerate them, so they've received the message to fall in line."

"And Ultra Violent?" Butch asked, missing nothing.

Wolfgang stared back at him in a way that made my powers flare protectively. "I'll handle her, Captain. You just mind your own."

For a moment I worried someone was about to throw hands—or Hand—but Butch stood down with a clipped nod. "I will. Let us know if she becomes a threat."

"Consider it done," Wolfgang replied, although he looked uncharacteristically pained. "Although, I do hope it doesn't come to that."

All at once, I understood how serious he was about not letting anyone threaten his family. According to Wolfgang's morally gray morals, *anyone* who stood against a Suarez must die, so the moment our parents crossed that line themselves, *they* became his enemies.

He actually cares about the rest of us.

This realization shook me so intensely I barely noticed as he headed for the door, said his goodbyes, and disappeared.

Butch blew out a forceful breath, bringing me back to the present. "Shit. I'm glad that crazy fucker is on *our* side."

"Yeah," I absently murmured. "Me too." Clearing my throat, I refocused on my two favorite things: Butch and making Butch blush. "You know, sweetheart, if you keep up this swearing, we're never going to leave the lair."

Worse things could happen.

To my delight, he got a little pinker, still peeking at me shyly, despite everything we'd done together. "I told off my father, by the way—when he shared the news of my engagement. I swore and everything."

He says such sweet things.

I groaned and brought Butch in for a kiss, grinding against him through our suits. "What bad words did you say, baby? Will you whisper them in my ear when I bounce on your cock?"

"*Xaaaaan...*" he dropped his head back and whined, although his shoulders shook in laughter. "I swear, you better deliver the ride of your life for all this big talk you keep torturing me with."

He just makes it so easy.

"Oh, I'll deliver something big," I cackled. "But let's kick some ass first before I give you this ass. Sound good?"

He tried to protest, but I quickly distracted him with my tongue down his throat and my hand slipping inside his suit, finding him hard and ready.

Good boy.

Butch was desperately thrusting into my hand when my phone vibrated with an incoming call. I ignored the interruption, but whoever it was immediately called back—as if their minor emergency was more important than me making my *inventus* come.

I am not above killing someone for that.

Because I was a pro, I kept stroking Butch while wrestling my phone out of my pocket with the other hand, bringing it to my ear when I saw Kai's number flash on the screen.

"Someone better be on the brink of death, or so help me—"

"Well, that depends entirely on you, Xander. And my son." A voice I now recognized darkly chuckled on the other end of the line.

Vortexio.

I swallowed hard, releasing Butch as panic flooded my veins. He tucked himself back in without question, focusing entirely on whatever was causing me distress.

Letting his solid presence ground me, I hit the speaker button, forcing my voice to remain steady. "Hello, Harold. What can we do for you?"

Apparently, Vortexio was in no mood for niceties. "You can both meet me at Dead Man's Ravine in ten minutes," he hissed into the phone. "Or your pink-haired human dies."

CHAPTER 47
XANDER

Kai stroking my hair. Kai camped out on my couch, binge-watching *Trophy Wives*. Kai brattily demanding that I spill the dirty details from my hookups. Kai bringing me weird healthy soup when she heard me puking through the walls. Kai getting way too excited when I gave her fingerprint access to my apartment—as if I'd proposed. Kai cat-sitting, despite Meowson despising her. Kai tap dancing on stage during RHPS, stealing the spotlight with her joy.

Kai finding Butch for me.

My dread threatened to suffocate me as we raced through the air to Dead Man's Ravine. There was no doubt in my mind Vortexio would kill Kai if we arrived a second too late. He might kill her anyway, even if we got there in time.

I didn't know what I'd do if that happened. The thought of no longer being annoyed daily by a manic pixie dream girl made my blood boil with vengeful fire.

A gentle pulse of power washed over my skin as Butch attempted to soothe me from up ahead. I reminded myself that this was the kind of situation he faced regularly—no matter what else he was dealing with, and no matter how personal it was. As much as I relished being in control, the thought of Butch handling things instantly calmed me, allowing me to mentally prepare for whatever awaited us.

I need to let him lead this time.

The sun had set by the time we arrived, but between my supe-vision and the full moon illuminating the jagged cliffs, I spotted our target immediately.

"Just in time—how disappointing," Vortexio casually drawled, glancing at his watch for effect. "I never understood the fascination with humans. Such weak, fragile creatures... although this one proved useful."

He was hovering high above the ravine with a terrified Kai clinging to him. Her tearful eyes widened as she spotted us, but at least she looked relieved at the sight of Captain Masculine, even if she had no idea who was behind the mask.

I should have told her everything.

I should have kept her safe.

"Butch and I are here now, Kai!" I called out, unconcerned about blowing our cover. "It's all going to be okay." I didn't know if my words were for her benefit or mine, but I was determined to ensure they remained true.

Most normies were incredibly far removed from the reality of a supe's perilous life—and we were expected to keep it that way—but I didn't give a shit about the rules anymore. I ripped off my headgear without a second thought, wanting Kai to know exactly who had come for her.

Her friends.

"What the *fuck*, Xander?!" she yelped, momentarily forgetting her terror long enough to scold me before her attention shot to Butch again. "Wait. Are you telling me you've been fucking THE Captain Masculine all this time?"

Of course, that's *what she'd focus on.*

"Silence!" Vortexio snarled, carelessly shifting Kai in his arms so she squealed in fright. Ignoring me completely, he turned to address his son. "This joke of a 'relationship' ends now, Butch. Heroes belong with heroes. You *know* this."

Butch crossed his arms, impressively calm and collected despite the fury I suspected was roaring beneath the surface. "The only joke here is how there's nothing separating heroes and villains besides a bullshit piece of paper. *You* know this. It's why you eliminated Iron Axe—so you could continue this charade of superiority. But I don't care who Biggs Enterprises deems a hero. Xander is more of a hero than you'll ever be— not to mention my fully bonded *inventus*—so you have no hope of ending our relationship or defeating us. It's over, Vortexio. Hand over the human and surrender, and I'll appeal to the USN for a lighter sentence. It's my one and only offer, and more than you deserve."

"Well, dang," Kai muttered, echoing my Captain Masculine fanboy thoughts exactly.

Unfortunately, her commentary brought Vortexio's attention back to her, and he expertly flipped his captive, dangling her by the ankle over the ravine far below.

"Xander!" she screamed. "Xan, help me!"

I gaped. Kai wasn't calling for Big City's greatest superhero to save her—she expected *me* to do it. The guy who didn't even think he *had* superpowers until a couple of days ago, who'd never been close enough to another person to care what happened to them, who didn't consider himself anywhere near the definition of 'heroic.'

NOT ALL HIMBOS WEAR CAPES

"What makes you think you're not capable of those things as well?"

For some Freudian reason, Dr. Ownit's words from our last therapy session echoed in my head. I'd been describing traits I loved in Butch—before I even realized what I was feeling was love—yet stubbornly believed there was no way I could ever embody them myself.

Because I'm a villain.

Except Butch had waxed poetic about how heroic he thought *I* was, despite the villainous blood in my veins. This same man—the best man I'd ever known—was ready to become a villain for *me*, to switch sides without hesitation, despite the long lineage of so-called heroes in his family.

Like the famous 'hero' currently dangling an innocent normie over a ravine.

"Don't think I won't end you, Vortexio!" Butch shouted, flames blasting outward as his control wavered. "Father or not, I will scorch you from this earth."

If he could stop being so sexy, it would help me focus.

Vortexio threw his head back and laughed, the sound so eerily similar to my villainous father that I startled. "Oh, Butch. For being such a good little student, you never learned how to play this game. Rule number one: Never threaten what you can't deliver. You *can't* kill me—which means your *inventus* can't either. It's over, son. Time to get back in line with the other heroes, where you belong."

The slightest curl to Butch's lip told me to get ready to dive for Kai. "I'm exactly where I belong," he sneered. "And I always deliver. Tell me, *father*, does *this* feel like it's over?" With a flick of his finger, Captain Masculine sent a fireball sailing past his father's cheekbone, taking half the skin on his face with it.

Gross.

Vortexio bellowed, but I didn't have the chance to enjoy how much of his expression held pain, rage, shock, or fear, because Kai was suddenly falling to her death.

I dove after her, trusting that Butch was occupying Vortexio enough that he wouldn't interfere, trusting my *inventus* had enough power to beat his formidable father. Most of all, I had to trust in myself—that I could reach Kai in time.

I've got you, bestie.

Despite only learning to fly earlier today, I instinctively supercharged my speed. Scooping up a shrieking Kai only a few feet above the turbulent water, I shot straight up and veered toward the nearest cliff. The sounds of battle told me Butch was holding his own, but I forced myself to focus on getting Kai to safety before joining the fray.

Not that I know anything about how to fight like a supe.

I landed and attempted to untangle myself from Kai, but she was having none of it. "Don't you dare leave me," she angrily sobbed into my chest, clinging to me like a pink-haired spider monkey. "I can't believe you got me into this shit!"

Don't you dare brat me right now.

"Jesus, fuck, Kai, can we not… I have to…" I twisted my body with her still hanging off of me, needing to see what was happening with the love of my life.

My heart nearly dropped to the rocks below. Butch looked like he'd been through a meat grinder, with his suit shredded in so many places I might have appreciated it under different circumstances. Vortexio didn't look much better, but it was clear they were evenly matched, each man violently pummeling the other with hurricane-force winds—waiting for their opponent's strength to give out.

NOT ALL HIMBOS WEAR CAPES

I need to help him!

Kai had blessedly gone quiet, staring at the scene above us with her mouth hanging open. Finally understanding the severity of the situation, she quickly released me and backed away with a fierce expression that erased her lingering fear.

"Go do your hero thing, bestie." She gave me a sassy salute. "Wipe the ravine floor with that asshole villain."

She thinks I'm the hero...

Well. Why the fuck not?

Not wasting another second, I shot into the air, positioning myself in Vortexio's blind spot while I determined how to attack. More wind might knock Butch off balance and it would be pointless to throw fire into the middle of opposing cyclones. I couldn't just stand by while he took the brunt of this, but there were no other supes nearby to pull power from.

Or so I thought.

Razor-sharp ice formed on my fingertips the exact moment I spotted my mother standing on the opposite cliff. For a second, I panicked, thinking she was here for Butch, but quickly realized her fury was aimed at Vortexio alone.

Sucks to be him.

Glacial Girl couldn't fly, but a frozen tidal wave rose beneath her feet, lifting her up to meet her old enemy on equal ground.

"This isn't your fight, Signe!" Vortexio shouted over the howling wind. "After I teach my son a lesson, you and I can settle the score over Gemstonia's death."

The look on my mother's face was murderous. "I didn't kill your pretty little pawn, Harold—unlike how *you* snuck into my *home* to finish off my husband!"

Say what now?

After a stunned silence, Vortexio laughed. "Not my handiwork, but good to hear Ender won't be joining us. I've been waiting decades to destroy you on my own."

Every supe knew of the legendary face-offs where Vortexio and Smoldering Siren battled Apocalypto Man and Glacial Girl. But my father was dead—with Harold Holt apparently framed for his murder—and Butch's mother was notably absent.

Although she could show up at any moment.

Vortexio probably thought the odds were in his favor, which only proved that *he* was the one who didn't understand the game.

He may have eliminated Siren's *inventus*, but it was done as an afterthought, without due diligence of what that bond meant. I now had pure ice running through my veins—courtesy of an extremely pissed off supervillain—which meant my *inventus* did, too.

Three against one, fucker.

Wrongfully assuming my mother was the biggest threat, Vortexio sent a punishing gale in her direction. The blast met a substantial wall of ice, knocking him backward several feet, and causing the cyclone he'd been holding Butch back with to falter.

A costly mistake.

I wasn't sure if the *inventus* bond came with shared intuition, but Butch and I both took the opening to release a volley of ice arrows, relentlessly slicing through flesh and bone as Vortexio bellowed in pain.

"You don't deserve to call yourself a hero or a Holt," Vortexio bellowed, whirling on his only son. "I provided you with opportunities others could only dream of, and Biggs Enterprises gave you the adoration of an entire city as Captain Masculine. Yet you repay our generosity by traitorously joining the most disgraceful clan possible?"

How dare *he talk to Butch that way?!*

Enraged on his behalf, I prepared to fire again, but when I glanced at Butch, I was surprised to find a resigned sort of calm on his handsome face. "At least the Suarez clan takes care of their own." His quiet voice was somehow louder than the wind. "That's more than you ever did for me."

Vortexio's eyes narrowed, but before he could retort, Glacial Girl burst through her barrier with an inhuman growl that echoed off the surrounding cliffs. Turning her hands into daggers, she launched herself at her longtime foe, and sliced an icy blade across his throat.

"You fucked with my family, Harold," she hissed in his ear as he choked on blood. "And coincidentally, I've also been waiting for the chance to destroy *you*, one-on-one."

With their powers focused on maiming and killing the other, the two legendary supes plummeted toward the roaring river below. They hit the water hard—still violently battling for the upper hand, turning the inky surface choppy as they continued their fight beneath the waves.

Vortexio managed to come up for air, gasping in a single breath before being yanked underwater again. With a deafening crack, the entire length of the river was suddenly encased in solid ice, trapping him underneath to drown.

Along with Glacial Girl.

I felt as frozen as the water far below. My deeply ingrained *need* to defend my family warred with the realization that my mother probably hadn't shown up to defend me at all.

Yes, I'd recently increased my value as a Suarez by manifesting powers, but the events of tonight were more about settling an old score than supporting a new beginning. This conclusion between our families was inevitable—accelerated by my brother, but also written in the stars long before I was born.

Endgame.

Butch was instantly by my side, slipping his bloodied hand into mine to soothe me and sighing as whatever natural comfort I provided soaked into his skin in return.

"They didn't deserve *us*," he finally spoke, and I turned to face the man I loved.

His pretty blue eyes were dulled with exhaustion, but he cracked a smile. Not the one he gave the cameras—all cocky and completely fabricated—but a soft one, just for me.

I see you, too.

The two of us could have continued this cycle of warring households and passed on the hatred for generations to come. Instead, we found love, formed an unbreakable bond, and healed ourselves.

"Fuck 'em," I replied, bestowing a kiss on my brave hero's lips—knowing there were thousands more where that came from. "We have our own family now."

CHAPTER 48
BUTCH

Things moved fast after the showdown at Dead Man's Ravine.

Despite her protests, Xander and I immediately brought Kai to a normie hospital to be checked for injuries after her run-in with my father. As they usually did, the press found out we were there, causing chaos in the lobby until a frazzled receptionist asked if we would mind making a statement so the camera crews would leave.

Better to just get everything out in the open.

"You go ahead, Butch. I'll stay here with Kai. It's Captain Masculine that the people want to see, anyway."

Oh, no you don't.

"Not gonna happen," I snapped, grabbing his biceps through his supersuit and hauling him to his feet. "It's time for the world to meet my *inventus*—Doctor Antihero."

Kai snorted from her hospital bed, barely visible among the mountain of gift shop stuffed animals Xan had bought for her. *"Doctor Antihero?* You couldn't come up with something better than that, dude?"

Xander glared at her with so much love, I almost swooned. "I didn't come up with the name. Butch's soon-to-be *ex*-boss did, although..." He paused thoughtfully. "Although, I do have several PhDs, and after the events of late, I don't mind the 'Antihero' label so much. *Anarchist* would be more fitting, but of course Marvel already used that one. They took all the good names, to be honest."

Probably why I ended up as Captain Masculine.

I patiently waited for Xander's mini-rant to be over, knowing he was simply stalling while getting his nerves under control. When he finally quieted down, we checked each other's headgear and headed for the lobby.

We still need to protect our private lives, after all.

Unsurprisingly, Captain Masculine being romantically involved with a mysterious supervillain from the Suarez family buried the news that Vortexio, Apocalypto Man, and Glacial Girl were dead.

Our story was spun as a modern-day Romeo and Juliet, and I somehow convinced Xander to do a themed photoshoot with the Big City Tribune's Sunday magazine, featuring him standing on a balcony while I flew up to kiss him. Just as I'd hoped, he hated every minute of the experience and took it out on my ass as soon as we got home.

All those brat lessons from Kai are really paying off!

'Home' for both of us became Xander's apartment, with Kai still living next door. I insisted my mother take back the hideous condo and firmly rejected the idea of us finding a bigger place. There was nothing I loved more than crowding Xander on the couch while we watched documentaries on man-eating fish or whatever. I usually wasn't paying much attention, since I couldn't seem to stop looking at *him*.

"I can *feel* your heart-eyes boring into my skull, Butch," Xander chuckled from where he sat at his worktable in the warehouse lair, tinkering with his microplastics ray gun 2.0. "Is my needy little cumslut not getting enough attention?"

Never enough.

"Excuse me, I'm right here, you sex-maniacs," Kai grumbled from where she was sprawled on the couch, flipping through our Sunday mag shoot.

Unruffled, as always, Xander scoffed. "When are you *not*, Kai? I swear, I could throw a condom wrapper in any direction and probably hit you." He swiveled on his stool to fix me with a heated look. "Not that Butch and I have ever used them."

Sugar...

I could feel myself blushing, less from Xander's words and more from the mental image of his cum flowing out of me... only to be pushed back in... or licked off and swallowed...

He smirked knowingly, but before he could torture me further, Kai piped in again. "Oh, on that note, I've been meaning to say that if you guys ever want to have kids, I'd be more than happy to be your surrogate."

Xander and I were still 'eye-fucking' each other when she dropped that bombshell, so I fully witnessed the sheer panic that passed over his face. I didn't take it personally. Neither of us had experienced *loving* parents, and I knew it was an automatic response on his part to go into flight mode before someone *else* could disappoint him.

Since we now go to therapy with Dr. Ownit together.

I also knew that it was my inability to hide my emotions that helped Xander open up and share his. So I let him see *exactly* how I felt about the idea of us having kids together—whether or not they had superpowers.

The answer will always be yes.

Because Xander couldn't deny me anything, his expression softened—a loving look just for me—before he buried it beneath a scowl and turned to Kai.

"That is something Butch and I will discuss *in private,* thank you very much. Besides..." He cleared his throat. "We would have to make sure a fragile normie carrying a supe baby wouldn't result in our spawn clawing its way out of you, *Alien*-style. You know, to be on the safe side."

Kai barely waited until he'd turned back to his work to roll her eyes. Then she winked at me before rising to stand—making it clear she'd noticed how much attention I paid to the overpriced baby gear commercials when we watched *Trophy Wives* together.

A true bestie.

"Okey-doke, I'm gonna head out and check on Meowson before tonight's performance," she chirped, striding toward the door before stopping in her tracks. "Oh! I almost forgot. One of our neighbors handed off some mail of yours that must have gotten mixed up with theirs." Kai dug around in her enormous purse before handing Xander a single envelope.

He was still frowning at it after the door shut behind her. "This is odd. All the donations I've made to Cerulean Crest over the years have been anonymous, so how the hell did the organization get my name and address?"

Oh, shoot.

I forgot about this...

For a moment, I panicked, thinking Xander might be legitimately angry with me for going behind his back. I shouldn't have worried. He'd opened the letter and was now staring at it with actual *tears* in his gorgeous amber eyes.

Happy tears.

"You did this?" he quietly asked, although it wasn't really a question. "When? When did you—"

I was blushing again—not from shyness, but more because of how much I'd *pleased* him. "Right before I flew to your parents' compound to make things right. Whether I lived or died, I wanted my money to go toward something *good*, especially as it originally came from such a horrible situation."

"This... this must have been *all* your money, Butch. I..." He set the letter down on the table with a shaking hand before bringing it to his mouth—uncharacteristically overcome.

He was correct that it was everything I'd 'earned' working for Biggs Enterprises since graduating from Superversity. I didn't miss it, especially as I'd picked up more than enough endorsement deals since becoming a free agent.

And it's not like Xander lets me pay for anything, anyway.

My freedom was thanks to Sylvano Ricci. The USN took Solomon Biggs and Biggs Enterprises to trial for crimes against humanity, resulting in every 'contract' between the Biggs and Holt families being ruled null and void. A larger case was now being worked on to examine similar claims in other cities.

During the investigation, a warrant was issued to search the Holt residence inland, and evidence found there led to the discovery of Franco Marisi's body on the property. Unsurprisingly, Butch's mother knew nothing about this, and after paying her respects, surrendered the remains to Marisi's villainous family.

Xander and I had also donated blood for the cause—to prove there was no biological difference between heroes and villains, and therefore, no reason they couldn't be together.

But we already knew that.

All that aside, it wasn't often that I saw Xander at a loss for words—and I couldn't remember ever seeing him get *teary*—so I did what I could to make him comfortable.

"Yeah, it *was* all my money. I couldn't think of anyone I'd rather spend it on than *you,* but since you do a pretty good job of that yourself…" My attempt at humor fell flat as Xander was still staring down at his letter in a daze.

Just the facts, then.

"I donated everything with the stipulation that it be used to create a waterfront nature preserve on Rose Island. Additional funds were set aside for any legal fees needed to kick out anyone who'd built a mansion in critical habitat. I did it in *your* name, so those rich assholes would know exactly who to blame for fucking up their comfortable lives."

That did it.

Xander sprang from his stool and tackled me. Instead of the kiss I was expecting, he wrapped his arms around me in a crushing hug before burying his face in my chest—enveloping me in that smoky leather scent of his I couldn't get enough of.

"How the fuck are you so perfect?" he huffed. "Just think about those clowns trying to come for me only to get bitch slapped with the Endangered Species Act. That's spank bank material for years to come."

He was quiet for so long, I thought he might be done, until he suddenly *sniffled.* "And... j-just think about all the sea turtles this is going to save..."

Oh, Xan...

Pulling back, I tried to *see* what he was feeling. Of course, he still attempted to hide his emotions behind a smirk, but I grabbed his face in my hands and forced him to look at me— to look at himself.

"I know how important this is to you," I whispered, "which makes it important to *me.* It's okay to cry over sea turtles, Xan. It doesn't make you weak."

He stared at me like he'd seen a ghost before finally delivering the kiss I'd been expecting. Except it wasn't his usual domineering style. Xander kissed me so gently, I barely felt it, the salt from his tears somehow making it even sweeter.

"Thank you, baby..." he whispered against my lips. "For being everything I didn't know I needed."

We stood like that for a few minutes, softly kissing and simply staring at each other with 'heart-eyes,' until my phone buzzed in my pocket.

Regretfully abandoning Xander's lips, I saw I'd received a message from the USN, which was temporarily acting as law enforcement HQ while a non-Enterprises police force was created. With Xander's tech support, Sylvano and I had set up a 'bat signal' app, so I could be alerted to any crimes that needed a supe to get involved.

I'd already made a public statement to the citizens of Big City that I was now *volunteering* my time to defend them, and would continue to do so unless they wanted me to step down. I was honored when the overwhelming response was to keep me on as the deliverer of vigilante justice.

And who am I to argue with righteous bloodshed?

"Will you be at the office long, sweetheart?" Xander crooned, smoothing his hands down the front of my supersuit when I went to kiss him goodbye.

"I shouldn't be more than a couple of hours," I smiled, stealing two more kisses just because I could. "It's a normie crime, so I can't rough them up too badly."

Xander hummed. "Mmm, so it's safe to say you'll have some pent up energy to get out of your system afterward?" I bit my lip and nodded, already thinking about what we might get up to later.

True to form, Xander simply refocused on his project and adopted a casual tone. "Very well. I'll see you at Ars and Invenio in two hours. You're going to sit through dinner and drinks like a gentleman before *anyone* thinks about touching that beautiful cock. Sound good?"

Fuck.

Shaking my head, I snuck in one more kiss on his cheek before heading for the door. Knowing he was expecting an answer, I called over my shoulder. "The answer will always be yes, Xan."

"Good boy," he murmured, filling every long-neglected corner of my soul with the warmth of his praise. "I'll see you later, baby."

Always.

EPILOGUE

XANDER - A FEW WEEKS LATER

"There you are, sweetheart. I was worried you might stand me up."

Butch laughed as he landed on the roof next to me. "Never! The visit with my mother just went longer than I'd planned." He awkwardly rubbed the back of his neck. "She baked *cookies*. I don't think I've ever seen her do that before."

"Sounds nefarious," I crooned, pulling him close, unable to keep my hands to myself any longer. "We'd better keep an eye on it, in case baking turns into world domination."

He rolled his eyes with a smile. "It would be just as weird if *your* mother had baked or… if *Wolfgang* suddenly did."

I barked a laugh. "Yeah, if Wolfy ever cooked anything, the main ingredient would probably be *people*. Luckily, Betsy is still keeping my siblings fed at the compound."

Most of them, anyway…

There was still no word from Violentia, and I could only assume she blamed Butch and me for our parents' deaths. It wasn't entirely accurate, but I knew better than to throw Wolfgang under the bus for his Hand in the Holt-Suarez house cleaning, especially since he was the head of my clan now.

Blood is thicker than murder.

Wolfgang had promised to handle the situation, and he'd been busy—systematically preparing to personally check each of the Suarez-owned international properties for traces of our sister.

Since his 'system' eerily resembled a conspiracy theorist's wall covered in grainy photographs and string, I offhandedly mentioned he should find an assistant to help him stay organized. The manic gleam in my brother's eye caused me to immediately regret the suggestion. There was no doubt the idea of employing a full-time minion fulfilled all of Wolfy's villainous fantasies.

Thoughts and prayers to that poor soul as well.

"Sylvano was at the condo," Butch abruptly added, bringing me back to the present. "Apparently he's there a lot…"

So it wasn't about the cookies.

"How do you feel about that?" I recited the open-ended question Dr. Ownit encouraged us to use when giving each other the floor.

Butch was quiet for a long moment, giving his answer careful consideration. "I'm feeling this irrational *need* to defend Vortexio's honor or something, even though my mother and I were nothing more than pawns to him. The truth is… I would have killed to have someone like Sylvano in my life growing up. I've looked up to him for a while now, so as far as step-dads go, I could do a hell of a lot worse. Plus, my mother deserves a second chance at love after losing her *inventus,* so I'll support whatever makes her happy. Family is what you make it, right?"

I nodded. It was extremely rare for a supe to get remarried—and unheard of for it to be with a normie—but Sylvano Ricci was a good man who'd always treated Butch with the respect he deserved.

Unlike his own father.

Butch was gazing at me so hopefully, I couldn't resist a tease. "As long as you don't start calling *him* Daddy, I'm fine with it. What else is bothering you, baby?"

Since I can read you like a book.

He deliciously blushed. "Well, all this talk of family reminds me I wanted to ask you something..." He dropped his gaze, and I braced myself for where I assumed this was going.

He hesitated long enough that it was clear he needed a nudge. "If this is about kids, you know the answer will always be yes, Butch. Although, full disclosure, the idea of being put in charge of living creatures who are *not* self-sufficient cats or famous superheroes scares the crap out of me."

Might as well be honest.

Butch shot me an indulgent smile. "I dunno, Xan, you took pretty good care of me when you thought I was just a really muscular yet fragile normie." He sobered before continuing, "But no, it's not about kids—not yet. I want to wait until we know if Kai can be involved and, well… I kind of like having you all to myself for now."

Same.

Apparently, the 'scientific' study conducted by the USN to determine if supes and normies could safely procreate had been illegally influenced by Biggs Enterprises. Tobias Johnson—the little shit who'd interrupted us in the archives—was exposed as the insider behind the corruption. He was unceremoniously fired and Sylvano was now working on organizing a new study with unbiased experts.

Butch and I had already discussed how we'd prefer Kai as the surrogate over anyone else, even if it meant our kids wouldn't have powers. I also begrudgingly agreed that we should probably wait until we knew it was safe for her—since I *did* care about her. Kind of.

Okay, a lot.

I'll take that secret to my grave, though.

"Very well. The spawn discussion is tabled for now." I rubbed a lecherous hand down his very muscular arm. "Talk to me, Butch. Tell me everything that's on your mind."

He blew out a slow breath before gazing at me earnestly. "Okay, I was hoping that maybe I could… you know, if it would be all right with you… take *your* last name at some point…"

You've got to be kidding me.

I backed away and bent over as uncontrollable laughter burst out of me, delighted at how consistently *not* in charge I was with this man.

"Butch," I finally found my voice again. "Did you seriously just steal my thunder *again*? First with the 'I love yous' and now this?"

He looked so adorably perplexed that I cut to the chase, promptly dropping to my knee and fishing a small box out of my pocket.

It's now or never!

"Oh, my god," he gasped in that breathless way that simultaneously made me hard as a rock and melt into a puddle. "Are you—"

"Just let me *do* this, Jesus," I chuckled before clearing my throat and adopting a serious tone. "Butch Holt, will you do me the honor of becoming my husband, of *taking my name,* and starting your villain arc with me?"

Then I popped open the box.

Butch's euphoric expression turned to confusion once again. "W-what is that?" He leaned down for a closer look, only to straighten with an amused sigh. "That goes on my dick, doesn't it?"

"Sure does." I licked my lips, enjoying this exchange immensely. "I didn't know your actual ring size, so thought I'd start with a more *adjustable* alternative before we go to Cartier tomorrow for something that matches."

"Is it gonna… hurt?" Butch asked, his eager gaze fixed on the 18 karat yellow gold cock ring with channel set princess-cut diamonds.

Only the best for my inventus.

"No," I chuckled, rising so I could deliver a sloppy kiss. "I got the XXXL size, so it will only strangle that thick cock just enough. We can't have you popping off like a two-pump chump later tonight just because you're finally in my ass."

Butch's head swiveled so fast I was surprised *it* didn't pop off and roll away. "For real? Tonight? Please don't mess with me. Xan. I don't think I can take any more teasing."

Oh, you'll take it.

"Yes. *Tonight.*" I laughed, even if it was partly to mask my own nerves.

Good little student that he was, Butch had been stretching me for weeks now—with his fingers and my 'murder weapon' plugs—although it wasn't the size of his monster cock that concerned me.

This act would demolish the final barrier still remaining between us, and although I'd already put my full trust in him, I still got squirrelly thinking about it.

Intimacy issues don't just go away overnight.

The truth was, there was nothing I wanted more. That I'd ever believed I couldn't be close and open with another person seemed ridiculous at this point. Even if I didn't realize it at the time, my misguided insistence on facing life alone had disappeared the moment this hottie himbo entered my life.

How did I get so lucky?

"So… we're going home right away, right?" Butch was crowding me against the low brick wall at the edge of the roof, his hard cock desperately straining toward me and its fancy new bling.

Oh, sweetheart—have we met?

"No," I stated, drinking in his growl of frustration like the smoothest bourbon. "I bought us tickets to go see *The Rocky Horror Show* on stage. The London cast is in town and I simply couldn't pass up the opportunity to see Richard O'Brien revive his role as Riff Raff. It felt appropriate, since *your* first time was after we went to see Kai debut on stage, remember?"

Since the only reply I was getting out of Butch was his Captain Masculine Blue Steel stare, I went in for the kill. "Oh, and speaking of Kai. She'll be joining us with her new girlfriend—the one she *really* wants us to meet."

Gotcha.

He hung his head with a groan before rallying. "Fine. Fine. I'll do it for Kai, *and* because I know how much you love torturing me."

I shot him a decidedly villainous grin. "Guilty. Although, I believe *you* love it as well, baby."

Butch bit his bottom lip, his pretty blue eyes sparkling. "I do love it. I love everything you do—especially when you call me baby."

"Good boy," I replied, delivering a playful pat on his glorious ass. "My car is downstairs, and I brought civilian clothes for us to change into. But first... You still haven't given me your answer to my marriage proposal, sweetheart."

The sparkle in his eyes turned mischievous. "You know what the answer will always be, Xan... but I don't think I'm going to say it out loud until I'm buried in that tight virgin hole."

What a fucking brat.

"Well played," I sighed, grabbing his hand and leading him to the stairs. "C'mon, baby, let's go edge ourselves a bit more before the very *big* grand finale."

Thirsty for more skintight supersuits?

Sign up for my newsletter for the BONUS epilogue: **Only Good Boys Get to Top Their Xaddys**, and preorder Wolfy's story: **Gentlemen Prefer Villains** (Ignore the Amazon date! We're aiming for March 2023)

REVIEWS

If you have enjoyed **Not All Himbos Wear Capes,** please leave reviews! It helps other readers find my work, which helps me as an indie author. *Thank you!*

Amazon
Goodreads
Bookbub

But don't stop there: Tag me in your reviews, stories, edits, videos, and fan art on social. I love to share these posts with my followers!

VILLAINOUS THINGS PLAYLIST

Please enjoy the Spotify playlist that inspired the Villainous Things series (and let me know if you have a song to add):

(CENSORED) BUTCH & XANDER PRINTS AVAILABLE

LINK TO ORDER PRINTS ON THE BOOKS BY C. PAGE

(CENSORED) BUTCH & XANDER PRINTS AVAILABLE

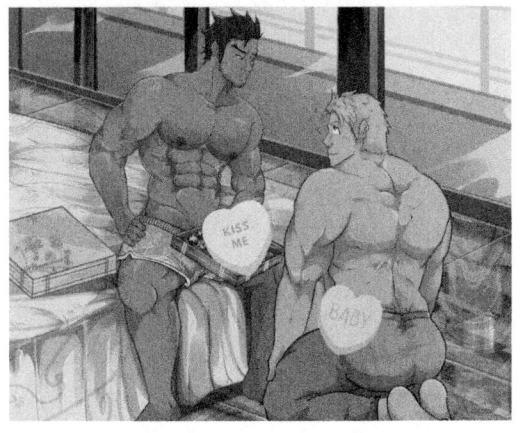

And more!

BOOKS BY C. ROCHELLE

Looking for signed paperbacks, N/SFW art prints, bookplates & other goodies? My store can be found at **C-Rochelle.com/shop** (and **Patreon** members get discounts on art prints and signed books, plus extra swag and personalized inscriptions in their books!)

VILLAINOUS THINGS - SUPERHERO/VILLAIN MM ROMANCE (COMING SOON TO AUDIBLE):

Not All Himbos Wear Capes *(sign up for the newsletter to get the Only Good Boys Get to Top Their Xaddys bonus epilogue)*

Gentlemen Prefer Villains *(sign up for the newsletter to get the Yes Sir, Sorry Sir bonus epilogue)*

Putting Out for a Hero *(sign up for the newsletter to get the Idiots in Love bonus epilogue)*

Enter the Multi-Vers (the twins)

Villainous Book 5 (reunion book)

Want More Villainous Tales? The evil author is already scheming multiple spin-offs!

MONSTROUSLY MYTHIC SERIES (ALSO ON AUDIBLE):

The 12 Hunks of Herculeia (Herculeia Duet, Book 1)

Herculeia the Hero (Herculeia Duet, Book 2) *(sign up for the newsletter for the bonus epilogue: Three Heads Are Better Than One)*

Herculeia: Complete Duet + Bonus Content *(includes Calm Down Monster-Fucker, Three Heads Are Better Than One, & the Thanksgiving Special: Get Stuffed, plus UNcensored art)*

More Monstrously Mythic Tales:

Valhalla is Full of Hunks (Iola's story)

THE YAGA'S RIDERS TRILOGY (ALSO ON AUDIBLE):

Rise of the Witch

A Witch Out of Time

Call of the Ride

The Yaga's Riders: Complete Trilogy + Bonus Content *(The Asa Baby Christmas Special & the Too Peopley Valentine's Day Special)*

More Yaga's Riders Tales:

A Song of Saints and Swans *(Anthia spin-off novella, which includes From the Depths & the Halloween Special: It's Just a Bunch of Va Ju-Ju Voodoo)*

Wings of Darkness + Light Trilogy:

Shadows Spark

Shadows Smolder

Shadows Scorch

Wings of Darkness + Light: The Complete Trilogy + Bonus Content *(Oversized Cupids V-Day Special, The Second Coming Easter Special, & the Sexy Little Devil Halloween Specials Pt. 1 & Pt. 2)*

More from the Wings Universe:

Death by Vanilla (Gage origin story novella)

Current/Upcoming Anthologies:

Creepy Court: A Monster Mall anthology (featuring my tale - **Vampires Totally Suck**)

And there will be a bonus Monstrous holiday special in the forthcoming **Snow, Lights, & Monster Nights** charity anthology

ABOUT THE AUTHOR

C. Rochelle here! I'm a naughty but sweet, introverted, Aquarius weirdo who believes a sharp sense of humor is the sexiest trait, loves shaking my booty to Prince, and have never met a cheese I didn't like. Oh, and I write spicy paranormal/monster Why Choose + MM, MFF & MMF romance with dark, naughty humor. #loveislove

Want More?

- **Join my Clubhouse of Smut on Patreon**
- **Subscribe to my newsletter at C-Rochelle.com**
- **Join my Little Sinners Facebook group**
- **Stalk me in all the places on Linktree**

AUTHOR'S NOTE & ACKNOWLEDGMENTS

The first huge (as huge as Xander's cock) thank you goes to everyone who's read this book—whether my loyal paranormal/monster Why Choose romance readers or existing fans of MM who decided to take a chance on me.

I have never been as nervous about a book release as this. It wasn't that I'd never written an MM relationship before—my other books are chock full o' sweet 'n' spicy man-love—but I'd never focused solely on the guys, and wanted so badly to do them justice.

I'm a rabid reader of the genre (especially contemporary MM), but knew I needed objective input as I wrote Himbos, to make sure I was hitting the notes and not wandering (too far) off the path.

Thank you to my alpha readers, authors Cora Rose, Lily Mayne, Vera Valentine, and Ariel Dawn, as well as my hype queen team leader (and even more thirsty MM reader) Michelle Kardolus. And an extra butt pat to my proofreader, Lindsay, who survived my hot mess process to make sure I stuck my commas in the correct holes.

Another group that was invaluable to this book are my Clubhouse of Smut members on Patreon. Himbos started as a patron-only serial (mostly because I was skerred to dive in), but the feedback and support I received from these earliest of early readers gave me the confidence to put it up for preorder (and write like a woman possessed).

A smutty shout-out to my Va Ju-Ju Voodoo Queens patrons: Adrienne, Emily, Fawn, Jasmine, Kaitlyn, Kaylah, Kelly, Kristina, Kyla, Lauren, and Stephanie. Thank you for supporting my author journey in this way!

Some lecherous love to my monsterly horndog author friends —the ones who are there for inappropriate memes, legitimate industry questions, and real-life support. I appreciate you fucking weirdos more than I can say.

And as always, extra sloppy kisses to Little Sinners admin Kristin and my ARC and Street Team—my loudest, proudest Ho's. I appreciate every bit o' hype you can spare for me and my dirty little books.

Thank you to everyone who believed in this little smut engine that could! Hop on my caboose and hold on tight, sweethearts.

Printed in Great Britain
by Amazon